THE TALE OF TWO CROWS

ABELIA SUMPTER

This book is a work of fiction. Names, characters, places, and incidents are the product of the author's imagination or are used fictitiously. Any resemblance to actual events, locales, or persons, living or dead, is coincidental.

The Tale of Two Crows

Cover Design | Rose & Lavender Press, LLC

Formatting | Rose & Lavender Press, LLC

Proofreading | Taylor Necko

Scene Breaks & Chapter Heading | Kyta @nocoats; nocoats.ink

Note from the Author

The Tale of Two Crows is not suitable for those under 18 years of age. Please see abeliasumpter.com for a full list of content warnings.

Prologue

Knox

P-AR 4035

“He’s only five. How could he know better?”

“Mrs. Arris, it was the work of a monster, not some misunderstood child.” Vicar Minthra folded his hands together behind his robes. He was the kind of man who looked permanently scorned. The kind no child would want to call “grandfather.”

Knox pressed his back into the wall, staying hidden in the shadows just outside the too-small kitchen as he eavesdropped on the three adults exchanging heated words. Through the doorway made of branches, his father and mother stood across from Minthra, one of the Vicar elders. The bitter stench of his laurel berry cologne overpowered the usual burnt leaves and damp timber of their worn-down hut.

The Vicar turned his attention to Knox’s father, his frown deepening. “That’s the fourth household pet reduced to carnage this month." Minthra's wrinkles deepened in a disgusted scowl, and Knox barely contained a laugh. "Another infraction and we'll have a more serious conversation, Councilman."

"Minthra, Knox can do better—he can *be* better—I know he can," Knox's father said. "He is just a boy; one that can improve with a bit more discipline. The gods know I don't spare the rod."

Knox instinctually reached for the tender welt on his upper arm.

Vicar Minthra lowered his head. "I don't have to remind you what the elder council has suggested."

"You won't touch my boy!" Knox's mother sobbed into her hands, her words morphing into incomprehensible cries.

"Zareena, please, get a hold of yourself." Knox's father cleared his throat and leaned against the wooden counter. "That won't be necessary. I will get him under control."

"Good, for if things do not change, you won't have a choice. Callisto, I say this as a friend, but I can only keep the council at bay for another few months. However, if Knox inflicts his ailment on any of the children, I cannot guarantee you even that long. The council will do what they must for everyone's safety." The Vicar's brown cloak swayed by his calves as moved toward the door.

Knox didn't understand what the big deal was. So what if he had too much fun with the neighbor's cat? It was old and would have died, eventually. All he did was help it along. It was probably suffering . . . or at least it was once his fingers were around its neck. It just took a small jerk to break the bones, followed by a thrilling bliss. A surge of power. His smile hadn't faded, even as his neighbor slapped him across his face. Nor when his father brought out the whip.

After Vicar Minthra left, Knox sprinted to his bedroom and threw himself under the covers. The sun would rise in a few scant hours. Not much time remained before his father would awaken him.

Other children may shiver knowing a beating awaited them in the morning. Knox never understood why other kids got so worked up over punishments from adults. Pain was something he experienced but didn't process, not unless it was happening to someone else.

As the moon luminesced through the window, Knox tucked himself deeper under the scratchy comforter and drifted off to sleep.

Before Knox opened his eyes, he breathed in the morning dew wafting through the cracked window. It rained more often than not in the Mountains of Eskdale. Once upon a time, the mountains were coated with white, pillowy snow. Knox wondered what it would be like to sled down the rumored powdered slopes in the time before the snow melted into muggy swamps.

The door creaked open behind him, and Knox didn't bother bracing himself. Any quiet entrance was bound to leave bruises.

His father never understood that the harder he beat him, the less Knox cared.

Knox lay in bed, waiting for a hand to grip his blonde curls and drag him from the room to the whipping stump. But no hand came. A small form leapt onto the side of his bed. Tiny hands shook his shoulders, and he groaned with annoyance.

"Knox, get up! I'm here to play!" the shrill voice shouted, straight into his ear.

Great, Milo's here. Knox would have rather been whipped than spend a single hour with his bubbling cousin.

Without another thought, Knox shoved him off his bed and onto the floor. "You must be four or older to sit on my bed. Remember my rules?"

Milo huffed on the floor, arms crossed, and blew a strand of black hair out of his eyes. "That's not fair! I'll be four on my next birthday!"

"Bummer." Knox hopped off the bed, landing in a squatted position next to Milo. "Is your papa here?"

"Yes, dummy." Milo scooted away from Knox toward a set of wooden toys.

His cousin wore his patience. But Knox didn't have any siblings, and neither did Milo, so their parents expected them to converse like brothers.

"Let me play with these." Milo raised his palms to Knox, four small wooden animals held within: a rabbit, a tiger, a horse, and a monkey.

"Fine, but only one."

Milo's gaze darted between the toys, as though the thought of choosing only one was agony. After a minute, he dropped the rest and hugged the wooden monkey to his chest.

Knox seldom played with his toys. The outdoors interested him more. Nature.

Animals made of warm flesh and flowing blood.

"Knox! Milo!" Knox's mother shouted through the house.

Knox grabbed Milo's arm and pulled him to his feet. "Come on, you heard her."

The boys ran to the kitchen where Knox's father and uncle sat around the table in hushed conversation. The sun reflected off his mother's golden hair as she washed dishes.

"Uncle Balistar!" Knox ran to his uncle, dressed in a loose tunic and pants. Most Vicars dressed in robes, but Knox's uncle hadn't recently. Something about being banished from the council.

"Ah, there's my favorite nephew!" Uncle Balistar embraced Knox, his long, snow-blonde hair tickling Knox's nose.

"I'm your only nephew," Knox joked.

The adults laughed, and Balistar ruffled Knox's hair.

Knox surveyed the kitchen. "Where is Aunt Imory?" As much as he loved his uncle, he adored his aunt.

Milo, he could do without.

Uncle Balistar exchanged looks with Knox's parents. "She felt under the weather this morning, but don't worry, she will be at the feast. You can see her then, all right?"

Knox nodded. It wasn't like her to be absent, but if she was ill, he couldn't protest.

"Can we play outside?" Milo interrupted, tugging on the edge of Knox's tunic.

"That sounds like a great idea," Knox's mother said. "It will give us and Uncle Balistar some time to . . . discuss things."

More and more, Knox took notice of the secretive conversations between Uncle Balistar and Vicars. But *meetings* and *politics* were a grown-up ordeal, and Knox was in the business of fun.

"Come on, squirt, you heard her." Knox grabbed Milo's hand and pulled him to the door.

The boys ran out of the crooked hut and into the yard filled with patches of swampy grass. Grayish-blue rays from the sky paled their already-light skin.

"Let's play catch," Milo beamed, grabbing a wooden ball from the play bin.

"Only if I get to throw first." Knox smiled.

Milo stomped his food into the mud. "You always get to go before me." But still, he didn't argue further. Instead, he placed the ball on the ground, folded his arms, and kicked it over.

Knox rolled the heavy ball over the backs of his knuckles. A simple toy, but it could really hurt someone if used by the wrong hands.

He gained momentum, charging his throw, and released it at Milo.

His younger cousin caught it but barely. The ball thumped against his chest and he squeaked.

Knox's lips parted. He didn't mean to cause Milo pain. In fact, he had never hurt another Vicar before, only animals. He never knew the suffering of humans could cause that same weave of power. Still, he pushed it down. If he hurt his cousin, what would his father think? What would *Uncle Balistar* think?

The boys tossed the ball a few more times. His crows taunted him every time the ball hit Milo too hard.

Once more, the ball was in Knox's hand. He closed his eyes and took a deep breath, remembering what the elders taught him about control. He didn't have to give into every violent temptation that popped into his mind.

The caws grew louder, amplifying the violent thoughts. When he obeyed the caws, his powers increased, and he could hold on to the energy longer, strengthening and harvesting it. Already, at five, he had surpassed all the older kids in the Vicar school and even some at the temple.

The wooden ball left his fingertips, flying across the yard with more speed and power than he'd ever thrown before. Milo, fear in his eyes, dove away but not quickly enough. The ball slammed into his shoulder, throwing him to the ground. Silence stretched, Knox holding his breath with gleeful anticipation.

A glorious cry escaped Milo's lips. "Papa!"

Knox raced over, and with a single touch of his fingers to Milo's forehead, his cries fell silent. That didn't mean they stopped. Milo's screams rang out in Knox's mind, held within the Vicar trance.

Sedating Milo with crows was forbidden, but it kept Knox safe from the adults. The ones who couldn't understand what the crows demanded of him.

His magic wouldn't last long against Milo. His cousin was an untrained half-Vicar, after all. He could only be controlled for a few minutes. In a few years, Knox would have no bearing over Milo.

Knox took the wooden ball and stood over Milo. If the council heard about this, Knox would pay dearly. He could get a few more jabs in to satisfy the crows then erase the last few minutes of Milo's memory.

He raised his arm above his head while his crows cawed in excitement. Rare opportunities like this cleared his mind. Like this, he was his true self, not the child his father wanted him to be.

A strong, calloused hand gripped Knox's arm as though it were nothing and threw him many feet away. Knox landed on his side in a patch of grass. Pain shot through his shoulder, but he barely noticed it.

He stared up at his uncle, knowing that the pain of being thrown was nothing compared to the pain of disappointing him.

But, to Knox's surprise, Balistar did not appear angry or even disappointed.

"Knox, no!" His mother screamed, falling to her knees. Her weeping filled the entire yard.

The blue-gray sky grew dimmer as Balistar turned from Knox and scooped Milo into his arms before pressing his fingers to Milo's forehead, undoing Knox's crows.

Knox's father's face was nothing short of devilish, furious, but it was also frightened. The use of a whip seemed to be an unfruitful daily occurrence, as if his father could bring control back to the world with it. Though deep down, Knox knew his father didn't enjoy hurting him.

"Zareena, go inside! The neighbors will hear you!" His father kicked open and entered the run-down wooden shed, then he emerged back outside with a whip in hand. "Knox, get over here, now."

Knox stood, keeping his head held high. No one liked to be whipped, but Knox tolerated it better than most kids. When would his father understand that? Besides, the scars weren't as beautiful on his back as they were on others.

Uncle Balistar quickly placed his hand on Knox's father's shoulder, halting his steps. "Callisto, let me handle this."

His father hesitated, a stare passing between them for several long moments. Knox's heart raced. A whip from his father he could tolerate. But wielded by Uncle Balistar. . .

"It's my son that suffered. It's only fair."

His father glanced back at Knox, then at the surrounding yard. His breath shook, his voice quavering. "No one can know about this. If the council finds out that Knox—"

"Don't worry, brother. When I'm done, he won't even dream about it."

His father handed over the whip. Knox took a step back.

"I have no need for that. There are other ways to get a point across."

Knox froze. What could his uncle do that was worse than the whip? The only thing Knox hated more than disappointing Balistar was that uncertain and unpredictable air he had to him.

Balistar strode forward, his face unreadable. He took Knox's hand with a gentle grip and led him toward the forest behind their house, which was a bit of a walk. Knox's steps were slower than his uncles, but he was pulled along without any thought.

The Akumu Forest was said to be haunted, and the other kids were terrified of it. Knox wasn't, of course, but he was forbidden to enter. Sometimes, he hung around the outskirts, never walking in more than a foot or two.

His cousin slept peacefully in Uncle Balistar's arms, unaware of his surroundings. Unaware of the forest.

What was his uncle capable of?

Far from the hut, Balistar stopped at the edge of the forest. Leafless branches hung from the trees as though they were weeping. Despite the daytime, the spaces in between the trees were as dark as night.

Uncle Balistar laid Milo on a large stump off the path, his cousin curling into a ball. Balistar knelt, cradling Milo's face for a brief moment. He stood, smoothed out his tunic, and faced Knox.

Instinctively, Knox took a step back.

His uncle laughed. "Knox, don't be afraid. I'm not going to hurt you."

Knox tightened his muscles. He couldn't relax until he knew his punishment. Would his uncle make him run into the forest of nightmares and face his worst fear? Or hand him over to the rumored spirit-monsters that inhabited the trees?

"Come sit by me." Balistar motioned to another large stump and took a seat.

With hesitancy, Knox slowly made his way over to the stump and hopped up on it, but he kept a good foot in between him and his uncle.

Balistar stared out into the forest as if it was some gorgeous landscape and not a place that people entered, never to be seen again. "You hurt my son. That's not something I take lightly."

"I'm sorry, Uncle." Knox twiddled his thumbs together. He wasn't ashamed of the pain he caused Milo but of the disappointment he brought to his uncle. He could handle the Vicars cursing him, wishing him dead. But Uncle Balistar? That was another story.

"I've heard reports from the tutors at the school. They say your crows are strong."

Knox didn't answer, unable to gauge his uncle's next move.

"Your tutors would never admit it, but you've surpassed many of them, haven't you?"

Knox nodded slowly.

"I think your crows have the potential to be even stronger than my own. You've found a way to increase their strength. To take power from others when you hurt them. Am I correct?"

"I feel strong when they're in pain."

Balistar nodded, and Knox sat up straighter. Uncle Balistar didn't seem upset at all. In fact, he seemed . . . impressed?

"The council wants you gone because they fear you, Knox. They see you as a vessel of destruction, but I see you as a catalyst for real change. Your crows make you more powerful than any of those old Vicars. In fact, even in the darkness you carry, you could do some good. Maybe in time, you could even save this decrepit planet." Uncle Balistar rested his palm on Knox's shoulder. "You're a weapon, and we shouldn't be suppressing that. Weapons can do immense good in the right hands."

Knox never thought of himself as a weapon. The Vicars spoke of nothing but peace and religious rituals. If they heard the way his uncle spoke now—

"I-I can't stop myself from feeding them," Knox croaked. "The crows take and take, no matter how much I seem to give."

Balistar's jaw clenched, and he breathed in deep. "Rather recently, I've dealt with similar issues with my own crows."

Knox beamed. "You have?"

"In my own way. I've learned that it is all about balance. Light cannot exist without shadows to tame it. Your crows tempt you by rewarding you every time you give in. I know that. It's why the Vicars are ashamed of the gifts they carry. There are ways to control your crows while keeping your parents happy."

Balistar placed his fingers on Knox's forehead, connecting their minds. A swarm of crows descended from the skies, blocking out the sun. In the thousands, they flocked to the forest, eating away at the trees and leaves. Soon, Milo disappeared from view.

A cloudy realm of dark reds and yellows surrounded them.

Around Knox's feet, white birds pecked around at food on the ground. Not crows but doves. For the first time in Knox's life, he had no urge to stomp down on them. They were beautiful. Peaceful. They held the crows at bay, holding back the whispers. They were there to help him—to help Balistar.

"There are other powers out there, my nephew. Powers that are waiting to be utilized. Powers the Vicars will never teach you. The doves balance my crows so they don't take more than I need. Now, I'm lending some of them to you."

Knox bent over and stroked a dove's soft head, its beady eyes depthless and infinite. "And that's all it will take? I'll be free?"

"Mostly." Balistar snapped his fingers, and the illusion faded. The forest reappeared where Milo still laid fast asleep on the stump. "I trust you will keep this between the two of us? Not even your parents can know."

Knox stared in wonder at his uncle. "Yes, I won't tell a soul."

Uncle Balistar pushed off the stump and swiped Milo into his arms. "In time, I will show you more forms of complementary magic besides simple doves. As with most things, control will take time. Before then, as long as I'm alive, your crows will not torment you."

Uncle Balistar strode back to the house, and Knox walked by his side.

Chapter 1

Margot

D-AR 4061

Sweat soaks my tank and shorts, bleeding into the sheets. This is the third time this week I've woken up in a panic with my heart racing. At least this time nobody violently shakes me to jostle me awake. To my relief, the other rebellion girls stay fast asleep in their bunks.

Peaceful dreams are a luxury few can afford. I certainly can't. To think there was a time when most of mine were pleasant. Those days are nothing but a childish fantasy. Most of the time, I dream of the torture in restless fits. That's when I wake up screaming, unable to catch my breath.

But this morning, I dreamt only of *him*. I was imprisoned in a realm where his fingers gripped my hair, his lips devouring mine in desperation. Our bodies moved together while gasps escaped us.

"I could never love someone like you," I said.

He peppered needy kisses along my neck. *"Liar."*

I push myself to the edge of the bed and rest my forearms on my thighs while I catch my breath. Fluorescent lights from the cracked sliding door illuminate the black diamond ring snug on my thumb.

Milo's ring.

My fingers curl around the ring's edges, my ribs twisting into knots.

I should've pawned it off a long time ago. Found a broker in the city who could sell it off planet. It's worth a fortune and could supply the base with months worth of food. We wouldn't have to rely on Joriel or our other donors for once.

But I can't muster the strength to take it off. I don't know what stops me. It's not like it would save me if Milo ever found a way into our base.

With no hope of falling back asleep, I get up before the wake-up call and get dressed.

I make my way down the white-brick walls of the tunneled hallways toward the meeting room, my boots moving over portions of metal grated floors as I pass by weapon and training rooms. Considering how early I am, I'll be the first one there. The ground rumbles as a train passes through the nearby subway.

The paneled lights flicker. I flinch then curse.

I'm just glad Dimitri didn't see. Anytime he witnesses my physical reactions, I have to find some half-baked excuse to avoid talking about why I just visibly shuddered. He's not stupid, though. I know he knows. It's why he's done nothing but baby me since I returned months ago. Sometimes all I want is space from him or to go on a city excursion by myself.

Nobody has been able to leave safely for months. I suspect it's why Lucinda is holding a meeting today. I miss the outdoors, despite the lack of breathability. When I needed to clear my head, I could sit on the roof of a tall building and admire the Merth skyline with its colorful, dancing lights. I won't stop fighting until that freedom returns.

When I arrive at the conference room, I pause at the threshold, surprised to see someone has already arrived.

Imory sits at the long presentation table holding a warm cup of tea in her hands, a soft smile on her lips. The hexagonal mission screens along the walls illuminate her glowing skin. "Margot, how are you?"

She's the kind of person I have to take in every time I see her, not just because of who she resembles, but how she, with her gentle smile and kind eyes, could have survived Balistar Arris. How her son followed in his footsteps.

"You're here early." I take a seat at the table.

"I find it beneficial to ground myself and soak in the quiet before the chaos." Imory sets her tea down. "I suppose you and I are similar in that sense."

"I just had trouble sleeping and wasn't sure what else to do with myself."

"I know things must be difficult since . . . well I don't have to say. All I know is that it's hard to lose someone you love."

"I *don't* love him."

Imory smiles and runs her thumb over the teacup's rim. "I was talking about Lleu."

My chest tightens. "Well, regardless, I don't . . . Milo, I mean."

Her smile grows sympathetic. "I know." Imory has that way about her. Without even trying, she exposes the contents of my heart like they're tattooed right on my forehead. "I hope you don't still blame yourself."

"I fell for their trap. So easily too. How could I sneak into my own base, steal confidential information, and give it to the Colum? I should have remembered everything the second I stepped over our rebellion's threshold. Because of what I did, we lost so many members."

"What *you* did? Coerced and tortured by dark men? Memories erased by proditor magic? Margot, if anything, it was because of what *my son* did."

"Tell that to the rebels who mourn their loved ones."

"They know what proditors are capable of. People are sympathetic."

"I don't need their sympathy. I know how they view me. Tainted. Like I'm some ticking time bomb or a sleeper agent. A dormant virus waiting to consume them."

"Crows will only taint you if you let them."

I pinch my lips together because she's right, even if I don't want to accept it. Whenever she looks at me, it's like I'm made of glass.

"Look at you, arriving before me." Dimitri strides through the door, Oliver in a headlock, snacks tucked under his other arm. Normally, it's the other way around with those two.

Oliver grabs hold of Dimitri's arm and pushes him off before smoothing back his black hair.

Could he have arrived at a worse time? His ability to read a room has always been subpar. I shake my head. "You have way too much energy this early in the morning."

He tosses the snacks on the table as more rebels spill in behind him. "Why the long face? Today is going to be a good day. I can feel it. Right, Oliver?"

Oliver folds his arms. "Margot's right, you *are* exhausting today."

"Take that back." Dimitri tries to put Oliver in another headlock, but Oliver fights him off with a few swipes of his arms. While Dimitri laughs and plops down in the chair next to me, more rebels trickle in, lost in conversation.

A few of them pass by me, offering pitiful smiles. Some avoid eye contact completely, like I don't exist. Even if they won't say it out loud, I know many of them blame me for the Colum getting ahold of their faces. It's my fault we have to have this meeting to begin with.

Lucinda enters, her white-blonde bangs resting on her forehead, and approaches Imory and me. "It's good to see you, Imory. I hope Joriel didn't give you too much trouble."

"Just a twinge more than the last time," Imory admits. "But it seems whatever you paid him has let you off the leash for a little while longer."

"I better hope. It was a dent in the treasury." Lucinda's eyes scan the room. They hesitate upon me. "Margot, have you been sleeping? You have dark circles again."

I rub my temples. "I'll sleep when Lavenai can grow wheat again."

Lucinda shakes her head, and I can almost see the memory of my father that flashes behind her eyes. "Spoken like a Tavish."

Dimitri pushes his snacks in my direction.

"This is a meeting, not a buffet," I say.

"Don't tell me you're going to pass up chips made with real lab-grown potatoes?" Dimitri slides one of the bags over.

"I'm not hungry."

"So you finally ate breakfast?"

I turn my head away.

Dimitri opens the bag of freeze-dried apple crisps and shoves them in my hand. "That's what I thought." He ruffles my hair.

I smack his hand. "I can take care of myself, you know."

"Clearly."

Lucinda calls out for everyone to take their seats and a few minutes later she raises her hand until the chatter ceases.

"The Arris's web has tightened planetwide, especially here in Merch. Even in the surrounding regions, they're increasing their civilian shakedowns. We lost two informants in the Staeziemie region who were crossing into the Dhuaan region. They were apprehended during a random search," Lucinda says. "With our current predicament, we're unable to send personnel to help escort contacts through borders. Which leads us into why Imory Nolan has risked everything to be here. Imory?"

Imory nods and trades places with Lucinda, then she activates the holographic projector. "Thank you. As most of you know, I've been hiding out in Lavenai's Oro region since the inception of the Arris Reign, and there I've made hundreds of connections and partnerships with ex-proditors and defectors. Before my travels here, one of my own spies working undercover as an Ashtanaban guard was able to determine the central server hub for Lavenai's facial database. That includes your rebellion's faces. Not only that, but he informed me the base is completely mismanaged and undertrained, from traps not being fixed to doors being left unlocked."

The holograph projects a 3-D image of a base. It's large and filled with ships and garages. I see why they would keep the database there. Nobody would ever suspect it to be hidden inside a shipyard base within driving distance.

Imory continues, "Another anonymous party has provided me with Ashtanaban guard uniforms. If we can send a team of you undercover to destroy their facial-recognition servers, you may not have to be locked underground much longer."

Lucinda nods. "A day may come where Sinclair is unwilling to let us out through his entrance, and our vehicle exit near the outskirts of the city is not conducive for traveling into Merth." She folds her hands behind her back as she paces behind a few cadets. "We've begun construction to add new entrances, considering our current ones are compromised. Once we're able to complete missions back in the city, our primary mission will shift to disabling Ashtanabo's proditor temple points."

Imory smiles. "Yes, as a few of you know, there is a lead I received from an ex-proditor. There's a girl in Susuku that has the power to change everything."

"Change how?" Oliver asks skeptically.

"She has a power different from the proditors. A power my contact interacted with firsthand in a prison there. While with her, his powers ceased working as if she were a walking hyssopite plant. We theorize that, if she is within close range of a temple point, the tower will deactivate."

It's hard to believe there are other kinds of magic out there besides the gift of the crows—even the crows are a bit of an anomaly. The Vicars who originally held it used it for worship, and they essentially believe having it made them cursed. Their whole way of life focuses on atoning for some sin they believe they must have committed in order to wield it.

"Is she dangerous?" I ask.

Lucinda shrugs. "Depends on who you ask. Any proditor would say she's deadly. To normal humans? Unfortunately, we aren't sure. If she's not liked by the proditors, that probably flows both ways. Though the girl is irrelevant if we can't wipe our faces from the database."

A hologram model of the base expands upon the table as Lucinda points to a few key locations. "We have a small window to access the base itself. An opportunity like this doesn't come every day, so we're sending two teams inside—one to destroy the servers, the other to compromise the backups. Dimitri is leading the first and Oliver the second. I'm taking volunteers to join them. No more than ten total."

Is this how I can rectify things? How I can show the other rebels I'm not the pseudo-proditor they fear? I can quell my guilt and right my wrongs, all while undoing the very thing I did to them.

"I will go," I say.

She shakes her head. "No, Margot. You're needed for the Ashtanaban mission. We can't risk you getting injured or worse."

"With Knox's crows, I may be the only one who can fight a proditor if the time comes, and I'm the only one in the rebellion who knows how to fly a ship if anything were to happen within the base. Besides, if this mission isn't successful there will be no Ashtanaban mission."

"Actually, Lucinda," Imory interrupts, "I may agree with Margot on this one. Flying is hard enough as it is, and if I know Balistar, he would've taught Knox how to fly, which means Margot can too since she holds his muscle memory."

I straighten in my seat as I wait for Lucinda's answer. Her eyes dart past my shoulder, trying to find an excuse to stop me from going.

Finally, she sighs. "I will allow it for the time being."

Hours later, I train in the recreation hall. Since I returned to the rebellion, I don't go a day without combat training. I'm on the mat almost as much as Dimitri and Oliver because what once felt optional for a spy is now a necessity.

I head into the locker room to freshen up. As I turn on the shower, the lights flicker. I hold onto the shower handle to steady myself.

You are safe.

You are not on the Imnicus.

There are no proditors here.

I say it enough times to just barely believe it then step into the shower, letting the warm water bead down my skin. With my eyes closed, I hum a tune.

If we're successful on this mission, maybe the other rebels will forgive me. Half of them already seem to. But the other half? I've known most of them my entire life and it only took one amnesiac mistake for that trust to shatter forever.

I focus on the shower, my muscles relaxing under the warm water, and my paranoia dissipating. But the relaxation is short-lived, fear trading itself with thoughts of *him*. The memory of his kisses. How he'd press me into the tiled wall.

You don't love him, I think repeatedly.

A shadow passes over my lids, and my eyes shoot open.

On the ground, a single crow dances and bathes itself in the shower puddles.

It can't be real. This is a dream, right? I stumble back and jam my heel against the shower wall, the pain confirming that I'm truly awake.

The crow moves its head rapidly a few times before focusing on me and cawing.

I kick my foot, and it backs up slightly before spreading its wings. Black eyes stare straight into my soul. Its neck moves erratically, caws echoing off the surrounding tile.

I rub my temples, massaging the hallucination away, but it remains. "Get out of here!" I kick water at it.

Three beaks poke through the drain, pecking like their lives depend on it. Before I can lunge for it, the drain comes free and an explosion of crows shoots out. I scream and fall to my knees.

It's not real. It's not real.

I close my eyes and count, starting in the five-hundreds. I steady my breathing as crows circle above me with their beckoning call.

"Five-hundred and sixty-one. Five-hundred and sixty-two. Five-hundred and sixty—"

All at once, the caws stop and the wind storm of crows ceases. When I open my eyes, all that remains is shower water that grows colder by the second.

Perhaps the rebels are right to fear me. The crows they fear haunt me. They control my waking thoughts.

And this is far from the first time it has happened.

Chapter 2

Milo

"Her vitals are stable, Colum," the humanoid says through his silver lips. His blue, metal thumbs rub together nervously. "But we must wake her soon to avoid complications. We have suspended her in a medically-induced coma for far too long."

I've been inside the intensive ward of the medical bay only twice. It's rare anyone's wounds are fatal enough on the Imnicus to warrant such high-level care. It's even rarer that I choose to visit them.

Lleu floats in the light-green gel of the healing chamber, a bullet-sized scar on her lower belly. Her dark skin is somewhat mottled—a side effect of the treatment. It will go away within a day of removal. But her complexion isn't what I'm worried about.

I want to know who gave her that damn letter.

Whatever was inside helped Margot escape, and when I catch who wrote it, they'll pay dearly.

The humanoid adjusts his stance to face me. "Healing chambers can be harmful when patients overstay their welcome. I'm beginning to worry for her well-being."

I glare at him.

"I-It's all just recommendations," the humanoid corrects, "for her safety."

Despite the adverse reactions, the healing chamber is the safest place for Lleu. Releasing her means handing her over to the torture and interrogation that Arris Law demands. My father found punishments to be an art form and his laws reflect that. A necessary evil, one I never participated in against a woman until Margot. An evil I never want to enact so directly again. It's something that haunts me, guilt gnawing at my chest day in and day out. In the moment, it felt like any other interrogation, but hers left an aftertaste. One I still struggle to scrub off my tongue.

But the rebellion could play their next hand any day now, and if that happens, I need to know who on the Imnicus betrayed me. If there is a rat on this ship, Lleu knows exactly who it is.

"Wake her today," I tell the humanoid. "Then transfer her to one of the nobility prison cells. Make sure it's one with keycard access, and only allow access to those I personally approve. I'll assign one of the proditors to oversee her, but other than that, no one will visit her without my approval, and that is an order."

"Is she that dangerous?" the humanoid asks.

"*She's* not who I'm concerned about." I turn to leave.

"Yes, right away, Colum."

As the humanoid types commands into one of the computers, a team of medics enter to prepare the transfer.

I stand over Lleu in the white-walled luxury prison cell I know she doesn't deserve. Right now, it's the only way to keep *him* and the law away from her. If he had his way, she'd be in the south wing enduring proditor interrogation.

I remember Lleu's first day on the Imnicus. She was resistant at first, but after a few threats, and some Imnicus maid training, she naturally fell into her role as Margot's lady's maid. Lleu adapted so well I often forgot I had kidnapped her.

Lleu stirs slightly and rolls on her side, and it seems like she's about to fall into a deeper sleep before she coughs once. Then again. Soon enough she's violently hacking and on the verge of gagging. Green gel stains the white sheets.

I sit there silently while she expels the remnants of the healing chamber.

Slowly, she catches her breath before rolling in my direction and sitting up with watery eyes. The second her gaze meets mine, she jolts back into the headboard hard enough to leave a bruise. "Colum."

"Good, you're awake." I take a handkerchief from my pocket and toss it to her to wipe her mouth. "Did you sleep well?"

Lleu cleans her face and presses a hand over her abdomen.

"The gunshot barely missed a major artery. Still, it's a miracle you survived," I say.

"How long was I out?"

"Months."

Her lips part. "But . . . it feels like . . ."

"It happened minutes ago? Yes, healing chambers have a tendency to distort time."

Lleu hands the handkerchief back to me. "Why did you save me? I pushed Margot away from Knox and into the escape pod."

"That's not why you're here, but you're right, normally that would be cause for execution in itself."

Lleu's hands shake slightly at my words. "Then why?"

"I'm after information. I know you delivered a letter to Margot the day she escaped. We saw you remove it from your pocket through the cameras shortly before you entered the bedroom."

Lleu presses her lips tightly together.

I rest my forearms on my thighs. "Maybe you don't know the situation you're in. Should I enlighten you?"

"I thought it was a goodbye letter," she snaps.

"A goodbye letter from whom?"

She stays silent yet again.

"Maybe it *was* just a goodbye letter. So prove it to me. Who sent it? A maid? A soldier?" Margot grew close to a lot of people while she was their Columess, but who would have gone far enough to help her escape? Far enough to betray me? "If you tell me, you'll see your parents again today in Msanii and we can pretend like none of this ever happened."

Lleu pauses, takes a deep breath, before closing her eyes right. "I'm sorry, Colum."

"Do you not understand that I'm trying to help you? That if you refuse, I may not be able to protect you from things worse than death?" If I had kept a better eye on Lleu, studied who she kept close to outside of Margot, maybe I would have a suspect—a lapse in judgment on my part.

Lleu watches my fist tighten. "Why are you trying to protect me?"

"You know the horrors of what happens in the south wing. The things every maid and soldier try not to think about. I'm giving you mercy."

"I've been on the Imnicus long enough to know how things work. If you wanted, I would have woken up in a torture chamber, not a cell made for the elite. It wouldn't even take much to get it out of me, I'm sure of it. I'm not strong like Margot. I'd break faster."

I bite my tongue. If she keeps trying to read me, I really won't be merciful.

Lleu lightly scoffs. "It's her, isn't it? You're afraid that if you hurt me, she really will hate you."

I slam my fist down on the bedside table and she jolts. "Don't mistake my mercy for kindness. I could easily send my proditors to Ashtanabo right now and turn your family to dust. I'm still your Colum."

At the mention of her family, Lleu keeps her mouth shut and nods, but I know she doesn't believe me. To her, this all happened a moment ago. That emotional core still runs hot. She needs time to sit in this cell and let solitary confinement do its job. Silence leaves room to think, and the threat of the inevitable will have her crawling toward freedom, eventually. Dread is my ally here, and dread takes time to form.

I move to the door, using Margot's old ring to open it. "One of the proditors will check on you often, as well as a very select few maids. If anyone unauthorized comes in, press the button behind your headboard, got it?"

"Colum, would you like more water?" Sloane asks.

Around the dining room, servants are busy bringing out appetizers and the rest stand quietly in a row by the wall.

With a frustrated sigh, I nod. Lleu's words chip away at my thoughts. How she defied me because she knew she could. I need to be more careful in the future. Showing too much of my hand is dangerous.

The seat across the table is empty, as it has been for months, yet the place is still set because I'm too stubborn to tell them to stop. They never ask about Margot, and they have no right to, even though I can practically read their thoughts through their unsubtle expressions. It's their blind obedience and fear of reprimands that made deceiving Margot so much easier.

The arbitors were trickier to fool. A false attack on the Imnicus was hard to stage. But Monicas is a romantic, and the easiest lies to accept are the ones you want to believe. He teared up when I told him I secretly got married and he wept when I told him the rebellion poisoned Margot with psychedelics on her last mission.

"Oh, and after how much that poor girl has been through already," he had said.

The dark walls cave in on me. Every noise in the room is louder than normal and infuriating. A servant clears his throat. Two A.S.O.P. units zip around the table, clanking uneaten dishes together.

An A.S.O.P. unit rolls by my chair and over my long cape. Its wheels stutter over the fabric and it beeps nonsense while it tries to free itself.

"Dammit." I tug the cape away from it, but it worsens the snag, the fabric climbing up the wheels into the internal hardware.

The robot screams through a series of beeps and tries to roll away faster, only adding to the jam. It yanks my neck back, my head slamming into the chair. Why did my father insist on utilizing these incompetent machines?

Sloane and another servant rush forward and kneel in front of the robot.

"Turn it off," I say through clenched teeth.

"Yes, of course!" Sloane picks up the robot. Its wheels still gnaw up the fabric.

The other girl frantically searches for the kill switch. "This is one of the newer models. I can't find it!"

My teeth clench together as the robot zips out of Sloane's hands and partially cuts off my breathing.

I fumble around for the cape's latch and release its hold. The A.S.O.P. unit shoots across the dining room, smoke pouring out from its slats. The fabric is stuck far up enough to require repairs.

My head pounds. The servants rush to catch the robot as it zigzags around the room, slamming into table legs and servants. The yells and clangs push me over the edge.

I fly out of my chair, summoning my crows.

The world slows ever so slightly.

I stomp forward, my heart pounding, my anger seething. I push servants out of my path. In their eyes, I'm quick on my feet as I pass by them.

I swipe the A.S.O.P. unit up by its circular head. If it had successfully freed itself from the fabric, maybe I could find patience somewhere deep within me. Perhaps I could have let it go.

Instead, I summon as many crows as I can into my palm and squeeze. The robot's squeals fade with its broken voice box as I crush it slowly in my fist, my bicep shaking.

Soon, its frantic beeping stops, and the blue lights that line its circular edges die out.

One of the servants gasps as I drop it, its dented body clunking against the tiled floor.

The humans know better than to move, but a humanoid takes a cautious step toward the kitchen. A V.I.X. unit outright flees the room.

A pressure pounds against my temples. I can't take it anymore. "Everyone, leave now!"

I close my eyes as the stillness turns into quick steps while everyone funnels around me and out the door.

I rub the back of my neck, breathing in the blissful silence.

Until a slow, methodical clapping breaks my concentration. "Well, well, Colum, that was quite the show."

Knox leans against the doorway, his gloved palms clasped together. My jaw twitches. He's the last person I want to see right now.

"You know, as much as you've always hated those things, I never expected you to destroy one so openly," he says.

"It was wrong of me." In fact, it's illegal. To the humanoids, I may as well have just killed someone. I head back to my chair and slump into it. I lift my glass and take a large gulp of red wine.

Knox shuts the door and removes his disguise, plucking a grape off my plate. "You know, the last time I picked food off your plate, you almost cut my finger off."

"Do you need something or are you here to further piss me off?"

"Is it wrong for family to visit family?" Knox sighs and leans back. "But I'll cut right to the chase. I want to know what's being done about the actress."

I run a hand down my face. "Don't even start with that. Tensions with Lavenai are higher than ever. Any minute there could be an uprising and you're concerned about Lleu's judgment?"

"She is overdue, and if Uncle Balistar were here, I know he would agree."

"My father wouldn't torture someone for no reason."

He smirks and pops another grape into his mouth. "Maybe you didn't know him as well as I did."

I fly out of my chair and grab Knox's collar. He has no right to speak about my father that way.

"Is it a lie?" Knox's voice strains under my grip but still contains the usual amount of cockiness. "The man he showed you and the one he showed me are two different people. Are we going to continue to ignore the way he really felt about you?"

My arms are on the brink of shaking. He knows it's a low blow. It's like he's trying to make me lose control and it nearly works.

I release him and step away. "I'm his heir. He showed me what it took to be a leader."

"And he showed me what it takes to be a fist. How to truly keep two planets dancing upon your fingertips." Knox slides off the table and takes a roll from the breadbasket. "So what's it going to be, Milo? Are you going to give Lleu to me? Or are you going to keep her all to yourself just like you did with Margot?"

"The terms of Margot's fate changed. You deserve nothing."

"You mean your feelings for her changed."

"She means nothing to me," I rasp. "Like any man would, I fell slave to my urges."

"How about now? If we found her again, would you finally give her over to me? Would you let me use her skin as a canvas?"

I turn my head and say nothing. I have no rebuttal, no answer that wouldn't be a lie.

"I see." Knox chuckles and paces around the room in deep thought while he tears off a section of the bread with his teeth. "You're funny, you know. I'm sure you spend your every waking moment believing Uncle Balistar favored me because of my powers. Resenting me for inheriting three forms of complementary magic. Yet, you fail to see the real reason—you're soft. Maybe even as soft as Alarik. I wonder, what would the Arbitor Council think of this?"

My eyes darken. My father instated the arbitors to protect his laws from being overturned by any future leaders, including me. They're the reason our government isn't considered a dictatorship, though the rebellion would say otherwise.

Knox parts his lips. "Ah, interesting. Doesn't the law say . . . "

"I know what it says."

"Section 41:B of Arris law states all acts of treason must be dealt with swiftly and harshly. Three months is the required time frame. Physical punishment and execution are the only acceptable judgments."

I frown. Since when has Knox made himself familiar with the law? "Subsection C," I say, "Lists the exemptions and special circumstances, including prisoners with potentially critical knowledge."

Knox rips off another chunk of bread. "If you say so. As long as the arbitors are aware."

"You know they aren't," I say. They're as unaware of Lleu as they are of who Margot really is.

Knox smirks. "Well time is ticking now, isn't it? As your cousin, I will be kind and give you time to figure things out, but just know, Lleu is heavy on my mind."

"Once I have the information I need, her life will be unimportant to me. Even if the time comes to dole out her sentencing, there is no law stating that *you* personally have to be the one who carries it out."

Knox frowns and repositions his mask and hood. "Tick tock, Colum, the law awaits."

The door hisses shut behind him, and I collapse into my chair.

Knox and I haven't had an amicable relationship even at the best of times, but there's always been a level of disrespect he wouldn't cross.

Those threats were different. They were real. If the arbitors find out everything I've been hiding from them, I'll be forced into the Nymbing Program my father instated. Even I'm not immune to reconditioning.

But would Knox truly follow through? He is a man of whims and passions. All he craves is satisfaction.

I just need to keep him from breaking his cage.

Chapter 3

Margot

Alone in the training room, surrounded by aged equipment and tattered sparring mats, I pound my fits into the frayed punching bag. I've been at it for an hour now. My knuckles ache and my body is overheated, but I push through.

The old me never trained like this. The old me would have slept in before the mission. But here's where I find the new me every spare second, training myself half to death, finding any semblance of control in this universe controlled by a bloodline who can entrap anyone's mind with a single brush of their skin.

I'm strong on my own, I think to myself. *I don't need crows to survive the proditors.* I push down Knox's crows anytime they try to take over. Instead, I work on training my innate strength that nobody can take from me.

The door of the recreation room slides open. "Margot?"

"I'm busy, Dimitri." I stop to re-wrap my knuckles.

He finds a spot near a piece of equipment and leans against it. "We're leaving in less than an hour and you're not close to ready."

"I just needed to warm up."

"You know, Lucinda said you didn't have to go. Maybe it would be best—"

"Stop that." I return to my spot in front of the punching bag. "I'm going."

Dimitri sighs as I continue punching. "You know, when I agreed to train you, I thought I was doing you a favor, but it seems I've created an obsession."

"The ability to protect yourself isn't an obsession," I pant. "Besides, I may not always have crows, so I need to be confident in my own strength."

"Yes, but even with my years and expertise in training, I don't think I could defeat a gloveless proditor."

Crows and fear flood the veins of my forearms. My next punch shakes the punching bag and the force nearly knocks the chain off the hook.

Dimitri visibly swallows but says nothing as he pushes away from the equipment. "Get dressed and meet me in the parking garage. Don't be late or Oliver will have an aneurysm."

I reach out and stop the punching bag from moving. "I'll be there soon." Once he's gone, I move to a mat and stretch to cool down.

I know what Dimitri thinks. The words he's too fearful to say out loud or admit to himself. When he watches me train, he can't deny the tick in my muscles. How I'm not myself when I swing a punch or land a kick.

And he's right. When I do those things without resisting the crows, it makes me feel like *him*.

And I don't want to be anything like Knox Arris.

I nicknamed the crow link as the "Nexus"—a sick bond I share with an even sicker man. As long as Knox is alive, I will always feel this knot of his power.

It usually only manifests when my adrenaline peaks. My skin crawls anytime my gait feels foreign or when I pick up a utensil in a way only he would. At worst, it's a specific angle of a punch toward the solar plexus, taking the air from sparring partners' lungs. Or to their kidneys where they writhe in pain for just a moment longer than usual. It's something I'll have to resist leaning into on the mission.

When I'm done stretching, I head to the locker room to get ready and my communicator beeps. Dimitri's name pops up on the translucent purple screen to let me know the vehicles are almost ready.

I quickly slip my boots on then sort through the supply shelf, packing medical supplies into my side satchel for the mission. As I reach for a bottle of rubbing alcohol, my arm stiffens.

All at once, my nostrils fill with the rubbery scent of the torture room. I can feel the cool metal against my back and the leather tight against my wrists. Fear as sharp as razor blades slices through me.

"No, sweetheart. You don't get the mercy of looking away. You're going to look at him. Know that your weakness caused this."

A high-pitched ring pierces through my eardrum.

Breathe, breathe, I tell myself as I fall to my knees.

Phantom pain shoots through my forearm. I yelp and my eyes water.

Crux isn't here. This isn't real.

I pull myself up and lean against the lockers, placing a hand on my sternum, barely keeping up with my breaths. *You're safe. You're safe.*

I roll up my sleeve.

The scars sit in a line on my forearm as they always have. Un-bloodied and completely healed. The ones that Alarik gave me so many months ago.

I try to push his tortured face out of my head. The way Crux forced him to hurt me. If it wasn't for Alarik, I would still be imprisoned. I may even be dead. Because of him, I have a shred of sanity left.

I muster up enough willpower to put the rubbing alcohol in my satchel with the other first aid supplies without triggering another episode before heading out.

The heavy vapor of gasoline replaces the normally stale air of the vehicle warehouse. Light poles hang from the cave walls. The floors are sleek and black—the design taste of the base's former owner, whom Lucinda doesn't like to talk about.

Rows of vehicles line the garage. A handful of them are parked in the center for the mission. Rebels run around, performing last-minute maintenance and filling up the trunks with supplies.

Oliver fuels his motorcycle while one of the newer rebels, Kaia, jabbers on to him about something while she should be working.

Besides Kaia, a few volunteers joining the mission are newer recruits in training. Like everyone else in the rebellion, they are here because they've lost nearly everybody in their lives. Being in our organization means no connections to the outside world, meaning most of us are orphans as a result of Balistar. Lucinda is the only mother most of us know.

Dimitri stands next to a motorcycle with a helmet tucked under his arm. "Careful, if you don't perk up, you'll get frown lines like Lucinda."

I grab another helmet off the nearby rack, unable to force a smile. "You mean the ones she has because of you?"

Dimitri laughs. "There she is."

I wince. It's comments like that, when he tries to patch the strange unexplained rift between us, that wear at my tolerance. When he sees me like a defenseless animal trapped in a well. He hasn't accepted it yet—that I'm not trapped. I'm here, standing next to him, while he searches the well for a girl who no longer exists. But saying that would only break his heart.

Oliver gathers everyone for the mission briefing. "There will be three teams, which you've already been separated into. One of those teams is Margot and Dimitri, who will override the primary server. My team of four will be responsible for taking out the backup servers. The third team will monitor the guards and, if needed, take out any that pose a threat. Nobody, under any circumstance, is to veer off path without my explicit direction. If there are any emergencies, use your earpiece to communicate. Any questions?"

After the briefing is complete, Dimitri turns to me while everyone else loads into ATVs or hops onto motorcycles.

"You riding with me?" he asks.

I nod. "No sharp turns this time. There's no need to show off in front of the new recruits."

Dimitri laughs and revs the engine as I hop on behind him.

Once everyone's respirators are secure, the door of the vehicle exit opens. Engines fired up, we head out into the large field on the outskirts of Merth.

We ride for hours over dirt hills as the sun sets, shining a lilac glow over the patchy hills. The branches on the scattered trees weep and their stumps slouch. Most of Lavenai's flora barely survives. Regions that should be filled with jungles became desolate deserts and it hasn't snowed since I was an infant.

Periodically, we pass small homes or small warehouses, the majority of which are abandoned. Most people don't have the survivalist skills to live away from most of the population. Those who can afford to live away from civilization are considered rich, not primitive. Nonetheless, the few elite of Lavenai still choose to live in Merth or other big cities.

I lower my mask from beneath my tinted helmet, taking in the air. In these more reclusive parts of Lavenai, away from the bigger cities and factories, the air is somewhat breathable without a mask. I'll never forget my first breath in Ashtanabo's capital of Heidl. At the time, I hadn't realized it was the first fresh breath of nature I'd taken in my entire life. If I had, I would have savored it. I wouldn't have listened to a word Lady Lorne or Bruis said, sat on the ground, and simply breathed.

In the sky, a ship descends toward the base and I instinctively lower my head. A large circular structure appears on the horizon and searchlights emerge. Oliver shoots a hand up.

We follow him into a sect of scattered trees and slow down to minimize the sounds of our vehicles. He parks and hops off his motorcycle.

I step off Dimitri's motorcycle and stretch my legs, honing in on the sounds of the base in the distance.

One of the rebels pulls the bag of guard uniforms out of a trunk and distributes them between us. I hold mine out in front of me. Dimitri once killed someone to get a guard's uniform for me. It's how I was able to sneak into the Imnicus. Though that one had a red stripe and nearly got me caught before I stepped foot on the transport ship.

We all quickly change into our disguises while Oliver re-briefs us.

The last few buckles click as I place the guard's helmet over my head and adjust the sleeves.

Dressed and ready, all ten of us emerge from behind the trees, splitting into three groups and keeping to the shadows as we near our target. Dimitri stays close to my side.

The octagonal building is a metallic coliseum with fences, towers, and searchlights. It looks more like a prison than a base. A few guards patrol the tops of the base, but not as many as I'd expect for a structure of this size.

Dimitri and I stick to paths that skirt around the lights. Though when light does touch us, our uniforms keep us safe from detection.

The purple shield atop the base vanishes. A ship slowly ascends out of it—a ship model similar to Knox's. My pulse skips. A rush of air moves the surrounding grass, a buzz rumbling the ground under my feet. The ship's engine whirs loudly before tilting at an angle and accelerating toward the sky. A boom resounds before the ship becomes nothing more than a star in the distance.

If it wouldn't compromise our original mission, I would say we should steal a ship to fly straight to Ashtanabo.

We find a lower area of ground—a drainage ditch with tall grass right next to the tall wired fence.

Once, when we were teenagers, Dimitri and I went exploring with Oliver and stumbled upon a fence like this one. Oliver dared me to touch it, as we challenged each other a lot back then. Dimitri tried to stop me. Needless to say, that was the last time Oliver and I dared each other to do anything.

Dimitri and I move toward the fence as if we're patrolling before coming to a stop in front of it.

"You think Imory's intel is right? That the electricity is broken?" I ask. "What if they fixed it?"

Dimitri shrugs. "That's the thing. Her intel also included that this is the most mismanaged Ashtanaban base on Laven soil."

"You want us to just risk it?"

He pulls a device from his belt. A voltmeter. "You don't think I'd come that unprepared, do you?"

"You're saying I am?"

He chuckles and tests the wires while I study the rest of the base. Even though there are spotlights and cameras everywhere, not a single guard patrols the exterior. That's not typical for Ashtanaban-run bases and I'm sure if the Colum learned of this base's practices, he'd have their heads.

"It's clear." Dimitri kneels and pulls out pliers. He cuts the bottom of the fence until he can bend the metal upward. "I'll go first."

He crawls on his stomach beneath the wire. After he's through, I follow behind.

We quickly make our way to the base's exterior and head to the nearest door. I'm ready to put my pick-pocketing skills to the test, but Dimitri pushes the button beside the door first. It opens.

"I haven't been on a mission this easy since we broke into that clothing warehouse a few years back." Dimitri steps inside.

"Yes, as it turned out they had nothing worth stealing."

The room seems to be a breakroom for the guards. There's a vending machine, a fridge, and a television that tunes into Ashtanaban media. Crumbs cover the hexagonal tables, and wrappers lie inches away from the trash can.

"The server is on the west side of the base," I say. "We're still south of that. We'll need to walk naturally, especially since we are without guard-issued firearms."

"You're saying I walk too Laven?"

When I snuck aboard the Imnicus, it was my gait that prompted Milo's suspicion of me. "Very. Straighten your posture and lengthen your neck too."

"How fancy." Dimitri opens the next door into the primary hallways. "Stay close."

I huff as I stride past him. "I'm not a child."

He stabs his elbow into my side and snickers. "Yeah, but when we were kids, you had better comebacks than that."

Irritation rises with his words, but I bite my tongue.

We stay quiet as we trail through the halls. Every time we see a guard, I nudge Dimitri so he remembers to walk properly.

My mouth goes sour at the sight of the hallways. They remind me of the Imnicus's smooth walls and electronic sliding doors. If this hallway were cleaner, it could be the cousin of the south wing.

Four guards turn the corner toward us. Dimitri and I stiffen, keeping a hold on our composure.

Their uniforms aren't as pristine as I'm used to, their zippers and buttons loose, the fabric slightly wrinkled, and their postures are relaxed.

As they near, one turns their head in our direction. The string inside me pulls taut.

"Hey, you two coming to the party tonight?" he yells over to us.

After a second too long of silence, I look up at Dimitri through the helmet's visor. A female voice may be suspicious, considering Ashtanaban women aren't mandated to join the military.

Dimitri finally gets the hint. "Oh . . . uh! You got it, boss."

Boss? I shake my head.

"Nice! Smith is sneaking in drinks for it." He places a finger over his helmet where his lips would be. "Don't tell the higher ups."

"Wouldn't dream of it," Dimitri says.

After they disappear across the corner, I pinch myself to settle my nerves. That could have been close.

A few halls down, we find the server room, and the two guards at the entrance let us by without a security check.

The room glows purple from the walls covered in tech panels. Server structures are stationed side by side in neat rows. Somewhere within are the facial scans of our people. According to Imory's contact, all we need to do is find the correct port and insert the string of code that would destroy the records without any unwanted attention.

"This place makes our own server room look like a bootleg black-market job," Dimitri says.

"Because it was a black-market job. Our whole operation is held together with gum and confiscated goods."

He nudges me. "Remember when we would play tag in there?"

My patience flickers, my tone becoming short. "You don't need to keep saying stuff like that, you know?"

"Like what?" Even through the tinted helmet, I can see Dimitri's eyes narrow.

I shouldn't bring this up right now, but I can't take it anymore. "It's like you're always trying to bring me back and remind me of who I was."

He frowns. "We're family. It's because I care about you. You think it's easy for me to watch you deteriorate after what that monster did to you?"

"Just . . . forget I said anything."

"Margot—"

"I *died* on the Imnicus. Why can't you accept it, Dimitri?"

Dimitri falls silent and clears his throat. "Let's just finish the job, all right?"

"Gladly." I push past him. Back then, upsetting Dimitri would be enough for me to cry. But now—nothing, because it doesn't matter what he says. I will never be who he once knew.

After following the rows of organized servers to our destination, we stop in front of one of the tall, glowing structures.

"Here it is. Server 12-B." Dimitri pulls out the attached computer and types away.

I pull out the corrupted drive and insert it into the port, then I speak into my earpiece. "Oliver, we found it."

"Got it. We just finished up with the backup servers." Oliver says back through the frequency.

"You remember the code to activate the virus?" I ask Dimitri.

"Of course I do!" Dimitri snaps as he types harder than he needs to on the keyboard. He works through the prompts for a good ten minutes and the upload begins.

Oliver's voice reignites in my ear piece. *"We need backup in the shipyard!"*

"Shit," Dimitri and I say in unison.

The upload bar is only ten-percent complete.

"Finish up here. I'll see what's going on," I say.

Dimitri says nothing. My chest stings.

I rush out of the server room. What on earth could have happened? They had just finished their task, and it's not like Oliver for his teams to get caught.

Sirens wail, the hallways turning a deep red, and guards rush out of rooms toward the shipyard. I pick up the pace, staying a few steps behind the guards when I should really be sprinting ahead.

I rush into the yard filled with an endless amount of docked ships.

Oliver and Kaia brawl in hand-to-hand combat with a handful of guards near a small tactical ship. Where is the rest of Oliver's team?

No matter what happened, I have to stop this before more Ashtanaban backup is called.

I pull two sedation syringes from my belt and jog forward behind the circle of guards. With a grunt, I leap and plunge them into the necks of two guards.

"What the—" One rips the syringe out of his neck.

The other turns to charge at me. "I'll teach you a lesson!"

But his threats are short lived, his eyes rolling into the back of his head. Both guards fall with a thump to the ground.

Three guards spin around. I ready my fists.

"Another one!" a guard shouts.

I sprint at the first one with raging adrenaline. Without trying, the Nexus kicks in. I curse. There's no time to try to meditate the crows away. I need to fight.

My fist meets one of the guard's visors and it shatters like glass. He falls over with a thud.

Another aims his gun and his finger presses down on the trigger. Bullets propel in my direction and I duck, barely missing the assault.

"Bastard!" The guard moves to re-aim. "I'll end—"

I leap and wrap my legs around his waist, slamming him to the ground harder than necessary. His head hits the side of a ship, knocking him out cold.

Control your rage, I tell myself.

I look to my right to choose my next target and something jams into the back of my visor. Before I can stop the next blow, my helmet twists, leaving me blind. Before I know it, hands pry it off my head.

My vision clears in time to see a barrel pointed at my chest. The crows ready themselves, absorbing any fear.

The guard tilts his head. "I think I'll get a promotion after this one."

I drop flat against the ground as the muzzle flashes, spraying bullets into the wall behind me. I swipe my legs to knock the guard off his. With all my might, I elbow the side of his helmet, ensuring he won't be conscious again for another hour. Oliver finds his bearings and jumps into the brawl, knocking another guard out.

The two of us form a small bubble of safety among a sea of chaos. Between us, stands Kaia, completely frozen, limbs locked in fear.

I hear another set of shouts from a balcony, the rest of Oliver's team rushing down the steps in our direction.

The last conscious guard lunges at me with a dagger. I deflect the lunge easily, grabbing his wrist and elbow before he can scramble away. Energy surges through me, and I forcefully bring his arm down upon my knee. The crunch of bone sends shudders of blissful energy through me.

I stop to take in the surrounding scene of groaning guards and sprays of blood. A painting of violence that fills me with satisfaction.

Oliver stands there wide-eyed with a border-line horrified look. "Margot, I've never seen you do that before."

I shake my head. "There is no time to—"

A guard at my feet wails and grabs a dagger from his belt, quickly shuffling to his feet before aiming his dagger straight at Oliver.

I don't have time to think things through, so I lunge at the guard, grab his skull in my palms, and break his neck with a single movement.

All the rebels go still. My limbs freeze.

I'm not an assassin like Dimitri or Oliver. I'm not a proditor. I've never killed anyone before.

And the worst part is, power surged through me, like I could take on ten even stronger men now, even though I should be completely exhausted and winded.

What is happening to my body? To my mind?

Dimitri catches up to the group. "It's done. Now what the hell happened here?"

Oliver shoots a glare at Kaia. "This rookie thought it was wise to go off mission and steal a ship for the rebellion."

Kaia is in absolute tears now. "I—I just thought . . ."

"No, that's the problem. You didn't think!" Oliver yells. "You ignored my direct instruction to not stray from the mission. Because of you, I had to leave the rest of my team behind to save your ass!"

"The base is on high alert and more guards will be here any minute," I say. "We need to get out of here while we still have a chance." I'm as angry as Oliver at the rookie, but there's nothing to be done about it now. Punishing her will be a job for Lucinda.

The alarms blare overhead. Dark-red lights spin and metal gates fall over all the doorways, locking us in.

"Fuck." Oliver lets out a few more curses before glaring at Kaia.

Dimitri scans the shipyard for possible exits before staring at the night sky. "Looks like the only way out is up."

"With that shield? We're not going anywhere." Oliver jabs.

"I remember similar shields onboard the Imnicus, though you could fly through those to keep oxygen in. The ships would simply fly toward the hangar exit, and the secondary shields would lower once they got close enough. There must be a sensor onboard for authorized vessels," I say. "Besides, an alarm like this wouldn't override the sensors. They'd want ships in the air during any other incident. Nobody would have had time to manually lockdown the hangar yet."

"Then what do you suggest?" Oliver folds his arms.

"I'm not trained for most of these ships, but I can manage that model." I point to a ship on the other side of the yard. It's golden and similar to the one Milo trained me on. I may not remember a lot, but with Knox's muscle memory, this may just work.

"Then there's no time to waste. Let's go!" Oliver commands the group.

At the sound of a shrill beep, all of our heads shoot to the same part of the yard. One of the hangar garages slowly opens.

"What the hell is that?" Dimitri asks sharply.

The garage is so dark, I have to squint to make out anything. Are those ships? They're so horizontal, with something on top like a metal . . . head.

I suck in a breath.

They're not ships. They're machines. And not just any machines . . .

Large, obsidian-colored robots stand in a line, all of them at least ten-feet tall with gigantic arms and legs. Their cubical heads rival the size of car engines and their fists are strong enough to knock over a boulder. They're nothing like the robotic servants on the Imnicus. No, these aren't meant for serving royalty but for punishing humanity.

Gallow Machines.

I've heard of these from Lucinda and others old enough to remember the takeover. Balistar used them as one of the final blows to win the war against Lavenai. One of them could take on an entire squad of trained military fighters. We're just a ragtag group of spies and assassins facing down five killer machines.

"Run!" Dimitri shouts.

We sprint just as their power cores whir. I run harder and faster than I ever have in my life. To be caught by one would be lethal. A complete blood bath.

I peek over my shoulder just as their heads rise and their eyes glow red.

All at once, the five Gallows run at us.

It only takes a few of their heavy steps to bring a rumble to the ground, strong enough to slow down our run. The vibrations shoot up to my kneecaps, but we can't stop running. In their hands, they'll pop us like grapes.

My heart is in my throat, and my muscles burn and ache. The heave in my lungs grows worse from the fear raging through me, fueled by memories of gory stories about the Gallows.

"Margot!" one of the boys yells behind me. Tatum.

Before I can turn my head, I wince at his ear-splitting scream. The splatter of blood against the ground.

No. Stop. Don't do this to them. They're only on the mission because of what I did. Punish me instead.

My composure takes a second blow as I hone in on the reflection of one of the ships. Kaia.

Don't stop running, Margot. You can't save—

I can't watch as a Gallow swipes her up. As it snaps her spine in half as she screams in horror.

"Shit!" Oliver curses and gags.

Dimitri slaps himself while he runs a few strides in front of me.

My fingers and toes go numb as another rebel is swiped up by a Gallow. Then another. Lightheadedness takes over at the stench of blood.

This is your fault, a voice whispers in my head. *You caused this.*

When we get to the ship, Dimitri and Oliver leap inside. I follow after them, sliding in to help pull the survivors up.

The last guy tries to jump in, falling on his torso on the ramp.

Dimitri reaches for him. "Get up! Hurry!"

The boy is too late. A gallow is on us in seconds, grabbing the boy and dragging him off the ship. Dimitri yells and I pull him back before he gets snatched too. With all my might, I slam my hand onto a button, closing the ramp and securing us inside.

At the control panel, Oliver hits buttons nonsensically.

"Go check on the survivors." I nudge him aside and flick a switch. The panel lights up and I work the controls until the ship slowly ascends. The engine whirs as the ship's legs hover off the ground.

But the ascension stops. We're being dragged down.

"What's going on?" Oliver shouts.

Dimitri peeks out a window. "They're grabbing onto the ship! Margot, get us out of here!"

"I'm working on it!" I grit my teeth and fumble with a few more buttons. I can't remember all of what Milo taught me. Parts are coming back bit by bit but not fast enough.

My throat goes dry as three Gallows punch the front of the ship.

I have no choice. I have to use the Nexus . . . intentionally.

I close my eyes, ignoring the nausea that Knox's crows bring as I let his shadow step into me at full control.

My eyelids shoot open and my body moves without my mind telling it to. My hands move over the panel, pressing buttons and pulling levers. Screens light up and the engine kicks on.

I pull back one of the thrusters, the ship ascending with an even force.

As we ascend, higher and higher, the ship goes as light as a feather as one of the Gallows loses its robotic grip.

The other ones grab on too, but I fight back, accelerating the ship until a burning smell overtakes the cockpit. One by one, the Gallows lose their hold.

The shield opens for us, and once we're past it, the last gallow falls.

I bite down on my inner lip as my hand automatically hits a silver button, launching the ship far from the base.

We're only a few hundred feet away before the engine sputters. I aim the ship toward the forest, gritting my teeth.

Come on, you can make it.

The ship loses altitude, the screen lights glitching as we propel toward trees.

"Brace!" I shout.

Everyone gets on the ground and covers their heads. I bend and reignite Knox's crows, my hand instinctively pulling back a lever.

In the reflection, Oliver and Dimitri fall over, grasping for something to hold onto. I hold onto the control panel for dear life, my knees going out from the force.

The ship slides through the forest, raking over tree roots. It's thrown around by trunks before catching on mud and skidding to a complete stop.

My abdomen loosens and my arms fall to my side as the Nexus releases.

Dimitri sighs in relief and Oliver slumps to the ground, grabbing his hair.

I place a hand on my forehead. This isn't how this was supposed to go. I was supposed to fix everything, and the rebellion was going back to normal. Yes, we cleared our faces. But at what cost?

We lost half our team. Two of them were rookies, and they weren't supposed to die on their first mission. They would still be alive if I hadn't compromised our faces to begin with.

The Nexus rages through my veins, and I punch the control panel once, then twice, and again until my knuckles bleed.

Oliver catches my arm before I can land another blow. "Stop it. This is Kaia's fault, not yours."

"It doesn't mean she deserved to die."

The drive back to the rebellion is quiet and somber. Dark and piercing. Lavenai's moons stare down at me, their cratered eyes sunken.

Chapter 4

Milo

My head rests against the wooden wall as I let the steam of the room take over my muscles. Normally in here, I lose myself to the heat, mentally exhausting myself to the point where I can't think of anything besides tolerating it.

Today, not even the heat is enough to push out Knox's threats.

It's true that my father trained Knox in forbidden Vicar magic—ravens, owls, and finches, and without my father around, he's careless with it. If only my father had given him the ability to use doves, then maybe I wouldn't be dealing with how sick Knox's crows truly are. The second my father died, every dove in Knox's body left him, leaving him consumed by vicious birds with no way to tame them.

Knox can cause hallucinations in the environment without having to touch a person's skin, as long as they're in his line of sight. When his power is at its peak, he can even break into minds without skin contact. Though, he cannot cause any real pain to a victim in that state—not unless he utilizes the power of another proditor's touch.

I step out of the steam room and into the adjoining shower area, lathering my hair in shampoo.

I hear the door swing open and I step further back inside the tiled nook. Only proditors and myself have authorized access into this room, so there's only one of five people it could be.

My muscles relax when Dune speaks from behind the wall. "Colum?"

"Yes?"

"The maids said you forgot your change of clothes."

I turn my gaze to the empty bench, then to the hamper where I've already discarded my old clothing. *That I did.* "Leave it."

I hear the stack of clothes hit a bench before he returns back behind the wall. Dune was gone for so long tracking the rebellion that he only met Margot once—when I sent her on the mission to Lavenai. Little did she know, Dune was watching her until she disappeared into the underground, just in case something went awry. I also wanted Alarik to have backup in case Knox lost control of himself while flying her there.

My crows reach the wall and they relay the tightness of his chest and the tension in his upper back.

Dune sighs and I hear his leather armor adjust as he leans against the partition separating us. "Do you ever forget about our bonded crows?"

"In truth, yes."

Dune's family joined the Vicars when I was barely able to walk. They were from the tribe of Nonaka and traveled the planet to find us after they discovered they also held crows, which was unusual outside of the Eskdale Mountains. After my father took over, Wayra Catawnee swore his family's eternal allegiance to ours. They allowed his crows to intertwine with my father's so that if my father was ever in danger, Wayra would know. They bonded Dune and me with the same dark magic as well, yet it didn't have quite the same effect.

"The bond felt more ceremonial at the time," he says. Dune takes his family's oath seriously, even without the tangible feelings of our linked crows. For instance, if we both had children, Dune would expect his child to watch over my son or daughter.

"Your point?" I ask.

"The distress you're bearing . . . It's painful to be around. I don't only feel it in the same room with you, but I feel it across the Imnicus too."

I turn off the shower and reach for my towel to dry off my raven hair. "Whatever you're feeling is in your head. I'm half-proditor, so we can't sense each other's states the way your father could mine." Most of my magic is perception-based to begin with.

"That's what I've always thought too. But now—" Dune's communicator beeps and he stays silent.

"What?" With a towel around my hips, I walk around the wall and grab my clothes.

"It's the rebellion." Dune lowers his communicator. "They're infiltrating a base."

The command center is pure chaos; My hair is still wet. Live security footage plays on every monitor at every angle. At a station, Dune communicates with Laven-stationed proditors to put them en route.

"How long have they been within the base?" I ask.

Aisil scrolls through the footage. "We estimate less than twenty minutes."

In the base's shipyard, two rebels fight off a cluster of guards. I don't notice the lone guard running toward the commotion until they pierce syringes through two guards' necks.

Another rebel wearing a guard's uniform?

The rebel fights off the guards tooth and nail. It isn't until the rebel loses their focus and their helmet falls from their head that I slowly sit, my pulse raging.

Margot.

It's her.

I can't take my eyes off her long lashes or her golden locks as she ruthlessly fights off my guards, barely blinking while she takes them down like flies. She's so different like this. So similar to the girl I had interrogated with rage in her face.

I grip the arm rest when she breaks someone's arms like a flimsy board—Knox's signature move.

She absorbed more of him than I thought, and I'm not sure if I should be more worried for my reign's well-being or her own. Margot having Knox's combat skills could be lethal for the Arris Reign in the long run. My cousin is as skilled at fighting as he is with dark magic. But he's also sadistic and unmerciful against his enemies.

I unbind the knots in my abdomen and push her out of my head, focusing back on the big picture.

What is the rebellion's game? What are they trying to do?

I have a thousand questions but no time to ask Aisil them all. The rebels are at the base *now*. I can end this *now*—the rebellion; the woman who plagues me.

I'll take them all dead or alive.

I stand and rest my palms on the surface of a control panel between two officers. Their bodies tense while they replay footage, piecing previous events together.

If any of them recognize Margot, my supposed wife, they don't show it. Regardless, I'll have every last one of them sworn to secrecy on threat of death if they utter a word of this to anyone outside of this command center.

"Release the Gallows," I say.

Aisil's eyes widen. "You can't be serious? They haven't been used since—"

"I said do it!"

Aisil shouts orders to the surrounding officers. They promptly override the Gallows software to control the robots' movements from the Imnicus.

Every child on Lavenai knows the stories of the Gallows. They're what my father used to bring Lavenai to complete submission. As long as Margot has Knox's muscle memory, on top of everything she knows, she's dangerous to the Arris Reign. I should have taken her out the second she got back from her mission on Lavenai like Crux suggested.

Now, I'll rectify that mistake.

The hangar opens.

The rebels sprint for their lives.

Margot's composure breaks little by little as she runs, the veins in her neck sticking out.

My gaze locks on my ring snug around her thumb and my chest tightens. I lean forward on the desk.

In the corner of my eye, Aisil picks his cuticles raw as he watches the Gallows in hot pursuit. A few of the officers wince when the first rebel gets swiped up and blood splatters across the shipyard. I sit back in one of the chairs, cross my legs, and lean on the arm rest as a rebel girl's spine snaps.

Aisil lowers his trembling voice for my ears only. "I don't see how we'll explain this to the arbitors if something happens to Margot."

"Keep the pursuit going. That's an order." My eyes are locked on Margot's heaving breaths.

Her fate is in my hands. I could stop the Gallows with a single word.

Considering how quick Gallows are, most of the rebels cannot outrun them. A lucky few make it, the group of them piling into one of the ships. The Gallows grab another rebel before Margot shuts the ramp.

The ship ascends, and it takes everything in me to maintain my composure.

Aisil turns to the officers. "Take that ship down!"

They type commands to the Gallows to bring down the ship, and as they grab on, smoke emits from the bottom of the ship. *You're not getting away that easily, Margot. Not when you barely know the basics of flying.*

But the ship fights against the Gallows' grips. Then it performs an advanced maneuver that I certainly didn't teach her.

My anger simmers, and I internally curse. I knew Margot could use Knox's combat skills. But his aerial ones too? He gave her too much of himself.

The Gallows lose their grip and the ship shoots off in the distance.

My jaw and shoulders tense.

"I'm sorry, sir." Aisil bows his head. "We'll have a team track the ship at once."

"They'll be long gone before soldiers get to them."

Even without me yelling or cursing, everyone stands on edge, waiting for my next command.

If Knox wouldn't have gone overboard with his crow transfer, the rebels wouldn't have gotten away. Margot wouldn't be a true threat to the Arris Reign. Not to mention the base staff, which turned out to be so incompetent that we had to fight the rebels from the Imnicus.

I don't know what the rebellion was after. If their goal was to steal a ship, they were unsuccessful. There is no way they'll be able to fly it back to Merth before soldiers track them.

The only way I'll catch her is by hunting her down myself. Face to face. She wants to break into my base? Reignite her rebellion? Now that I know their organization is coming up for air again, I won't let them get much farther. Not without a fight.

"Aisil, prepare my ship. We're going to Lavenai."

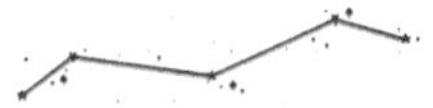

"You all say it's everyone's fault and nobody's fault. Which is it, then?" I ask. "Am *I* to blame for placing a base in the middle of nowhere? Or is it the bulk of you for allowing rebels to infiltrate it?"

Commander Aisil and Proditor Onyx stand behind me near the ramp of my ship. The line of guards keep their eyes trained on the blood-stained ground of the Laven base's shipyard.

Many of them are bruised and battered from Margot and the rebels; others stand completely unharmed, the ones who didn't respond to the breach alarm quickly enough before the Gallows were released. Sweat forms on their necks as they look at one another. All of them are quick to blame, but none of them are willing to step forward. Not with a proditor mere feet away.

I pace up and down the line with my hands laced behind my back. "A battalion lives and dies by its leader's competence. Aisil, which one of them is in charge?"

Commander Aisil steps forward, his voice off kilter. "T-that would be Major Fletcher, and unfortunately, he was among the deceased."

Past the carnage of rebel bodies lies the major who has yet to be put into a body bag. "Who comes next in the chain of command?"

Aisil shakes his head, holding back for a second before speaking. "Captain Maguire."

I motion to the line. "Step forward."

A young man with sweaty hands takes a pained breath before stepping out from the row.

I stop in front of him, his eyes filled with fear he's so desperately trying to control. "Major Maguire, explain to me how a base can be so mismanaged that a handful of rebels entered undetected without any security clearance?"

Captain Maguire swallows. "It seems they knew of weak spots around the base and were able to break in through there. We found one of the barbed wire fences completely cut open. It led to one of the unguarded employee entrances."

"And why was it left unguarded?"

He breaks eye contact and looks to Onyx. "Major Fletcher—"

"Major Fletcher is dead. Answer my question."

"It was late in the evening, and a lot of us shower around that time. We've never had anyone break in before so—"

"This base got lax. Is that what you're telling me?" I reach forward and grab his jaw, bringing his eyes back to mine. "Don't be scared. There's no need to look at the proditor. You came out of the ordeal without so much as a scratch while those who ranked lower fought your battles. Tell me, where were you while this was happening?"

"I got the transmission late as I was showering. Colum, we will do better in the future, I assure you!"

"I'll make sure of that."

I squeeze his face tighter before releasing him sharply. He steps back and falls to his knees.

I turn on my heels to face my ship. "Lieutenants, teach your superior a lesson."

As I ascend the ramp, the lieutenants form a circle around the captain. Punches, grunts, and yelps ring out as they beat the living daylights out of him. Under my rule, rank has nothing to do with who can punish who. I find that ordering lower ranking soldiers to punish the higher-ranking ones gets the job done. Humiliation brings a level of order to the Ashtanaban army. It keeps everyone in line. It shows that no matter how high someone's rank is, they can still be reduced to nothing. It was a belief my father passed onto me.

"Did we find out what the rebels were after?" I ask as I take my seat on the ship across from Onyx.

The commander doesn't meet my eyeline and my crows relay the perspiration forming on the back of his neck. "You see, Colum—"

"Let me," Onyx says, crossing his legs and resting an elbow on the arm rest. "One of the technicians told me the rebels wanted to wipe their faces from Lavenai's database so they could freely move about the capital on missions."

I completely forgot that this base was responsible for the facial database. It makes me all the more furious that this base was so incompetent. "And? Were the rebels successful?"

Onyx hesitates. "Yes."

Every muscle in my body coils. This can still be rectified. "When will their faces be re-uploaded?"

Onyx rubs the seams of his gloves together. "They can't. The backups have been compromised too."

I sit back in disbelief, barely able to contain my anger. With the rebellion's facial data destroyed, that would include Margot's. I never thought to have a scan of my own created on the Imnicus, and it's impossible to have reliable data drawn from recordings.

Margot, when I get my hands on you and your rebels, it will be the end for you all.

Chapter 5

Margot

Lucinda stands solemnly in front of the crowd of rebels, all of us fighting the urge to tear up while she delivers a eulogy. The projection screen displays a picture of Kaia, along with the other deceased members.

I clench my fists. My death toll is climbing. We wouldn't have had to go on the mission if it weren't for me. Lucinda keeps reminding me that the operation would have had a successful getaway if Kaia hadn't gone off-mission, but I can't push the blame out of my head. Kaia wouldn't have tried to steal a ship if we didn't have to go on the mission to begin with.

After a moment of silence, Lucinda dismisses everyone for the day. I stand in place as rebels funnel around me back to their rooms.

Dimitri says nothing to me as he leaves, but his muddled gaze catches mine. Lucinda still hasn't noticed he and I are quarreling, but the less she knows the better.

Now that our faces are wiped from Ashtabano's database, we can begin the next phase—traveling to Ashtanabo, freeing the hyssopite-like girl from prison, then taking out the temple points one by one.

It's something I have to do. To quell my guilt. To avenge their deaths.

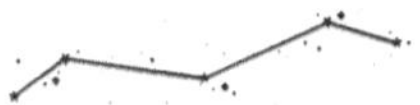

Dimitri, Oliver, and I take a seat at the conference room table with Imory and Lucinda. I keep my arms folded, unable to raise my head.

"We can only move forward," Lucinda says.

"Wonderfully said." Imory nods in agreement. "Margot, are you all right?"

I can't control the flash of heartbreak that washes over my face. "Good people died yesterday. I know *he* was controlling the Gallows. The Imnicus has had primary control over them since Lavenai's occupation. He killed all of them."

Imory purses her lips. "He will always honor his father's wishes, and that's protecting the Arris Reign at any costs."

"You say that as if he has a single ounce of good left in him."

"He's my son, so I have no choice but to believe that a part of him is the boy I once knew. The boy who found the value of life in something as small as a mouse."

"After the way he annihilated rebels like ants?" Dimitri scoffs. "The boy in him is long dead."

Imory's lips form into a straight line.

Lucinda clears her throat. "At the end of the day, it's done. Our faces are erased, and though we lost too many rebels, we need passage to Ashtanabo. A team of rebels will travel to Diyu Prison to free the girl. Once you have her, you'll use her powers to take down every last temple point and restore Lavenai's stolen life force. Ashtanabo will no longer be able to thrive at our expense."

Oliver chimes in. "I want it to be just the three of us. I know we spoke about sending a team of five, but less is better."

I settle back into my seat. "But there are over a hundred temple points, right? This could take months if not years."

"It's something to consider before you trek out," Lucinda says. "I suspect you'll be out for three years, even if you're efficient. There's too much travel involved to be optimistic about it taking less time than that."

"Sacrifice is what we signed up for, right?" I say. "I'd do it even if it takes decades."

"About that, Margot." Lucinda tightens her face. "Though you're essential to this mission, I need to know you can handle it."

I frown. "What do you mean '*handle it*'?"

"The mission report included your combat choices. You ruthlessly broke arms. Hell, you even added to your death count for the first time. I worry about your composure."

My throat burns. "The assassins do the same things in combat, and I don't see their mental state being questioned."

"I was there, Margot," Oliver interrupts. "You weren't . . . *you*."

Dimitri stays silent, his gaze searing into the side of my face.

"Margot, you know my past in crime organizations. I know what it's like to lose control. Between your anger and your increased strength, I worry for you." Lucinda laces her fingers together. "Can you look me in the eye and tell me you can complete this mission without giving into emotion?"

I bite down on my tongue. She doesn't realize how truly horrible Knox's crows are. The way they've haunted me. But I won't let it stop me from going to Ashtanabo. "I can handle it."

"Glad to hear it."

Dimitri asks more questions about the mission, like specifics on the prison's location and potential obstacles. I barely listen, unable to banish the Gallows and Kaia from my head.

Imory's words snap me back into focus. "I think we should focus on the crime lords. With their dubious connections, they could help us."

Oliver pinches the bridge of his nose. "Aren't we on thin ice with them?"

"Joriel may have connections to the military and pilots, and I suspect he's been to Ashtanabo before," Imory says.

I part my lips. It's not something I ever considered. If he gets black market shipments of luxury foods and products from Ashtanabo, why wouldn't he be able to fly there whenever he wants? I'm sure the only thing keeping him from living there permanently is his lack of proper identification. Then again, Joriel is the kind of man who gets off on controlling others and living as if he's king of Merth.

"I'll talk to him," I say. Convincing Joriel is the only time-sensitive way to get off Lavenai. I won't spend another second in endless planning sessions, letting my shame and guilt fester. I need rectification, and if not rectification then a noble distraction.

"Your last interaction with him is the reason I had to dip into rebellion funds," Lucinda says.

"Trust me on this one. It's me he's angry with. Let me settle things with him."

Imory stands, stretching her back. "Maybe it will soften things over in the long run."

Lucinda frowns. "At the very least, bring a weapon."

I ride a motorcycle over dirt paths between mushroom fields. This route takes an hour since the vehicle exit is in the outskirts of Merth, but I want a mode of escape in case things with Joriel go awry. It isn't considered one of our primary entrances and is usually not documented in our files, considering it's not usually conducive to rebellion activity within Merth itself unless we're transporting large amounts of goods.

Even with our faces wiped from the database, I keep the helmet snug on my head with a respirator beneath as a secondary precaution.

I enter the city, purple and pink city lights bending as rain pours over my poncho. Ashtanaban ships fly over the skyscraper city, their engines echoing through the streets. Some back alley restaurants are still open, despite it being late at night. The food isn't worth the cost, no matter how they try to disguise the chemical taste.

I weave my motorcycle between lanes and down alleyways. Guards patrol sidewalks as the nightlife comes into full swing. Music pours out into the streets. If there's one thing Lavens love, it's a night out. There's a part of suffering that breeds debauchery.

I slow my motorcycle and take a turn down a darker street. The lights slowly fade from pink to a deep red, and the music grows more sultry with every business I pass. The scent of alcohol pricks my nostrils.

I park my motorcycle in an alley and secure the kickstand before disappearing into a convenience store to change. The worker doesn't bat an eye at me as I stride past and into the cramped leaky restroom. If I had left the rebellion looking the way I intend to, Lucinda would have locked me away, as would Dimitri, if he were still talking to me.

I carefully remove my pants and shirt and slip on the tight black dress, avoiding grazing against the dirty toilet at all costs. Balancing, I slip off my shoes and throw on the heels one at a time. In the reflection of the murky mirror, I tie my curls into two low buns, squinting as the dim hanging bulb sways behind me.

When I emerge, passing the less-than-edible food on shelves, the convenience store clerk's eyes widen.

I keep to the long awnings of the sidewalks to evade the trickling rain. Sinclair had them built for the long lines that form in front of his club on particular days.

Sinclair's brothel stands in better shape than any of the surrounding buildings. The large, red mirrored sign reflects and bends light throughout the street.

As I approach the entrance, a drunk man stumbles out with lipstick covering his neck. I sidestep to narrowly avoid his stumbling gait.

When I enter, a draft brushes my neck. The music thumps loud enough for my chest to resonate with the deep bass. I take my respirator off, and the scent of alcohol and tobacco collides with my nostrils, only quelled by a hint of cinnamon. Dark-red lights bleed into the mirror-shard chandeliers.

A modded V.I.X. unit erratically flies toward my head to pick up a glass behind me. I duck to avoid it.

I push through the crowds of dancing, kissing, and drinking games, evading any hands that pull me in to join.

In the center of the club, on a slightly raised platform by the dance floor, is Joriel's empty throne. I scoff. Everything in the club is modeled around it for his viewing pleasure. Or at least that's what he wants people to think.

Where is he? Normally when I enter, he drags me to him in ten-seconds flat. My stomach sours. Nobody enters his club without his knowledge. His eyes are on me somewhere, but it seems he wants me to find him first.

I head into the back rooms, shielding my eyes from the depravity of people who didn't close the doors to the private rooms. That or they like being watched, their full passion on display against walls.

When I find two goons with arms bigger than my head guarding a door, I know I've made it to Joriel's office.

I bite down on my inner cheek and approach them. The goons eye each other but ignore me completely.

I thought they'd see the dress and get the hint. I flutter my eyelashes. "Is Joriel here?"

One of them folds his arms and puffs his chest out. "What for?"

"It's about a business proposal."

The goons laugh before one speaks. "Trust me, Joriel has his fair share of *business proposals*. Go enjoy yourself somewhere else, little girl."

"I'll be the judge of that, lads."

My muscles tense at the voice. I turn around slowly.

The young crime lord, dressed in a fitted wine-colored suit, studies the contour of my hips and waist while he leans against his gold cane. His dark-brown hair frames his face and is a bit longer than the last time I had a run in with him.

"Tavish, I'm surprised to see you here. Last I checked, I ordered a hit on you."

My bottom lip twitches. "That was months ago. Let's keep the past in the past."

"To me, it feels like yesterday." Joriel takes a few steps forward. "Don't forget, you took advantage, love."

"Is that what you call it? You changed the terms of our agreement at the very end."

He leans down until his head is at level with mine. "And that's why I'm the best in the business, and it's how I always get what I want."

Not everything, I think to myself. "Can we talk? Alone?"

Joriel's expression grows curious, then he smiles. "Never thought I'd see the day where you asked me that." He motions to his goons to part the way. One of them presses a button on the wall, and the office door slides open. "After you, Tavish."

I straighten my shoulders, ignoring his body heat as he follows close behind me.

Joriel's den is exactly what I'd expect from him. Dark-gray walls surround leather chairs and couches. Books with metal covers line the shelves and frame the blue-flame fireplace. Many of the decorative items in the room are geometric in nature. Very Ashtanaban. Maybe Imory is right about Joriel's travels.

"Please take a seat." Joriel motions to one of the couches while he approaches the minibar and pours two glasses of Ashtanaban whiskey. "How is that cousin of yours?"

"Dimitri is fine," I say, "and employed."

Joriel smirks over his shoulder at me. "I'm recruiting more assassins with his skills."

I tilt my head. "Assassins? Is that all?"

"What can I say? It's hard to find male courtesans when most Laven men work in the factories." He turns, holding the glasses in his hands. "A drink?"

I nod and he hands me the glass, his finger lightly brushing mine. He takes a seat a few feet away from me on the couch. I frown. Here I was thinking he doesn't trust me.

"Now, what is so pressing that you begged to be alone with me?" Joriel asks.

"I didn't beg." I narrow my eyes. "I was wondering about your travels."

Joriel raises an eyebrow. "Travels?"

"Well . . . you're wealthy. I have to assume you've been all over the place."

"Yes, as you'd expect I've been to every region on Lavenai at some point. My father was rich even before the takeover. As a boy, he dragged me on his trips. Though if you're asking presently, still yes."

"And only Lavenai?"

"What are you implying?"

"I'm asking if you've been to other planets?" Of course, he could visit one of the other thousands of planets in our galaxy, but Lavenai and Ashtanabo are the only ones in this solar system. I doubt he's in deep enough to have been to those. Most ships aren't equipped for such speeds, though I've heard of occasional trades occurring with far-off planets. Thank the gods we've never been in a galactic war.

He takes a swig of his drink. "There is, from time to time, a need for a gentleman such as myself to make personal visits to the properties in which I invest."

So it's true. He has been to Ashtanabo "I'm surprised you're not *off-planet* all the time."

"If you're insinuating what I think you are, planets of comfort are boring. Mundane, safe, and filled with routine. Region after region, city after city, and island after island, I could never find what I was searching for. It's what made me realize a human can't reach their full potential without some risk. My father taught me that. It's why, even while Lavenai thrived, he was a crime lord." Joriel's eyes dip to the exposed part of my thigh. "So, you're wanting to travel? Or can I assume your rebellion wants something?"

I set my drink down. "A few of us rebels need passage to Ashtanabo, and I believe you're the only one capable of pulling it off."

Joriel laughs and motions to my body. "Is that what this dress is about? And those heels? You're trying to use your beauty against me? Well, Margot Tavish, that won't work." He sets his whiskey down.

"Joriel, please—"

"Let's say I can get you to Ashtanabo. What's in it for me?"

"I'm sure Lucinda will make it worth your while."

"I have more than enough money."

I can't leave here with a no. It's Joriel or years of finding an alternate solution. I thought my hold on him was stronger and that dressing up for him would be enough to push him into a dazed *yes*.

What can money not buy that would convince Joriel Sinclair to give me passage to Ashtanabo? What's worth risking his business and life?

I scoot closer to him, positioning my body in his direction. This is *more than* a last resort. It wasn't even on the menu. Yet after I offer it, I have no intention of giving it to him. Once I'm on Ashtanabo, I could be there for years to disable temple points. This could work without having to uphold my end of the bargain if he agrees. So yes, I'm manipulating him.

"Margot?" He scans my new position and moves back, like he's unsure if my next move is lethal.

My thigh touches his and he flinches slightly. I take his hand and move it to my waist. "Let's make a deal."

His smile drops and his breath hitches, thumb moving against the fabric on my waist. "What kind of deal?"

"Hmmm . . ." I move over him, straddling his waist from where he sits.

His eyes grow hungry like I'm the last morsel of food on Lavenai. He quickly turns his head. "You're playing a dangerous game bringing that to the table."

I run my hands down his chest. "But I am."

"I want to hear you say it." Anger and arousal lace his breaths, but he doesn't pull his hand away.

"Well, you're a businessman, so let's treat this as such. We both *need* something from each other."

"Clarify it. Quickly." His fingers dig into the fabric, and if I don't lay out the terms quickly, I'll be pinned to the ground beneath him, my dress ripped from my body.

"Firstly, you must successfully complete your end of the bargain before you reap the reward," I say. "Meaning you won't have my body until I return."

His grip around my waist loosens. I move my hands under his shirt and trail my fingers up his abdomen, feeling his muscles twitch under my touch.

"What do you say?" I tuck my head into his defined neck that's beading with sweat, keeping my lips from touching his skin.

"You're a viper." His voice is breathless, his abs moving rapidly with his increased respirations. He holds my waist like it's the only thing keeping him a gentleman. "My life would be on the line if you were caught—"

I put more of my weight on his lap.

"Margot—" Joriel hisses. I know it's taking everything in him not to grab my hips and grind me against him. He moves one hand from my waist up to the back of my neck, scared that if he doesn't hold on tight, this moment will end.

"If you can get me to Ashtanabo, and I make it back to Lavenai alive, you can have me. Fully."

Joriel's grip tightens as he rests his forehead on my chest. He's a man who has everything he wants except one single thing, and now I'm offering him that, but it will cost him.

Joriel moves quickly, tossing me back onto the couch and boxing me in. His breaths shake. "And what if you don't make it back? What do I get out of this?"

The Nexus isn't kicking in like I'd expect, and I don't see the chain of his necklace. Is he hiding hyssopite somewhere else on his body? Or is this a situation Knox would invite, so his crows are appeased? "It's all about risk, isn't it?"

Joriel pinches his eyelids together and forces himself off me. "I accept your offer, Tavish."

I sit up and reach my hand out. "Shake on it?"

He keeps his hands by his sides. "If I touch you again, I won't be able to stop."

Seeing Joriel Sinclair show restraint actually makes me believe him. "All right. Then it's a deal."

"One more thing, Margot."

"Yes?"

"Sleep here tonight in one of my guest rooms. That I insist upon."

Chapter 6

Lleu

How many days has it been now? Two? Ten? My hair hangs matted, my skin dry. At least as a lady's maid, I got to keep up with my routine.

The only time I see anyone is when guards drop off barely edible meals and dried, nutritional mush. Many of them avoid eye contact, pretending like we weren't acquaintances months ago.

There was only so long I could go along with the Colum's plans. It's not like I ever came to the Imnicus willingly, after all. He ripped me from my family, and I'm sure they're worried sick.

Though I'm terrified of what will happen, I'm glad I helped Margot escape. Until her, I never felt . . . purpose. Until her, the height of my potential was making it big as an actress and marrying well. But now I am working for a greater good. I just wish I had the strength to endure the inevitable proditor interrogation. Will my resolve shatter the second they begin?

Around dinnertime, I overhear the robotic food cart squeak down the hallway. The first time I tried the prison food, I nearly vomited, but it only took skipping a few meals for the mush to become palatable.

As the door opens, I brace my nose for the intolerable food along with a grumpy guard. Or maybe even the Colum.

Instead, a proditor stands at the threshold.

I flinch back before my shoulders soften at the sight of the knotted patterns in his metallic mask. He whispers something to the guard before stepping inside, the cell door shutting behind him.

"Alarik." My abdomen tightens at his presence the way it always does when he's around. Though I don't fear him like I do the other proditors. Around him, things are . . . different. Warm. Safe. But mostly I become a ball of nerves incapable of forming a coherent thought because . . . I've never liked anyone as much as I like him.

Alarik sets a tray filled with meats, breads, and vegetables down on the small table. "I thought you could use a break from all the mush."

My mouth waters at the sight of the food. "Thank you."

I sit at the table and it takes everything in me to stay ladylike and not ravenously devour the meal. I pick up the sourdough bread and take a well-mannered bite.

There are so many things I want to ask him, but I have to be careful. Questions sit on the tip of my tongue, and I try to communicate through my eyes what I want to say to him.

Alarik sits down at the small table with me, and after a prolonged, uncomfortable silence, he speaks. "This cell isn't bugged, you can speak freely."

"Thank the gods." I drop my head before cutting into the meat. "Alarik, this is serious. Oh, it's my fault isn't it? I shouldn't have inspected the letter in the hallway."

A flicker of guilt passes over his visible features. "You're apologizing? You should be angry at me. In fact, I thought you'd throw something the second you saw me. I wasn't truthful with you and I got you involved in something I shouldn't have."

"What did you write to her?"

"The less I tell you the better, but it led to Margot's escape, and that's all that matters." Alarik folds his gloved hands together. "Lleu, I won't let them hurt you for what I did. If we plan and time it well, I can sneak you off the Imnicus. Your safety is my sole responsibility."

My body warms at his words. "You know that I'd never betray you, though I don't see a world in which this ends with me still breathing."

Alarik exhales slowly. "I will figure something out."

His promise shifts my despair into hope. It will be nearly impossible to get me off the Imnicus without Alarik also being detected, but he speaks with enough conviction that I believe him.

I swallow another bite of food. "Can I ask . . . why did you do it?"

Alarik exhales slowly. Even with his disguise on, his exhaustion is apparent. Like he's spent every waking moment covering his tracks. "I've spent years numbing myself to the pain of hurting others for a life I never chose. When Margot was captured, I guess the boy I buried awakened again. I didn't know her, but I knew I had to help her."

I lower my fork. "What do you mean?"

Alarik's under eyes darken. He's always kept to himself the way Dune does. As much as we've spoken in passing and at Milo's impromptu meetings regarding Margot, I don't know much about him.

"Milo had us torture her in shifts to get her tablet's code. But when I was alone with her, I couldn't do it. The other proditors broke her so badly that she was hardly responsive when I came in. Something shattered in me and sparked an idea. If I could keep her intact and get her back to Lavenai alive, her rebellion would have more information than ever before about the interworking of the Imnicus. So I used my crows to reverse theirs in any way I could. But Crux caught me and made me torture her as punishment. If Milo found out I spared her . . . ".

"Alarik." I place my hand on his arm. His warmth radiates throughout my body.

"I also took her to the coroner after Knox murdered that innocent girl during the ball. I knew the second she saw those burns, she would see the connection and hopefully unravel Milo's plan. When everything fell apart after her mission, the only thing I could do was help her escape. Truly, I'm sorry I involved you without your permission."

"Don't be sorry." I squeeze his arm tighter. My heart thumps into my throat at the prolonged contact. I'm sure touching a proditor without permission is an execution-worthy offense, but Alarik places his hand over mine. I bite down on the inside of my cheek. "You said you didn't choose this life?"

Alarik closes his eyes, almost like he's in pain. "My father was on the Vicar council and blocked a lot of Balistar's fanatic ideas, so they didn't get along. When Balistar occupied Ashtabano, he made one last stop at the Eskdale Mountains and took me by force. As I aged, I was forced to train as a proditor, all for Balistar's revenge on my father."

My heart drops. Balistar . . . kidnapped him? Pulled him from his parents and thrust him into a life of service on the Imnicus? He was just a boy. "Where are your parents now?"

"Likely still in the mountains. The Vicars eventually used their magic to seal themselves off from the rest of the world to remain untouched by the Arris regime. It's the only place Milo cannot touch."

I let go of Alarik, processing everything he's telling me. It's not Milo he's retaliating against but Balistar himself. "We *both* need to get off the Imnicus. You can't stay here any longer, Alarik. Eventually, Milo will connect the dots."

He shakes his head. "Quite honestly, this cell is the safest place for you right now, at least until I think of a plan. Right now your safety, not my own, is my priority."

I hate that he's right. That a prison cell is safer than hijacking a ship to hide out in Msanii.

Alarik stands and turns to leave but stops. "Lleu?"

"Yes?" I swallow.

"I don't think I'll be able to handle it if Knox ever hurts you again." He curls his fists.

My pulse quickens. What is Alarik saying? What does he mean he couldn't handle it again?

"For that, I will certainly kill him."

Chapter 7

Milo

I stare over the city of Merth through the floor-to-ceiling window at the Cymru hotel, watching vehicles pass over the sleek black streets, neon lights reflecting off their paved surfaces. I press my forehead to the cool glass and close my eyes.

The base's laxness allowed Margot to escape, and I'll be sure nothing remains of their former training. I've already assigned a pair of proditors to oversee the reconditioning. They'll be up to Imnicus standards by the end of the quarter. The intensity of the training alone is enough to break the strongest of men. If those soldiers want to act like cadets, they'll be treated as such. Captain Maguire was lucky all I did was have him beat.

My communicator beeps on my bed. I step away from the window and grab it. A message from Onyx lies dormant on the screen.

Come to the conference room. It's urgent.

What now? I quickly freshen up and step out of the hotel room.

I walk down the white-gray hallways. When I pass guards, their knees shake slightly. It's not something I witness often. On the Imnicus, most are used to my presence. I have maids with more confidence than these planetside soldiers.

The conference room door opens to Aisil sitting across from a man I don't recognize. Onyx leans against one of the walls with folded arms.

Aisil turns in his seat. "Colum, thank you for joining us. This is Lieutenant Jacobson. He used to work on the Imnicus if you recall."

The name sparks a vague memory but not as much as Aisil might expect. If he's stationed on Lavenai, and only as a Lieutenant, it would be because I sent him here for low performance scores.

"If he's here for another demotion, I think you can handle it yourself, Commander." I turn to leave.

"Colum, wait." Aisil's brow sweats. "It's about Margot."

I barely glance over my shoulder. "What about her?"

The guard swallows. "Lady Arris—I saw her at a brothel here on Lavenai." My eyes meet his and he shrinks back into the chair.

I pace around the table, hands folded and my face neutral. A brothel? A strange jealousy flickers through me. Why there of all places? This guard doesn't know what he's talking about. It couldn't have been her.

"You must be mistaken." As I slowly walk behind the guard, the hairs on the back of his neck stand on end. I stop right behind him and he stays completely stiff, staring just past Aisil.

Sweat coats the man's palms. "It's a possibility, Colum. The establishment was dark and hazy, and I had a couple . . . " He clears his throat and straightens his back. "But I would recognize your ring anywhere."

If it's true, this is troublesome. Even the guards at the base didn't know the rebel they fought was Margot. Besides the arbitors, barely anyone outside the Imnicus knows what the Columess looks like. "I'm more interested in why one of my lieutenants frequents a Laven brothel."

The man turns to face me with absolute horror in his face. "Sir, Colum, I only wished to—"

I raise two fingers to stop his next words, as I have no interest in what he could possibly say next. "Thank you for your report. Your diligence has been noticed by the Arris Reign. You may go now."

He clutches his chest and stands, bowing his head. "T-thank you."

As he leaves, with too much speed in his gait, I stop in front of Onyx, my gaze pinned on the closing door. "Take care of him."

My crows sense the curl of Onyx's lips. "Certainly, Colum."

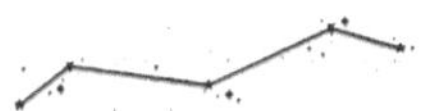

As my vehicle pulls up in front of Sinclair's brothel in the middle of the day, everyone on the sidewalks stops in their tracks at the model of my car. Onyx gets out first and people scurry down alleyways and into other businesses.

The guards get out next. One opens the door for me, and I step out with a respirator on. Music booms through the street. The only thing clean on the entire street is the establishment's red sign.

There was once a time crime lords practically ran the city of Merth. My father respected them, as did Proditor Kyouya Tanaka, for mostly different reasons. I never agreed with my father's point of view on their usefulness. Crime lords may consider themselves royalty, allowed to run brothels while a blind eye is turned on their illegal activities. To me, they're nothing but a silver coin atop a pile of compost.

Let the people have their fun, my father once said about Lavenai's nightlife. The Arris Reign didn't rise with honorable tactics, but at least it is consistent.

Inside the crowded brothel, I peel off my respirator. At first, the patrons don't notice my presence or the guards funneling in behind me, too distracted by each other's bodies or the drinks in their hands. Onyx can't hide his amusement toward the unspeakable acts occurring.

On a platform sits a man on some makeshift throne. One girl straddles his waist with her tongue down his throat and another one sits on the arm rest, nibbling his earlobe. The only person I know who is shameless enough to get laid so openly in public is . . . well . . . Onyx.

The speakers screech and the people murmur before a few gasps rattle throughout the dark club. A few people run out the door, but most are frozen in place.

The young man on the throne breaks away from the girl's lips and shoots a glare at the DJ. "What in the bloody hell is going on? Turn that back—" He goes still as he locks eyes with me. If he has any ounce of fear, he doesn't show it.

I raise my voice to the patrons as we near the platform. "This will only take a moment."

The man sits up and takes a hold of his cane, placing it between his legs, and leans forward. He doesn't even stand for me. "Why, Colum, it's an honor. Is there something here I can provide you with? A drink? Girls?"

"I'd like you to introduce yourself."

"My name is Joriel Sinclair. To what do I owe the pleasure?"

I slowly approach the throne. If Mr. Sinclair understands the implications of my presence, he doesn't show it. "Two nights ago, a base was raided by a terrorist group out of Merth. They avoided detection, took lives, and stole a transport ship just to crash it in the forest. Does this at all sound familiar, Mr. Sinclair?"

"Only with the rumors, Colum, and I never pay much mind to those."

"Somehow, I very much doubt that."

He smiles and sits back, crossing his legs.

"Thankfully for you, I'm not after a rumor. There was one among them, a fugitive, that I was told you may know a thing or two about—"

"One moment, Colum." Joriel stands and passes me, standing on the edge of the platform and projecting his voice to the rest of the club. "What are you all looking at? This is a nightclub not a show, so get back to it! And if a single one of you even breathes in our direction, I'll see to your timely demise."

My lips part. This man—Joriel Sinclair—is fearless. Not even Commander Aisil, who I've known since I was a boy, can really look me in the eye. But this club owner doesn't seem to care what I think or what I can have done to him.

Who is he to have Lavens fearing him as much as they do me?

He returns, twirling his cane before leaning against the side of his throne. "Sorry about that. I suspect this conversation is best left between us. And, please, call me Joriel. Mr. Sinclair makes me feel like my father, and I suspect you might feel similar. We are roughly the same age, I take it? Inheriting young brings a certain stigma I try to avoid." Joriel extends a hand. "Are you sure you and your proditor don't want drinks?"

I don't take his hand. "We're here for one purpose alone. I'm looking for a girl. She goes by the name Margot Tavish. Have you heard of her?"

Joriel tilts his head and stands straight, intrigued. "The Colum himself came all this way from the Imnicus to ask me where some girl is? Well now I'm curious, Colum Arris. She must be quite special."

My crows reach out to him. Even through his charismatic and chaotic facade, I feel hints of deception through his pulse. Though my birds aren't lie detectors, and his pulse could be spiking for other reasons.

I take a step toward him. My chest nearly touches his, but his face doesn't break even as his blood pressure notably increases. "So you don't know of her? Blonde, curly hair?"

"You have no idea how little that narrows it down." Joriel chuckles. "But I will be happy to keep an eye out for anyone with that description."

I don't know if I believe him, but torturing him isn't the wisest decision right now, not with so many people around. Thankfully the music covers our conversation. "That is unfortunate."

"Though I must know, why are you searching for this girl?"

I suppress a smile. *Curiosity only leads to demise*, my father always said. If Joriel didn't know Margot, he would have been grateful I was about to depart. He would keep his mouth shut. Instead, men like him have no choice but to quell their desire even at the threat of danger.

I lower my voice. "Do you know why people fear the proditors?"

Joriel's chest rises quickly. He tries to hide it, confidently motioning to Onyx. "Of course, I do. They are strong, agile, and intimidating. Breakers of minds. Fascinating specimens, if it's not too crass to say. People fear only what they don't understand."

I take a step toward him. To my surprise, he finally steps back.

"It's not just the breaking of minds but the way the pain lingers for a lifetime. How life will truly never be the same," I say.

Joriel smiles, but I know it's not genuine in any regard. "As I said before, if this girl shows up on my doorstep, you will be the first to know. Please come back anytime. And if you stay, anything you want is on me."

I study his face, searching for any additional signs of deception with my crows, but his vitals stay steady. "We will speak again."

Joriel sits down on the throne, his posture relaxed. "I do look forward to it."

With a sharp turn away from Joriel, I head toward the front door. My crows relay his gaze burning into the back of my neck. People at the bar can't look away. A man by the door tries to sneak a photograph of me before Onyx twists his arm, the communicator falling to the ground. Onyx shatters it under the sole of his boot.

Once Onyx and I are back in the vehicle, being driven back to the Cymru, he crosses his legs and rests his arms behind his head. "I didn't anticipate leaving there without you having him viciously interrogated."

"I didn't either, but we have to be tactful, Onyx."

"I don't mean because of Margot."

"What?"

"You didn't feel it? Your crows weakening?" Onyx asks. "Wait, I forgot. You half-proditors don't have quite the same reaction."

"What do you mean?"

"The man was wearing hyssopite."

That's highly illegal on Ashtanabo and Lavenai. An execution-worthy offense. But I can't shut this club down until I'm certain about Margot. Not yet, anyway. "It explains his confident mannerisms around you."

"And his guilty ones," Onyx adds.

Chapter 8

Margot

I stand next to Sinclair's throne with my arms crossed where Joriel oversees the activities with amusement. Sinclair's brothel bustles with depravity, even with the sun out. I should have left hours ago to deliver an update to Lucinda, but Joriel is taking his time for reasons that are beyond me.

"Any news from your connections?" I ask.

Joriel sighs and kicks his legs over the armrest. "You worry too much."

"The rebellion prefers to stay organized and on schedule." *Unlike you.*

"I have everything taken care of, Tavish. You needn't be concerned."

Anger bubbles in my chest. "Have you even contacted anyone?"

"Of course I have. Why so impatient?"

"This mission isn't a joke."

"You should know better than anyone that I have a vested interest in you completing your mission and returning safety."

"I'm starting to think you just like tormenting me."

Joriel arches a brow before grabbing my waist and hauling me into his lap. "Maybe it's because I have a sense that you like it, Tavish."

"If that was the case, I wouldn't be complaining." I try to stand, but his arms stay tight around me. Today, he's actually wearing that damn hyssopite necklace. The Nexus is even weaker than when he subdued me before.

His thumb runs over my hip bone before moving my hair off my neck and whispering against my pulse. "Would you like an appetizer of my torment?"

I tap into my innate strength and tear his fingers from my waist to push myself off his lap.

Joriel grins. "You were so receptive on my lap last night. Why the change of heart?"

Just because I'm willing to compromise my morals to get to Ashtanabo doesn't mean I want to. I open my mouth to say the words, but one of his goons rushes up the steps.

"Sir," the goon says.

"This better be worth the interruption." Joriel frowns.

The goon looks to me in a panic before nearing Joriel and whispering something in his ear. Joriel's eyes flash in annoyance before widening.

"T-thank you."

Joriel's stuttering? What's going on?

He motions frantically to two courtesans. They climb the steps quickly and position themselves on his lap. He rakes his fingers through his dark hair, as if primping, before resting a hand on one of the girl's hips.

I roll my eyes. "What? Too deprived to wait?"

"Margot," Joriel says firmly. "Go to the back rooms quickly. Don't come out until I say."

"Wait, why? What's happening?" A goon pulls at my arm.

"Just go!" Joriel holds the neck of one of the girls and brings her lips to his, burying his tongue in her mouth.

"What the—" If it weren't for the unusual franticness, I'd flip him off.

The goon guides me to the back rooms. He points to a door near the back before rushing back into the main room.

I grumble and stay put. What is Joriel hiding from me?

Does it have to do with one of his contacts for the mission? Maybe he doesn't want them to see me yet. But if the contact is dangerous, I need to know. I also want to ensure Joriel isn't selling me out.

I find the back kitchen door and move past the metal counter to the door leading back into the main room. I peek through the small, circular window. Nothing is out of the ordinary. Joriel's still making out with the girls. Patrons dance. Goons monitor the festivities.

My chest tightens as the music fades before people murmur.

I can't see what's happening; my line of sight is partially ob-structed from my height. The murmurs turn to gasps and panicked gawks. The entire club is fearful. Whatever is happening is beyond Joriel's crime network.

I find a small stool and drag it to the door. I step on top and peek through again.

My chest constricts to the point where I cannot take in a full breath. Time stops completely.

Guards and a proditor surround a dark figure. People cower back as they move through the club.

The Colum . . . he's here.

The club lights magnify his black hair and stern face. The cut of his royal attire amplifies his strength. Either that or he's been training his body since my escape.

He nears Joriel, who doesn't acknowledge him while he sucks the faces off both girls.

I can barely think or move when Joriel finally pulls away, when he introduces himself to the Colum, nor when he converses with the Colum without a lick of fear.

Joriel shouts something to the club. I can't hear anything they're saying through the door. I can only deduce Milo is here for me, and if he finds me—Oh gods, will he kill Joriel? Torture him? He brought Onyx, after all.

As Milo questions Joriel, Onyx's eyes scan over the room then the wall next to the kitchen door. I quickly duck before he sees me.

Milo could already have guards positioned on the outer exits in case I try to escape the building, and I can't get to the basement undetected from here. I rush out of the kitchen's back door, into the halls, and back to the room I was supposed to be hiding in all along.

Seductive contraptions and tools fill the room, and I'd grimace if I wasn't in such a panic. I turn the lights off and hide behind the bed, lying on my side.

Milo's last words still haunt me. The thought of them sharpens my breath. *"I may very well kill you."* His ring tightens around my thumb, burning into my flesh.

If he catches me, I'm doomed.

I lie there, waiting for the worst. Waiting for the moment he calls for a search. I imagine the doors flying open and Onyx barging in, dragging me by the ankle through the club. For him to throw me at the Colum's feet. For Milo to stare down at me without a shred of mercy and compassion.

Could he really kill me? Or would he turn away while Onyx carries out my sentence?

I jolt when the door slides open with a beep. With my eyes squeezed shut, I curl into a ball, shrinking myself. Maybe with the contraptions, they'll be put off enough to skip this room before searching it. Then again, this room wouldn't disgust Onyx.

I don't hear the stomp of boots or the clank of firearms.

A cane and dress shoes tap against the ground. "I think you have some explaining to do."

I sigh in relief and sit up as the soft overhead lights ignite. Joriel leans on his cane in the center of the room.

I move around the bed, sitting on the side facing him. "The less you know the better, believe me."

"I understand guards being after a rebel. I even understand a proditor hunting you down. But the Colum himself?"

I bite back my confession. Anything I tell Joriel, he will only use against me. If I don't tell him, he could threaten to ruin me and the mission. "Let's just say there was a reason Lucinda thought I was dead. A reason why I was gone for so long."

"And now you're getting me involved?" His calm demeanor shatters. "With the Colum, no less!"

"You say that as if you haven't been in cahoots with the rebellion since you could barely walk."

"Yes, but that was with the Arris Reign as a whole. The Colum himself is personally looking for *you* of all people."

"Part of you must know you're doing the right thing. Otherwise you would have turned me in already."

Joriel presses his lips together. He walks closer until he's a few feet in front of me. "Tell me. What really happened on that mission that had the rebellion thinking you were a dead woman?"

I choose my words carefully. "All I'll say is this: That mission got me very close to Milo Arris. Enough that he knew my name."

Joriel's angered expression turns to one of amused curiosity. His hands press into the bed on either side of my hips. "You could have gotten me killed today."

"And you saved me. Maybe there is an honorable man living inside that dark heart of yours after all."

"Honorable?" Joriel shins press against my kneecaps. He captures my chin, lifting my gaze to his. "What makes you so certain I won't punish you for this?"

"The sooner you get me on a ship, the sooner I'm out of your hair." I swallow when he slides his leg in between my knees.

"I'm less confident about your return with him on your tail. Perhaps we should renegotiate, considering you've put me in more danger than I anticipated." Joriel moves my legs apart with his, his face lowering to mine.

I keep my expression unchanged, even as my heart leaps into my throat.

Joriel tilts his head, his thumb skimming over my bottom lip. "Haven't you ever been curious? About what I would feel like? What I would *taste* like?" He pushes me back slowly onto the bed and climbs over me, his arms boxing me in.

My body reacts slightly, a warmth filling my inner thighs. Never, in the entire time I've known him, have I ever considered Sinclair. He's horrible and wicked. A crime lord who wouldn't hesitate to betray me at any given second.

But Milo's face flashes in my memories. It wasn't too long ago that he had me entrapped beneath him. Every day while we were together, I craved him more and more. Not just his body, but every interaction brought about new ways to express love through pleasure.

I'm responding because of the Colum, not Joriel.

I snap back into reality.

Joriel is teasing me, trying to get me to submit and give him what he wants before he delivers his end of the bargain. Well, that will never happen. My body is the only piece I have in play.

"I respect those who keep their deals." I push him to the side and slide off the bed. He'll keep his end of the bargain. All I have to do is look at his pants to determine that.

"Thought I had you there for a second." He lies back and folds his arms behind his head. "And I will deliver. You think I'll let you stay here another second with him watching me? My entire establishment is going to be under external surveillance for gods know how long."

"When do we leave?"

"Tonight, when we can use the dark to our advantage."

Oliver and Dimitri sit in the brothel's basement with me, the music leaking through the ceiling. We have no choice but to stay hidden down here since Milo may have sent undercover agents to spy on the brothel.

Dimitri stuffs his face with complimentary snacks imported from Ashtanaban. We still haven't spoken much after everything. A neutral word here and there. I want to slap some sense into him for how childish he's being, but it seems insignificant in comparison to the mission.

"You said Joriel has a plan but hasn't told you what it is?" Oliver questions me. Unlike Dimitri and me, Oliver's parents are still alive, though he has never told anyone where they are and why he chose the rebellion over family. Anytime anyone brings it up, he grows cold, and he's always had quite the temper as it is.

"If he was going to turn us in, he would have done it when Milo was here earlier today. All I know is he wants us out of here as quickly as possible," I offer.

The basement door squeaks open and sets of heavy footsteps, along with a cane, descend the staircase. Goons stand behind Joriel as he approaches us with a bag in his hands. "Oliver, Dimitri, good to see you again."

Oliver narrows his eyes. "I still don't like this one bit."

"Oh?" Joriel tilts his head. "You still don't trust me?"

"Not as far as I can throw you. For all I know, you could be leading us into a trap."

"Why, I'm insulted. And after I provided so many goodies to go along with your excursion." Joriel motions to the bag.

I frown. "Goodies?"

Joriel throws the bag into Dimitri's chest. "See for yourself."

Dimitri reaches inside and pulls out a currency device, which looks similar to a communicator and contains electronic Ashtanaban geeds, along with clothing to help us blend in once we're there. Not even Imory could get her hands on their currency. Oliver shakes his head in disbelief.

"It's nice you've come around to supporting our cause in a more active way," Dimitri says.

Joriel smiles. "Yes, of course. I love . . . justice . . . or whatever it is your rebellion is always rattling on about."

I stiffen at Joriel's words. The last thing I want is for Dimitri, or anyone else in the rebellion, to question what I offered Joriel to get him to agree. If I told Dimitri, he'd sock Joriel in the face and call off the entire thing.

"We could have handled obtaining geeds and clothing ourselves," Oliver says.

"What's the alternative? Leaving you broke *and* without a proper change of clothes on Ashtanabo? Though don't thank me too much. It's only a thousand geeds, which doesn't go far over there. My Ashtanaban assets are harder to liquify on such short notice." Joriel grins. "Now, change into the clothes. Both sets. Ashtanaban clothes first then jumpsuits over."

"Jumpsuits?" I frown.

"It's what all dock workers wear."

"I thought you had your connections? That you'd put us on a private transport ship with a pilot sworn to secrecy?"

"Yes, well, you see, they weren't so receptive this time around. Something about the Colum being less forgiving as of late. Perhaps you'd know something about that. Hmm? No worries, I have everything handled."

How Joriel plans to get us through a base entrance without detection is beyond me. All I know is that if we go down, so does he. I have no choice but to trust him.

We change behind the partitions meant for courtesans. I zip up the olive jumpsuit before emerging with Oliver and Dimitri.

Joriel scans our bodies. "Wonderful. The spitting images of Ashtanabo cargo workers. Now, follow me closely."

Joriel ascends the staircase. The three of us follow after him with the goons close behind. As we quickly move through the back hallways, I side glance into the main room anytime we pass one of the thresholds. Nothing seems out of the ordinary for Sinclair's Brothel. Is it true Milo is having the club watched? Or is Joriel just being extra cautious? A goon stands on my right, blocking the rest of my view.

Inside the parking garage, the goons form a semicircle around us. As much as Joriel likes to think he owns the structure, he's far from the only club owner who utilizes it.

"This one." Joriel motions to a limo.

When we open the door, I do a double take. A group of scandal-clad courtesans are inside giggling. Oliver and Dimitri look at me in shock.

I turn to Joriel, out of hearing range from the girls. "What is this supposed to be?"

He grins. "A possible distraction once we're at the base."

"Gods, you couldn't think of anything better?"

"What's a better distraction than sex, love?" Joriel winks.

It's not something I can fight him on, mostly because I don't know what I'm fighting against. I nod to the boys and they reluctantly pile inside. Through the windows, I watch the goons enter a second limo that I assume will follow behind.

The three of us sit close together with me in the middle of them. The girls giggle at Oliver, one of them sitting up close to him. Dimitri looks away as a girl plays with his hair.

Joriel sits across from the three of us with his legs crossed and arms splayed out on the seat while two girls nuzzle up to him. "Comfortable?"

Oliver politely puts his hand out, coaxing a girl away from him. "Whatever you want to call it."

Dimitri tries to ignore the girl running fingers through his hair. He distracts himself with the currency device, messing with the buttons.

"It taps and scans, just like the Laven ones," Joriel offers.

"They have a completely different keyboard from us. The Y is where the S should be. The N where the Q should be," Dimitri says.

"To be honest, I prefer theirs," Joriel says.

The limo passes over a divot as we leave the parking garage and pull into the neon red streets.

The second limo pulls out behind us and before we turn down the next street, a third vehicle pulls out of the adjacent parking structure. Some kind of van.

I watch the van closely. The way they pulled out seemed . . . off. It was the kind of maneuver I do on missions when I'm following someone closely.

When we take the first turn, they do the same. It happens again at the next intersection.

"Please tell me that's one of your vans." I tell Joriel.

Joriel looks out the back window and frowns, then he shouts to the driver. "Snake through the neighborhood twice." He pulls his communicator out of his pocket. "Keep an eye on that vehicle."

I grip the leather seat, keeping a close eye on the van. Sure enough, every turn our group takes, they take too.

"We've got company," Joriel says into his communicator. "Lads, let's lose them. You know the drill."

"You got it," a voice says back.

"We'll take them through Sinclair Avenue. But use the scanner first to ensure there are no dash cams on their car."

"Sinclair Avenue?" Oliver questions. "I'm familiar with every street in Merth. You don't have one named after you."

"It's a little nickname I have for a stretch of road I personally paid to repave . . . with a few adjustments. No cameras or surveillance, among other things."

Dimitri's relaxed attitude finally snaps. "This is never going to work. We need to go back."

"You're acting as though I've never had a run-in with the military before. Or that I've never been under surveillance." Joriel's muscles relax further. "Just sit tight, enjoy the show, and try not to scream."

Both limos speed down the freeway, snaking between cars and pretending to race each other. Horns honk and the courtesans shriek and laugh every time the car turns sharply.

The unmarked van matches our speed and more horns blare. Others slam on their breaks as our vehicles cut them off. Our limo swerves and skids toward the off ramp, and my body slams into Dimitri's, enough to make us both grunt. A girl falls onto Oliver's chest and she grabs his jumpsuit collar for dear life after we've already slowed. I roll my eyes.

The cars turn down a long stretch of road, but there's no other cars in view. Both limos drive evenly next to each other, still pretending to race.

The van matches our illegal speeds, staying a few car-lengths behind.

Joriel curses and speaks into the communicator. "Persistent bunch. Stay close then begin the protocol."

We turn onto an even more secluded street, and Joriel is right about it. There are no cameras. Anything could happen.

Just before we make it around the curve, I'm able to see through one of the van's back windows.

A proditor. *Shit.* "Joriel!" I yell.

"Yes, yes, I see him." He turns to the driver. "Speed up. Tell the other driver too." He pulls a device with large, square buttons from under the seat. How does he plan on getting them off our tail without word getting back to the Colum?

"Now let's see . . . " His fingers hover over the buttons. "Ah yes, this one. Would you like to do the honors, love?" he asks a girl next to him.

She smiles. "Of course, Mr. Sinclair."

"On my signal."

The courtesan takes the device while Joriel communicates with the other limo. "Gain some distance from them . . . good . . . break slightly . . . accelerate . . . "

My belly is in knots and I pinch my toes together. If this doesn't work . . .

"Now!" Joriel says to the girl.

She presses the button.

Spikes pop up from the cement, lodging themselves in the van's tires.

I bite down on the side of my pinky finger. Their van swerves, the screech of rims audible from within our limo.

Dimitri's jaw releases. "My gods—"

The van rolls into a ditch. The limos quickly take the next turn and then the next, still pretending as though they're racing.

"How do you know they won't trace that to you?" Oliver grits.

"I have my ways. I wouldn't be helping you unless I had the utmost confidence in my own survival. Believe me." Joriel speaks to the communicator one last time. "Don't follow us. Split up and assure nobody follows you back to the brothel."

Our limo turns down a familiar street and large hangars come into view. Ships lower inside of them while others speed into space with rumbles that shake the car.

It's a place I never thought I'd see again. It's where I stood in line dressed as a guard and snuck onto a ship to board the Imnicus.

I instinctively duck my head beneath the tinted windows.

Oliver and Dimitri lower their heads too but keep their gazes locked on Joriel.

We near the gate's checkpoint, and Joriel's car is waved through without inspection.

"I'll get the limo close to the cargo ship. All you need to do is get onto it without suspicion." Joriel says.

I peek over the window, watching the patrolling guards and pilots as we drive deeper into the shipyard and into a hangar. "Why the girls then?"

"Cargo workers aren't supposed to stray too far from their ship in regards to Ashtanaban protocol." Joriel looks out the window and swallows. "Additionally, there may be an inspection on my vehicle after all."

The cargo ship comes into view. It's the size of a warehouse in itself. My stomach sours when the car comes to a stop on the opposite side of the hangar.

Two officers stomp in the direction of the limo with weapons in hand. Dimitri grumbles curses.

"We don't have much time," Joriel leans forward and pulls up a hidden hatch on the floor. "Go out through the floor."

There's nothing to be done now. Either we go along with Joriel's half-baked plan or risk getting caught. I peer over the windowsill, taking in the surrounding ships. Any minute now, the commanders will be here. I need to plan a route and exit the vehicle in less than that.

I take note of every ship and employee, mentally drawing a discrete line to the cargo ship. "The more natural our walk is, the less likely anyone will question us."

Dimitri nods a second after Oliver does, seemingly hesitant to listen to me now that I'm on his bad side.

"See, look at you three already working things out. Now, I have some officers to deal with. You shouldn't have any problems."

"Like hell, Joriel," I shoot.

He blows me a kiss and I quickly slip through the bottom hatch and onto my stomach. Dimitri and Oliver follow suit.

It's sick how far Joriel's talons reach into the Ashtanaban military. It's like he's living on an entirely different planet than us with how little he fears the realities of being Laven.

I hear the limo door fly open. "Mr. Sinclair—"

"Ah, gentleman. So good to see you again. Remember those presents I promised you for the last time? Well, I've brought that and more."

"Which way?" Dimitri whispers harshly.

"Wait just a minute more, and when I say so, follow me." I look at the ship.

The officer lowers his weapon. "Listen, we enjoy our deals with you. But we told you, you can't just—"

Joriel grabs one of their collars and pulls him into the car with him. Female hands grab the other officer who can't help but laugh. The doors slam shut. If it weren't for the rocking car and the moans and giggling reverberating through the limo, I would have thought Joriel ambushed them.

Dimitri mockingly sticks two fingers down his throat, fake gagging. Oliver slaps his shoulder.

"Stand and walk. We have a short window," I say.

I push myself up and the boys follow suit, fast walking as naturally as possible past mechanics working on ships, a guard patrolling the open garage doors with his back turned, and pilots taking water breaks with their helmets tucked under their arms.

I time everything perfectly, only stepping forward when I know there will be no eyes directly on us.

As we near the cargo ship, I guide us beneath a large ship so I can reassess.

Dimitri places his fingertips on the belly of the ship above him. "There's too many of them loading crates for us to go up the ramp."

"We may not have another option." I study the demeanor between the cargo ship employees. Though they are technically military, they're more relaxed. More open to suggestions if I had to guess. "But if anyone says a word to us, stay silent. Let me talk."

"Are you crazy?" Dimitri frowns.

"Less crazy than Sinclair." Knots form in my neck from my positioning under the ship. I don't wait for either of their opinions. I don't know how long Joriel's charades are supposed to last, but the sooner we get on this vessel the better. After a pair of guards turns their backs, I move out from under the ship. "Quickly."

We move past stacks of crates, and I keep us hidden behind them as long as possible. I want to curse Joriel for having such a risky plan. With no other choice, I emerge from behind the last obstructive crate and toward the long ramp.

Nobody processes us with the jump suits. So far so good. Once we're inside, we can hide behind crates for the journey. We'll be on Ashtanabo in no time.

"You three," a voice says.

Or not.

I turn as a man with an identical green jumpsuit approaches with a clipboard. "What section are you assigned to?"

Section? Gods, I don't even know how to form the lie I need. Are the sections in letters? Numbers? A combination of both?

"We keep getting reassigned," I say. "Where would you like us now, sir?" I bite down on my inner cheek, praying to the gods to get us out of this unscathed.

The man eyes us before scrolling through his electronic clipboard. "I can't keep anything straight these days. Uh . . . go to section epsilon. There's more than a few boxes that need to be organized and secured before departure. Then we'll need inventory taken during the journey."

"Oh, yes, right away, sir."

"Stop calling me sir."

"Right—sorry."

The man turns on his heels and barks orders at a few cargo workers incorrectly moving boxes.

The three of us quickly disappear inside. The cargo ship is humongous. Palates are stacked upon each other. Robots work alongside humans to load the ship. We find section gamma then delta, before standing in front of section epsilon.

It's in complete disarray compared to the other sections.

"So . . . " Oliver starts. "Are we really expected to organize all this?"

I place my hand on one of the small metal boxes. "If we want to arrive in Ashtanabo undetected, then yes."

Chapter 9

Milo

I lean back in my seat, twisting Margot's ring around my pinky finger. The proditor's face me from different positions within their lounge, waiting for my next words.

It's times when I'm alone with the proditors, where no guards surround us, that I'm reminded of the simpler times on the Mountains of Eskdale. How we'd play games at ceremonies together while our parents spoke in cordial conversation. Where the only care in our world was who got to climb our favorite tree first. The times before my father betrayed the Vicars and converted many of them into proditors.

The boys I once knew are men now. Killers and torturers. Feared by the galaxy. Molded by my own father.

Their guards are down when it's just the six of us. Nobody wears their masks and my cape is detached, lying over one of the chairs.

"Tailing the crime lord has been a dead end," I say. "There is no sign of Margot in or around his facilities. The only report I've gotten is about a flat tire when they tailed him one evening. Does Merth still not use street cleaners?"

Onyx sits crossed-legged on the table. "He was clearly hiding something. I say proditors should raid his facilities and be done with it."

"We need more surveillance and a sliver of tangible evidence before that happens. If we move too quickly, Margot could get away again. For now, nobody will touch the crime lord."

Knox kicks his feet up on one of the game tables. "You know, you could always release her face to the Laven media. That way he'd have no choice but to give her up if he has anything to do with her."

Onyx flips and catches his sheathed knife. "Sounds like a great idea to me."

I shake my head. "No. The arbitors will be up in arms and I'll have to tell them—"

"That you lied?" Knox leans on the arm rest.

My jaw tenses and Onyx stops tossing his knife abruptly. Dune's attentive posture stiffens and Alarik unlaces his folded hands. Crux stays perfectly still from where he leans against the wall.

"I did what I had to do to end the rebellion." I sit back in my chair, forcefully relaxing my muscles before I lose all composure.

"I suppose you're right. At least we still have the rebels identities—oh wait." Knox shakes his head.

It's also when we're all alone that Knox loses control of his mouth. My father would have had Knox beaten by a swarm of guards for the blatant disrespect. But that was the thing—Knox never disrespected my father.

Dune cuts in. "It's not public knowledge that the facial scans are stored at that base. The rebellion clearly got intel from an Ashtanaban source. And we never could have anticipated the backups would be corrupted too."

"Alarik, report on the prisoner," I say quickly to interrupt the conversation. I can't let Knox dwell on this a second longer.

Alarik looks between Knox and me before speaking. "Besides the slew of complaints, she's doing well. Though she still refuses to give me the name."

Knox smirks. "I'm sure you could make her if you put your mind to it."

Alarik's fist tightens a bit more than I'd expect from him.

Knox hasn't killed anyone unauthorized since the ball. *That I know of.* Even through his smiles and jokes, there's a slight twitch behind his eyes. His crows are hungry, and Knox has been intentionally starving them to amplify his next rush.

"None of you are to torture her and I'll say no more on the matter," I command. It's the way my father would have worded things. Stern and direct. It's how he kept control of them when they were teenagers who did nothing but eat, train, and repeat. "Am I understood?"

"Yes, Colum," they all say at once.

"Alarik, report any changes with Lleu to me at once. Until we find who gave Margot the letter, the entire Imnicus is at risk," I say.

"I understand." Alarik nods.

"Anything more to report?" I ask. When none of them says anything, I send them off with their updated tasks.

Onyx slings his arm over Crux's shoulder as they leave, no doubt telling him about whatever unorthodox activity he's planning for his next leave. Onyx is just like his father, and one of the few whose father is still alive or in their life. Even though I don't dictate how often Kyouya Tanaka is allowed to see his son, I don't let him visit the Imnicus. Even in his middle-aged years, he's insufferable.

Alarik leaves next in the direction of the prison cells. He's obedient though too soft in the heart at times, which is why I keep him exclusively on the Imnicus. His already pale skin has suffered for it.

"Dune, stay," I call out before he can step over the threshold.

Knox gives me a final look, which borders more on a glare, before he heads out to his assignment.

After the doors are secured, Dune stands at attention with his hands behind his back. "Yes, Colum?"

Dune is the proditor I choose when I need something done off planet. The proditor who connects the Imnicus proditors to the ones on land, overseeing missions and facilitating ones of his own. But now I have a task for him within the Imnicus.

I rest my elbow on the arm rest, resting my temple against my fist. "There is something I need you to do for me."

"Anything."

"Keep an eye on Knox, and if you see him loitering around the prisons, inform me at once."

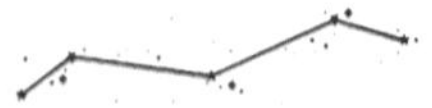

Past: D-AR 4048

In the middle of the throne room, Alarik screams and yelps while a group of soldiers beat him senseless. If he fights back at all, it will only lengthen the duration of the punishment.

My father sits on his throne, resting his chin on his fist as if he's growing bored. I stand at his right, flinching with each blow. If Alarik wasn't fully proditor, he would be out for months, but he will heal in mere days. Yet it doesn't make it any less painful to watch.

With the simple lift of his hand, my father pauses the assault.

The soldiers step away, folding their arms behind their backs. Proditors are spread out throughout the room, including Dune's father, Wayra Catawnee, watching the ordeal. When anyone is punished on the Imnicus, my father sees to it that those of lower rank are the ones who carry out the beatings on their superiors. Alarik being only fifteen means nothing to him. *Age is never an excuse for weakness*, Father always says.

Alarik slowly unfolds until he's kneeling before the throne once more. Blood drips down his face and bruises cover his body. He can barely catch his breath or lift his head, forcing him to stay bowed.

"Must I teach you the same lesson every time?" My father questions, sighing like Alarik's infraction is a minor inconvenience.

Alarik gathers enough oxygen to speak back. "I-it's too cruel. I won't do something like that to another person. The gods never wanted our magic to be used this way."

Though Dune, Knox, Crux, Onyx, and Alarik have been training basically since they were children, it's only recently that my father has taught them how to truly utilize their abilities for the Arris Reign. Once they are fully trained, they'll be required to wear proditor garb.

My father leans forward, his crown unmoving upon his head. "You're a proditor. The subjugation of the mind is not optional. You were born for greatness. Born to bring the planets into submission."

"I was not! I'm a Vicar!" Alarik yells, his voice steady. But his eyes flicker, a shimmer of doubt that my father will exploit.

My father doesn't lash out. He's always been slow to anger until the last possible minute, which is sometimes scarier than the alternative. Sometimes I wish he would yell. At least then I would know what he was thinking.

"Bring him in," my father says to a nearby guard.

Alarik sits back on his legs, his arms shaking. He looks to me for support that we both know I can't give him. I'm thankful for the shouts outside the room that tear his eyes away. Two guards drag a middle-aged man into the throne room, his head slumped and clothes ragged.

I don't recognize the man, and Alarik doesn't seem to either. The man's face is haggard and covered in bruises of his own. The guards toss him down before Alarik.

I lean down slightly to speak to my father. "Who is that?"

With his focus still on Alarik, he shoots his hand up to silence me.

The proditor beside my father unclips the knife from his belt, tossing it upon the marble tile before Alarik.

He stares at the knife and then at my father with horror in his eyes. "No."

Father tilts his head. "No?" He laughs. "You don't have an option."

"I'd rather be beaten."

"That will be arranged, regardless." My father sighs and crosses his legs, getting comfortable on the throne. "The man before you is an Ashtanaban smuggler who was caught transporting illegal firearms to Lavenai. His execution is scheduled for now, and you, Alarik, are his executioner."

Alarik doesn't say or do anything. He just tightens his fists on his lap.

They stare at each other, the moment stretching out like an eternity.

"Alarik, if you do not kill him, I will have you nymbed."

Alarik's face swirls in horror. Never in the history of the Arris Reign has a proditor been nymbed. Most are too strong to be forced into it. But Alarik hasn't been fully initiated yet, and there's no way he could fight off the fifteen proditors who stand in the throne room now, and that's not even including Knox and the others.

My father pushes himself up from his throne and descends the steps of the dais. I stay glued to my spot while he bends down next to Alarik and picks up the dagger, placing the hilt in Alarik's hand.

"Tell me, Alarik. Is this man's life worth losing your ideologies over? Is he worth not being able to think for yourself?" Amusement passes over my father's face when Alarik's eyes pinch together.

Alarik squeezes the hilt, like he's actually considering being nymbed.

Crux stands off to the side next to Knox and Onyx, his face slightly turned into a smile. And Crux never smiles.

"Go along now. Don't keep me waiting." My father takes a few steps back.

Alarik stands and takes a few steps forward, towering over the man.

The man shakes at the sight of the dagger. "Please don't do this." His voice is coarse, broken from hours of screaming. "My family doesn't even know what happened to me. Please!"

Alarik turns his head away and takes a deep breath before raising the blade over his head. "I'm s-so sorry."

To his credit, Alarik doesn't wait. He knows the longer he drags it out, the more it will hurt for both of them. Still, Alarik's contorted face sickens my stomach. I want to hide behind the throne, but if I close my eyes my father's wrath will extend to me.

Something glazes over Alarik's features. A darkness I've never seen even in my father or any of the other proditors.

The blade punches into the man's chest, just above the heart. Alarik's hesitation keeps the blade from sinking in far enough, the blow unlethal. I can barely stand the sounds from the man as Alarik pulls it free. He tries again. My jaw tightens, and my lips tremble as Alarik plunges the knife in two, three, four times until the man stops screaming.

The entire time, my father watches in silence, not reprimanding or shaming Alarik. Nor does he praise him. He knows well enough that not acknowledging something can make it hurt even worse.

Alarik takes a step back, blood dripping from his trembling fingers as the blade clatters against the tile. He falls to his knees, eyes staring at the corpse before him.

My father pulls a handkerchief from his pocket. "Well done, Alarik. Tomorrow, you will begin your first *full* day of interrogation training alongside Crux. I know I don't have to emphasize what will happen if you don't comply." He drops the handkerchief in front of Alarik for him to clean the blood off his face.

My father waves a dismissive hand while he ascends the dais. "Guards, twenty lashes for him, then take him to the medical bay."

As the guards prepare the electric whip, I watch the boy I once knew disappear from behind Alarik's face.

And I never met him again.

Chapter 10

Margot

For hours and hours, we work aboard the cargo ship, staying to ourselves to remain undetected. My head pounds from inventorying every last box in our section.

When the ship lands, we pretend to stretch inside the Ashtana-ban hangar before blending in with a group of workers and exiting into the city.

We stand there now with our mouths gaped. Even for me, it's like seeing the city of Heidl for the first time.

The sun rises above the capital, washing the streets, white two-story buildings, and shops in a soft pink glow. Most build-ings grow plants on their flat rooftops, creating greenery that vines down building walls. Silver vehicles drive leisurely down the streets. A woman with rosy cheeks pushes a straw bassinet down the egg-white sidewalks.

Oliver scoffs at the sight. "I'm not sure if I should be angry or mesmerized."

Dimitri rakes a hand through his hair and takes a step back. "Is this heaven?"

It's paradise, and it's only possible because of what Balistar took from us. What he's *continuing* to take from us long after his death.

"Come on," I say. "We need to change into the next set of clothes." Not to mention, we're not safe to stay in one area for too long. Off-duty Imnicus soldiers could recognize me if we're not strategic.

We find a secluded alley between two white buildings and face away from each other to change. At the moment, Milo still thinks I'm on Lavenai. Unless we do something that draws eyes, or a soldier recognizes me, it's unlikely he'll know I'm here. Still, we have to be mindful of lingering eyes.

I hear the ruffle of pants behind me before Oliver speaks. "It feels like treason to dress like them."

"A small price to pay." I pull the poncho over my head.

Once we're all dressed, Oliver rolls his shoulders back like he wants to jump out of his own skin.

Whereas Laven fashion is industrial, functional, and protective, Ashtanaban fashion, at least when worn casually, is loose yet formfitting. I'd call it desert-like with the relaxed tan, white, and light brown fabrics. Though their formal-wear is much more outlandish—colorful gowns structured with harsh angles. I only witnessed it once at the ball, but it made me thankful the Imnicus has their own standards for fashion.

No matter how disgusted I am with Ashtanabo, it's hard to deny its beauty. It was a stunning planet before it started to die, or so

I've been told. A part of me wants to feel some sympathy for how they struggled. After all, it was Lavenai's refusal to aid Ashtanabo in any significant way that gave Balistar no apprehension when destroying us.

I avoid eye contact with the smiley people who pass by. "We need to get to Susuku and find the girl. Then we can destroy the temple points."

"Something tells me Susuku isn't a walk down the street," Dimitri points to a domed statue with the regions detailed out, as well as the "*You are here*" star. We're regions away. On foot, it would take weeks.

"How was I supposed to know what region we'd end up in? Had I known we'd land in Heidl, I would have planned better."

"I wasn't accusing you," Dimitri bites.

Oliver grumbles something before pointing to a silver sign. "Would a train work? We could use the geeds Joriel gave us to pay. Does that sound simple enough, children?"

Oliver has no idea what's going on between Dimitri and me, but it's becoming impossible to hide too. Both of us need to get a grip.

Dimitri seems to have the same thought. He jumps over Oliver and gives him a noogie. "You make it sound so easy."

Oliver shoves him off. "Tone it down. You'll bring us unwanted attention."

The train station is spacious and not at all like the dirt-coated subways on Lavenai. The ceiling is made completely of glass. The ticket counter sparkles as if it's cleaned every hour on the dot.

A woman stands behind the counter, wearing an electronic badge with her name on the screen. Not a single strand of her hair is out of place. "Hello. How can I assist you?"

I fold my hands together on the counter. "We would like three one-way tickets to Susuku."

Her smile cracks slightly. "That's quite a long trip. Wouldn't you prefer flying?"

Trains are safer with little to no security checks, according to Joriel. It's our only option unless we muster the gall to walk. "Three tickets please," I say again.

She types into her computer, her eyes a little too happy. "Three tickets will be nine-hundred geeds."

Dimitri chokes on his own spit. I forgot Ashtanaban geeds are practically a different currency than Laven ones. After this trip, we'll only have one-hundred geeds left.

"That's insane . . . I mean, why is the price so high?"

The woman raises an eyebrow, as if most Ashtanabans don't bat an eye at cost. "Well it is nearly a forty-eight-hour journey with all the stops. Food and beverages are included, so . . . "

I want to find another way, but what choice do we have? Other modes of transportation are too risky or time consuming. Flying would be even more expensive. And we need to reach the girl before Milo catches wind that I'm on Ashtanabo. At the very least, we won't have to worry about food. Still, once we get to Susuku, we'll have to pinch our geeds unless we can find a way to make more money. "I'll take them."

Dimitri holds onto my forearm, like he's trying to stop me, but he doesn't do or say anything else as I scan the currency device.

"Enjoy your trip," the woman says.

Once we're out of earshot, Dimitri stands in front of me with narrowed eyes. "We'll never be able to make more geeds once we get to Susuku. We have no documentation."

"We can't rent a vehicle without identification either," I counter, "and we certainly can't take a ship, so we are left with only one option."

Oliver takes his ticket from me and stares at the golden inscriptions. "It leaves in ten minutes, so are we going to keep complaining or are we going to do this thing?"

Dimitri grumbles under his breath. "The food better be good."

We wait on the platform with people holding suitcases as the brass-white train pulls into the station, a vine-like design embossed into the sides. I wouldn't be surprised if people took entire vacations on one of these things. It's unlike Lavenai's underground trains where you're more likely to survive a night in the wilderness than a ride across the city.

After the attendant checks our tickets, we file onto the spacious train with dark blue walls and circular windows lined with gold and white trim. It's the kind of place you never want to leave. To Ashtanabans, this is considered normal, not something meant only for the elite but for everyday people.

There truly isn't anything on Lavenai like this. Even with Joriel, the richest person I know, nothing he owns comes close to this train's interior. I elbow the boys to keep their dazed expressions in check.

A woman leads us to our cabin. Blue lights line the baseboards in the white-walled room, fit with two sets of bunk beds, a desk, and a private privy. A glass drink fridge is tucked in the corner. A room this size would fit eight at the rebellion.

Dimitri falls onto one of the bottom bunks and sniffs the soft, clean mattress. "If I could live on this train the rest of my life, I would."

I run my hand over the blinding white sheets that promise a good night's sleep. At the rebellion, I usually wake with a shooting pain in my neck and a sore shoulder if I accidentally roll onto my side during the night.

Oliver touches one of the plush decorative pillows before gripping it and throwing it off into a corner. I don't blame him for being conflicted. When you've been deprived for so long, it's easy to get lost in the comfort while also feeling shameful for enjoying it.

Dimitri rolls on his side to face me. "You really lived like royalty every day, didn't you?"

I stiffen. "It wasn't a vacation."

"You have to admit that a part of you misses it."

"Miss what? Living a lie? Thinking I was part of the Arris Reign? Finding out that everyone around me was faking friendships to manipulate me into destroying everyone I loved?"

Dimitri sits up and grips the edge of the bed. "Every time I look at you it's like you're still there."

"Because part of me is!"

"Why can't you move on? Why can't you let it go?"

My muscles twitch. I sacrificed my soul for the rebellion and for him. And now he has the gall to—

"Enough, you two." Oliver's legs hang over the side of the bed. "I don't know what has been going on with you guys, but we have a mission to do, so save the family drama for back home. Remember what Lucinda says? Emotions are how you get killed."

Dimitri and I glare at each other before he stands and heads to the door. "I'm going to scope out the train."

I shake my head as the door slides shut behind him. I'm not sure how much more of it I can stand.

Oliver hops off the top bunk and folds his arms. "Just so we're on the same page, he's being a jackass."

Inside the foot cart, we're served food at round metal tables along with others on the journey.

"Gods, this is the best thing I've ever tasted." Oliver groans as he chews a marinated piece of beef.

"Pass the pasta over here, Oliver, I'm starving." Dimitri motions.

Ignoring the fact that the pasta is closer to me than Oliver, I bite into my roll, chewing angrily. Our quarrel reminds me of the times we'd bicker as teenagers, but in the end, one of us always apologized.

The waitress stops by our table with a bottle of wine. "How is everything?"

"Divine," Oliver says.

She smiles. "You three must be hungry. I don't think I've seen anyone eat so quickly!"

The other guests are still halfway through their meals, whereas many of our plates are licked clean. There are a few passing glares and grimaces in our direction.

The waitress holds up the bottle. "Can I interest you in wine? It's complementary and pairs nicely with the beef."

Dimitri nods over enthusiastically. "That would be—"

"We're good with our current drinks," I interrupt. "But we appreciate the offer."

The waitress nods and moves onto the next table to offer them the bottle.

Dimitri folds his arms. "What was that all about? It would have been free!"

"We can't risk being intoxicated right now," I retort.

Oliver holds his stomach. "With the food coma we're in, we may as well be. Though Margot's right. We need to stay sharp."

Dimitri shoots up. "I'm going to head back."

"Don't you want dessert?" Oliver asks.

"I'm full. I'll see you back in the cabin." Dimitri strides through the dinner cart. The train car door automatically slides open for him before he disappears out of view.

Oliver leans forward. "Listen, I don't know what's going on, but it needs to stop."

"You tell him that," I say.

"Did something happen on the base mission?"

"No—yes. It's more than that."

"I know how Dimitri can get, especially when it comes to family matters, but you both need to sort it out."

"I've done nothing wrong. He's the one who needs to apologize to me."

"I don't doubt that. He's the most stubborn man I know. But, just know, every second you two spend bickering is another percent raised that we don't make it back alive."

I bite down on my tongue because Oliver has a point. But what am I supposed to do? Pretend the Imnicus didn't happen? Pretend I'm still the girl Dimitri grew up with?

After dessert, Oliver and I head back to the cabin where Dimitri is already asleep or at least pretending to be.

Oliver stretches his arms and lets out a long yawn. "I'd say we deserve some shut eye. None of us have slept in who knows how long."

I nod. "Goodnight, Oliver."

Oliver climbs into his bunk and I follow suit, slipping into the bottom bunk. A part of me wants to be on the other top bunk, so when I roll over I won't see Dimitri across the room.

When I hear Oliver's breaths soften, I sit up and hug my legs, keeping guard with my eyes locked on the door.

I know I'm being paranoid, but I can't help it. I know proditors and they would probably wait until we least expect it to attack.

My eyes are heavy as I watch and I don't know how much time has passed until my head dips and I jolt up. But more time has passed than I thought, sunlight no longer streaming through the train's window.

Dammit, I really did fall asleep.

There's a crashing noise from somewhere outside the cabin and I physically recoil. What the hell was that?

Dimitri and Oliver snore away on their bunks. How could I have been the only one who heard that noise?

I whip out of bed and quietly slip out of the room to investigate. For all I know, a waitress dropped a bucket of utensils, but still I need to check for my own sanity.

Darkness fills the cabin cart, only illuminated by a few electronic sconces with virtual wicks. It's even later than I thought. Everyone's holed up in their cabins. I would expect some people to be up for late-night drinks, but the bar and entertainment cars are completely empty.

The train rocks slightly down the tracks, beams of moonlight shining through the windows as the carts move through the countryside.

I inspect the next five cars down and don't find a single soul. Not even an employee.

Where the hell is everybody?

I enter the restaurant cart and stop in my tracks. One of the windows is shattered. An icy chill drifts into the cart.

I bend down and pick up a piece of glass, careful not to knick myself. My blonde curls move from the outdoor wind while I search for what broke it.

As I set down the glass, a gentle caw sounds through the cart.

I shoot my gaze up to the windowsill, my blood running cold.

A single crow perches on the edge of the glass, watching me with black beady eyes.

Chapter 11

Margot

Where there are crows, there are proditors.

My nerves are on fire, lungs on the brink of popping. I look at one car door and then the other. The hairs on the back of my neck stand on end. I can feel someone watching me, waiting in the shadows for an opening. My body is telling me to sprint out of the restaurant cart and into the next, but my mind screams at me to stay put and that I'd only risk crashing into a proditor.

I take a step forward and the ground divots as if stepping on a pillow. A crowd of crows explode from the floor beneath me.

Their caws blend with my screams. My ears ring from the noise. *No. Stop it. Go away!*

I fall back as they attack me, their beaks pecking at my arms and abdomen. I swing punches with one arm and protect my eyes with the other, but it isn't enough as they make contact.

Something is strange though. My arms don't bleed and their pecking doesn't break skin. It doesn't even hurt.

Slowly, I uncover my eyes and look down at my body. Three sit on my torso, pecking gently at my ribs and abdomen.

They aren't trying to attack me. They are trying to get my attention. Others fly around me like an impending tornado.

I suck in a breath and force myself to my feet. "Stop it, all of you."

Their pecking stops and their caws cease as they fly away from me, perching themselves on chairs, tables, curtain rods, and picture frames.

I calm my breathing as the Nexus burns from my neck to my fingertips. What I'm seeing isn't real, but I also know I'm not in a proditor entrancement.

The crows' heads turn rapidly, their eyes flickering. An energy overtakes me as their minds join with mine. I can feel what they feel. Hear what they speak.

These are my crows—Knox's crows—demanding an audience with me.

Feed us, they say, *and we will reward you.*

"What?" I turn in a circle to take in the sight of all them. "You can't be serious."

Feed us. We are hungry. We desire blood.

"Never," I tell them. "I'm not Knox and I'll never be like him."

I sense their anger and bitterness. *It will only be a matter of time.*

I swallow rapidly, remembering Milo's words about Knox's sick crows. How he can't help but obey them and deeply enjoys fulfilling their requests. Now, they're trying to force me into the same submission, but I'll never listen to them.

They caw again, shrill and unbearable.

I cover my ears, the high pitch forcing me to kneel. "Stop it!"

They take off toward me. I cry out, feebly covering myself with my arms. Their black forms spiral above me like a twister, jagged wings brushing my skin.

"I do not have Vicar blood!" I shout. "I'm a waste of your time!"

They don't listen. They caw and cackle, mocking me. One lands on my shoulder, talons digging into my skin. I shoo it away, but it leaves its mark. I push forward to escape their torment.

The train jolts forward, accelerating, and I lose my balance. Only the edge of a nearby table keeps me steady. Loose plates whoosh past me, shattering against the walls.

I duck as a butter knife almost pierces into my arm. I need to get to safety before a sharp object lodges itself in my eye. With everything in me, I strain to keep upright against the unnatural speed of the train.

Two more windows shatter, glass flying into the train. I block the shards with one arm while holding on for dear life with the other. My hair blows wildly while the crows continue to torment me.

As the glass settles on the floor, I peek over my forearm and freeze.

At the threshold stands a figure and I shudder with every fiber of my being.

Raven hair, broad chest, and all, he stands there, a dagger wrapped in his ring-clad hand.

No, not a proditor. The Colum.

Moonlight dances across his indifferent expression, his eyes locked on me. Yearning and fear collide in my chest.

Milo takes a step forward.

I grip the table edge harder, my ribs tightening for more reasons than one. "Here to kill me?"

The Colum says nothing, taking another step.

I grab for one of the fallen utensils, pointing it at him, as if that will protect me.

He lifts his chin slightly. "Would you do it for me?"

I lower the butter knife, wrist trembling. "What?"

"I promise. It feels otherworldly." His voice isn't his own.

This isn't Milo.

The train accelerates again. Glasses fly around the restaurant cart, narrowly missing Milo as he steps closer, completely unaffected by the wind, speed, and shards.

One crow flies between us, blocking the view of his face. When his face emerges again from behind the feathers, he's been changed, features matched to the beholder of the voice.

Knox grins as a crow perches on his shoulder. "And after all the crows have provided you . . . "

My arms shake and my fingers freeze in fear. *He's not real*, I tell myself. "There is no temptation that will ever be great enough. I will never be like you!"

With his chest inches from mine, he stares down at me sadistically. "Aren't you already?"

He grabs my wrist and squeezes it like I'm made of cotton. My tendons ache before I have no choice but to drop the butter knife.

"Knox—" I bite out his name with a pained gasp.

He brings my inner wrist toward his mouth, brushing my pulse point with his lips as he keeps his eyes locked on mine.

I shrink back.

Knox speaks against my skin. "Did you like the way it felt? When his neck snapped?"

The officer on the Laven base—I've tried putting him out of my mind. I've told myself every night that I did what I had to do. "It was self defense!" *Wasn't it?* "He would've killed Oliver."

I swing a fist at him but he catches that wrist too.

"We all have a choice," he rattles back. "And don't deny it, Margot, that a part of you enjoyed it."

The train tilts on its axis. I lose my balance, my feet desperately trying to stay glued to the floor. The only thing that keeps me from falling is Knox.

"Our time is up. Mark my words, we will meet again." Knox unfurls his grip and gravity takes me.

I land flat on my stomach and slide down the tilted cart. With desperation, I grab for a table leg and then the edge of the bar, but my fingers slip past each one of them. All I can do is yell.

Knox tilts his head and waves goodbye.

I scream as I fly out the cart door, my body sucked beneath the train—

"Margot, wake up!"

I jolt awake at the shake of my shoulder. My fist swings into a chest.

Dimitri winces and falls back. "What the hell, Margot!"

The dream still overtakes my limbs. I slap at Oliver before he catches my hands.

I slowly come to as I take in the sight of the cabin and the boys watching me, Oliver with concern and Dimitri with anger.

Oh gods, it was just a dream. A dream where I felt real pain. Whereas Milo and Knox felt like figments of my subconscious, the crows did not.

I sit on the side of the bed and rub my temples. "I'm sorry, I just—"

"Just what? Swing at people for doing you a favor?" Dimitri stands and brushes off his clothes.

I narrow my eyes. "It was just a nightmare. Get over it."

Oliver throws a pillow at Dimitri. "We still have a long way to go before we arrive in Susuku. Both of you are driving me up the wall."

It's an understatement to say Dimitri hasn't been himself since I returned from the Imnicus. But never in our time growing up together has he ever been so . . . so . . . arrogant.

After passing through countrysides and mountains, the train reaches a city filled with pink trees and homes with pyramid-hip roofs.

Susuku.

Unlike the capital of Ashtanabo, this region is less technologically dense. There are fewer vehicles and plenty of ponds and streams with wooden bridges to cross them.

And somewhere in this region is Diyu prison where the hyssopite-like girl is being held. According to Imory, it's one of the roughest prisons in all of Ashtanabo and is typically used for political prisoners who have the capability of ending the Arris Reign.

"We have one-hundred geeds left," Oliver says as we walk the streets. "Any ideas?"

I scratch the back of my neck. On Lavenai, a hotel stay may cost only ten or twenty geeds, but on Ashtanabo, one may cost between fifty or even one-hundred, and that's not including food.

Dimitri scoffs. "I fully expect to be sleeping on the side of a wolf-infested hill and eating grass for dinner."

A few streets over, there is a festival with food carts, dancing, and women in long, robe-like dresses. Families eat lunch together on blankets under trees while they watch men play instruments on a small stage.

The three of us take a seat on the grass, watching the festivities. Oliver lies back with his arms outspread. Though the train ride was luxurious, it was also long and exhausting.

The scent from the food carts fills my nostrils, enough for my stomach to rumble. The train ride ended shortly before lunch, leaving the three of us to sit in hunger.

Dimitri holds his own abdomen. "Gods, how are we supposed to make it through the next few days without food? We should have found another way to Susuku."

"We know what it's like to be hungry for long periods of time," I say. "Perhaps you need to be adaptable."

"Yeah? Well what about when we run out of money? What will you do then?"

I shake my head and look back at the festival. My back muscles grow tighter with each passing minute. Our mothers are sisters. Did they ever fight like this? What would they think from the heavens if they knew their children were constantly bickering with one another?

A few helmetless guards patrol the streets, though the ones here aren't hostile in the slightest. They have conversations with vendors, tipping them extra with an appreciative smile.

My body stiffens as I catch a ripple of black in the corner of my eye.

At a food cart, an old woman bows in appreciation as she hands a Susukan proditor a fruit-filled dessert, and he bows back to her.

I lose control of my breathing, my ribs flaring out. The dream on the train comes back, along with the memories of the torture on the Imnicus.

Everything goes stiff. Any second he could stare straight at me. What if he senses my crows?

The scars on my arm burn and I hold onto my forearm, a pained sound exiting my throat.

"Margot?" Dimitri asks before following my gaze.

His mouth gapes and he takes hold of my upper arm, scooting me toward him. "Count the grass."

I focus on the vibrant green strands, barely able to catch my breath. There was a simulation during the torture where I couldn't inhale for what felt like a thousand years. *Seven, eight, nine . . .*

When I get to one-hundred, Oliver speaks. "He's gone now."

His words bring air to my lungs and blood back to my fingertips.

When I look at Dimitri, his eyes flicker in pain.

Oliver sighs before standing. "You two have a lot to talk about. I'm going to see if anyone is handing out free samples."

Dimitri places a hand on my shoulder. "Margot . . . I didn't realize . . ."

"I'm prepared to die," I say shortly. "Even if torture is on the table, I'm prepared to lie down and take it again, even though the thought of it is enough to shatter me. That's how serious I am about this mission. I am a daughter of Lavenai. A Tavish. My life is not my own—it belongs to my planet. I can say the same for Oliver, but what about you Dimitri? Are you prepared to die to stop the Arris Reign?"

A sharp silence fills the air between Dimitri and I.

"I'm not scared to die for Lavenai," he says.

"Then what is it? All you've done is complain about your hunger and about the decisions I've made to protect us all."

His hair covers his eyes as he watches the festival. "When you never returned from the Imnicus, it took me weeks to accept that you were dead, and when I finally did, I . . . I didn't know how to handle it. I lashed out at everyone who would come near me, even Lucinda. It got to the point where she threatened to kick me out of the rebellion if I didn't get my emotions together. She told me to be strong because it's what you would have wanted, so I did. I shoved down the pain, the misery of basically losing my sister, and trudged on. So when you came back . . . "

My chest tightens. I knew Dimitri had a rough time while I was away, and understandably so, but I didn't realize to what degree he suffered.

". . . it felt like the gods had finally answered my tear-filled prayers to save you. Though shortly after I realized that, even though you were safe, you weren't . . . you. You still aren't. It was like the gods dangled your survival in front of my face only to rip you away again. But this time, I could still talk to you; still see you. It's so hard to be next to you when you're not really . . . here. You're constantly spacing out, and when I look at you, it's like I can see the inside of the Imnicus." His eyes turn to glass even as he tries to hide them further under his hair. "So whenever I see hints of the Margot I knew, it feels like if I reach far enough, I can pull you out of there and away from him."

I place a hand on his shoulder, my heart breaking. It may not be an excuse for the way he's been treating me, but it's like I found him again, buried under layers of pain and agony.

"Dimitri Flynn, you're a real bastard, you know that?"

He laughs slightly, and I know if he would let it, a tear would drop.

I soften my voice. "I'm still Margot, you know. And I'm still the girl who played games with you all throughout our childhood. That being said . . . " My ribs pinch together. "What happened to me cannot be undone, and though I am still your cousin, things will always be different. All I can promise is that I'm not some spawn of the Imnicus. I may not be the girl you once knew, but that doesn't mean we can't make new memories with who I am now. Ask me questions, even if you're scared of the answer or of the question itself because, at the end of the day, the only thing worse than losing you to death is losing you to hate."

"You're right." He reaches forward and squeezes me in one of his tight, back-breaking, bear hugs. "I had no right to treat you like that. I'm so sorry. I've been an asshole, haven't I?"

"Yes, you have." I push at his shoulders. "Now let go, I can't breathe!"

We laugh and joke more, and when Dimitri isn't trying to force it out of me, I really can connect with my old self again in small glimmers here and there. As much as he missed the old me, I also missed the old him. The one who wasn't trying so hard. The one who simply is fun and down to earth and has no qualms picking on me in good fun.

Oliver finds us again with three small toothpicks, a piece of breaded chicken on top of each. "I have some good news."

"You found food?" I accept a sample from him and swallow the chicken with only a few short bites.

"That and there's a hotel near here that only charges thirty geeds a night."

My eyes light up. It's still on the pricier side, but it buys us three days with a roof over our heads. "Where?"

"The vendor drew a map." Oliver pulls a napkin from his pocket and hands it over. "It's just a few streets north. It's probably family owned. He was very pushy."

"Thank the gods," I say. "There's no time to waste. Let's go."

We make our way through the crowded lantern-filled festival and follow the path on the hand-drawn map. The scent of food is overwhelming against the pangs of hunger, which aren't close to how bad they'll be in a few days.

The hands on the clock tick, counting down the seconds we have to break this girl out of prison before hunger turns into fugues of starvation.

I admire the sights along the way, taking in the vendors and the little competitions that take place with light crowds watching in awe. There is music, dance performances, and ritualistic ceremonies. The Susukan people wear genuine smiles. It's bittersweet. It's that joy Lucinda has been fighting for since the Arris Reign began.

It's something I've always wanted for Lavenai, but I can't help but want it for both. There must be a way for both planets to thrive once all is set and done. Normal Ashtanabans are just as innocent in this as Lavens are. It was Balistar who forced us to become enemies.

But unless we think of an alternative, destroying the temple points and regaining control of our planet is the only way.

"Just past here." Oliver points to a building.

We turn the corner and Oliver's eyes glaze over. I take in the sight a second after him.

The hotel's sign reminds me of the neon ones in Lavenai—specifically the crime district. A seductive silhouette of a woman hangs above the door. And though the name of the hotel is in Susukan lettering, I don't need a translation to guess what the establishment specializes in.

"Could you have found a sleazier place, Oliver?" Dimitri shakes his head.

Oliver glances at the map scrawled across the napkin, turning it around this way and that. He sighs and lowers it. "He never specified what type of hotel it was. I told him my price, and he drew me a map. He said we'd be taken care of . . ." Oliver pinches the bridge of his nose. "I wondered why he was so pushy."

Dimitri rubs the back of his neck. "Maybe I really would rather sleep in the woods with the wolves."

"We won't be here long. Our money situation will make sure of that," I say, even though I don't want to stay here either. It's like Sinclair's all over again. "Besides, it's close to the prison."

Oliver's shoulder slump as he nears the door, and it slides open.

I follow in behind him. A mixture of colognes and perfumes cover the scent of faint body odors and other smells I'd rather not identify. Considering how clean and beautiful the rest of Ashtanabo is, it's a wonder a place like this is even allowed a permit.

Erotic paintings fill the lobby, which I try my best to ignore. Outlandish lopsided furniture takes up the open space. Dimitri is the most put-off of us three, keeping his eyeline low.

At the counter stands a middle-aged man wearing a formal vest, and to our relief, he doesn't only speak Susukan. He stares between us, a thin smile cracking the corner of his mouth. "One room I assume?"

I sigh and pull the payment device out of my pocket. "Yes, thank you."

The man types a few things into his computer. "What kind of room?"

"Excuse me?" I raise an eyebrow.

"Some groups prefer the ropes room. Others like rooms with more *devices*." He hones in on Oliver. "You look like a chains guy, if I had to guess."

I've never seen Oliver go red before, the hue creeping across his neck.

"J-just the most basic room you have please," I say quickly. Of course we should have expected lewdness in a place like this, but a part of me thought things would be more anonymous. That it would be a 'no questions asked' kind of thing.

"Suit yourself, though couples of three typically prefer our more premium stuff."

I practically gag. Besides Dimitri basically being my brother, I've seen far too much of Oliver over the years to see him that way—witnessed every awkward phase, heard every gross boyish noise, and nearly strangled him more times than I can count.

Dimitri searches for words to clarify. "Just so you know . . . "

I elbow Dimitri before he can correct the man. We can't exactly tell him we're only here for the cheap rooms so we can break an inmate out of prison.

After he hands us our keycard, we head upstairs with our heads down, being careful not to make eye contact with anyone we pass. Others are the same, trying to leave their rooms with as little interaction as possible with the other guests .

As we step into the hotel room itself, all of us wince.

"You've got to be kidding me." I rub my temples.

Even without a theme to it, it's the last place I want to be staying with my cousin and a guy I've seen eat rotten food off the floor over a dare. That one had him in the infirmary for a week.

Nothing in the room seems meant for rest or relaxation. Hand-held devices charge on every surface. Silky sheets. A strangely shaped chair.

After we throw every device we can find inside drawers or cover them with towels, I know that it's going to take at least an hour before I can fully look either of them in the eyes.

Oliver opens one of the closets. "There is a cot in here that one of us can use."

"And it seems like the couch is a pullout," Dimitri adds, pulling the cushions off of it. "You can have the bed, Margot."

I roll my eyes. "How kind of you."

"I'm sure they clean it well in between guests," Oliver says sarcastically.

With our hunger leaving us no time to rest, we sit in a circle mapping out our plans.

Chapter 12

Lleu

I swipe nail polish over my thumb nail, careful not to smudge the crimson color on my cuticles. It took me a long time to decide on a color, so a dozen discarded bottles of polish rest beside me. Normally the day itself would call for its own color, the outfit demanding an accent. But in my cell, clad in dull gray day after day, any color would do. Too many options, really.

But I shouldn't complain. The fact I can paint my nails again is a luxury I don't deserve. I've even had a chance to curl my hair thanks to Alarik smuggling in some of my personal items. Now I feel somewhat like myself again.

As I move onto the next nail, the door opens quickly and I smudge the polish.

It doesn't matter how many times Alarik enters unannounced to keep me in the loop about Margot and Milo, I still tense when he's near. My belly fills with knots and my throat goes tight before flutters take over my chest.

"Margot is still safe," Alarik informs.

I mask my hitched breath as a sigh of relief and start on the next nail. Most pleasantries these days are skipped in favor of the only news I truly care about. "Do you think Milo's closer to finding her?"

Alarik shrugs. "There's a crime lord who may have something to do with her, but it's too hard to say."

"Crime lord?" I shake my head, laughing slightly. "There's a lot I have to learn about Margot."

Alarik moves closer, inspecting my half-polished hand. "You're shaking."

"I'm left-handed, so painting my left hand can be tricky." It's not fully a lie, but I'm too coordinated with a brush to let that be a proper excuse.

Alarik sits down at the table with me, peels his gloves off, and takes the brush from my hand.

"What are you doing?" My heart pounds when he takes my hand and holds it steady. His skin is so warm and soft, his touch shooting heat across my ribs.

"Helping." With meticulous precision, Alarik moves the brush over my nail, not a drop of polish touching my cuticle. It's impressive. "I don't know many left-handed people."

My throat bobs. "Both my parents are left-handed."

When he touches me or he simply looks at me, it becomes impossible to deny the way I feel about him. From the first moment I met him, even before I saw him without his mask, I knew. No crush or partner has come close to flustering me the way Alarik does.

As Alarik works on the next nail, small sensations zap along my fingers from where he holds my hand steady. A second later, there's the faint flap of crow wings in my ear.

I smile. "I think someone is cheating."

Alarik laughs, but keeps his concentration locked on my nails. "Would you believe me if I said this was my first time painting nails?"

"If I hadn't felt your crows, I'd have to wonder if you work part-time at an Ashtanaban spa."

"Who says I don't?" Strands of dark auburn hair fall over his brown eyes, and even with his mask, I can tell he's grinning ear to ear.

Gods, his eyes.

Once he completes the final stroke and lets go of my hand, my skin prickles at the loss of contact. If my mother knew I've fallen for a proditor, she would do more than scold me. She would say they are dangerous and born manipulators. My father would be more concerned with my wellbeing and how proditors are worked to the bone. He would warn me that a proditor wouldn't have time for me.

But I may never make it off the Imnicus. In fact, every day I wake up breathing is short of a miracle. Milo could have me tortured and executed, or worse, he could change his mind and have me handed over to Knox.

"Are you all right?" Alarik gently touches my forearm.

I hold my breath. "Yes, I am fine. Just a little stuffy in here is all."

"You know, it's within my right to let you out for a little fresh air."

I know well enough that, even though it's his right, it touches dangerously close to the line. "But the Colum—"

Alarik guides me to the cell door. " . . . doesn't have to know."

The thought of being away from the stuffy cell slowly overpowers the rest of my caution. "Okay."

Alarik leads me out of the cell and into the white halls lined with prison doors, nodding to the guards on the way out of the unit.

"We'll stay in the south wing and keep to the unused hallways," Alarik says, ushering us down the lesser-used passages.

"Those halls give me the creeps." Though it's for the best we keep as many eyes off us as possible. Besides avoiding other proditors, I'm completely underdressed in my plain dress.

"Yes, but they also give Milo the creeps, so we won't have to worry about him." Alarik winks and my breaths deepen.

Once we are in the unused hallways, the lights buzz and flicker. I know it's because of Alarik's crows, but it doesn't fail to make every nerve in my body fire warnings for us to turn back. Even so, it's nice to be up and about. Already, my joints feel looser and my head clearer.

Besides the thrum of the Imnicus, everything between us is too silent. Normally, words and conversations come easily to me. Often, I find myself so lost in conversations that I completely forget the original topic. That or I don't realize that the person has long stopped listening.

But around Alarik, my head blanks, and it's not that I'm nervous, as much as I'm enthralled to the point of speechlessness.

Alarik pierces through the silence. "What kind of plays were you in before . . . you know?"

"Oh. Well I was supposed to star in a romantic tragedy before I was taken. Guess you can say my understudy lucked out."

"As the lead?"

I nod. "But it's behind me now. I'm sure the play has run hundreds of times now without me." I stifle down the pain of that loss. How missing the theater has become the least of my worries. "Do you have any siblings?"

"Two . . . I think. An older brother, and when Balistar took over, my mother was pregnant, so likely a younger sibling as well. You?"

"Two older sisters."

"Ah . . . do they envy you?"

Envy me? "What do you mean?"

"Because of the three of you, you must be the pretti—" Alarik pinches his eyes.

I stop in my tracks, my legs forgetting how to work. "The what?"

Alarik takes a deep prolonged breath, stretching his fingers. "I . . . well . . . your beauty is unmatched."

I don't move from my spot and watch the tips of his leather gloves press into each other nervously.

"Alarik—"

"I like you, Lleu," he says abruptly. "Enough that I'd give my life to protect you. Enough that I'd get on my knees and beg you to forgive me for the mess I've placed you in."

I open my mouth to speak, but no words come out. We'd be foolish to say we've hidden our feelings well from each other, yet I'm shocked.

He turns toward me, the hall shrinking in on us. "I don't want another second to pass without you knowing that. But even if you don't share my feelings, nothing will change. I would still trade my life to save yours."

I bite down on my bottom lip. With this confession, everything rises to the surface. He cares for me as much as I do for him. I part my lips, absorbing the silence before speaking. "Yes."

"Yes?"

"I have always felt the same. From the very beginning."

Alarik lifts his hands slowly, cupping my face and tracing my cheekbones. My body goes warm, the skin he touches on fire.

I raise my hands to his mask before undoing the thin straps and lowering it, exposing his smooth, freshly shaven skin. I study every contour of his needy face, moving dark auburn hair away. He's an angel.

He runs his thumb over my bottom lip and I shiver. I stifle a gasp as he quickly backs me into the wall.

His mouth presses against mine, softly, yet all-consuming. I melt into a puddle.

It's like a fever dream, slow and silky. The kind of kiss that is only supposed to happen only in stories. For months I've fantasized of Alarik kissing me. With my predicament and our stations, I never thought it would happen. A part of me even believed I didn't deserve one of the most powerful proditors in the galaxy, to which most girls would scoff.

He holds me tightly against him as I wrap my arms behind his neck. He moans softly when I inch my tongue into his mouth and he breathes me in. Nothing about him is rough. His heart pounds through his armor against my chest.

He caresses my ribs and hips. My body heats, and if we don't stop soon, nobody will be able to pry him off of me.

I break the kiss, both of our breaths heavy. His hood has fallen, and if anyone found us like this, I'm sure they could report us for breaking at least five different Arris laws.

Alarik rests his forehead against mine. "I'm going to save you from Milo, even if it kills me."

"And you'll leave the Imnicus with me?"

Alarik's hands tighten on my hips, and I understand.

He can never leave Milo or his life as a proditor. Once a proditor, always a proditor. Part of me has to believe there could be a future for the two of us. Either on Msanii or some other place. He doesn't want to be here. I know he doesn't.

His hands leave my body. "We should keep walking. I'm sure your legs are stiff from all that time locked away."

I nod, my heart aching and burning at the same time.

We roam through the halls past flickering lights and blocked off doors. The Arris Reign is the life he's known since he was a boy. To him, this is his only tangible reality.

But does Alarik really find himself so stuck that he cannot leave? No path that ends with him escaping the Imnicus and hiding out with me on Ashtanabo? Is throwing all this away really that much of a risk?

Am I not worth the risk?

An icy chill passes over the back of my neck, so cold that I grab the back of my neck. Alarik's attention is focused straight in front of him. Does Alarik not feel it too? There are no vents in our path or behind us to explain the freezing temperature.

My vision cracks like shattered glass and I can't move any of my limbs or even my fingers. The world around me grows uneven like a broken mirror, and I can't even find it in me to scream. *Oh gods, what's happening to me?*

The worst part is, Alarik doesn't seem to even notice.

Everything around me disappears, including him, and my stomach drops like I'm falling off a tall building.

Fingers press into my temples and I try to scream but can't.

Even through it all, I can still feel my physical body walking calmly next to Alarik's. None of this makes sense. If this isn't Alarik's doing, then what is going on?

"Hello there," a voice says. "It's been so long. Too long."

Phantom arms wrap around me, my back pressed firmly into a chest. I yelp and fight against him, but his grip stays firm.

"I've been watching you," Knox says softly.

Has he been watching this entire time? Waiting to strike?

"Get the hell off of me!"

"Not yet." His lips brush over my hair.

"You couldn't have touched me! Alarik would have noticed! I would have felt it!"

"An expert on crows, are you? Who's to say what I have or have not done."

"I know enough. This isn't an entrancement. It isn't real."

"Consider this more of a middle ground to a proditor entrancement. Believe me, it's real enough."

"Milo will find out what you're doing."

Knox chuckles. "Will he? I'm shaking in my boots."

"You can't hurt me here. I know that much!"

One of his hands snake around my neck, thumb stroking my windpipe. "There are tortures of the body and tortures of the mind. Over the years I have learned that anticipation can be worse than pain itself."

I want to cry and scream and beat my way out of his talons but he's holding me so tightly I really do almost hurt.

"Have you ever heard of raven magic?" he asks.

I shudder. Is this the darker proditor magic I've heard rumors about? A magic that Balistar practiced behind closed doors? I shake my head.

"Then let me put it lightly." His lips lightly brush under my ear as he speaks. "If Alarik or any other proditor touches you, the next time you dream, it will be only of me."

My lungs heave. "That's impossible."

"With ravens, I can spread my crows through Alarik's skin and into your mind like a wildfire. One mishap and you'll be mine. He won't even be aware of what he's doing. My power is contagious if I allow it to be."

Does Alarik know Knox can curse me through him? That the smallest brush of his skin from this point forward will hand me over to Knox the next time I sleep?

If I avoid touching Alarik, I will be able to sleep without being in danger of Knox. "He has no reason to touch me."

Knox laughs. "You think I didn't see that kiss? It's only a matter of time before you'll crave his touch between your thighs. If I were him, you would have fallen apart in my hands already."

I shudder. Months ago, Knox arrived back on the Imnicus one morning with hickeys covering his neck and jaw. I didn't want to imagine what the girl looked like after that encounter.

"The second I get out of here, I will tell Alarik everything." I wriggle in his arms.

"No, I don't think you will."

I wince against him. "And why is that?"

He smiles against my neck. "Because Alarik will certainly attempt to murder me. And when backed into a corner, I kill."

No. Knox wouldn't really kill Alarik, would he? They grew up together. Then again, he's done far worse than death to me as it is.

The ground gives way beneath me as Knox's grip loosens. My stomach plunges as if dropping thousands of feet.

"See you soon, Lleu."

I suck in a deep breath, my eyes catching up with reality. We're back in the prison wing, long white halls and empty cells passing with each step. Alarik leads the way, completely silent. Did I respond to anything he said while I was in Knox's entrancement? Or did he think we just walked back to the cell in an awkward silence? All I know is he didn't notice a thing.

Gods, this isn't good.

When the cell door opens, Alarik walks in first and I follow in at a safe distance behind him. Besides the area between his hood and mask, every part of his body is covered with proditor armor. At least I don't have to worry about accidentally touching him for now.

When Alarik turns around, he pulls down his mask and nears me.

I take a step back and extend my hand. "Not now."

His eyes flash. "I'm sorry—I shouldn't have—"

"No!" I say too quickly. "I mean, I just want to take things slow if that's all right?"

My heart breaks at rejecting him. There's nothing I want more than to kiss him. To strip him of his dark armor and taste every inch of his skin. But right now, it's too risky for both of us.

"Will you visit me tomorrow though?" I ask.

"Yes, of course. How could I not after . . . "

My face heats up. "You could bring a game. It gets lonely being locked up here, you know?"

Alarik nods. "Then yes, tomorrow we'll simply play a game."

Chapter 13

Margot

"You see anything?" I ask Oliver upon the rooftop of a shop covered in greenery.

Oliver lies on his stomach next to me, holding a pair of techy binoculars pointed at the entrance of the prison.

Diyu prison is half the size of a skyscraper and looks like a black cube surrounded by high fences and black rocks. It seems out of place compared to the rest of Susuku, especially this close to the city. It's heavily guarded with security cameras pointed every which way.

"There may be a couple of weak spots we can try." He pulls out his communicator. "Dimitri, those fence bars on the left of the prison, check those next."

Dimitri's voice comes in fuzzy. *"Roger that."*

Oliver puts down the binoculars and rests his head in his hands. "Gods, I'm exhausted." He holds his stomach as it growls. "Something tells me there aren't soup kitchens on Ashtanabo."

Sleeping last night felt impossible. Turns out sleazy hotels are most active at night. Between the grotesque noises and the blaring music, resting was done in shifts. Not to mention, it's hard to sleep when your stomach is completely empty. Our window of breaking this girl out of Diyu is completely dependent on how long our stomachs and geeds can last before we take to stealing, which is a last resort given the risk. Though our hunger is still a moderate discomfort, eventually we'll become ravenous.

"After we pay for tonight at the hotel, we'll have forty geeds left," I say. "If we spend some on food, it will help us think through the mission clearly."

"We may be on the planet for months or years though. Shouldn't we ration it more?"

"We need something in our stomachs even if it's something small." I can't imagine breaking someone out of prison while dizzy and starving. It's why Lucinda always made quality food a priority for the rebellion. "If we're going to invest in a big meal, it should be right before the mission."

Dimitri's voice plays over the communicator. *I think I found something. Meet me back at the hotel.*

Oliver and I breathe a collective sigh of relief as we sneak off the rooftop. The entire way back, my head spins, and I hold my breath when we pass restaurants, mouth-watering scents filling the streets.

When we enter the room, Dimitri is already sitting on the edge of the bed with a smile on his face.

"You better have something good." I slump onto the floor, crossing my legs. What I wouldn't do for something as simple as sugar water. We may be the only people starving on this entire planet.

Oliver leans against the wall and folds his arms. "Good enough to break out a tier-one inmate at that."

"First thing is first," Dimitri says, "the security is next level. In fact, it has more safeguards in place than most Laven prisons. They have everything from scanners to motion sensors, V.I.X. units, and an electrical moat—"

"Well that's not very motivating," I interrupt. "You're making it sound like it's not even possible to sneak in."

Dimitri crosses his legs on the bed. "Because it isn't."

My chin falls to my chest. "Shit."

Oliver throws his hands up. "Way to get our hopes up."

"Both of you, would you just let me finish? I know we're hungry but please have patience." Dimitri clears his throat. "Anyway, Diyu has quite a few visitors. Family and friends of inmates. It seems that Ashtanabo is a bit lax with visitations."

"So, you want us to just waltz up to the guards and say we're visiting their most highly-guarded inmate?" I ask mockingly.

"That's exactly what I'm suggesting," Dimitri says with too much confidence.

Oliver looks like he wants to tear his head off. "Gods, we don't even know her name yet."

"Anali Matsumoto." Dimitri pulls a tablet from under the pillow next to him and offers it to Oliver.

"What the hell? Did you steal this?" Oliver pushes off the wall and swipes it quickly.

I rub my temples. I'm a spy and have trained my entire life for missions exactly like this. I like to be cautious and careful, scope out locations for days at a time if possible, and explore every avenue before taking the first move.

But time is something we don't have anymore. I don't have the luxury of ironing out every detail. I'll have to see this mission like the one on the Imnicus and take everything as it comes.

After we spend too much time bickering and agree on Dimitri's plan, I take the currency device to the convenience shop and buy the cheapest energy bars I can find and throw them at both boys once I return.

We sit on the floor, devouring the bars like a pack of animals. My ravenous stomach turns this bare-bones meal into a delicacy on my taste buds.

Dimitri clicks through the channels on the holographic television while we eat. Lavenai doesn't have shows like this that are purely for enjoyment. Most of what we have are propaganda or news channels. Even commercials are rare.

It surprises me that I was ever allowed to watch television on the Imnicus when anything damning could have played. But now that I think of it, the channels were very limited. Only five or so to choose from. Even when it came to the library selection, it's very possible books were removed to ensure I didn't stumble on the truth of how Ashtanabo came to rule Lavenai. That would explain why I couldn't find resources on proditor burns too.

Dames of Ashtanabo plays on one of the channels and the food in my stomach goes sour.

Most days, I try not to think of Lleu, but right now it feels impossible. Even if she didn't die, being alive can't be much better. Not when the alternative is her being held captive in an Imnicus prison cell while they torture her for days on end.

She was a girl in the wrong place at the wrong time, forced onto the Imnicus, and trained to con me to maintain Milo's charade. All so they could get the code to my tablet and use my face to infiltrate the rebellion. Anytime she tried to rebel or help me, she suffered.

I click past the show, unable to bear the reminder of Lleu. Of how much I miss her.

But a few channels later, my finger freezes mid press.

Milo's face appears on the screen. A younger version of him.

"In the year 4050, after Colum Balistar Arris was mysteriously assassinated, his son, Milo Arris, took the throne at the age of seventeen." The camera angle changes to Milo standing on a stage in front of thousands, being crowned Colum by Arbitor Monicas. Milo's face is emotionless as the crowd claps and cheers before he's led off stage and onto a ship. *"Though many rumors circulated of him killing his own father, those whispers quickly died down after Arbitor Gareth Monicas temporarily took over operations until Colum Arris came of age."*

Dimitri tries to swipe the remote away. "Margot, you shouldn't."

I quickly lean to the side, keeping it out of his reach, my eyes pinned on the television. On Milo, who has fully come to power. And though he looks young, there's a coarseness to his expressions that adds to his capability, even at that age.

"At the age of twenty, Milo Arris fully came to power and became the spitting image of his father." Milo stands around a long holographic table with a group of politicians, pointing to the images to review plans. *"He continued his father's policies alongside the arbitors, ensuring Ashtanabo stayed healthy as a planet."* He exits a ship, surrounded by guards and proditors. They lead him into a government building to escape a crowd in Heidl. Never once does he smile. Not at his people. Not at the cameras. Not even at other politicians.

"However, Balistar Arris will always be missed. Many agree things haven't been the same on Ashtanabo since his passing." Balistar Arris smiles and waves in a compilation of quick clips, blowing kisses to cheering Ashtanabans, his white-blonde hair kept perfectly in place by his ivory crown.

Finally, it cuts to a clip of Milo at the age of twenty-six, two years ago, overlooking a crowd. His jaw twitches in the way it does when he's uncomfortable. Everything about him has matured through his now eleven-year reign—his hair longer, eyes darker, face more defined. My heart pounds and my hand sweats as I grip the remote harder.

Whereas Balistar wore his rule on his sleeves, Milo looks like he wanted to rip his sleeves off and burn them in a fire.

This version of him is closer to the one I know. The one I loved. Still angry and constantly scowling, but a boy who really became a man, shrouded in darkness, lost in purpose.

I don't catch my lips parting until Oliver crawls forward and turns the holographic television off on the device itself.

"I think we've all had enough for one day," Oliver says in a slightly awkward tone. "We should finish up our food and get to sleep. Tomorrow will be a long day."

Dimitri's hand is frozen around his energy bar, his stare coarse, though he doesn't voice any suspicions.

I peel my gaze from him as I finish my food.

Chapter 14

Lleu

I force down the last few bites of my bland lunch, food passing over the lump in my throat.

Last night was filled with tossing and turning. Nightmares that fluctuated my body between hot and cold as the dreams ebbed and flowed.

Dream after dream, Alarik's hands worshiped me, fingers tracing my face and working between my thighs as he whispered words of love.

But each one ended the same, with the environment warping to Knox standing over me, his hands wrapped around my neck, a slick smile painted across his face.

You lose, he said a second before I shot up from the dream.

One mishap. That's all it will take for Knox to trap me in a world of his creation without even touching me. I've been there before, and I never want to go back. The infliction of proditor magic is the kind of thing you wouldn't even wish on your worst enemy.

Knox's obsessions defy logic. His sickness, filled with sadistic desires, has brewed for months. It's no secret it's Margot he truly wants. But it doesn't matter; he'll torment me in the meantime.

When I finish my meal, I stand and stretch, pushing the potential horrors out of my mind.

The door slides open and I instinctively take a step back.

Alarik enters with a wooden box in hand, and his eyebrows raise slightly. "I suppose I should announce myself since I'm in uniform. I'm sorry."

"Please don't apologize. I've just been on edge." I bite down on my inner lip.

Alarik secures the door and removes his disguise.

I want him to kiss me. To tell me everything's going to be all right. The nauseating knot in my chest tightens when I remember Knox's threats. What he'll do to Alarik in retaliation if I reveal anything.

Alarik sets the box down on the table before taking a step toward me. Again, I take another step back before cursing internally.

A wave of hurt passes over his face, but he tries to cover it with a smile before sitting down at the table. "I brought *Micheqo*. It was my favorite game back in the Vicar village. Sometimes, I'd ask to play it so much that my father would fake a headache and make my brother play instead."

I laugh weakly. It must be hard for him to think of his family in any capacity. All the childhood memories he lost out on. "So it's a children's game?"

Alarik shrugs as he sits. "It's a bit advanced for most children, but I fared well with it. It may be the one thing I'm better at than most people." He dumps out the contents of the box, setting up the circular wooden board and the tiny glass birds. When he removes his gloves, I suppress a sharp breath at the sight of his skin. Skin that will hand me over to Knox at the slightest brush.

I shouldn't play with Alarik. I should lie and tell him I'm not feeling well. But he'll ask me to explain myself and how can I? What lie is believable enough?

"It's easy enough to learn." Alarik places the clear glass pieces on my side of the board and the black glass ones on his. "Simpler than chess and also faster, because you have to beat your opponent to the middle space while also blocking them from getting there. Sort of like king of the hill. There aren't turns, only strategy." He explains what each piece is allowed to do at any given time and what the different colored spaces mean.

"You start at the spot closest to you marked in gray and every piece you set has to be next to or diagonal to another. They have to connect like a snake from your starting point all the way to the middle. It's like solving a puzzle. But remember, you can block me at any given moment, or use your owl piece to branch off and steal one of my pieces to make the entire chain fall."

"You played this as a child? You were basically a toddler when Balistar took over."

His face is unreadable as he stares at the board. "Like I said, it's the one thing I'm good at."

"That's not true. You're good at fighting and at strategy. Not only that, you may be the kindest person I know. Oh and you're good at putting Onyx in his place."

Alarik smiles, his cheeks reddening slightly. "Do you mean that?"

I nod. "You should shun anyone who says you're not talented. Though, please go easy on me."

"You'll do great, and I'll go slow since it's your first time playing *Micheqo*." He reaches for his first piece, unable to find his next words between his smiling lips. "We'll both start with our opening moves, then after that we can begin finding our way to the middle."

I nod and the game starts.

Within minutes, Alarik is already halfway to the center and I'm only a few pieces in. It isn't long before I forget all about Knox and my competitive side takes over. The game is enthralling and I can see why it's Alarik's favorite game. I decide to go on the offense toward his chain instead of the middle, but by the time I get there, he's already won.

"I thought you said you would go easy on me." I fold my arms.

"I'm sorry, I got carried away." He sets the board back up for the next game. "Don't worry. This time I will hold back."

"Well, don't patronize me. I think I'm getting the hang of it so give me your worst."

"If you say so."

The next game starts fiercely, and this time I don't waste my first few moves. I go straight for the center. To beat Alarik, I'll need to be on defense and offense at the same time.

I work aggressively, using offense every other move, until we're both tied, which is a lot better than I did last game. His confidence slowly fades from his face, as if he's regretting going easy on me. Something competitive flashes in his eyes, which only makes my own will to win increase ten fold.

We're both moves away from winning. I inch off my seat a bit when I'm two moves from victory. But Alarik is quick to block me, staying barely ahead of me as I move toward the center. He's not quick enough though.

My hand comes down for the winning move, but the room twists before my piece reaches the board. Shadows pass over my skin, and I hear the caw of crows. My heart thumps wildly and my eyes widen.

I can't bring myself to move as I stare down at the edge of Alarik's hand pressed up against mine, my fist gripping the game piece.

I flinch away, hurling the small glass bird as if it were scalding hot. Alarik fumbles to catch it before it hits the ground. My hands clutch my collar, my breathing rapid.

The next time I sleep, Knox will be in my head. The horror of it is almost too much to process. Too much to think or imagine. I don't know whether to cry or to scream, so I just sit there with unblinking eyes and trembling hands.

Alarik stays completely still, staring at me with a thousand thoughts behind his eyes. Did he feel what I felt? If he did, would I feel relieved or horrified? He stays quiet and rises, staying in place for a moment, before rounding the table.

Tears fall down my cheeks as he kneels in front of me, taking my hands into his.

If he's hurt, he doesn't show it. Instead, he traces my fingers gently. "Lleu, I hope you know, I would never hurt you." He brings his lips to my knuckles, kissing each one.

"I know," I manage to say. "It's just—"

"You've been through a lot," he interrupts. "If I could take your pain away I would, even if that meant I had to wear it as my own."

With the damage done, I let him bring his palms to my face as he swipes away the falling tears. I don't know what hurts more: the anticipation of the end or the fact that he truly believes I'm afraid of him.

Why is it when everything is going well, something has to come and rip it away? Like Milo tearing me from Msanii just as my acting career was taking off. My new friend disappearing without a trace, even though I'm glad she's safe. And now it's this. Knox stealing my ability to touch Alarik without the threat of torment.

But there's no risk now. What has been done cannot be undone. The next time I sleep, I will be bound to Knox for him to do with me as he pleases.

Alarik's throat bobs. "Every time I look at you, I fight the urge to stay a gentleman."

I melt at his words, taking in every part of him—his dark auburn hair, the dimple on just one side of his face. He glows as he traces my cheekbones, his body carved to perfection by the gods themselves.

I slip off the chair, joining him in kneeling.

His eyes dip to my mouth. All I have to do is nod and Alarik leans forward, his soft lips brushing against mine.

Alarik is gentle with me as his hands move to my hips, pulling me closer until my chest presses into his. He wraps his arms around me while he tastes me. His hold is tight and protective. Like if I stayed in his embrace forever, Knox would never be able to have me again.

He pulls his mouth away. "I'm sorry, I know you said you wanted to take things slow."

I laugh, the tears drying on my skin. My mind may not even be my own by tomorrow. This may be the last chance I have to hold him. To cherish and savor him. Because I don't know if I'll be the same woman tomorrow.

I keep my eyes pinned on him as I reach for the clasps on his proditor armor, keeping our gazes locked. Alarik's lips part as I slip his outer armor off his shoulders and undress the layers until he's down to his black tank.

His chest rises and falls, and his hands flex slightly as his gaze rakes across my body. "Can I take your dress off?"

A white-hot feeling courses through my body at his request. I nod slowly.

He finds the hems, the backs of his fingers slowly dragging along my skin as he raises the dress up my thighs, my waist, then my ribs, before lifting it over my head and tossing it to the side.

With a sharp inhale, Alarik's lips part as he takes in the sight of me with craving and longing, staring at me like I'm forbidden. Delicate.

I take his palm and set it on my chest. "Don't worry. I'm not glass."

He moves his hands over my breasts and down my ribs, circling his thumbs there. "Are you sure you want this? We could wait. I could make it special for you." His hands tell a different story as they pass over my underwear line.

"You're acting like this is my first time." I lean forward, pressing my lips to the pulse point on his neck, relishing in the quiet groan that vibrates in his chest.

"I want this to mean something, not just to me, but to you too."

I pull back quickly. "Now you're making me feel like it's your first time."

"I promise it's not." He bites his lip back at his own words.

I'm not jealous or upset that he's been with other women. All I feel is longing. Gods, I want him. I'm going to suffer the next time I sleep, and I may never be the same after. For that reason, I want to know I showed him how much I love him. Not just in voice but in the way that only two bodies intertwined can with tangled legs and small gasps between kisses.

I grab the ends of his tank and pull it over his head. "Don't hold back, please. Touch me. Taste me however you'd like."

Alarik takes one more deep breath before crashing his lips into mine, his gentle kisses gone. He drinks me in with need, unclasping my bra and discarding it.

My tongue explores his mouth and I can't believe his touch is real. That it's taken us this long to get here with the way we melt into each other.

His fingers slide down the hems of my panties, slipping them down my thighs.

I can't get enough of him, my mouth devouring his while I undo his pants and get him as bare as I am. I can't wait any longer. I need to feel every part of him.

Alarik presses me back into the cold floor and kisses my forehead. He keeps his gaze trained on me as he positions himself and joins us together.

"Alarik—" I bite down on my lip as he moves. My toes curl as the bind between proditor and human collides and we become bound by the stars themselves.

Between gasps and damp skin, we find a rhythm. I tangle my fingers in his hair to deepen my kisses. Alarik places one of his hands on my head to protect my skull from hitting the wall in the tight cell.

I want to tell him I love him, but something about it feels too soon. Instead, I show him with my mouth, with the roll of my hips to take him in deeper, and with the cries of pleasure when I finally break.

And as my body arches, Alarik stares into my eyes, cradling my face. He takes me in, my dark skin and my trembling lips. It's when I look through his eyes and into his heart, to the place he never lets anyone see, that he loses control and releases.

The euphoria on his face is almost enough for me to break again, but I hold back. I don't want to lose this moment. I want to watch him. To study him. To take in this rare version of him that I may never be able to appreciate again.

Chapter 15

Margot

My palms grow clammy as the three of us stand in line, just past the gated entrance at the intake area of Diyu prison. The air smells metallic with a hint of burning plastic. Guards patrol the lines, which lead up to a seated officer in a muted-gray uniform vetting every visitor.

Oliver lowers his head and whispers to me. "You remember what we talked about?"

I nod and exchange a knowing glance with Dimitri as well.

In line with us are the loved ones of prisoners. Some carry gifts that will be heavily inspected by the guards as well as the large metal detector run by V.I.X. units and a humanoid.

If I were the Colum, I would keep knowledge of Anali's abilities a secret and the nature of her incarceration a quiet affair, even from the guards. It's too early to tell, but nobody that's not of higher ranking in the prison should know of her importance if my theory is correct. She's like a valuable shipment sent via a courier instead of an armored car just to avoid being targeted. With that, the guards may be more lax regarding her. They also likely don't expect Lavens infiltrating any structure on Ashtanabo.

"Next," the officer calls out while he taps away at the screen of his tablet.

"I'll approach him first," I say quietly to the guys. "Follow behind and don't say anything."

Oliver takes a small step back near Dimitri as I walk toward the desk. Being a woman, I'll be seen as less suspicious than them. It's something I've used to my advantage many times on missions.

I stop in front of the officer who doesn't spare a glance as he pulls the keyboard up on his screen.

"Which inmate?" the officer asks shortly.

I keep my throat from bobbing. "Anali Matsumoto."

The officer pauses, his eyes finally meeting mine. "What is your business with her?"

Is my theory wrong? "I'm a childhood friend."

He shifts in his seat and types in her name. "It says here she's never had a visitor before."

I act as ditzy as possible. "My gosh, I've only recently heard she was here!" So it's true. This officer doesn't know about Anali's powers. If he did, we would have already been onto plan B—escape, survive, and try again.

"And these men with you, who are they?" The officer folds his arms.

Dimitri's breaths are heavy behind me.

"My older brothers. They knew her too."

The officer types on his tablet, grumbling as he searches for something. He eyes me a few times in the process. My fingers sweat and I can hear Dimitri's inhales growing more ragged. I want to reach back and slap him, but thankfully the officer doesn't seem to notice.

My intuition fires on all cylinders, screaming for me to run. It's not too late for us to pull the plug while we're still outside security. Feign ignorance, some deniability, or even illness, just to get out of line.

But the guard dismissively waves us off toward the prison entrance. "You're clear. A guard will escort you to her cell. She has a ten-minute visit limit so keep things short." He motions to the woman behind me. "Next!"

I smile and thank the man before striding past, keeping my breathing steady. A guard is assigned to us and I reach for Dimitri's hand, squeezing it tightly if only to tell him, *Phase one is complete, but we still have a long way to go.*

We follow the guard past large doors that lock behind us. There's no going back now.

The walls of the prison are grayish-blue and impeccably clean with a sleek shine. Vault-like doors line the hallways. Patrolling guards barely spare us a second glance.

On the second floor, there are open cells with bars with quiet inmates slump on their beds and against walls. The one time I had to break into a Laven prison for a mission, the inmates were rowdy, shouting and cursing through the steel bars.

Here, they stare blankly at the walls, mindlessly playing with threads on their jumpsuits or with their uneaten food. They're like robots, not even turning their heads as we pass. Oliver slows at the sight of them.

"This is my first time visiting a prison," I say to the guard. "I didn't expect it to be so . . . quiet."

The guard shrugs. "Well, this prison is different from any other. Most people here have been through the nymbing process. Don't worry, in just a few months they'll be as good as new and ready to be reintegrated into society."

Nymbing? I can't ask him what it is. He said it like I should already know. It sounds somewhat familiar. Whatever it is, they don't use it on Lavenai.

"Oh," is all I say.

An older defector's face lies between the bars, drool dripping down the corner of his lip.

We take an elevator up to level five and file out into a darker hallway filled with more vault-like cells with higher security clearance. These cells are more spread out. They're dark and isolating. I cross my arms when the temperature drops significantly. Oliver visibly shudders.

The guard leads us to the door at the end of the hallway. "She's been in solitary confinement for most of her incarceration, so she may not be the same person you three once knew. Figured I should warn you." He taps his wrist to the security screen. "You'll have ten minutes. For security reasons, I have to lock the door behind you while you're inside. When you're finished, knock on the door three times. I'll be waiting out here."

The draft from the door sliding open moves my curls slightly.

My heart stops at the state of the cell.

White scratches cover one of the walls. Some are even tallies. Others look scratched on erratically. Hooded stick figures and crows cover another, neither of them depicted in a positive light.

In the center of it all sits a girl in a chair wearing a straight jacket.

Her blue-black bangs cover her eyes and her head slumps, but it's not enough to shield her age. She's a few years younger than me if I had to guess.

I take a step closer and my crows immediately go dormant, landing back in their nests, shielding their heads from the nullifying energy that radiates up my veins.

"Anali, you have guests." The guard turns to us after a prolonged silence. "Keep it short."

As the door locks behind us, I flex and stretch my fingers. If we have any encounters with proditors on the way out and this girl is near me, I won't be able to defend us.

The weight settles in my chest. She's not just dangerous to Milo but also to me.

As I near her, I can finally see her opened eyes through her bangs. She stares at a drawing on the wall of two crows encircling each other.

Her lips curl. "Another proditor sent to test me?"

I startle at her tone—numb and weak, yet also amused. Has she been nymbed like the others?

"Hmm, your crows taste different." She rolls her neck back, her long bangs still covering her eyes. "You can report back to your superior that you're not immune to me either."

"There aren't any cameras." Olivers searches around the walls and the lone cot. "Tell her why we're here. Quickly."

"You're Anali Matsumoto, right?" I ask.

She grins with her tongue between her teeth before shaking her head wildly a few times. "Do I get a full pardon from the Colum if I say yes?"

Dimitri stands at my side. "I'll unbuckle the straight jacket. Keep her talking."

"Wait." I grab his arm. "We don't know why she's in it or what her powers can do."

"Do we have a choice? We can't exactly sneak her out if she's in this."

I bite down on my tongue as Dimitri kneels behind her and undoes the first buckle.

I clear my throat. "Anali, we're not here to test you. We're here to rescue you."

"Rescue?" She lifts her head, finally clearing her face of her hair. Her Susukan features glow in the foggy light.

"There's not a lot of time to explain," I say, "but I know you can help us. In return, we're going to save you from this hell hole."

She drops her head again. "Can I really be saved, Proditor?"

"I'm not a proditor," I say. "

She stares at me, eyes curious. "They're crying out. So loud. So *hungry*." Her eyes soften to pity. "How do you bear them?"

Dimitri undoes the last strap of the straight jacket, and I help him pull it over her head. Her arms fall limp at her sides.

"How do you want to play this Oliver?" Dimitri asks.

"I'll take down the guard and Margot will guide the girl out."

"I have a name," Anali rolls her shoulders back. She has enough muscle that I doubt they keep her in the jacket all the time. Still, I worry if she has enough strength to walk.

I kneel in front of her, taking her hands into mine. "Are you able to turn your powers off?"

"Why? So you can defeat the proditor that roams these halls? He hates me, you know. He hates how *human* I make him feel."

So, no. She can't turn them off.

"How close do they have to be for your powers to work?" I ask impatiently. There won't be much time before the guard comes to get us and we need the element of surprise.

"They've done measurements. Every day. When I'm sleeping. After beatings. When I'm eating. It's all the same. Ten feet." she says.

Which means if we do encounter a proditor, it would be in our best interest to keep her within range of him. "Can you walk?"

"Of course I can walk." Anali pulls her hands away and stands. I follow suit.

I thought she'd have more questions or apprehension. But it seems she wants out of here like any prisoner would, no matter what stranger shows up to take her. No matter the intention.

Her legs go weak.

Oliver quickly rushes forward and catches her under her arms. "You sure about that walking thing?"

"They're just a little out of practice, is all," Anali grumbles.

Oliver holds her up. "This isn't good. She'll only slow us down."

"Watch it," she bites, her energy slowly returning.

"She's the reason we're here." I take Anali from him, wrapping her arm over my shoulder.

"And if we encounter that proditor, what then?" Oliver asks.

"Then he and I will both fight as humans," I answer. "Good thing I've been training."

Oliver narrows his eyes before he motions to knock at the solid door. "Ready everyone?"

Dimitri and I nod. Anali gives a weak thumbs up, and I adjust to put more of her weight on me. I pull her to a corner to keep her out of the guard's initial line of sight.

Dimitri knocks three times and takes a step back. Oliver stretches his wrists before curling his fists.

I hold my breath as the door opens.

The guard steps forward. "How was she—"

Oliver lunges and takes the guard by the head, slamming his face into his kneecap. The helmet cracks and the gun clatters to the ground.

"Son of a bitch!" The guard yells, cradling his face.

Dimitri rushes to the door to crack it, masking the noise from the rest of the prison.

The guard reaches for the gun, but Oliver is faster. He rips the helmet off and kicks the gun away.

With a swift motion, Oliver swings the helmet, thwacking the guard's skull. The guard falls over, and his eyes roll into the back of his head.

Oliver bends down and drags the body off to the side.

Dimitri flings the door open while Oliver steals the security band off the guard's wrist. I guide Anali over the threshold and into the hallway.

"Which way?" Dimitri asks.

"Let's go left," I answer. "With the security band, we can escape through the back exits."

"So many have tried and so many have failed." Anali chuckles.

"What is that supposed to mean?" Oliver bites.

Anali shrugs. "Just wait and see."

Oliver frowns. "Ignore her. Let's keep going."

We get to the end of the hallway and turn. With a closed-circuit television system, we have to be quick. Once they pick us up on the feed, the entire prison will go into lockdown.

Dimitri helps me guide Anali down the sets of echoey metal stairs and onto the first floor.

Someone clears their throat at the end of the hall, and my bones stiffen.

I turn, my jaw clenching at the dark figure standing at the end of the hallway, hooded and masked.

Dimitri's muscles visibly tighten. "Shit."

The figure tilts his head curiously.

Anali waves across the hall. "Proditor Tatuc, I'm finally leaving this shithole. Aren't you happy for me? You'll finally be able to grow balls with me away." She says it like she's talking to an old friend.

I shake her. "Stop! What is wrong with you?"

Though, I shouldn't have expected anything less from the only human immune to proditor power. Or maybe she's just that bold. Or completely insane.

Oliver and Dimitri take a step back on the brink of petrification. I've seen them defeat men twice their size, but they've never fought a proditor. Especially one his size.

The ebony-skinned proditor narrows his eyes.

As long as Anali is near, we're safe. Relatively. Though none of it will matter if guards surround us.

"All four of you, put your hands up and get on your knees," Proditor Tatuc says.

I push out the petrification that threatens to take over. I know I am capable of fighting even without the Nexus but not if I'm in range of Anali.

"Keep her away from me," is all I say before I push Anali to Dimitri. I sprint toward the proditor.

"Wait!" Dimitri yells, but I ignore him.

My eyes are locked on Proditor Tatuc, who chuckles. It may be the first time in his life someone who isn't a proditor has taken a run at him, besides maybe Anali of course. He gathers himself, raising his gloved fists.

I have to keep his hands busy. His skin is more of a weapon than his punches, and because I'm not a real proditor, I can still be entranced. His gloves need to stay on at all costs.

"Find the path to the exit!" I shout as I throw the first punch at the proditor.

"On it!" Oliver yells back.

The proditor blocks it seamlessly, and he's quick to retaliate, throwing one back at me that I narrowly miss. It takes a series of punches and kicks for me to pick up on rhythm. The subtle flaws in his fighting style that I can exploit.

The proditor is a great fighter, an expert by most standards. However, there was a time I fought Imnicus proditors. If I was battling one of them, I may not stand a chance. But the Nexus against a regular Ashtanaban proditor? My skills excel what I thought I was capable of.

"A female proditor? Or a rogue Vicar?" He shakes his head in disbelief while he fights. "Either way, your crows are the most despicable ones I've ever been around."

If he thinks I'm a proditor, he's less likely to entrance me. Still, I don't want to test that theory.

He pulls a knife off his belt and swipes at my torso, and I jump back before he slices me. The Nexus quells my fear, and I pretend like it's a game, jumping back at the quick movements.

I catch onto what he's doing.

He's trying to get me closer to Anali. To put me in range to quell my crows while keeping him powerful. I shoot my gaze over my shoulder. Oliver is still off somewhere trying to find an exit. Dimitri holds Anali's wrist, pulling her further back.

Anali laughs hysterically. "This is the most fun I've had in years."

We near the end of the hallway. I can't go back anymore without Anali being in range.

A few of my crows fall asleep. My fighting becomes visibly weaker.

"Margot, roll back!" Dimitri yells. "I got this."

He's got this? Against a full-blooded proditor?

I can't overthink it. I have to trust him.

I control my fall, catching the floor with my palms and rolling backward.

Dimitri runs forward with Anali.

The proditor's brow rises and he backs up quickly, but he's not fast enough. The second they're ten feet away, and Anali's nulling energy zaps his crows, Dimitri is on him. He kicks the proditor to the ground, the knife clattering to the floor.

Dimitri gets a few punches in, nearly cracking the proditor's mask, before he takes a punch of his own and falls back. The proditor overtakes Dimitri and throws him far out of Anali's range.

Dimitri's eyes widen as the proditor leaps on top of him. He holds Dimitri's biceps down with his knees, before peeling off a glove.

No. I sprint and grab Anali's hand, yanking her with me. If she falls, I'll drag her.

"Some warning would be nice!" Anali grumbles.

As the proditor's fingers touch Dimitri's skin, Tatuc flinches as his crows simultaneously fall asleep. Proditor Tatuc huffs before readying a jaw-shattering punch.

I grab the knife off the ground and lunge at the proditor, grabbing him and shoving him off Dimitri. I throw my weight onto Tatuc, straddling him.

Anali must be on the cusp of ten feet away, her sphere of influence just on the edges. She's still close enough that the proditor can't entrance me but far enough that I can feel a sliver of crows. Enough for their whispers to caress my ears as I aim the dagger at Tatuc's throat.

Kill him, the crows say.

I try to shake free of their influence, even as the proditor's bare hand catches mine just above the hilt. His hand shakes as he keeps the knife from his neck. If Anali takes even one step back, I'll be trapped within his entrancement if he catches on that I'm not a proditor, but that's hardly what occupies my mind.

I bear all my weight down upon the knife, edging closer to the soft skin of his neck. I stare into his dark brown eyes, seeing the well of life behind them.

"Don't do this," the proditor says.

I frown and shake my head clear. "Stop talking."

"Your crows are sick. If you give in, they'll only want more."

Oliver runs around the corner. "I found the exit. Let's go!"

I don't need to kill this man.

A part of me simply wants to.

It wouldn't make any difference to Dimitri or Oliver if I ended him. They're assassins. This is their every day. No one would care.

The crows swarm around my head, promising me a euphoric rush if I obey. In fact, they promise me something even better.

"You can never go back," Proditor Tatuc warns. "You'll be trapped in a cyclic hell where you have no control over your own motivations. It's why Vicars like you are normally put to death."

If I do this, a door will open. It will lead to a path that will take me on a journey I can never turn back from.

The journey of becoming Knox.

"Margot, wrap it up!" Dimitri yells. "We need to get out of here!"

I grunt slightly, pushing back against the urge, stuffing crows back into their nests.

But the crows are ruthless, pecking at my mind in one moment and giving me tastes of euphoria the next. In both, a promise of what will await me at the end of each choice.

We could make you feel better, the crows tempt. *Let us numb your pain.*

"Put your hands by your head," I tell him.

Tatuc doesn't move.

I bite down on my lip. "Please. I won't hurt you." I loosen my grip upon the knife, releasing some of my weight as a show of faith.

His jaw clenches and eyes stare into mine. Then he sighs and slowly unwraps his fingers from my hands, placing his wrists above his head in surrender.

I take my own breath of relief as I keep the knife pointed at him and stand.

Oliver points down the hall. "We don't have long. Come on!"

"What if he comes after us?" Dimitri looks to the proditor, who's still lying on his back with his hands by his ears.

It's silly seeing a proditor put in a position of complete surrender. Proditors are the glue that holds the Arris Reign together. Without their power, everything falls apart.

"Then we'll need to get a head start," I answer.

With her muscles warmed up, Anali does a small jump. "Wait, I need to say goodbye."

"Goodbye?" I shake my head.

She skips over to Proditor Tatuc.

"Anali, stop!" My pulse rages. Dimitri should have held onto her!

She kneels beside Tatuc. "It's been fun, but now it's time for me to go. Don't miss me too much, all right?" She gives him a peck on his forehead, the way a family member would.

Proditor Tatuc doesn't move from his position. He stares blankly at us as she skips back.

I hold onto her hand tightly, too worried to let her out of my sight. "Are you insane?"

"What is he going to do to me? I'm immune."

"He could have grabbed you!"

"Then I would have beat him senseless."

"What?"

Anali smiles. "They didn't keep me in the straight jacket because it was fashionable."

My mouth gapes. "You can subdue him? Then why did you just standby while—"

Oliver interrupts. "We can talk about it later. Now let's get out of here."

Chapter 16

Lleu

I spend the next two evenings forcing myself to stay awake by requesting tea and splashing water on my face.

The only thing keeping me alert, besides pure fear, is drawing. I sketch the symbol of Msanii, the house I grew up in, and some of our native flowers. Though there is a stack of books, if I try to read I know I'll nod off.

This time, Knox won't show me a shred of mercy. I need to stay awake.

And it's easier than ever to stay awake when Alarik is in my cell, our bodies joined together.

Like right now as my hips roll on top of him as he moves deeper inside me.

"Y-yes, don't stop," Alarik says, the pleasure on his face intoxicating and addicting. If I could watch him like this forever, I'd never need to sleep again.

So I won't sleep again, not until my body forces me to. Not until I learn every angle of Alarik's body.

I relish in the pleasure and even in the pain. My fingernails run down his chest, leaving soft lines in their wake.

"Lleu—" His voice stays somewhere between a gasp and a sigh. "Stop for a second."

I slow down. He moves his hands to my waist and repositions us so that he's behind me. I place a hand on the wall as he wraps my hair around his hand.

When he enters me again, I bite down on my lip.

Alarik buries his face in the crook of my neck while he thrusts, gliding his tongue just below my jaw.

"Oh . . . Alarik." My body seizes up as the pleasure explodes.

Alarik moans into my neck as the sensations overtake him, his hips stuttering.

Being with him like this makes me forget. It makes me want to be taken by him again and again.

My own climax comes down as Alarik relishes in his. Relaxation floods my body. Fatigue. Exhaustion.

You'll break soon, a voice somewhere deep inside my mind says.

I tense from the hallucination of Knox's voice, causing Alarik's release to last even longer. All the warmth in my heart turns icy cold, shattering everything as fear becomes my controller.

All my body wants is sleep. And all I want is to lie in an embrace with Alarik. To have his fingers tracing my spine as we fall into our dreams together. But if I do, it's a dream I'll never wake up from. At least not unscathed.

I just need more moon tea. More drawing supplies. I heard traditional Imnicus training includes a period where the soldiers don't sleep for five days straight. If they can do it, then so can I.

Alarik sits back. "Lay with me."

I should refuse him. If I lie down, there's no telling how soon it will be until I fall asleep against my will. But if I refuse, he'll ask questions. I need him to fall asleep first, then I can get up and draw or douse myself in the coldest water the Imnicus provides. Or maybe I can get him to leave for the day.

"Don't you have other duties?" I scoot next to him.

Alarik rubs my arm. "Not at the moment. Milo thinks I'm questioning you about the letter."

I guess I should be relieved. If Milo ever finds out what Alarik and I are *actually* doing in this cell, I could be assigned a proditor who will truly make me suffer, even if it's against Milo's wishes. But what would happen to Alarik if Milo found out? Would he have him executed? *Nymbed?*

Alarik settles back in the small bed and rests his forearm over his eyes. I remember how busy he was while Margot was around. This time together may be the most rest he's gotten in almost a year. With the servants and most military personnel unaware that Margot wasn't actually the Columess, the proditors were the ones assigned to scour the library for books on Lavenai for removal. The ones who limited the channels on the Imnicus television, which of course nobody dared to question.

I run my fingers through his dark auburn hair, studying his features. His eyes flutter shut and his breathing slows.

"You don't have to say it back," Alarik says softly. "But I'm in love with you."

I freeze, my heart on the brink of melting completely. He loves me.

He loves me.

By the time I can even consider telling him how I feel, he's fast asleep. For just a second, I lie against him and rest my head on his shoulder, listening to his soft inhales and taking in his warmth. I close my eyes and imagine the life we could have together if he wasn't sworn to the Colum.

He'd move to Msanii with me and we'd have two daughters, because everyone in my family can only seem to have girls. He'd help me in the mornings, getting them ready for school by braiding their hair. He'd smile at them and wipe any crumbs from breakfast off their honey skin. Afterwards, he'd walk me to the theater for a long day of rehearsals. I don't know what he would do, but as long as he's not working as a proditor, I'd be over the moon. What would he want if he was merely human? I don't think he knows either.

A small gasp escapes me as I nearly nod off. I sit up quickly.

That was close. More than close. I was practically dreaming.

I slip out of bed and find my dress scattered between Alarik's proditor armor and slip the fabric over my head.

Inside the bathroom, I turn on the water spout. Icy water fills my cupped hands and I splash it on my face.

Gods, that's cold. Borderline agonizing. But it added at least a few more hours before my body will force me to give out.

I grab a hand towel and dry off, hating how much the fabric feels like a warm pillow that I could get lost in.

As I lower the towel from my face, I flinch back at the sight of the mirror.

The glass ripples like stones dropped in a body of water.

I've officially entered the part of sleep deprivation where my mind is playing tricks. I run more cool water over my inner wrists, but still, the mirror doesn't return to normal. I move a finger toward it.

My lips part when my skin never hits glass, my hand and then my wrist moving into the vertical water.

I yelp when something grips my forearm. My body jolts as I'm yanked forward.

No . . . what is this? I lean back with all my weight, using my foot against the vanity to pull against the force. My shoulder, on the brink of tearing, gives out and I'm wrenched over the sink, diving head first into the rippling mirror.

I can't breathe, the water all consuming.

Finally, air meets my lungs again and I'm thrown to the side. My body rolls across the sandy tiled floor.

I'm in the south wing with its dark-gray walls and hard furniture. None of this makes sense. I know I'm sleep deprived, but this is another level of hallucination.

Lying on my stomach, I reach forward and grip a handful of sand, letting it pour between my fingertips. This is no ordinary beach sand. It's Msaniian sand from the Napane desert.

"He just couldn't keep his hands off you, could he?"

I freeze at the voice, dark chills dancing down my spine. As quickly as I can, I move back until my spine hits the side of a table.

Knox leans against the door frame, legs crossed over each other and arms folded. Blonde curls frame his face and his smirk. Sadistic eyes crawl over the length of my body.

My body shakes, a numbness passing through me. It couldn't be. "You're cheating. I-I never fell asleep!"

Knox pretends to check the time on his wrist. "Oh? A twenty-minute nap isn't considered sleep anymore? I suppose I made a mistake then."

"What—"

"Right now, Alarik is lying asleep next to you, his hand unconsciously caressing your skin. All the while, I'm in your head and have you all to myself."

The time I thought I almost nodded off—

No, gods, no.

Knox snaps his fingers, and the sand rises like flooding water, trapping my limbs like sinking sand.

I scream, but no matter how hard I fight against it, it overtakes me. I beg internally, trying to communicate with my real body. Maybe I can command myself to stir violently in my sleep. Maybe I can wake Alarik and he'll know something is off.

Knox steps through the sand effortlessly, crows zipping behind him, cawing and gliding.

I search my surroundings but stop short. I'm not like Margot. She'd probably fashion a cord into a noose or transform a pen into a weapon. This is Knox's world. Items are only here because he allows them to be.

The sand takes me down deeper, covering past my ears. I squeeze my eyes tight, like how I do when I'm desperately trying to wake up.

Knox kneels down with his legs on either side of my hips. He dips his fingers through the sand and scoops me up under my neck and lower back, pulling me out slightly. Sand spills off my body like drops of water.

My skin crawls as his warm chest presses into mine.

Knox's soft breaths pass against the side of my mouth. "When you were younger, did you ever play hide-n-seek?"

A children's game? I force a nod.

A gloved finger presses under my chin and turns my head. "Don't be rude. Look at me."

My mouth trembles as our eyes meet. He stares past my soul, learning all my fears and stealing the knowledge of what makes me tick. My deepest secrets drain out, childhood phobias leaving my psyche and entering his. A tear drops from my eyes. Never have fear's talons leached into me so deeply. He's right. The anticipation of it is worse than the real thing.

My skin goes numb as he cradles my face, moving my tears out of the way. "Now, now, don't cry. You have an entire palace to hide, don't you?"

"Please, Knox. I'll do anything, just let me wake up. Don't hurt me." I babble out the words like an idiot, but I can't help it. This moment has been what I've feared. He now knows everything I'm scared of. The things I try not to think about. Of course, none of those compare to my fear of *him*, not even my fear of the dark.

"Here's what's going to happen." He keeps his hold on me. "You're going to hide, and I'll seek."

"You can't keep me here forever," I choke out.

"We'll play until your body gets enough rest to wake up on its own. If you would have just slept initially, you wouldn't be here for so long. Ironic, isn't it?"

I try to shimmy out of his grasp, wishing for the sand to overtake me again, but the grains and all surrounding furniture disappear. Knox drops me, my back slamming into the ground. I cry out.

"Lleu, oh, Lleu. You're going to make a fine substitute until Margot gets back. But lucky for you, I'm saving the worst for her. Now be a good girl and find a place to hide." Knox steps off me and extends one arm toward the door.

I don't want to do this. If this was the real world, I could pretend to lose consciousness, but here I don't have that luxury. I have to endure him until the very end.

Gods, Alarik. Help me.

I can't waste another second. I push up to my feet and sprint out of the room.

Knox likes challenges. Even though he could torture me right now if he wanted, I know he enjoys the chase enough to let me genuinely hide from him in this projection of the Imnicus. There is still a chance I could come out of this unscathed. Already, this feels different from any proditor entrancement I've been in. Perhaps something about his ravens having to utilize Alarik's crows gives him a little less control. It doesn't make it any less terrifying. Anything Knox asks from me I would give him just to be free of this trance.

I stop to catch my breath, more winded here than I would be in the real world. The halls are quiet, Imnicus engines humming.

The humming grows louder before the pitch increases. It's so shrill, I cover my ears.

Blue lights shatter one by one. I quickly kneel, holding my ears while also covering my skin from glass.

They fracture in a line until the last one goes out and I'm left in total darkness.

My skin crawls. Anything can lurk in the dark. Right now, Knox could be standing behind me, grinning, and I'd never know.

I sprint through the pitch black, even though Knox could be waiting for me around any corner. As my eyes adjust to the dark, I make out the outline of doors. I test every single one, searching for an unlocked one.

The chime of the intercom plays overhead.

"Lleu, hide quickly," Knox says in a sing-song voice. "And if you're scared, remember, it's all a dream." I hear the grin behind his words.

I can hardly breathe. The worst part is, he still exists in the real world. For all I know, he's relaxing in bed in the proditor quarters, arms resting behind his neck with his eyes closed and a smile on his face.

Finally, I find an unlocked door and slide it open. I quickly secure it shut behind me with the deadbolt.

A bed sits in the middle, surrounded by furniture strewn throughout the room. There aren't supposed to be bedrooms in the south wing. Candles are on every surface and along the mantle. Real candles with actual flames, something strictly forbidden on the Imnicus.

Candles are part of Msanii culture as a part of our monthly feast to celebrate adolescents moving into adulthood. Not only that, but these are the same black candles with the golden candelabras. The sight brings an ache to my chest and memories of my parents flash over my face.

My eyes stay locked on the door as I slide under the bed, making sure my dress isn't visible from the sides.

Everything falls silent and I can't hear the thrum of the Imnicus anymore, only my labored breaths against the dead air.

Minutes pass, and then ten. A paralyzing numbness keeps me glued to the floor. I keep blinking, trying to coax my body awake.

"Lleu? Are you there?"

My limbs startle at a voice outside the door. But it's not Knox's. It's not even male.

It's Margot's.

She knocks at the door, then pounds. "Lleu, please, he's after me too. I came back here to save you. Let me in and we can wait this out together!"

She's not real. She's not real. But to see Margot again even in a dream . . .

I don't let the cloudy emotions move me from my spot.

Another set of footsteps echoes down the hall toward her.

Margot knocks with such force that the door vibrates. "I know you heard me that day! You knew what Knox was doing to me in the drawing room. You heard my screams and you ignored it, just like you're ignoring me now! He made me suffer when you could have saved me!"

I bury my face into my hands, remembering that horrible day. The day I had to stand outside the drawing room, waiting for Knox to erase Margot's memory a second time. Her screams were piercing, her cries pained. Milo had stood next to me as we both waited for Knox to complete the partial wipe, neither of us knowing what to expect once she fell completely silent. Even though Milo directed Knox to be quick and discreet, we both knew deep down he invaded her mind too. It was Milo's face that crushed me the most. That brokenness in his eyes as he had no choice but to let his cousin do whatever sadistic thing he wanted to her.

I cover my ears as Margot screams in the exact way she did that fateful day, but it isn't enough to drown out the sounds. I can still hear her body slamming against the door, the sound of a knife unsheathing, and her guttural noises as the blade is driven into her body.

When blood seeps in under the crack of the door, illuminated by candlelight, tears stream down my cheeks. It doesn't matter that, in reality, Margot never knew that I was outside the drawing room. It doesn't matter that, even if I tried to save her, Milo would have held me back. I was complacent. A girl simply doing what she was told.

My tears are cut short as the door opens. My heart lurches at the sight of black proditor boots stepping through blood.

"Lleu? Are you okay? Where are you? I know what he's doing to you . . ."

My heart melts at Alarik's voice. I knew, in time, he'd wake up before me and realize what was happening. That he would sense Knox's crows.

I push myself from under the bed and run to him, wrapping my arms around his neck and kissing his face. When I pull back, he wipes the tears from my cheeks.

"I should have told you, but I was afraid you'd get yourself killed," I cry.

Alarik kisses my forehead and holds me tighter. "This is darker magic than I'm used to. It's a hard entrancement to break. No matter what happens, I will protect you."

"There is no time to waste." I try to free myself from the hug, but he doesn't let me go. "Alarik, come on, there's time for that later."

I gasp as he squeezes so tightly that my ribs ache. "That's too much, Alarik, you're going to break my back." Stars cloud my vision. The adrenaline is enough to make me lean back and slap him clean across the face.

Alarik unlaces his arms and steps back, cradling his cheek. "Lleu?"

I lean against a nearby chair, trying to catch my breath. This isn't right. Alarik won't even kiss me without permission, let alone crush me with a simple hug.

When reality hits, I slump to the floor still cradling my ribs.

"Knox," is all I say.

Alarik stares at me blankly, and I expect him to morph into Knox at any second.

No, I know this isn't really Alarik. He would never hurt me. He's the only one I can trust.

Another set of leathery boots squeak before stepping over the threshold into the room.

Knox stares at me with a grin and folds his hands in front of himself. "You hid well, though I've seen better."

"You're using him against me!" I yell. If this was reality, Alarik would have snapped Knox's neck. But in this realm, he just stands there, face blank, waiting for instruction, like clay waiting to be molded.

Knox steps toward Alarik and puts a hand on his shoulder. "You're the one who lets him permeate your subconscious to such a degree that I have no trouble personifying him here."

"But I know it's not him. You've lost."

Knox only shakes his head and directs the faux Alarik to take a seat. "Why must you taunt me? Do I need to remind you of the position you're in?"

I pinch my lips together. "Give me another chance. Let me hide one more time. I'll do better this time."

Knox cocks his head and chuckles. "If you insist. I'll give you ten seconds."

He snaps his fingers and every candle in the room dies out, leaving us complete darkness.

My heart pounds and, any second, Knox will reach for me. His body was last between me and the door. If I am going to escape, I need to go around him quickly.

I side-step, palming around for the furniture as quietly as I can.

"Come out. Come out," Knox taunts from somewhere in the room.

My mind is a wreck and I keep losing track of the door's location.

A gasp leaves me as my thighs hit the end of the bed.

I was off my mark. I misjudged my own sense of direction.

"Ah, there you are."

The candles reignite as I spin around. Knox stands there, cracking his neck. Alarik still sits in the chair, his posture relaxed.

I scream and lunge onto the mattress to escape off the other side. Hands grip my ankles and pull me across the comforter. As I claw at the sheets, I catch a glimpse of Alarik. His eyes widen, a glimmer of empathy, though he stays glued in his seat.

"Alarik!" I scream and fight with all my might. It doesn't matter if this Alarik isn't real. I need him. How can he just sit there and watch!

Knox pulls me off the mattress, then bends me over the bed. Gripping my hips, he spins me onto my back and pins me down.

"This could be so much easier if you would just accept it. Embrace it," Knox says.

I turn my head toward Alarik. "I know part of you has to be in there. Don't let him break me!"

Alarik's caring eyes stay put, but he doesn't move.

Why does he have to look like that? Why couldn't Knox make him unfeeling and blank? If it seemed like he didn't care, then at least I could separate it. I could truly convince myself that he is nothing but a figment of my imagination.

"Alarik . . . please." Why am I begging him? I know he's not real. But part of me must believe that, even in a projection, the true Alarik couldn't help but save me, even under the control of Knox's puppet strings.

It brings me enough anger to knee Knox's thigh, narrowly missing his groin. He grunts and loses his hold on me. I pull my body back.

Knox recovers quickly, crawling onto the bed with me, matching my pace. He keeps his hands next to my waist, preventing me from rolling off the sides. He moves his face until it's inches from mine. "Dearest, you put up a good fight. I'm proud of you. But unfortunately, it wasn't enough."

"Get Alarik out of here!" I tear up. "I can't bear seeing him!"

When my back hits the headboard, Knox's fingers find my chin, tilting up my gaze. "But that's part of this isn't it? Proditor entrancements aren't just about physical types of pain." He pulls me to lie on my back and straddles my gowned waist. I flail around until my hands find one of the buckled leather straps on his armor. I grip it and try to throw him off, but he's a pillar of immovable steel.

He laughs as he slips his gloves off and throws them on the pillow next to my head. "There are different layers of this realm, and I want to show you all of them. While he watches, of course."

I cry and beg. My bargains go in one ear and out the other.

He traces my jaw. "Tell your monsters I said hello." His hands slam against my temples, propelling me into a deeper world of nightmares.

Alarik won't save me.

He can't protect me.

And if even Alarik can't help me, then what hope do I have?

So I submit.

Chapter 17

Milo

I sit back in a lounge chair in my bedroom, my legs kicked up while I scroll through security footage on a tablet in search of more clues. Anything to lead me to Margot.

I rewatch the videos repeatedly from beginning to end; from the moment her helmet was removed to when she disappeared inside a ship before stealing it.

For all I know, she could be deep underground again behind those impenetrable doors. Sometimes I wonder if I'm willing to destroy half of Merth if it means getting inside her base.

At one angle, she stops to talk to one of the rebel guys. I pause and reverse, slowing down the clip as much as the tablet allows me. I work on reading her lips, trying to make out what they were so furiously discussing.

Her mouth looks so soft.

I zoom in and place my finger on the footage of her face before moving it down her jaw and along her chin.

I tense and quickly move my hand back. *What am I doing?*

My gaze dips to her uniform. Even with it, I can make out the outline of her hips and waist. I remember how said body parts once looked completely bare.

The bulge in my pants strains against my zipper. I curse under my breath.

The thoughts consume me—her body tucked into mine every night. The way I'd slowly unbutton her night clothes, kissing across her upper back to rouse her before tasting between her silky thighs.

I stifle a groan and set the tablet to the side before resting my head on the back of the chair. No, I can't do this. Not to the thought of her.

Another memory assaults me. A night where she surprised me and woke me up for it. I'd never seen her so needy and almost thought I was dreaming, even as she placed delicate kisses on my neck, down my chest, and over the front of my pants.

The room grows hotter, and my pants tighten more as I unbutton my shirt to cool off. The cold draft from the vent hits my chest, chills spilling down my skin. Everything becomes more sensitive. It's like I can feel her kisses again and her delicate hands undoing my bottoms.

Except I'm the one throwing my belt to the floor and freeing my aching length from my trousers. And it's not her hand that's stroking it.

There may come a day where I have to kill her; I shouldn't be thinking about her like this.

I pump quicker, imagining her tongue coating me. Every movement curves my back as I move my hips with the rhythm of my strokes. My thoughts unravel completely. They're uncontrollable. Poison to my soul. Dangerous.

I miss her. I miss her.

The pressure grows so great, it's like I'm burning from the inside out. Sweat coats my neck and chest and around my ribs where my undone shirt bunches up.

The memories from the day she escaped overtake me. Her hips rolling and her tongue swirling.

Gods, she was using my body, manipulating me to escape, yet I'd never been undone the way she drove me to that day.

I groan, spilling out.

My strokes slow as I draw out the pleasure and the memory. How I wanted to strangle her as much as I wanted her to do it again.

My arms slump to my sides and a dose of reality hits. I swallow.

A knock at the door makes me flinch, any relaxation now replaced with rage.

"Didn't I say I didn't want to be disturbed?" I yell across the room and through the door.

"Milo, it's me," Alarik says through the door's intercom. "I need you to get ready quickly. Something is wrong with Lleu"

Lleu? My face hardens, not just at the possibilities of what could be wrong, but by the shake in Alarik's voice. The informal use of my first name. Something happened, and I doubt it's that she finally caved and spilled her secrets.

I clean up and get ready quickly before smoothing out my uniform and letting the door slide open.

Alarik leads us through the Imnicus, his face ghost white while we rush to the south wing prison cells. His strides are so quick, we arrive in half the time it normally takes me. My shoulders are already tight again.

The energy shifts the second I step into the prison cell.

"I found her like this," Alarik says.

Lleu lies on the bed in a nightgown, restless and writhing, eyes half open. But she doesn't seem awake.

"What happened?" My jaw clenches. I kneel at her side and hold her jaw to keep her head from moving.

Alarik sits at the end of her bed. "I can feel the crows, but I can't stop them. They're untraceable and impenetrable."

I let my own crows seep into her psyche to investigate, armed with accusations and a suspect. No, not a suspect—an accused. Being half-proditor means I can identify the owner of a stray crow more accurately than someone like Alarik can.

Diving deep into her mind, I walk beneath the canopy of her subconscious. The tall trees of Msanii rise like spires far, far above. Impossible proportions of a world as remembered by a child. Innocent, protective. Except there's darkness here, a thin layer, barely palpable.

I only notice the remnants at first. Jagged nests in the trees, feathers scattered along the leaf strewn ground. I stop at the cusp of a clearing with a great tree rising in the center. Among the dead branches are perched crows, their shrill cries piercing my mind.

Even now I can recognize their bitter cadence, the sharpness of their feathers.

Knox's crows.

At once, each of them fly toward me, voices cackling. They're . . . laughing at me.

Remember when we got to play with you? they say, mockingly.

I seethe. *And now I know how to block you out.*

I move past them, binding myself deeper within Lleu's mind. But I stop, seeing a pair of Alarik's crows perched innocently on one of the lower branches.

Alarik would never disobey my orders. He wouldn't torture her. He wouldn't have called me here, knowing what my powers can do, to expose himself.

There's something else in the tree with them. I grab hold of a branch, pulling myself farther into the canopy, pushing out the taunt of Knox's crows.

There are glimpses of a black presence above that I am not familiar with. My arms strain as I climb, Lleu's subconscious pushing back against mine. One last branch, one last bastion. My fingers ache as I push myself over the last limb.

My blood goes cold at the top. Staring back at me like a remnant shadow of my father himself is a wicked raven with death in its eyes.

I flinch back, my mind returning at once to the prison cell as my fingers leave her skin.

No. If Knox used those—

"At any moment did you take her out of this room?" I ask, unable to hide my steep breaths.

Alarik hesitates before answering. "Just once to take her on a walk for fresh air. But I was with her the entire time. Not once was she out of my sight."

"Alarik, null all your crows, even if they all feel docile."

When the last word leaves my mouth, Alarik curses, like the realization hit him all at once. Knox did the unthinkable. Something abhorred not just within Vicar circles but proditor ones too.

Alarik closes his eyes and within seconds Lleu stops writhing.

I place my hand on her pained, unconscious face, confirming that no more birds remain before turning to Alarik.

His fists curl so tightly that they shake. "I-I failed you."

I've never seen him like this before. He's failed missions before, but normally it's met with a cold apology and the half-baked promise to train harder.

I reach beneath Lleu, picking her up bridal style. "Take her to the medic bay. Have them give her enriched fluids. Keep the room dark."

Alarik stands and gently takes her from me before his voice turns to ice. "I'll kill him for what he's done."

"Leave the disciplining to me. For now, keep her safe in the bay."

"You know there's nothing they can do for her."

I go still at his words and contemplate my own before speaking. "Then do what you did for Margot."

Alarik takes a step back with widened eyes as he clutches Lleu tighter to his chest.

I share a look with him, not even needing to say Crux's name before striding out past him to the proditor quarters.

My hand tightens into a fist as I stomp from wing to wing, servants scurrying away from my booming steps.

He went against my direct orders. Tortured Lleu when I told him not to. Not only that, he used dark magic to do it.

I enter the proditor quarters at the same time Knox is leaving his bedroom. He doesn't see me at first, securing his door before turning around. When he takes me in, his eyes narrow.

"Knox!" I shout down the hall, snapping my cape off and letting it drop to a pile on the floor.

There are a lot of things I've let slide over the years. But this . . . this won't go unpunished. It's the fact that I've treated him more like family than a subordinate that makes this as much my fault as it is his.

"What are you doing?" He rolls his shoulders back.

I barrel toward him, fists ready.

Knox takes a step back, his stance already on the defense. "Colum—"

The second I'm in range, my fist collides with his already-braced abdomen. He grunts hard and I grab the front of his neck before he can recover and land another punch.

Onyx's bedroom door flies open. He rushes out of his room, his hair disheveled. "What the hell?"

I don't have to tell Knox why I'm angry. He knows damn well why I'm doing this.

I grip his gold curls and throw him to the ground. "Dammit to hell, Knox."

I topple over him, holding his chest down, ready to land a punch to his face.

Knox furrows his brows. "Don't even think about it." His proditor strength kicks in, overpowering me and shoving me off him. He lifts his fist, charging a teeth-shattering punch of his own.

Onyx's eyes widen. "Stop it, Knox! You'll kill him!" He jumps in and grabs Knox's arm in time, hauling him back.

I take the opportunity to land another punch, this time in his side ribs.

Knox unleashes himself from Onyx, pushing him away. He grabs my collar and slams me onto the ground with enough force to almost knock the wind out of me.

Crux and Dune round the corner. They pause in disbelief before sprinting over to help.

Knox manages to land a half-punch to my face before Crux catches its full force. I grunt, blood dripping down my mouth and jaw.

Onyx tackles Knox and places his forearm over his sternum, anchoring all his weight down on him. "Knox, I swear—"

Onyx restraining Knox creates an opening. I start to lunge.

"Stop!" Crux grabs one of my arms.

Dune curses and catches my other arm, helping drag me back.

Knox and I haven't fought like this since I was fifteen, and if I can remember it correctly, we were in this exact spot practically strangling each other over a comment he made about my powers during training.

"You went against my direct orders!" I yell.

"I have no idea what you're talking about." Knox's blatant lie turns my blood to ice.

"Don't even try to play that with me." I try to whip forward, but Dune pulls me back. I could practically kill Dune for the overstep. "Lleu may never be the same because of you!"

Knox forces a laugh then scoffs. "Lleu? How could I have possibly done anything with her kept under lock and key?"

"I felt your crows *and* your ravens."

The other proditors shift at the words. The only proditors I know who can wield ravens are Knox and my own father.

Knox doesn't let his face crack. "Alarik has his own secret temper. He probably got fed up and finally decided to interrogate her."

"Are you questioning my judgment? My powers? I could have you reassigned to Lavenai."

Knox purses his lips. "But you won't." He barely blinks, refusing to surrender his dominance in the conversation. That dominance that he will tell the arbitors what I did if I cross him.

It takes everything in me not to command the other proditors to stand down so I can beat him senseless.

"This isn't over." I shimmy out of the proditors' grasps and barrel out of their quarters. If I'm with him another second, I will do something I regret.

The other proditors know him almost as well as I do. They know he's lying. They also know when not to engage him.

My only hope is that they feel threatened enough to question him in my absence about the ravens. Ravens aren't just invasive to humans but to them too. To know that someone borrowed your crows without your knowledge is enough to make any proditor feel betrayed.

It takes me a hallway to notice Dune following a few feet behind, holding my discarded cape in his hand.

"I'm sorry, Colum," Dune says. "I thought I was vigilant enough. I even followed him on CCTV."

"For all we know, he may have also been watching *her* through the cameras." If so, he may have cursed her through there. "Alarik took her on a walk."

All ravens need is a visual target to curse minds. My father always found them more powerful than crow magic, even though they're complimentary.

A raven user whose power has been amplified can cause external visual hallucinations to an entire room of people. Sure it's not the same as breaking into minds, but causing a mass hysteria can be deadly, which my father often utilized.

Dune stops suddenly. I can sense his apprehension through my crows.

"You're dismissed, Dune."

"This is terrible timing, I know," he sighs. "But there is something I have to tell you."

I turn to face him. "Yes, Dune?"

"It wasn't a coincidence that we found you and Knox fighting. We were searching for you."

I raise an eyebrow.

Dune stays stiff. "It's Margot . . . she broke an inmate out of Diyu."

I take a step back. She's on Ashtanabo? In Susuku? Fury rages through me.

Why Diyu prison? And which inmate? Most there are nymbed and completely useless to her cause. I search the archives of my mind. Who imprisoned there would the rebellion find valuable enough to break out? Who isn't nymbed?

My eyes widen. *Matsumoto.*

With someone like her on the rebellion's side, it could only mean . . . Would Margot truly be after something so daring?

I suppress a laugh as I head straight for the hangar bay. Of course she would. The Margot I know wouldn't stop at a small victory.

She'd go straight for the throat.

Chapter 18

Margot

Dark-green forests surround us while we sit around a fire miles outside the outskirts of the city. Guards will be looking for us now and, with the cameras, it's only a matter of time before Milo finds out I'm on Ashtanabo. Hotels aren't an option anymore.

With barely any supplies, we struggled to make a fire. It took Oliver well over half-hour to catch a spark while the rest of us sat there shivering from the frigid night air.

Anali crosses her legs. "So, are we just going to sit around freezing or are you going to tell me why I'm here?"

Oliver stokes the fire. "Your powers are useful to us and we have work for you."

She pushes a few rocks around with the tip of her shoe. "And what makes you think I'll help you?"

"Well, for one, we broke you out of prison!" he shoots back.

Anali sticks her tongue out. "I don't see why you need me when you already have a rogue proditor on your side."

"For the thousandth time, I'm not a proditor," I bite out.

"It's not something you can lie to me about, so don't even try. My powers are practically strangling your crows to keep them down."

At this point I know nothing I say will convince her, so I don't even try. "Anali, we need your power to help us take down the temple points."

Anali goes completely still. "Why would you want that? The planet will return to ruins."

I need her to trust us. With her imprisonment, I doubt she's sympathetic to the Arris Reign. But I'll have to reveal more than I want to for her to come on board. "Because it's what any Laven would want."

Dimitri slaps my arm. "Margot, don't."

"If we're going to work together, we can't hide stuff from her." I turn back to face her.

"You're . . . Lavens?" Anali asks.

"Am I right in saying you want Colum Arris off his throne as much as we do?"

Anali folds her hands together and contemplates before speaking. "It's what I was created for."

Oliver cocks an eyebrow. "Do tell."

"Well . . . I don't have parents. But I'm also not an orphan."

"That's physically impossible," Dimitri says.

"I was bred from hyssopite by the Ashtanaban rebellion."

I can't believe what Anali is saying. Ashtanabo has its own rebellion?

She continues. "After it became apparent Balistar would always win with proditor magic on his side, a geneticist within the rebellion came up with a plan to artificially produce a human who could null crow magic by simply being in their presence. There was supposed to be more like me but . . ."

"But?" Dimitri asks.

Anali exhales deeply. "The rebellion was discovered and raided. After they found out what I was, they took no prisoners. As far as I know, I'm the only one who survived."

So their rebellion is no more. My chest aches that their efforts were cut short. To think how far our own rebellion could have come with them on our side. "How old were you when you were imprisoned?"

"Fourteen. Before then I was trained in combat to possess lethal fighting skills to take down proditors. I was supposed to be Balistar's downfall."

She was so young. To spend a quarter of her life imprisoned for something she never chose to be is cruel at best. "May I ask who your leader was?"

"She was a kind woman. Went by the name of Imory."

My jaw drops. "Nolan?"

Anali nods. "You know of her?"

Imory started the Ashtanaban rebellion? No wonder she had to flee to Lavenai. Balistar must have eventually tracked her down only to find his former wife starting an organization to defeat him. "Anali . . . she's who sent us to save you."

Though I have to wonder why Imory wasn't so forthcoming with this information. How she knew Anali's name, her fighting abilities, and even how she was created, and shared none of it. Whatever the reason, I know Imory has no ill intent.

"So she did survive." Anali forces a laugh and stares off into the forest. "And now she wants me to finish the mission she started."

If Anali is relieved or feels somewhat betrayed that Imory took so long to save her, she doesn't share it. Instead, she lies back on the ground, her arms behind her head. "There are over one-hundred temple points all stationed on Ashtanabo. It would take months or years. I guess the latter."

"We're well aware," Oliver says.

"On the bright side, they're largely unguarded. Not even a nuclear explosion can destroy them from the way the crow magic interweaves with the black onyx. Quite literally, I'm the only thing that can disable them. Natural hyssopite on its own isn't even strong enough."

"So you'll help us?" I ask.

"For Imory, yes."

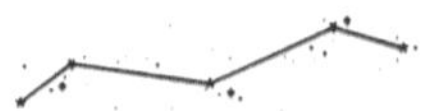

The countless-mile long hike begins at the crack of dawn after Anali cooks rabbits over a fire. Most animals on Lavenai are toxic, their blood lethal, so hunting is something we never learned in our rebellion's training. All our meat comes from shipments Joriel procures from Ashtanabo.

Anali walks in dance-like skips, unnecessarily jumping over rocks she could have gone around. She gawks at every animal that crosses our path. To be fair, so do I. Though I question her fascination with them after the way she flayed the rabbits this morning.

"Could you walk normally for five minutes?" Oliver snaps. "You're giving me a headache."

Anali dips her head back and groans. "I've been sitting in a cell for years. I'm owed some prancing, thank you very much."

I lean over to Oliver. "Just let it go. Focus on the sights. I mean, have you ever seen this much green in your life?"

Oliver grumbles. "She's a soldier one second and a child the next."

"Can you blame her? Who knows what kind of sick torture they've been inflicting on her."

"Are you guys talking about me?" Anali says from where she stands on another large rock.

"Nope!" we say in unison.

She swings her arms back and forth. "Are all of you related?"

I answer for us all. "Dimitri and I are first cousins."

"What about you Oliver?" She nudges his shoulder. "Where's your family?"

Oliver's breath hitches and my own muscles tense at the question. The truth is, not even Dimitri and I know much about his past, only that he joined the rebellion as a teenager and his last name is Parrow. Besides that, we know all he cares about is taking down the Arris Reign.

Oliver gathers back his neutral expression. "My parents were Balistar sympathizers and helped him establish his rule in Lavenai. He rewarded them greatly for their service, basking them in wealth and turning them into the few who stayed rich on Lavenai post-takeover. Even as a child, I knew what they did was wrong, and I despised them for it. The way they filled their own pockets at the misery of their own people. I eventually couldn't take it anymore and ran away. For over a year I lived on the streets, hiding from my father and his men. But it was Lucinda who found me first and, well, . . . here I am now."

His parents were sympathizers? I knew many crime organizations joined up with Balistar shortly before he took over, but I didn't know the upper class was in on it too.

Anali takes the biggest loud sigh. "Didn't mean to dredge all that up."

Oliver shrugs. "There's always the possibility we won't make it off this planet. No harm saying it now."

Dimitri and I share a look.

As the forest clears, and we near the edge of a path, a massive structure comes into view.

Red neon glows through the crevice of a black structure made of cubes and rectangular prisms stacked like blocks. Even from a field away, its power pulls at my crows and rouses them. The Nexus fires up, a knot forming in the pit of my stomach. To think this temple point is absorbing Lavenai's energy as we stand here.

Ten feet. All we have to do is get Anali within ten feet.

Oliver wipes the sweat from his brow. "I'd say we have about a half mile."

Dimitri takes a seat on a fallen log and takes a large gulp of water.

I stretch my legs. "Let's get down this hill. It's an open field from there."

The four of us trek down the hill and step over a creek before starting the walk through the wide-open plain. It's strange how the temple point's field is mostly barren yet surrounded with hills and mountains lush with flora. Maybe a bomb was detonated to clear the land before the temple point was built.

"Should we anticipate any catastrophic land events when this point is destroyed?" Dimitri asks Anali.

Anali walks backward ahead of us. "It's theorized to be a slow process, from what I've heard."

"Theorized?" Oliver cuts in. "So you're saying there's a chance that there will be an immediate earthquake?"

"Well, this is Susuku . . . we get those on a good year . . . "

I nudge Oliver. "Risk is part of our job, so you may as well stop anticipating the possibilities."

Oliver brushes me off. "Forgive me for wanting to be prepared in case we are toppled."

Though I'm not worried about an earthquake, I can't help but wonder what will happen afterwards. Once it's destroyed, we should take cover in the forest. Even if nature doesn't betray us, it will only be a matter of time before ships will come searching for us.

My ears perk up at something in the distance. Something low and rumbling. My body seizes up. It's a thrum that sounds all too familiar.

"What were you saying, Margot?" Oliver leers.

"No, that's not an earthquake!" I yell.

Even without seeing it, I know it's riding low against the planet's surface.

"Should we hide?" Dimitri asks.

"No, we need to make it to the temple point or we may not have another opportunity." I say.

The four of us take off in a full on sprint, and I keep shooting my gaze over my shoulder, trying to catch a glimpse of the ship that's still hidden, obscured by the tall forest.

A metallic glimmer flickers in the corner of my eye and I shoot my gaze in its direction.

My knees threaten to give out. No . . . not him. Not now!

"Dimitri, it's the Colum's ship!" I shout.

Dimitri curses. "Stay close."

Oliver places a hand over the dagger hilt on his belt. Dimitri whips his head back as the ship descends in our direction.

I yell over to Dimitri. "No matter what happens, focus on getting Anali to the temple point. Make sure she escapes this alive, even if I don't. Promise me!"

Clenching his jaw, he doesn't say anything back.

"Promise me!" I scream. If I had time to beat some sense into him, I would.

As the ship touches down, the grass blows fiercely like it's on the brink of being uprooted. The ship descends with a low hum, blowing our hair back.

Gods, Milo is here. To face me himself.

Directly in our path, the ship lands with a violent rumble. It's impossible to run with the wind like this.

The vibrations shake our knees and we fall back with silent thuds. My back connects with the ground and I curse before shooting my gaze back to the ship. I push my torso up, raising my head.

My heart leaps into my chest as the ramp touches down and the engine wanes. A brief silence takes over.

I hold my breath. I'm ready to fight him to the end if I have to. He won't stop us. Above everything else, I will protect Anali at all costs.

A figure emerges at the top of the ramp.

Staring at me with darkened eyes is a proditor. Above his carbon-fiber mask, his vindictive stare burrows into me. The scars on my arm burn.

I grip a handful of grass. "Oliver, take Anali, now! Get her to the temple point!"

"On it." Oliver stands and helps Anali to her feet. "Think you can outrun him?"

Anali grins. "I've never been more up to the challenge."

The two take off in a sprint in the direction of the temple point.

Crux looks at me first and drags his finger over his throat as he descends the ramp. I shudder.

He's going to hunt them. Hurt them. And the worst part is, I can't protect them, at least not yet.

Crux runs after Anali and Oliver, his boots thumping against the grass.

A cloud passes over, darkening the field as another figure stands at the top of the ramp.

My heart pounds in my throat, seizing every emotion, my nerves unsure of which to hang onto.

Collar-length black hair, sharp features, a hardened gaze. Murderous, tortuous, and ready to deal with me himself—the Colum.

Milo locks eyes with me, his stiff expression softening. I'd give anything to know what he's thinking. If he meant it when he told me the lengths he'd go to stop me.

A lifetime passes before he takes his next breath. His brows furrow as he takes the first step down the ramp.

Dimitri grimaces and helps me to my feet. "Stay back. I'll deal with him."

I brush the dirt off my pants. "He's half-proditor, Dimitri. You'll only get yourself killed."

I've never fought Milo like this before—as two true foes willing to stop the other's cause no matter what. In the torture room, I'd punched him once. It made me feel powerful. Invigorated. I let that part of myself take over now because if I let myself feel the way I once did for him—

As the soles of his boots meet the field, I ready my stance.

Milo's cape flows in the wind, his dark hair slightly tussled. "Maybe I was naïve to assume you'd never leave the confines of

Lavenai ever again. That you'd finally learn that nothing you do will stop the Arris Reign."

Dimitri raises his fists. "Really? Because we have plans to end it right now."

Milo tilts his head. "And who may you be?"

I shake my head at Dimitri. *Don't tell him.*

He ignores me. "I'm her cousin. And you must be the asshole who erased her memories and made her the Columess."

Milo paces in front of us. "It was a role that suited her. Honestly if your leader never sprayed her with hyssopite, she'd be a fine Columess ruling at my side."

I push down his words. That if my memories never returned, he would have kept me as his wife forever.

Dimitri scoffs. "I know Margot and she knows evil for what it is. In time, she would have realized what you really are."

Milo's gaze focuses on my thumb where his old ring rests. "You didn't tell him, I see."

My chest tightens. No, now is not the time and place for Dimitri to find out about that. Milo's using it against me to weaken my fortitude as well as Dimitri's.

"Tell me what?" Dimitri side-steps closer to me.

I don't know what to say, and I want to jump forward and cover Milo's mouth. This will only make things so much worse.

"It's nothing." I grit my teeth.

In the distance, Crux is on Anali and Oliver's tails as they sprint toward the temple point. Soon, he'll catch up to them, and though

Anali says she's a trained fighter, I don't know how much she's retained over five years of confinement.

Milo scans my body. "The bed feels so cold and empty some days. Tell me, do you miss it? Do you miss my hands on you?"

"What the hell are you talking about?" Dimitri lunges at him.

I grab his arm, yanking him back. "Stop it, Dimitri!"

"Let's not hide the obvious. You were my wife. It's only natural that we . . ."

"It was a mistake!" I yell at Milo.

Milo's expression turns somewhat amused.

"How many times does an act need to occur before it's no longer a mistake?"

Dimitri shimmies out of my grasp. "You told us he didn't touch you."

"He never did . . . by force."

"You mean you slept with the enemy . . . *willingly*?"

"My memories were *gone*, Dimitri. He wasn't an enemy to me, at least not in the way he is now. If I remembered even a fraction of what he'd done to me—to us, to our parents—I would have slit his throat!"

I shoot Dimitri a gaze that tells him everything he needs to know and he purses his lips before nodding. He understands now. Understands that I didn't just sleep with the Colum out of marital obligation, but that I loved Milo Arris, through and through.

There's no time for either of us to be angry about it. Crux has nearly caught up to Oliver. Even with Anali depleting his proditor magic, I'm not sure how long the two of them will fare against Crux's strength.

"Anali will destroy the temple point, then the next, and the one after that," I say. "You have a habit of not killing the people most dangerous to you, and now you'll pay for it."

Milo frowns and readies his stance. "And it's a mistake I'll never make again."

I swallow, his expression not matching his words. Like he's trying to make himself believe it.

If he's truly willing to fight to the death, then so am I. I charge at him.

"Margot!" Dimitri shouts.

When I get within range, I swing my fist and he quickly ducks out of way. He evades my punches at a speed that seems inhuman. Not even full-blooded proditors can move that fast. I time every move, adjusting my stance rhythmically, but each blow misses. I'm reminded of our dance at the Imnicus ball. How I followed his lead, his eyes locked on mine while he looked at the place just past my heart. How he's looking at me now knowing full well there's a place only he holds.

It doesn't seem like he's memorizing my fighting style, yet he's predicting my moves perfectly.

Knox. Of course he'd know every move his cousin would choose, so he's able to guess what I'll throw at any given moment.

If I want to break up the flow, I'll have to try something he won't expect.

I lift my leg, hauling it up to his head level. I swing and kick. It lands against his skull.

Milo quickly steps back with an annoyed grunt. It barely left a scratch.

Dammit. I angrily throw a punch.

Milo catches my bare wrist, and before I process the warmth of his skin, my crows fall completely asleep. Fatigue washes over me. I expended so much energy with the Nexus that I can barely tap into my innate strength.

He unhands me and I trip back, landing on my bottom.

He can weaken my crows? Last time he had to use hyssopite.

"Looks like my theory is correct," Milo says. "Because your crows are borrowed, proditors and half-proditors alike can put them to sleep."

I grit my teeth at the revelation and pull my sleeves over my wrists. "That doesn't mean I haven't gotten stronger without the crows."

But I'm in no condition to fight, and my muscles completely drained. Still, I ready myself to stand.

Dimitri steps in front of me, facing the Colum.

"I've been waiting a long time to rip out your throat," Dimitri says with venom.

Milo waves him forward.

Dimitri charges and Milo blocks him effortlessly. Though Milo is strong in stature, I never knew until now how fierce of a fighter he is. He's not even a full proditor, yet he must have trained as heavily as they did. Maybe more so.

Milo catches Dimitri's collar and lifts him up before throwing him roughly to the ground.

Dimitri grunts in pain and quickly rolls away just in time before Milo stomps down on his chest.

In the distance, Oliver and Anali are less than fifty feet from the temple point. Crux swiftly slides along the grass and trips Oliver.

Oliver kicks up at Crux, but Crux swipes his legs out of the way before abandoning him and running for Anali.

I don't know where to focus—on Milo close to beating my cousin senseless or on Crux peeling off his glove.

"Anali!" I shout, even though she can't hear me from this far away.

Crux grabs the back of her neck with his bare hand, pulling her back to face him. His grip tightens before remembrance passes over his face. He has no power over her.

Anali rolls her eyes and socks him square in the face.

Crux stumbles back then looks down at his hands. He curls them into fists.

She mouths something that makes Crux jab at her. She blocks it and attacks him, landing punches in his side, his abdomen, and his mask.

Crux finally gets a handle on her, blocking her blows, fury etched into his face. He can barely keep up with her. Oliver jumps in and lands a kick on Crux's back.

My head snaps away from their fight as Milo grabs ahold of Dimitri's neck and slams him into the ground again. He digs the sole of his boot into my cousin's neck.

"Stop!" With my strength coming back, I rush forward and hook my arm around Milo's throat, pulling him to the ground with me.

I move quickly, sitting on top of Milo and throwing a punch at his face. He moves his head just in time.

The Nexus returns next, turning my focus to the dagger on my belt. The need to use it.

The crows' words seize my heart, threatening to excel the contents of my stomach.

Finish him, they say. *And enjoy it.*

Something flashes in my eyes that Milo seems to notice. He shoots his hand forward and grabs my hand, lacing his fingers through mine.

The crows sleep again, along with the aching words they brought.

I quickly roll off him, scooting away and panting.

Milo stands and takes a few steps back, disbelief painted across his face. "Knox's crows are tormenting you. I thought all he did was transfer some of his abilities over. Margot, this is serious."

I shove all of his words to the side. "He did it at your command so that I'd be strong enough for you to use me."

"Eventually, you'll no longer be able to control the urge. I'll give you a choice, Margot. Give yourself up willingly, and not only will I spare you, but I'll find a way to purge his crows."

I force a laugh as Milo extends a hand to me.

"Or . . ." Milo frowns and moves his cape to the side, pulls a firearm off his belt, and points it at Dimitri. "I won't give you a choice."

No. He's trying to use him as leverage. My arms shake from the rage. Dimitri lies there, still recovering. He wouldn't be able to escape a bullet.

I jump up and fly between the gun and Dimitri, spreading my arms out. "I won't let you."

Milo's jaw tenses. "Margot—"

I take a few steps forward until my forehead presses into the cool steel of the barrel. "You said you would never make the same mistake again. You can end it all right now."

"Don't!" Dimitri shouts.

I ignore him.

Milo's nostrils flare, his forearm shaking slightly. "Move."

A rumble vibrates the ground. Milo's attention leaves me and shoots to the temple point.

Anali sprints in our direction, and Oliver runs a few steps behind. Crux is on the ground, trying to regain his footing.

One by one, the red lights on the temple point die out, the ground shaking harder as each one does.

Oh my gods, she did it.

Milo slowly lowers his weapon as the grass around the temple point fades from green to gray. He stares back at me for a brief moment, but it feels like an eternity.

He knows I've won this battle, and he has to choose between capturing me or saving the temple point.

Crux pushes himself up and immediately slams his bare hands onto the structure.

Milo curses something before turning on his heels and running in Crux's direction.

I quickly help Dimitri off the ground. "We need to get to the forest."

Oliver and Anali arrive out of breath. The intensity of the rumbles worsens.

"This isn't good!" Anali shouts.

"Someone was wrong about earthquakes." Oliver mutters.

On his knees, Crux's hands are glued to the temple point, his arms shaking like he's in excruciating pain. Milo comes up behind him, touching Crux's hand, as if transferring extra energy into him.

There's no time left to watch. The four of us sprint out of the wide-open field and back into the forest, narrowly evading branches splitting off trees and wildlife running between our feet. Every plant we pass shrivels and streams dry up. The veil is slowly being lifted off what Ashtanabo truly was before it stole energy from Lavenai.

Suddenly, the rumbling stops.

I lean against a tree, panting. "What happened?"

Anali wipes sweat from her brow. "He saved it in time but not without consequence. Everywhere from the temple point to our feet is almost what it once was. It will take a year or so for the flora to recover. If the proditor had waited a second longer, the temple point would have crumbled completely."

Part of me wants to be disappointed that we only partially succeeded. The other part can't wait for Milo to explain this one to the arbitors.

"How did it happen so quickly?" Oliver asks.

"I was wrong about it being a slow process, okay?" Anali bites. "Lavenai's power is a bandaid to Ashtanabo's sickness. A sickness I can only assume has gotten worse since the takeover. It seems it doesn't take much to expose what the planet should really look like."

"We need to move," I say. "It will only be a matter of time before the Colum calls in reinforcements to search for us."

Chapter 19

Milo

In an Imnicus conference room, I lose control of my temper, taking a glass and shattering it against the wall. The proditors stay completely still, trying not to react.

The temple point was nearly destroyed, and if that would have happened, half of Susuku would have been ecologically devastated. If Crux hadn't come with me, it would have spread even farther than the mile it did affect. Thankfully, nobody in Susuku lives within a few miles of the temple point. Still, I will need to keep the military and arbitors' attention away from that portion of the planet.

Susukan guards and proditors have been on full alert for Matsumoto, searching the region high and low. But the group has disappeared without a trace.

My fist tightens. "I want the proditor at Diyu Prison demoted and any personnel that interacted with them fired."

I once thought that if I had the rebels' faces, my woes would be obsolete. That if I destroyed the rebellion—whom I swore to my father I'd one day bring to their knees—Ashtanabo could finally live in peace.

Instead, Margot keeps escaping and getting the better of me. I can't help but blame myself.

Onyx is the first to speak. "In the proditor's defense, nobody could have foreseen this. A Laven has never infiltrated Ashtanabo."

I grip the edge of the table. Until Margot is apprehended, I won't be able to rest. The entire planet is in danger with Anali on the loose. "Are there proditors stationed at every point yet?"

"Yes." Crux brings up a projection in the middle of the table. "Not only that, but construction plans are underway to make them inaccessible, though it will take time. Until now, they were once so indestructible that most used them as picnicking locations."

"Dune, assign guards to patrol the perimeters. I don't care if you need to draft more, just get it done," I command.

"Yes, Colum." Dune bows his head.

"And starting today, I want you to go personally to Susuku and track them down. She'll likely be on her way to the second Susukan temple point and you're the only proditor on the Imnicus whose face Margot hasn't seen."

Dune nods. "Of course."

"When you find Margot, bring her to the Imnicus."

"And the others?"

"Dispose of them. Even Matsumoto. It was a mistake to leave her alive." I turn to Alarik who sits in the corner of the room, his face still pale since the incident with Lleu. "What's the report on Lleu?"

"She's at least speaking now," Alarik says.

Knox disobeyed my orders. He kept her there a long time, and even though the ravens won't make her lose her mind like pure crows do, she'll be shaken up for years to come.

It's why Knox isn't in this meeting right now. I had Commander Aisil do the dirty work and send him to Lavenai on a tedious mission.

After the meeting, I head back to my room and step into the privy, scrubbing Margot's cousin's blood from under my fingernails at the sink. I hesitated when I should have acted. Not when it came to killing him but her.

She's a rebel. A traitor to the Arris Reign. What kind of Colum am I to even consider keeping her alive because of these juvenile feelings?

Yet again, you failed me, I hear my father say.

I slip off my clothes and step into the shower, scrubbing my hair vigorously, the water pouring down my back. As much as I blame that proditor and the guards at Diyu, I know at the core of it, her escape was my fault alone. It was my lies that prevented me from bringing a fleet of guards along who would've apprehended them at gunpoint. They would have recognized her and rumors could have spread.

The next time I see her, I won't fail my father. Once I'm finished with Margot, I will end her and the rebellion and maintain my duty to my father and to Ashtananbo.

Later when I fall asleep, I expect to dream of Margot.

Instead, it's my father who haunts them.

Past: D-AR 4049

The north wing is quiet, besides a servant here or there scrubbing the floors and walls. Alarik walks by my side, dressed in a black, leather uniform as opposed to his old training clothes.

Just last week, he received his full proditor garb, meaning anytime we pass a servant together, they lower their heads just an inch more than they do for me. Most people forget I'm half Vicar or rather they forget to connect the dots.

It doesn't feel like long ago that Alarik and I ran through the Vicar village together playing hide and seek with the other children. Now we're both sixteen and we roam the palace like men, though my father never fails to remind me that I'm not a man until he says so. But today, all of that will change.

"I passed the flight exam," I tell Alarik.

"Today?" He moves his head quickly to avoid an oncoming V.I.X. unit. "That's wonderful, Milo."

I smile to myself. It's taken me almost two years to finish the training. Not only that, but I decided to go for the advanced license, which includes galactic combat. I don't really like flying, but without full proditor-magic, there aren't many things that I can accomplish. "I'm going to tell my father next time I see him."

Alarik's pace slows slightly.

"Is there something you want to say?" I shoot him a look.

"Nothing! It's just . . . " His eyes sink.

"Just what?" My heart pounds.

"Forget I said anything. I'm sure he'll be proud."

I narrow my eyes and push down his words, refusing to feel their weight.

As we pass through a hallway, muffled laughter leaks out from the drawing room.

"We should go another way," Alarik says quickly. "Didn't you say you were hungry earlier? We could ask the maids to whip us up a midday meal."

"We just ate an hour ago." I slow my stride when I hear it fully.

The fatherly laugh. The boyish voice in response. Alarik visibly stiffens, watching my face with bated breaths. I clench my fists before approaching the cracked door to peek inside.

My father sits across from Knox in front of the holographic fireplace, smiles plastered upon both their faces.

A burning pain crawls across my chest. I can't think of a single time where my father sat in this room with me, laughing without a care in the world. I'm not sure he's looked at me with genuine love and admiration since . . . since . . . my mother was still in the picture.

Alarik tugs on my arm, silently begging me to step away. I yank away from his grip, my face set. We've been friends long enough for him to know when I won't be moved, and he knows better than to try.

"Go." I wave him away, gesturing back the way we came.

Alarik meets my gaze for only a moment before he drops his shoulders and disappears down the hallway.

"How is your owl magic?" My father brings a chalice to his lips while he waits for Knox's answer.

Knox leans forward. "I tried it in my last interrogation. I think I'm getting the hang of it."

"And your crows?"

I know my father's double meaning. "The doves still work, Uncle. The crows have not been sick since I was five." Knox fiddles with a wooden figurine of a raven, one I know my father hand-carved. He hasn't taken to carving much in recent years. The sight of it pulls at my chest.

Father smiles. "That's what I like to hear, my protégé. Heir to my magic."

My heart breaks in two.

Knox crosses his ankle over his thigh and leans back. "Heir . . ." He tastes the word like it's sweet wine in his mouth.

"I want you to keep practicing with the owls. Once you're ready, I will teach you ravens, the most volatile and strong of them all."

"I've felt them before, Uncle. When you used them through me to trick that politician."

My father laughs. "That was quite the charade we pulled off."

Knox's chin rises, pride bubbling into his features. "That it was."

I storm away from the door and into the next hallway, leaning against the wall to collect myself.

Owls, crows, ravens, finches, doves. Soon, Knox will have mastered them all. But I will never wield any of them but crows, and even then, I barely have those.

I stand there for a few minutes before hearing the drawing-room door open in the adjoining hallway.

"I'll see you at dinner, Uncle," Knox says. I peek around the corner in time to see him replace his mask and hood. He disappears down the opposite hall.

When I sense he's long gone, I stand before the half-open door with a thousand emotions rafting through me. I shouldn't disturb my father. But I want to tell him about my flight training. If I were Knox, he would want to hear it.

I pause before knocking.

My heart races for the full minute my father makes me wait before he says, "Enter."

The door slides open and I step inside the dim room. He sits in his chair, flipping through documents on a tablet. It takes another full minute for him to acknowledge my presence.

"Yes, Milo?" He stays focused on the screen.

I swallow. "I just wanted to tell you . . . I passed the flight course today. Starting tomorrow, I will be allowed to fly ships without supervision."

His finger pauses mid scroll. "That's very nice."

The silence goes on again, my palms sweating out of control. "And I was wondering . . . if you'd like to train me more in my crows soon. I know I'm only half-proditor, but my crows may have other uses, and maybe with some trial and error—"

"Don't . . . even." He sets his tablet down.

I wince. "I'm sorry. It's just—"

"Just what?" My father stands and strides toward me. "That you don't have what it takes? That no matter how many times I've trained you with proditors, you cannot perform even close to their level?"

I take a step back before I even realize it. "It's not my fault!"

My father grabs my collar, pulling it so tightly my throat constricts. Dots swirl in my vision and I'm barely able to focus. But I see enough. His face is full of disappointment. Full of hatred. "I believe a man can do whatever he puts his mind to. There was a time I believed you could be as great as your cousin, if you only tried hard enough. But you have shown me time after time that you don't have what it takes to wield the crows. You barely have what it takes to bear the last name Arris."

When he releases me, I drop to my knees, begging the tears in my eyes to stay back. If he saw a single one of them fall . . . But his back is already turned. I don't know what hurts more, his words or his dismissal.

"What more can I do?" I ask, pushing the knot in my chest to the depths of my soul. "To prove myself?"

My father does not turn from where he faces the fireplace. "Do you know why I only punish the proditors and not you, Milo?"

He doesn't wait for a response. "Because there is no potential to beat out of you."

Chapter 20

Margot

For days we hike through the terrain of the Susukan mountain range, stopping periodically to rest. Anali hunts for food and we drink from streams. With no tents, I thank the gods it hasn't rained yet.

Things with Dimitri have been slightly awkward since he learned about my physical relationship with the Colum. He's still friendly but that tense edge has returned. I don't think he knows what to feel. I know he's not angry, but whatever it is, he keeps it under lock and key.

Finally, after days of sore ankles and aching muscles, the temple point comes into view in the distance.

When we get close enough to see it with binoculars, our faces fall.

It's swarming with guards and proditors. There's a temporary fence with checkpoints set up to deter us.

"Shit." Dimitri takes a step back and sits on a rotted stump.

Anali throws her hands up. "Come on, we can take them, can't we? You saw the way I handed that proditor's ass to him."

Oliver folds his arms. "I fought just as well as you did."

"You wouldn't have gotten a single punch in if it weren't for me." Anali sticks her tongue out at him.

"It would be a suicide mission," I say. "Which maybe wouldn't matter if we didn't have countless more to destroy."

"All the points on Ashtanabo are going to be like this for the foreseeable future," Dimitri says. "We need another method of approach."

Oliver nudges Anali. "Still need your thumb, Anali? Perhaps your body parts are enough to disable one if we find a way to launch it at the temple point."

She reflexively holds onto her thumb. "I'd prefer not to test that theory."

"If we want to destroy this temple point, we'll have to find a way to get Anali close without detection. Are there any cities near here? Any that guards frequent?" I ask.

Anali nods. "Twenty miles away. If my memory serves me, it contains one of Susuku's luxury clubbing districts."

"That's what we'll do then."

Dimitri and Oliver both exchange a look.

"You mean we'll party?" Dimitri asks.

I frown. "We'll befriend guards until we can find ones that are assigned to the temple point."

"Yes!" Anali places her hands on her hips. "And then we can torture the information out of one of them."

"No." I roll my eyes. "We'll build trust and then find discreet ways to weasel our way into the base from there."

"Yes, I suppose that is the boring, practical way to do things," Anali grumbles.

Oliver leans against a tree trunk. "We're not exactly dressed for clubbing."

Anali hops. "Leave that to me."

"How?" he questions.

"Once we're in the city, I can find unique ways to acquire clothing."

"So you're a thief too?"

"Only when I need to be." Anali winks.

Anali and Oliver go on ahead bickering while I stay somewhat behind with Dimitri. Leaves crunch under our boots.

I speak first. "We can talk about it, you know."

Dimitri looks off ahead. "Talk about what?"

I roll my eyes. "That yes, I had sex with the Colum. Yes, I did it willingly. I'm sorry I lied. I just didn't know how you and Lucinda would take it."

Dimitri rubs the back of his neck. "Listen, I'm not mad. Confused, yes. But that is not why I've been at a loss for words. Needless to say, the last thing I want to talk about with a family member is. . .*that.*"

I fold my arms. "Then what's wrong?"

"I think it's obvious."

"What's obvious?"

He swallows. "You're still in love with him."

The blood drains from my face. "That's ridiculous."

"I saw it with my own eyes, Margot. The way you both looked at each other, even as you fought. It's what you were truly hiding from Lucinda."

I press my lips together, unable to accept Dimitri's words. "All my love for him dissolved the second I got my memories back. I will never forget what he did to me. "

In the middle of the clubbing district, a navy cocktail dress hugs my body and a cool breeze brings chills to my skin. People pass by our group, conversing and club-hopping. Strings of white lights hang between the sleek one-story buildings, creating the illusion of twinkling stars. I take a few steps back and lean against a gray-marble pillar of a coffee shop.

Anali studies our outfits with a look of satisfaction. "I'd say I did an amazing job. Don't you agree?" Wherever she obtained these outfits, she keeps her lips zipped. Sometimes, her impulsivity scares me.

Dimitri shoots her a glare. "Margot is more skin than fabric."

I cross my arms. "Anali's dress is just as revealing as mine and you don't seem to mind."

He keeps his lips pinched shut because he knows I'm right. This isn't the time for him to be protective. There are times I'm glad he's not my actual brother. Maybe then I'd have to listen to him.

Dimitri and Oliver wear their own masculine versions of clubbing attire. An olive long-sleeve shirt hugs Dimitri's torso, the fabric tucked into a pair of baggy black pants. Oliver's outfit is a bit more shocking, though somehow it suits him—a cropped black shirt and leather pants. A thin chain hangs around his waist. It's not something I'd ever envision him wearing, but Anali was the one who picked it.

"I think we should split up and go to different clubs," I say. "We'll cover more ground that way."

"Are you joking?" Dimitri throws his hands up. "If you think I'm going to just let you roam around dangerous clubs by yourself dressed like *that*, think again."

Oliver folds his arms. "We're spies and assassins—and whatever Anali is. Don't let your familial relationship sabotage the mission. And not to throw you off your high horse, Dimitri, but Margot held her own way better than you did against the Colum. I agree with her. We need to split up to make connections or else we'll be stuck on this planet far longer than necessary."

Dimitri's breaths are angry, and if I know him, he's more upset at the realization that he wasn't able to protect me. "If she gets hurt, I'm blaming you."

Music pours out of the clubs, but unlike the ones in Merth's crime district, these are a lot more tame. People don't seem like they're out for a night of sin but for a night of fun.

"We'll meet back at this spot in two hours," Anali says. "There's twelve clubs in this part of town. So if each of us hit three tonight, we'll have them all covered."

"Didn't realize you were the leader now." Oliver jabs.

"Maybe I have a natural propensity for it." Anali smiles.

Dimitri pulls me aside while Anali and Oliver bicker more. "Are you sure it's safe to go by yourself?"

I roll my eyes. "For the last time, I'll be fine. You saw the way I fought Milo, and he's half-proditor. If I can subdue him, imagine what I can do against a soldier."

"Just . . . be careful." He presses his lips together firmly.

After we all sort out who will visit which establishments, we split up.

Pink roses cover the ivory exterior of the first club I enter. Greenery and silver bulbs hang from the ceiling. There's not many people here, though it is a small establishment.

A humanoid working the bar tries to take my order but I tell them I'm waiting until a friend arrives. We don't have enough geeds to spend on alcohol.

As the club slowly fills up, a group of soldiers enter and I do everything to make myself appear alone and available, but none of them spare me a glance and immediately order a round of shots. The glassiness of their eyes tells me they're already past the point of drunkenness.

I try another tactic and head over to another stool where a man sits all by himself. "Want some company?"

He immediately stiffens. "No . . . I'm so sorry, I don't know why I'm out this late. I'm engaged."

Right, this is a club. Of course he thinks I'm hitting on him. Maybe this dress was a mistake after all. "Oh, that's—"

"I have to go." The man pays his tab and slides off the seat, booking it.

That didn't go as planned.

I wait another half-hour for more soldiers to enter but none do. This club is a dead end. I slip off the bar stool and out the door.

The Club Meridian is a lot more lively. Almost too lively, with bodies packed on the dance floor and not a single seat available at the bar. *Dammit.*

If I stand awkwardly in the middle of the club, it will only draw eyes, especially since I'm alone.

My stomach tightens when my gaze meets another pair of eyes, already staring.

A guy at the bar observes me, his elbows back on the counter and a drink in his hand. Pin-straight brown hair ends at his waist, tan skin adding to his shadowy, Nonakan features. I can't read his expression, but whatever he's thinking, it's not carnal—I think.

If I don't blend in soon, I will only garner more attention.

I step onto the edge of the dance floor and sway slightly, though his eyes don't leave me. I dance my way toward the center of the crowd, trying to escape his line of sight.

Part of me wonders if I should take advantage and ask him questions. He could be an off-duty guard who has information. But there's discomfort and unease in my gut. He'll be my last resort.

Most of the guys around me have a partner they're dancing with. Though some of the women could be soldiers, it's harder to pick out who is military and who is a date, as female enlistment is completely voluntary in Ashtanabo.

A V.I.X. unit flies over to me with a glittering drink in hand. It tries to hand it to me.

"I didn't order that," I yell over the music.

It nudges me and presses the tray into my arm until I accept.

I sigh and take the drink, mostly to make it go away. The drink is a swirl of blue, purple, and glitter, and reminds me of the colorful drinks at the Imnicus's night club, the Jupiter.

If anything, the free drink will help me blend in. I take a sip, and then another, until I've finished the entire thing faster than I should've. In no time, a buzz runs through my body.

I grow more comfortable dancing, using the newfound confidence to scope out people around me when I turn. The alcohol is stronger than I thought, turning any and every black-haired soldier into Milo. But instead of fear, my heart pangs and longs. I squeeze my eyes and shake it off.

There was once a time where Milo would have been jealous watching me like this. In a lewd dress with the eyes of other men on me.

If things were still the same, would he abandon his own pride to dance with me? Would he do it just to remind everyone I belong to him?

As the effects of the alcohol increase, I lose track of my thoughts. No matter how hard I try to push him out, I imagine what it would be like for Milo to be pressed up behind me, his hands on my hips, guiding my body into deeper movements.

Instead of the drink dulling my senses, it only heightens the depth of every color, sound, and emotion. A warmth rushes through me. I bite down on my lip to sever the lewd thoughts from my brain.

A body presses up against me from behind, and I stiffen for a second. My initial thought is to push the stranger away, but if he's a soldier, I could get close to him and gain intel on the temple point.

I relax my body and meld back into the chest, letting the music overtake me.

One of his warm hands slides onto my hip over my dress, and then the other finds its way to my ribs just under my breasts. The growing heat amplifies my thoughts of Milo.

No, I need to get him out of my mind. I turn, taking in the new face.

My breath hitches. The Nonakan man from the bar.

There is a hint of hunger under his expression. Hunger for me.

My heart beats faster as I take in more of his features while others dance around us. He stares back with desire. I can only assume by his build that he's a soldier. If I play into this, he may give me information on the temple points.

And I need to get my mind off of Milo Arris.

I wrap my arms behind the man's neck, swaying back into the dance with him. He moves slightly, never taking his eyes off me as he slides his hands to my hips.

Milo coats my mind once again—his warm body, the way he once groaned in pleasure for me, and even the way his breaths would soften when I would massage his head and shoulders in the bathtub.

No, stop thinking about him. Do something, anything to stop the memories.

I stand on my toes, and press my lips to the guy's mouth.

The man goes still and I quickly pull away with a slew of curses under my breath. What am I doing? I should have at least asked.

Just as I'm ready to apologize, he pulls me back and kisses me with even more intensity.

My pulse pounds as he explores my mouth and my body floods with chills. Even so, he tastes like Milo and his tongue drags like his. I softly moan. His hand tightens on my hip.

The buzz of the drink amplifies, and soon I'm not able to push the Colum out anymore. All I taste is Milo. All I feel is his hands. All I hear is his gasping breaths between kisses.

Before I know it, I'm pressed against the wall in a bathroom stall with a tongue on my neck and a thigh between my legs.

I want to close my eyes and imagine Milo's hands exploring me.

He moves back to kissing my mouth. I grab his hand, guiding it to my core.

The man immediately pulls his hand away and his lips slowly leave mine.

I shoot back into reality.

I'm on a mission. A mission that cannot involve this man taking me back to his place. A mission that I have made almost no progress in.

I place my palms on his chest. "I'm sorry. I have to go."

Urgency flies across his face. "Please, just a few more minutes." His voice holds similar low notes to Milo's.

My neck heats up. "My friends are waiting for me."

He steps aside and lets me out of the stall. I stop by the mirror to smooth down my hair, hyperaware of his eyes on the back of my head. In the reflection, his face is back to how it was when I first saw him watching me at the bar. Not a hint of lust. Like a light completely died out.

An alarm bell goes off in my head, even though I have no clue why. It screams at me, *Get out of here. Fast.*

"Have a good rest of your night." I walk to the door, pressing the button. It doesn't slide open. I grab the manual release. It doesn't budge either.

As I take a step back, dizziness washes over me and my fingertips tingle.

I stumble back into the long counter and turn around, staring into the mirror at my constricted pupils and pale face.

My knees buckle and I grab onto the edge of the sink for support.

I see the man in the reflection again. My body seizes up at his expression.

He leans against the stall with his head resting against the side, completely emotionless as he watches me fall to the ground.

Run. Get away! My mind screams.

I need to get back to the door and pound it down if I have to.

"You're not well," the man says.

I weaken more, only able to crawl on my hands and knees. It's like moving through jelly.

He walks slowly behind me, like he's in no rush at all, and I internally scream at my limbs to move faster.

The Nexus kicks in, enough for me to force myself to stand on wobbly legs. "I don't know what you're trying to do—"

"Shhh." His fingers stroke the back of my neck and I fall again. He catches me under my arms as I slump down.

Extreme fatigue overtakes me, but it's not enough to dull the fear. "Let me . . . go." When I try to fight him off, I realize all my crows are asleep.

My pulse pounds. His touch made my crows sleep, just like Milo's once did. I thrash with all my might.

His hold stays firm. "Milo won't like it if I deliver you scuffed up, so settle down, Margot."

My world shatters.

It all comes together. His dark expressions. His shock when I kissed him.

"That drink . . . you drugged me," I say.

"And it only just now kicked in," he says, almost annoyed that he had to kiss me to keep me occupied. I recognize his voice now too.

Dune Catawnee.

I need to find Dimitri. I promised him I wouldn't be caught.

Dune's thumb circles my temple before I can scream, his crows nuzzling my mind with their feathers, keeping my borrowed ones at bay. His touch paralyzes my body, and he lifts me into his arms bridal style.

I can't fail this mission. Not yet.

The proditor unlocks the bathroom door and carries me down the hallway. He kicks the back entrance open with his foot and readjust me over his shoulder.

My fingers twitch as they hang.

Please, let me go, I beg internally.

Space and time flicker, and I can only think of my cousin. How worried he'll be. The three of them won't know what happened.

Every time I blink, my surroundings change. One minute Dune's trudging through alleys.

The next I'm being carried up the ramp of a ship.

Chapter 21

Margot

Blazing pain fires through my neck, and I'm too dizzy to open my eyes. I can't think, too focused on the headache that has me in a vice. The hard, thin mattress pinches my back. I reach out to my right and smooth my hand over the cool wall. Sheets scratch at my arms.

A chain binds one of my ankles.

I jolt up and open my eyes. White walls enclose me within the small cell, only the thrum of the engines audible. An ivory prison uniform dresses my skin.

When the night before comes flooding back, I grip the edge of the mattress.

I'm on the Imnicus.

My bottom lip trembles. How could I have been so stupid? Why didn't I trust my intuition?

Did Dimitri, Anali, and Oliver get away? By the gods, I can only hope.

I imagine Dimitri back on Susuku, completely up in arms and Oliver stopping him from killing the first guard they see patrolling the streets.

Why did I accept that stupid drink?

I won't let Milo win. I've escaped the Imnicus before, and I can do it again and again. No matter how many times Milo drags me back here, I'll always escape him.

I flinch when the door beeps. It slides open to a dark hallway.

A figure emerges. He was the only proditor I never saw without a mask. Now I will never forget Dune's face or his kaleidoscope mask. The Colum's wildcard. The card Milo finally used against me.

I place a thousand walls over my persona. "You know as well as anyone the lengths I will go to stay silent. Don't waste your time."

Dune's eyes narrow. "I don't know what the Colum has planned for you. I'm just here to check in and make sure you didn't escape. You have an annoying habit of getting away."

"And I will again."

"Maybe. But you weren't so lucky with me."

I bite down on my tongue. He drugged me. Used my feelings against me. But I know I let myself be manipulated. "Why did you kiss me?"

"I seem to recall you're the one who kissed me."

"You pulled me back into you when you could have pushed me away."

"It worked to my advantage. Most don't recognize risk when lust is involved."

I let out a sarcastic chuckle. He says it like it's something clinical.

"And it seems not even you can resist a free drink," he adds.

The Nexus and rage explode as my failure comes into full light. The crows stir me on, and before I can rationalize my thoughts, I lunge off the floor toward Dune, my temper burning hotter than it ever has. It blazes hot enough that I don't care what the demonic crows whisper to me. All I want is to see him in pain.

Dune simply takes a step back into the hallway, leaving enough space for the chain to go taut and my chest to slam against the floor.

I huff in pain as I roll onto my side. He doesn't deserve to taunt or insult me. Dune was once one of my torturers. There cannot be an ounce of goodness in his heart.

Dune squats and rests his forearms on his thighs. "When was the last time your mind was clear, I wonder? When you truly knew your thoughts were your own?"

I reel back and spit on his boot. "Long before you tortured them out of me. The crows aren't my only demons."

Dune just stares back, expressionless. "If you don't cleanse your mind of Knox's crows soon, it will only get worse. Without proditor blood, you're even less equipped to handle them than he is."

"And if I get rid of him, I won't be able to save my planet."

"That was a pipe dream to begin with."

"It's my only dream."

He shakes his head before turning to leave. "The Colum will call on you soon. Be ready."

Hours pass and nobody comes to see me. I can only guess it's nearing the end of the day. Still, nobody brings me food and my stomach growls.

Milo's starving me. Weakening me for whatever he has planned.

I walk on wobbly legs to the door and paw at the security sensor, even going as far as trying to yank it off. I look down at Milo's ring on my thumb and press it to the sensor with bated breath, as I have hundreds of times today, but it immediately turns red. Not that I'm surprised.

I place my fingertips on the crevices of the sliding cell door, searching for weak points. I get on my knees to inspect the bottom.

The door flies open when I press on the edge. I yelp.

Standing across the threshold, two proditors stare down at me kneeling. One with a smirk in his eyes, the other with all the contempt the universe has to offer.

"Expecting someone?" Onyx winks.

I immediately shoot up.

Crux holds a large box in his hands. "More like she's trying to escape. And failing, I might add."

They both enter, forcing me to back further into the cell. When the door shuts behind them, I swallow. I don't want to be alone with them.

Crux sets the box down on the table.

"The Colum asked us to bring you to him," Onyx says. "And to get you dressed."

I step back until my back presses against the wall. "If he wants to see me, he can come visit my cell like everyone else."

With Crux, I know where I stand. Where I've always stood with him. He's never tried to hide how much he hates me and I'm sure his hate has only grown since I evaded him and Milo. Since Anali beat him senseless.

In terms of Onyx, I don't know what to expect from him. He was always friendly with me, even a little *too* friendly. But now I remember the ways he tortured me along with the other proditors. Of course, unlike Knox, his magic was more textbook. He didn't get any enjoyment out of hurting me. It was just another workday to him, but it doesn't make him any less terrifying.

"I'm afraid that isn't an option," Onyx says, "Save us the trouble and get dressed."

When I don't move an inch toward the box, Crux's brows furrow. "Screw your patience, Onyx." He throws the lid off, yanks out a dress, and throws it at me. "Get dressed unless you want me to strip you and dress you myself. One touch is all it takes for us to null your pitiful excuse for crows, so don't even bother trying to fight back."

I can hear his furious huffs under his mask and I tense when he places his hand over the dagger on his belt. He won't kill me, but if Onyx wasn't here, gods know what he would do.

Crux heads to the door, pulling Onyx by the collar. "You have five minutes."

I shudder before inspecting the billowy dress in my arms—black, long, and ornate. Fit for a Columess. It feels so foreign as I slip it on, yet there was once a time where I dressed like this almost every day.

Wearing this dress isn't luxurious. It's treasonous. My skin crawls at every point in contact with the fabric. Milo may force me to see him, but I refuse to wear this, at least, not in its current state.

I quickly work, counting the seconds, to tear the dress apart, using my fingernails when I have to. I don't stop until it exposes my abdomen and leaves only four pieces of thin chiffon fabric that tie around my makeshift waist garter. What once was an elegant dress is now a weapon. Maybe not one that will win a war, but one certain to piss Milo off.

When the proditors enter again, their faces fall.

Onyx rubs his temples. "Milo is going to be furious."

Crux's face goes hot, like he's going to explode from anger. Onyx places a hand on Crux's arm to ease him.

Crux folds his arms. "I don't give a shit what Milo thinks. She's his problem now, and he can punish her himself."

Onyx grabs the heels from the box and directs me to sit on the cot. "For obvious reasons, I'll need to put these on you." He motions to the sharp points before taking off his gloves.

"Of course you do." I slump down onto the side of the mattress.

While Onyx places the first strapping heel on my foot, I resist every urge to kick him in the face. He's gentle, but a proditors' skin is a weapon. I stay extra aware of his touch while he works.

My heart pulses when my crows fall asleep.

Crux is silent, his eyes darting. If he was alone with me, would he reenact the day he tortured me? Add elements beyond my comprehension for no other reason than punishment?

He leans back against the wall. "Even with your newfound strength, you still cannot hide your fear."

"Says the proditor who had his ass kicked by a Susukan girl half his size," I shoot back.

Onyx grips my ankle reflexively, like a warning. Then he slides on the second heel.

Crux slowly walks forward until he stands over me. I keep my head turned away, even as the cot dips when he sits down to my left.

He grabs my wrist and pulls my arm straight. I try to resist, yanking my arm back to no avail. His other hand traces my scars. "You really think you're not afraid of me? Or is it Alarik's tormented face that gives you the most trouble sleeping at night?"

"Crux—" Onyx warns.

My shoulders tense as flashes of Alarik's face wash over my vision. His tormented expression, like he was hurting more than I was.

Crux continues, "When they trained us as proditors, Alarik was resistant and soft just like his father. Balistar forced him to help with interrogations on Lavenai to harden him up." Crux grips the back of my neck roughly and I yelp as he brings my ear close to his mouth. "I haven't seen that kind of pain from him since that first time Balistar made him kill."

A white-hot anger slashes over my chest. I don't care if I'll regret it.

I spit on his face.

Onyx's eyes widen as Crux curls his left fist, the leather of his gloves audibly crinkling.

"Crux, careful." Onyx yanks me off the bed, out of Crux's reach. He pushes me behind his back, becoming the wall between Crux and me. "Let's not prolong our orders anymore than we have to."

I suspected they had orders not to touch me, but this only confirms it. Why put me in a dress if I was allowed to be bruised and beaten?

I watch Crux carefully from over Onyx's bicep, worried that, at any second, he'll push his friend away, grab my throat, and shred me apart.

Instead, he heads to the door. "Milo should have disposed of you a long time ago."

I bite down on my tongue. If I knew I'd win, I'd beat him senseless. I'd make it hurt. He's wearing gloves, so maybe I could get a few good punches in.

Onyx and Crux walk on both sides of me down the halls that turn from smooth to geometric as we transfer wings. If I had to guess, the only reason I'm not in handcuffs is because the charade hasn't stopped and Imnicus personnel still believe I'm the Columess.

I'm angry that we don't pass a single servant or soldier on the way to the dining room. I want them to recognize me as the Columess. For them to see my dress and for their perception of leadership to crumble. For them to start rumors within their circles until Milo can no longer control them. Mere speculation can cause towers to fall.

The dining room doors open, and I take in the aroma of the food. My stomach rumbles.

When I see him, my hunger dissipates into an insignificant ache.

Milo is faced away from me, reaching for a chalice, my old wedding ring snug against his pinky finger. He's dressed more formally than usual, his royal attire fitted with silver embellishments.

Milo doesn't turn to face me as he lifts the chalice. "Are you finding your new accommodations comfortable?"

"Very," I snap. "It must be the most luxurious room on this entire ship. You shouldn't have."

Milo shoots his gaze over his shoulder before his imperial facade cracks at the sight of my dress. Everything is on display—my cleavage, abdomen, and thighs. I can tell it takes everything in him not to react. "I see you didn't like the dress."

"It wasn't exactly suited to my taste."

"I see. If your tastes are suited to the rebellion, then I will treat you like the criminal you are." Milo signals to Crux.

Crux pulls me forward and throws me to the ground at Milo's feet. Pain blazes through my shoulder.

If that's how it's going to be, then two can play at this game. "Would you like me to lick your boot while I'm down here, Colum? Or was that more your father's cup of tea?"

Milo stares daggers down at me. "Who gave you the lead on Matsumoto?"

"And who are you to question me?"

"Your Colum."

"Then, by all means, wipe my memories and try your tactics again. You know well enough that torture doesn't work on me. It seems like you prefer more perverse tactics now."

"Like?"

"For one, Dune's mouth tastes woodier than yours."

Milo's lips part, his eyes flashing. Even Crux's eyebrows raise and Onyx stifles a laugh.

"Crux, Onyx, step outside," Milo says calmly.

My heart beats harder. Did I push too far? Will he torture me himself this time? The thought alone turns my blood to ice. My words are empty, for I might actually cave if it's by his hand.

This version of Milo isn't one I'm familiar with. I know the one who had me tortured—the one who saw me as a spawn of Lavenai. But I also know the one who adored me. Who worshiped me.

But this Milo more of the first with a hint of the second—completely unpredictable.

The proditors bow their heads before exiting out the sliding doors.

I push myself off my chest and back onto my knees, holding his dark gaze. "Where are the others?"

"Your rebellion friends? I have proditors and two guards searching Ashtanabo high and low. We will find them."

"And what will you do once you find them? Slaughter them with Gallow machines?"

"You know what I'm capable of. The lengths I'd go."

"Then what about me?" I shake the pain in my shoulder out and stand. "How far will you go to silence me?"

Milo crosses his legs and sits back in his chair. "You . . . are a more complicated case."

"You said you would kill me if you ever saw me again. Why haven't you?"

"Because I haven't covered my tracks yet. You're still the Columess to the masses, and the last thing I need is to piss off Arbitor Monicas right now."

"And that's the only reason?"

Milo grips the armrests. "There could never be any other reason than fulfilling my duty."

"Would your father be disappointed if he knew you've kept me alive this long?"

Something boils over in Milo. He flies to his feet and stomps toward me. I back away until I hit the wall.

What is he going to do to me?

His hands slam onto the wall, boxing me in.

A lump forms in my throat. My legs go stiff.

He leans his face inches from mine, the surrounding air filled with his dark cologne. The bare parts of my skin flood with goosebumps as his body heat radiates into mine.

His breaths are angry, exposing the open nerve that I now have full control over.

My breasts tighten and a silky hot wave of desire licks up my inner thighs. I unintentionally wet my lips before snapping back into reality. "You're too afraid to kill me, aren't you?"

Milo grabs my hips and hauls me to the table, bending me over it and grabbing the knife from his place setting. I wince slightly when he presses the tip of it into my side, just enough for me to feel the sharp metal without breaking my skin.

He leans over me, his breath in my ear. "You had the chance to kill me too, and you didn't. Should we both play this game, Margot? Is it one you think you can win?"

He withdraws the knife and lets his partial weight melt into my back. Neither of us speak, our inhales labored. I bite down on my inner lip when his hot breaths move from my ear to my neck, shooting warmth into my lower belly.

No, this isn't the time to feel like this. Milo Arris is a dictator and a killer who would rather enslave an entire planet than disappoint his deceased father.

His breaths are shaky, and his touch is hesitant. He sets down the blade and moves his hand to my hair, grabbing it tightly, like he's trying anything to resist. But his other hand betrays him, his thumb lightly tracing the bare sliver of skin along my lower back.

Chills flood up my spine and my body goes icy-hot. I'm sure I could shove him off, but I just lie there while his fingers tremble as they pass over my skin. I push away the urge to press back into him.

Milo tenses and finally pushes off me, stepping away. He faces the wall, leaning against it with one hand, collecting his thoughts.

I slowly move off the table, my neck rosy and hands clammy. If he hadn't controlled himself, how far would I have let this go?

I sit at the head seat and take a bite of food off his half-eaten plate. It's all it takes for arousal to be replaced with real hunger. It reminds me that Milo starved me, and judging by the presence of only one setting, I don't know that he had any plans of feeding me today. The dress was only a cover in case servants accidentally saw me.

Milo finally turns to speak. "You won't receive any special treatment just because you once meant something to me."

I arch an eyebrow as I finish off the wine. "I'm well aware."

He straightens his posture. "You are a prisoner of the Imnicus. A rebel. You will be handled like one."

I simply nod and cross my legs, bringing more attention to the dress. The one made of the finest materials an Ashtanaban can buy.

"Stop mocking me," Milo bites.

"I'm not mocking you. You're being delusional."

"As the Colum, I demand your respect."

"Yes, of course, Colum." I dig into the untouched dessert before another thought breaks through the veil—hatred, overriding any other emotion. "Where did you bury Lleu?"

To my surprise, Milo's face doesn't grow crass or solemn. "She's fine."

I lower the fork. "You mean . . . she's still alive?"

Milo nods. "It took months of recovery, but she healed."

"Where is she now?" I ask too quickly. "Did she go back to Msanii?"

"No, she's still here on the Imnicus. Unfortunately, she's been going through interrogation to find out who helped you escape. Though, if you tell me, I will send her back home."

Bile pools in the back of my throat. "You interrogated her? Tortured her!"

"No." Milo's voice grows harsh. "I've only let Alarik question her. Verbally. That is all. I have not hurt her, Margot. Nor have I let anyone else. You have my word."

I pause, pinching my lips together, before going back to licking the dessert plate clean. I shouldn't believe him, but if she's with Alarik, perhaps Milo is telling the truth.

"So, who did it, Margot? Who sent you that letter?"

"That is none of your business, Colum." I will protect Alarik as much as I will protect Lleu. If Milo knew one of his proditors was a traitor, there's no telling what Alarik's fate would be.

Milo's brows furrow, as if he thought sparing Lleu and me from pain would spill my secrets. "If that's how it's going to be then very well." He yanks me up from his chair and wraps his arm around my waist, bringing me into his chest. "You'll have plenty of time to think about your choice in your cell."

He maintains an intense stare while he pulls out his communicator and presses a button to call in the proditors.

Chapter 22

Milo

After Margot and the proditors leave, I adjust myself in my pants before summoning Dune on my communicator.

Why did she have to modify her dress? Gods, I could have taken her right there without a second thought. I almost did. Crux and Onyx should have warned me before they brought her. I would have sent a second one. It's not like she doesn't have the hundreds I bought for her.

I remember the way she laid beneath me on the table, not moving or fighting back. If I would have grazed my hand up her inner thigh and beneath her garments, would she have finally pushed me away?

I have to believe she would've. She sees me as a tyrant. The son of the man who killed her parents.

But no matter how cruel Margot thinks I am, I'm not even close to harboring the heartlessness my father carried. Her parents were quite young when they were executed, twenty and twenty-one.

I remember their names from the records: Enzo Tavish and Lia Flynn, and then Lia's brother Kai Flynn, who is also deceased. My father was only a few years older than I am now when he oversaw their execution. Oversaw. That's what the records say, but I've seen the footage. He personally dragged them to the noose.

There's no way Margot would ever forgive that. And there's no way I can ignore what needs to be done about the letter. Neither she nor Lleu will say a word about it, and soon I'll have to question Margot more. But I can't do that in front of the proditors or guards. I'll need to get her out of her cell and alone. If I'm not careful, the guards will wonder why I'm interrogating my own wife, who they believe has been in a treatment center. The proditors will wonder why I'm giving her preferential treatment.

Finally, Dune enters, lowering his head. "Colum."

I rise from my chair and approach him. "Proditor." My fist collides with his abdomen.

Dune stumbles back, breath wheezing.

"You *kissed* her?" I ask harshly.

"I'm . . . sorry, it was—" Dune struggles to catch his breath. "It ended up being the only way."

"Yes. Sticking your tongue down Margot's throat was *the only way*." I scoff before leaning back against the wall. Dune isn't nearly as promiscuous as the other proditors, more so because he never has the time for it. Or doesn't make the time.

For now, I'll let it go. "Any news on the other rebels?"

"Not yet." Dune straightens his back. "But Susuku is crawling with proditors in pursuit of them."

"And what of the rebellion?"

"No other suspected infiltrations at the moment, Colum." He swallows. "But Knox just arrived back from Lavenai."

I tense. "Early?"

"You know how efficient he is."

I press my lips together. "You are dismissed."

Every move I make, I balance on a razor's edge. A razor that Knox holds in his hands and can swipe out from under me at any given moment.

With the woman of his violent obsessions back on the Imnicus, I don't know that I'll rest soundly until she's transported to a private Ashtanaban prison.

I shouldn't be uneasy though. There is no way he can access her cell, and there aren't security cameras within the cells themselves, so he can't use his ravens. Every base is covered, and the prison guards have been given strict instructions to not allow Margot any visitors without my approval and that includes proditors.

Gods, Margot. You've let Knox check my king without even trying.

Chapter 23

Margot

Onyx drops off a tray of food, which I devour. It's not nearly as good as the food that Milo is served, but it's still better than most meals on Lavenai. Milo hasn't provided me with a change of clothes from the gown I tore apart, and I assume it's to punish me.

Every hour that passes, the cell grows smaller and smaller. There's the small cot with a stiff, dirty mattress and a scratched-up toilet in the corner. Speckles line the walls that I swear are blood from previous inmates.

I recall the Imnicus training I received when I was still posing as a guard. There are cells in the prison wing that may as well be luxury experiences. Ones with beds and private bathrooms. But this one is made for scum on the bottom of Milo's boot like me.

Not wanting to imagine how many people have taken their last breath in my cot, I lie on the ground with closed eyes. Though Lleu survived the gunshot, she still helped me escape. According to Arris law, she should be executed, but Milo has been protecting her.

He's confusing to say the least. But if I have to guess, he's using her safety to manipulate me. That, or he has something more nefarious planned. No matter his reasons, I'm relieved she's alive.

I wish I could see her again. Hug her while we dig into desserts and I listen to her endless rambling about Ashtanaban pop culture. I also wish I could shake her senseless about choosing my life over hers. I didn't deserve to be saved. She had no reason to risk her own life to protect me, yet she did.

I drift in and out of sleep, turning restlessly on the hard floor.

Margot! Where are you! Dimitri screams from deep within my dreams.

Milo's voice enters my dreams next. *Arrest the rebel boys. Make an example of them.*

The dream turns lucid. I lie in my cell with wide-opened eyes, yet I know I'm still asleep.

Crows circle the infinitely high ceiling above me. Some of them perch on my cot. Others land on the metal door frame and caw.

Usually when they're in my dreams, their caws turn to audible whispers or promises of pain. Promises of what they can offer me if I'd only submit to them.

But this time, they don't taunt or beg me.

Try your ring, they say. *Escape.*

I turn away, curling upon myself to try to shut them out. *I already tried it.*

Try it again, they counter. One flies straight at my face with its beak wide open.

I jolt awake with a heaving breath to nothing but an empty cell free of crows. Milo's ring tightens around my thumb.

I rest my hands on my stomach, spinning his ring around my finger once then twice. It's pointless to try, and what kind of person would I be if I listened to my nightmares?

But what if they're right?

I push myself up, sliding my empty food trays out of the way with my foot as I approach the scanner at the door. It feels ridiculous to try this; an insult to Milo's attention to detail as much as it is to mine.

I raise the ring to the sensor.

And as soon as the ring touches it, the door clicks and slides open. I take a step back.

This seems like an impossibility. Like some kind of technical error.

I half expect a guard to be on the other side or down the hall, but it must be late into the night on Ashtanabo right now, which means most of the Imnicus is asleep too. Still, there's those on the night shift, so I need to be cautious.

I carefully walk down halls, staying out of the view of cameras the best I can.

Where is Milo holding Lleu? The last thing I want is to leave without her again. My chest tightens to think of abandoning her a second time.

But the sooner I take down the temple points, the sooner all of us will be free. I have to trust that Alarik will get her off the Imnicus.

I avoid the command center, taking servant passages in the direction of the escape pods. Everything looks exactly the same as the last time I was on the Imnicus. It's a well-oiled machine thanks to the maintenance and vigorous cleaning schedules.

I turn a corner somewhere in the middle of the south wing. As I move down a corridor, I freeze at the sound of footsteps.

Footsteps that are only a few feet behind me.

"Is the Little Fennec strolling all by herself?"

I quickly turn, the sight of Knox bringing an indescribable nausea and fear. The scar on my back burns—the tattoo he carved into me with a smile on his face.

I'd rather be in the prison cell, protected by the high security, then here right now at the mercy of Knox Arris. "Stay back."

"Why would I do that when I'm all alone with my favorite toy?" He takes a step forward.

I flinch, showing too much of my hand, too much panic. I can't control my fear around him. The crows sense and obey him. "I'm not something for you to play with."

"Aren't you? My toy?" Knox takes another step. "And do toys have a choice if they're played with?"

"You almost killed Lleu."

Knox stares at me deviously. "And aren't you glad I missed all the vital organs? You should thank me."

"Thank you?" I scoff. "You're criminally insane!"

"I prefer the term 'divinely enlightened.' Don't you understand it now, Margot? True power is everything, but it's rarely given for free. Our crows itch. They demand to be fed. A sacrifice is in order, and we're meant to give it to them."

"That's your cup to bear, not mine." I take a small side-step toward a door, though I have no idea where it leads or if it's unlocked.

"Isn't it though? I hear what you hear. Sense what you sense. You're burning inside. I can feel it. They're hungry, and you're in need of something or someone to satisfy them."

I need to divert him to get a head start.

I look just over his shoulder.

"Are you paying attention?" he asks.

I shake my head, as if I'm communicating with someone behind him.

Knox takes the bait, following my gaze to the empty hallway.

I sprint to the door as fast as I can.

Knox curses.

I grip the manual release on the door, sliding it open. I run inside before pulling it shut.

But before it closes all the way, a gloved hand catches the side, knuckles tense. I quickly back away as he pries it open with a grin.

The room is a small kitchen for south wing staff, but there's only one way in and one way out, and Knox is currently standing in front of it.

As my panic grows, so do my crows. I run to the kitchen island, sliding over the marble surface. As I glide, I grab a knife from the metal block and land on the other side, creating a much needed barrier between us. I spin to see Knox lock the door behind him, barring us both inside.

I trapped myself . . . with him.

Knox pulls off his hood but leaves his paisley mask on. His eyes smile. "If you wanted to be alone with me so badly, you could have just asked."

My hand clenches the knife. "I'm closer to throwing this blade directly into your windpipe."

Knox laughs. "You think you can kill me? Just because you have a weaker clone of my strength? You can't even control the crows."

"Who says I'm weaker?" I hurl the dagger at his shoulder.

Knox slaps the knife to the side. It clatters onto a pile of dirty dishes. "Margot, Margot, Margot," he tsks.

I ready my stance as he leans over the island and pulls a knife from the block. He slides it over to me. "Want another go?"

Hesitantly, I pick up the blade.

"Cut down the skirt off your dress. If we're going to fight, I don't want you tripping over that pitiful gown."

Fighting Knox and succeeding seems like an impossibility. But I've trained mercilessly over the past months. Even without the crows, I really am stronger than the last time Knox and I met.

I cut the fabric off of my waistband until I'm left in nothing except the shorts and dress bodice. "Leave your gloves on. I want us to fight as equals."

Knox chuckles, his eyes glazing over my body. "Oh, my dear, we're hardly equal."

My arms visibly shake, but not from fear. After everything Knox has done, I want to see him suffer so badly that it's almost salacious. To see him crawl across the tile in fear of what I may do to him, not knowing if every breath he takes will be his last.

I shake my head, warding off the euphoria.

Knox paces the length of the large island. His breathing rises and falls to the chant of the crows. "Do you feel that, Margot? They demand retribution. Their reward is sweet, I can promise you. It's worth every drop of blood."

"It's nothing I can't resist. Unlike you, I have self-control."

"Let's test that self-control, shall we?" Knox zips around the island.

I throw the next knife at him and he knocks it away. Then he's on me, barely giving me a second to block the punch he throws.

I duck my head and spin, grabbing a frying pan out of the sink and swinging it. He narrowly evades it, then he smacks my wrist with the side of his hand.

I wince and drop the pan, meeting Knox's punches throw for throw, rhythmically blocking them. I can't let him win. I'll fight and evade him until my arms give up from exhaustion if that's what it takes.

He nearly gets the upper hand, so I change my fighting style from Onyx's to Alarik's to throw him off.

I land the first punch of the fight into Knox's abdomen. He falls back onto the tile. I don't stop, even in my shock, because if I give Knox even a second to collect himself, I'll never escape.

I rush forward, blocking a wild, retaliatory kick and leap atop him, straddling his waist. Blow after blow, I rain down upon him, fist striking his grim paisley mask. I lose control of myself, throwing my fist over and over again until my knuckles bleed. I take out everything on him—the torture, the pain, the manipulation. Every grunt from his throat feels like pure ecstasy. His mask cracks down the middle.

Deep within his throat, a laugh gurgles free, rising like a tide over the ocean. Blood drips down his lips, staining his white smile.

Inside my crows shriek at the sky, laughing with him.

No.

He let me overtake him on purpose. He hasn't tried to defend himself, even though his arms are completely free. It was his plan this entire time for me to give into my crows and have the smallest taste of what Knox devours daily.

"*You* re-enabled Milo's ring," I say. "You wanted me here."

"Guilty"

I try to climb off him but he grips my hips to keep me put. Rolling off him doesn't work either. His palms still hold me tightly. The only way to get off of him is to fight. But to fight him means to give into what he and the cursed crows want.

"Keep going, Little Fennec. You're not finished yet."

"Letting me win only makes you one thing—a coward."

His face darkens and I clench my jaw, preparing for his wrath.

"The crows may strengthen you . . . " Knox moves his hand to my thigh. A hand which is now bare. I hadn't even noticed he took his gloves off. "But they will always obey me."

His thumb caresses my skin, petting his birds. Their wings spread in excitement, but then tame until they are sleeping in their nests, out of my reach. When Knox weakens the Nexus, it's different from when Milo or the other proditors do it.

The crows fly away from me, flocking at his side, cooing at him.

I have no choice except to fight him with my innate strength.

I punch him hard in the solar plexus, freeing a gasp from his lungs. His grip loosens from my thighs and I leap off him, sprinting toward the door.

Even with the Nexus asleep, I'm riddled with shame. The voice of Crux echoes in my head. *You are nothing without crows.*

I don't make it far. Knox grips the back of my neck and yanks me into his chest. His other hand finds the bare skin of my lower back, tracing my scar. "A work of art."

"Screw you," I seethe, fear gripping my chest. He's touching me, skin-to-skin, and at any moment he'll throw me into hell.

He moves his mouth to my ear. "Let's make this a little more interesting, shall we?"

Knox shoves my head forward to slam my skull into the counter. But a split second before the blow lands, everything puffs into smoke.

I'm standing on my feet. The kitchen is no more, leaving me alone in a realm of Knox's creation within my own mind.

The illusion is an endless world of mist and mind-bending structures.

A city with curved buildings surrounds me, broken in two, only connected by an arm-length sliver of cement as a bridge. A bridge I'm standing on. My stomach tightens.

One wrong move will make me fall to my—well, not death. Knowing Knox, probably something worse.

Fear consumes me.

I'm trapped.

I balance on the cement bridge, taking careful steps. My palms sweat uncontrollably.

Fingers thread through my hair, yanking me backward. I yelp.

"We'll fight right here," Knox shoves me to the ground.

I nearly slip off the cement as my chest hits the ground. My head hangs over the edge, staring into the bottomless cavern. Screams echo up below—the unfortunate souls who have fallen before me, their psyche frozen in time.

Are some of his victim's minds really trapped here? Or is it something he's faking just to further my fear? I don't want to find out.

My legs shake as I rise to stand. "If you want me dead so badly, then why am I still alive?"

"You're a rare spectacle, Little Fennec. One that craves an encore."

"So you'll just toy with me and break my mind? Milo will notice."

"I'll ensure he won't, and I'm confident you won't tell." Knox steps forward and throws two punches.

I step back quickly, barely evading them, but a third punch collides with my shoulder. I lose my balance. The second my back hits the ground, I spin my body and my legs catch Knox's ankle.

Knox's eyes widen as he falls, but he catches himself before he tumbles into the abyss.

I push myself up and run in the opposite direction. My gaze stays pinned forward the entire time, because if I look down, I know I'll fall.

Once I'm to safety near the city buildings, I check over my shoulder.

Knox is back on his feet, but he hasn't moved from his spot. He simply stands there, staring at me with that horrifying grin, as if nothing I did actually hurt him.

A numbing horror grips my muscles. I dart along the sidewalks and past run-down buildings that look abandoned. Beds hang from the sky. Wooden toys move on their own on the sidewalk as if given a breath of life. A pile of storybooks sits in the middle of the town square.

I run past it but stop abruptly. A book on the top catches my eye.

I approach the pile cautiously, careful to keep an eye on my peripherals.

I thought I'd lost it. I grab the dusty book, charred at the edges. This is one of the books Lucinda liked to read to Dimitri and me every night. What is it doing here of all places?

Neon lights ignite over the city of illusion all at once, like a power switch had just turned on. Purple fog slowly moves through the streets, pooling up my ankles.

It can't be . . . this is Lavenai? This city filled with rubble and ash, like it just endured the remnants of a war. But it couldn't have been Balistar's war. Most of the buildings were preserved during that time.

These buildings aren't ruined from age but from fire and bombs.

This is what Lavenai would have become if Balistar hadn't found a use for us in factories and stealing our planet's energy. The revenge he truly wanted. Total annihilation.

"It's like walking into a painting, isn't it?"

The voice isn't Knox's, but the inflections are familiar. Soft and coarse all at the same time. There's a hint of Milo's voice too, but more mature. More bold and eccentric.

When I turn around, the devil of the galaxy sits on the steps of a building turned slightly off its axis. Despite the rubble, his dark uniform is immaculate. His boots scrape over the rubble of a dead planet, gold embellishments shining in the neon light.

I've only ever seen photographs and videos of Balistar Arris where history can paint him in whatever light it pleases. But here, in person, I see only the hidden evils that lay deep within.

His head cocks to the side as he waits for my answer, his long, white-blonde hair shifting off his shoulders. His fingers tap, tap, tap in anticipation, covered in thick silver rings. Where Milo wears his rings like grim mementos, Balistar wears them like a prize.

"You're not real," I say more to myself than to him.

"Does something have to be real to cause damage?" Balistar stands, kicking stray bits of wood and stone off to one side to make a path for himself. "Nobody can truly define the difference between illusion and fantasy, no matter how strong they think they are. It's what makes proditor magic so beautiful."

"The Vicars never meant for their magic to be used like this."

His face grows harsh. "The Vicars?"

The very air vibrates at his words, as if he wants the planets to know his anger. "The *gods* made the crows, and if they weren't meant to be used, why did they give us access? They left their texts but never specified their intentions. They gave us power but did not outline the rules. The *Vicars* live in fear of their gifts. But the gods wanted someone to learn their secrets. Someone to rule. To me, the crows are nothing but untapped potential. Potential I have made a reality."

Hearing the words from his own mouth, even if it's just an illusion, is horrifying. He may carry himself with poise and grace, but deep down, Balistar Arris was just as much of a psychopath as Knox is.

"You used it for massacre!"

"And who committed it first? Hmm?" Balistar tilts his head, the shadows passing over his sharp features. "It was Lavenai who ignored us. Lavenai who watched us crawl, die, and beg for mercy. If you want to blame someone, blame the Laven Colum who preceded me. We cried for help to our sister planet, and for decades they ignored us. So I had no choice but to take retribution from everyone who would not take the knee."

Balistar snaps his fingers and points in the distance behind me.

Don't turn your back to him.

A reflection in one of the building's windows betrays me, containing the full horror of what Balistar wants to show me. I ignore all apprehension, spinning in desperation.

Two bodies hang from the lampposts by their necks, swaying in a breeze I do not feel.

My lips tremble, and I fall to my knees.

There comes a time in every daughter's life where she realizes her parents were once just as young as she was. Naïve yet proud. Strong yet weak.

My mother looks just like Lucinda described her, with blonde hair in a fishtail braid and barely twenty years old. My father beside her with scruffy brown hair caked in blood. In their lifeless faces, I can see myself. My mother's soft beauty, the tenderness of her cheeks. And my father, the fighter. Bloody and beaten, resisting until the very end.

"They were just kids!" I scream, tears falling down my face. The neon lights glitch and I close my eyes, unable to stomach another second.

Balistar's boots crunch on the dirt until he's kneeling at my side. He grabs my chin, turning my gaze back to the horrific sight. "Their age means nothing in the wake of domination. Their naivety is chaff to me. They were an example to all who looked upon them. Resistance would be a foolish endeavor, and my power is absolute."

The worst part is, his example worked.

Lucinda was the only flame that stayed alight in those days. The only spark that didn't die out. Everyone else submitted under the heel of the Arris Reign.

I can no longer close my eyes or even blink, Knox's entrancement taking hold of my body. The lights flicker faster now, the neon bulbs popping and shattering up and down the surrounding streets.

"When are you going to accept that their deaths were pointless?" Balistar turns my head to face him. "The example I made of them worked. You see them as martyrs, when in reality, they failed."

My ribs tighten. I grieve time itself, that I'll never have the opportunity to have my personal revenge on him. Through death, he'll always be out of reach, unable to pay for his sins. If hell exists, I hope he's in it.

His face morphs and bends until I'm face to face with Knox. He keeps a tight grip on my chin. I try to peel away, even as his face flickers between Balistar and his own, the lights flickering in rapid intensity.

They're one and the same. Uncle and nephew. The devil and his demon.

Knox uses his crows to inject something horrible into me. An agony I've never known. I scream as a brain-splitting headache rages through my mind. I beg the gods to take my pain away. To make everything disappear.

Then it does. Darkness falls over the world and the pain dissipates, turning into exhaustion.

It isn't until the familiar scent of the Imnicus hits my nose that I realize I'm being carried by a set of arms down the darkened hallways and into my prison cell.

Knox holds me close to his chest before lowering me to the mattress and covering me with the thin sheet.

"One day, I will kill you." I force those words out in a whisper, my body slowly fading into slumber.

Knox traces my jaw. "You will try."

Chapter 24

Milo

Slow breaths, soft lips, hair as gold as an angel's—still in that diabolical dress, or a remnant of it, the skirts now ripped away too.

I stare down at Margot's sleeping form in the cell, holding a change of clothes for her under my arm. Only the gentle thrum of the Imnicus engines and her soft breaths are audible. With the sheets tangled around her legs, I imagine the way she must've tossed and turned last night.

She's the source of all chaos in my life. The reason I can't sleep at night. The ghost that haunts the Imnicus and my every dream.

Yet when I look at her, all those woes disappear for a split moment and I imagine having her. Caring for her. Being her protector, not the one throwing her into darkness.

But sooner or later, I'll need to find out who wrote the letter. Either her or Lleu will have to bear the torch of who did it. If they don't, I'll have to wait until we apprehend Margot's friends to further motivate her. Though I refuse to interrogate her properly ever again, her friends aren't exempt from my wrath.

I sit on the side of the cot and she doesn't stir. A small sigh escapes her throat and my breath hitches. I don't catch myself until it's too late—my fingers stroke her golden hair, which has flattened into waves. She unconsciously moves her face toward my fingers, unconsciously trying to nuzzle them. My lungs contract.

I remind myself of who I am, the billions of lives I'm responsible for, and Arris law, which I swore to my father I would uphold.

I curse, my forearm tensing. Quickly, I move off the bed.

Margot rolls on her side, facing me, and when her eyes flutter open she startles.

I lean my upper back against the wall, crossing my arms and an ankle across the other, inspecting my rings to avoid looking straight at her. "Somehow you're more naked than last time I saw you."

Her arms shake as she pushes herself up to sit. There's a new hollowness to her face.

I narrow my eyes. "Have they been feeding you?"

"I thought you didn't care if I was fed."

"I care that you're strong enough to answer my questions."

"Why? Have you changed your mind about torturing me?"

"Margot, I asked if you've been eating."

"Like royalty." She says it with such confidence that I'm surprised when she rests her arms on her thighs and slumps her head. She looks more like someone who just endured hours of Imnicus training than someone who simply woke up from a night of sleep. "I see you brought me clothes. And that they're not prison robes."

I place my hand on top of the stack. "There is still a front that needs to be maintained if guards or maids see you."

She stands and approaches the stack of gray clothing. It's a lounge style that a lot of Ashtanaban women wear planetside. If I give her another dress, she'll just tear it to shreds.

Margot picks the top off the stack. "Turn around."

It's also not safe for me to turn my back to her, yet I do it anyway, using my crows to monitor anything she may try to pull.

I hear the shift of clothing behind me. "What's stopping me from telling the first guard I see that I'm not the Columess?"

"You've seen how easy it is to spread a narrative. For all they know, you've been drugged and indoctrinated by terrorists. They'll assume you're simply not in your right mind."

"It won't stop the rumors."

"True, but there are always rumors. Word will inevitably get to the arbitors, and that won't help you as much as think."

"*They* won't waste time executing me. I'd avoid torture."

"You're probably right. And I surely wouldn't avoid the consequences either."

Margot scoffs. "And why should I care? You're the Colum so it's not like they have any authority over you."

"I see you didn't read up on Ashtanaban politics while you were planetside. The arbitors have every right to have me nymbed if they think I deserve it."

I sense Margot go still. Most Lavens don't even know what nymbing is. Whereas proditors control Lavenai, nymbing controls Ashtanabo. Ironic, really, considering the process was a Laven speciality before the Arris Reign. It's a process I find cruel. One that I would vanquish if my father hadn't set up the law the way he did.

"Worried for me, after all?" I ask her.

Margot shrugs. "Don't twist my silence. Diyu is the first I learned of the process."

"My father instated it on Ashtanabo to keep people in line without using proditor magic. To make their minds malleable and empty and recondition them to his ways. Though a Laven invention concocted by crime lords, its process was too lengthy to use there, but it worked nicely on Ashtanabo to free up proditor resources, considering the defectors were few and far between."

"And you never thought to use it on me to get the code to my tablet?"

I turn when I sense she's finished changing into casual wear. "There's a reason it's not used in interrogation, only in reintegration into society. It's more permanent than proditor magic is. You likely would have forgotten the code forever."

Her eyebrows raise with a flash of pity. "And Anali? You never nymbed her?"

"I had no reason to integrate her back into society. Not when her presence is enough to collapse an empire."

"Hmm." Margot considers something before pinching her lips shut. "Is that why you're here? To question me about my friends?"

I fold my arms. "I have more questions than just that, but it's cramped in here. Let's go to a conference room." In here, it would only take a few short strides to be standing chest-to-chest with her, to be touching her. After last night, I can't trust myself. I've already had the cameras disabled in the hallways we'll take in case Knox tries to pull something.

"You mean an interrogation chamber?"

I tense. "No. A normal meeting room on the west wing."

Margot relaxes slightly.

I don't wait for her to agree or nod before opening the cell door and motioning to it. "After you."

The silence is deafening as we move through the halls. Margot doesn't acknowledge the guards that bow or the maids that curtsy.

"Should I expect proditors in attendance?" Margot asks. An A.S.O.P. unit rolls between us as if we're the ones in its way.

"No, it's just us. No one knows I'm here. Not the proditors, not even Aisil."

She goes quiet and I offer her no response.

I have no choice but to question her in secret. It's something I need to do, but I am too wary of Knox to have any of them with me. Besides, I meant what I said. I will never do that to her again. But to question her in secret may raise eyebrows too.

This is the only time of day I can do this unnoticed. The proditors all have assigned duties and I know exactly where they are all at. I just hope Margot doesn't remember the Imnicus well enough to know I'm taking a round-a-bout way.

This conference room is colder than normal, the draft enough for Margot to hug herself as the door closes behind us. I pull a chair out for her and then go to the opposite side to sit.

Margot studies the lavish conference room filled with pillars and a black-marble table. "How many meeting rooms does one palace need?"

"The Imnicus is a military hub. There are dozens of meetings that occur every day."

She adjusts in her chair. "Milo."

"Yes?"

"Those prisoners at Diyu . . . I just have to know . . . "

I hesitate. "A person is tied to a table and specialty red lights are flashed into the person's eyes for two days straight. It's not meant to be a form of torture, but it's an agonizing process. It leaves an Ashtanaban defector temporarily mindless, so that they can have their mind remolded to the Arris Reign. Eventually, the person's mind returns but shaped around a new ideology."

Margot's mouth gapes in horror but also in slight anger. Part of her fire comes back. "And you agree with this method?"

"These days, it's not used often, except for political leaders like myself and those who are more valuable alive than dead. When Ashtanaban rebels and defectors are caught, they're given two options—nymbing or death. In my opinion, the cowards choose nymbing. They're the ones who aren't willing to stick to their own ideologies from fear of death. So, no, I don't support nymbing in any regard."

My throat bobs at the thought of being nymbed myself. In fact, it's one of the few things that strike fear deep into my core. As I am my father's heir, death is not an option for me under Arris law.

Margot's eyes contemplate, like she expected me to say I fully agreed with it. "But you still agree with proditor torture."

"It's what I have on hand."

"Spoken like a true Colum." She looks down at her folded hands.

"That is what I am."

Margot meets my eyeline again. "But you're not much like your father, are you?"

"I don't have nearly as much political power as he did, if that's what you're asking. Say what you will about him, but he did a nice job guaranteeing the longevity of his life's work."

"The way I see it, Knox is the one who resembles Balistar in both ruthlessness and ideology."

My fists clench. Where did this come from? And why does the mention of my father and Knox in the same sentence make my blood boil over? My next words are practiced and rote, but I can't help the touch of anger beneath. "Knox was his protégé and my father took great pride in training him."

She goes to open her mouth, but voices leak into the room from two people striding down the hall. There's laughter in his voice and a coy giggle in hers.

Onyx speaks loudly enough for me to hear. "Why don't we find a more creative place to enjoy each other?"

My back stiffens. Onyx is supposed to be patrolling the east wing this time of day. Why is he here of all places? And with a girl?

My eyes widen and Margot lifts an eyebrow, confused. I rush around the table and grab Margot's hand, yanking her from the chair.

"What are you—"

I cover her mouth before she can finish her words, pulling her behind one of the large pillars. I lean back against it and hold her back to my chest. She squirms as I tighten my hand over her mouth.

"Be quiet. Trust me," I say.

She tilts her head back to face me, her eyes quickly turning to realization. The realization that she and I shouldn't be here alone like this. Realization that I have been treating her as anything but a prisoner. Still, she struggles against me.

I pull her closer to my chest just as the doors open.

Onyx waltzes inside the conference room. If Margot weren't with me, I'd have him assigned to a mission on Lavenai for an entire month. He has responsibilities, after all. Responsibilities he's forgoing for the sake of pleasure.

"Onyx, are you sure no one will come in here?" the maid asks.

"Of course, baby, it's just you and me," Onyx says. "Firstly, give me your hair ribbon."

The maid groans. "Not again. Haven't we been together enough? You promised that one day you'd let me see your face."

"One day, my love. One day. But with it being the law and all, I have to protect us both."

I roll my eyes. It's the most classic proditor pickup trick in the book. The promise that a proditor would break protocol for her and her alone. Of course they're all lying straight through their teeth. Even when I told them to make an exception for Lleu to see their faces, all of them were against it. They finally listened when they realized how inconvenient it would be while we conned Margot.

I know she's blindfolded once the sound of kissing and moaning ensues, leaving Margot and I even more trapped against the pillar. She's finally stopped trying to shrug me off, and I know she feels stuck enough for me to lower my hand from her mouth safely. I feel like a fool hiding like this from my own proditor.

Gods, why did I hide from him? I should have hid Margot behind the pillar, then I could've reprimanded him and the maid and sent the pair on their way with disciplinary plans in place. Why can't I think straight?

With the frantic ruffle of clothes and buckles hitting the ground, my arms tighten around Margot's abdomen and chest, overly aware of her warmth and how her breaths are growing as heavy as mine. More aware of our past, where she and I would have been as uncareful as Onyx.

When the lapping of Onyx's tongue echoes through the room, Margot's chest stutters. The maid moans. An image pops in my head of Margot in the same position. Where she once made similar noises for me. I silently curse as all the heat in my body pools into one central location.

I don't know what to do. If I try to adjust our standing position now, Onyx may find us, which would be even more humiliating to explain at this point.

Maybe she doesn't feel it. Maybe—

She places a hand over mine and squeezes it slightly.

She feels it. But her touch isn't angry or rough. It's more like she's trying to keep her bearing.

Control breaks in me. I run my hand down her abdomen, lifting her shirt slightly to rest my palm against her lower belly.

Her breath hitches and her hand tightens around my wrist, but she doesn't try to push me off. She runs her delicate thumb against my skin.

I slowly press my lips to the back of her skull.

Gods, I need to get control of myself. She deserves capital punishment not . . . whatever this is.

The table rocks and jolts as Onyx plunges into the maid.

I snake my hand up Margot's shirt, stopping myself when my palm rests against her lower rib.

She sucks in a breath as I ghost my lips lightly against the side of her neck. I can still stop this. I haven't captured her lips yet. I've barely touched her.

Margot leans back into me, only adding pressure to my pants, tearing away my last shred of sanity. I suck softly on the side of her neck, and her head falls back on my shoulder.

This is a mistake and I need to stop. I once had her tortured.

Yet the Laven is leaning into this as much as I am.

I move my hand down her abdomen and hold her inner thigh but quickly grasp control before my touch advances to her center.

Stop it. Stop it. My sucking on her neck only turns into soft licks.

Margot's forearms flood in goosebumps.

Onyx captures the maid's shameless moans with his mouth.

Margot moves her own hand near her pelvis but stops short just as I did, resting her hand just above the spot I know she so desperately wants to touch. A bead of sweat forms against her neck.

Onyx groans low and long, just as the maid screams out, and I've never been so relieved to hear another man finish. It's enough to snap me into focus and wrap my arms around Margot's torso, my lips breaking away from her back. I rest my chin on top of her head and I close my eyes.

I take in her scent and her warmth here in my arms. My arousal wanes, replaced with a deep pain.

Margot and I listen quietly as the maid whines to Onyx again about not being able to see his face. They argue briefly before heading out of the conference room.

Even after they leave, we stay exactly how we are. The sound of our breaths intertwines with the agonizing tension in the room.

A droplet of water hits my hand. I watch another run down the side of Margot's face.

I hold her tighter. We stand there wordlessly, letting our thoughts communicate and refusing to admit anything out loud.

I don't know how long we stand there, but eventually she steps away and heads to the door.

In complete silence, I walk her back to her cell, ignoring the fact that I was supposed to question her about the letter. At least for today, that ship has sailed.

Margot steps over the threshold of her cell and turns to face me. We stare at each other, neither of us breaking or being the first to look away.

It's the sliding door that finally cuts me off from her.

Chapter 25

Milo

One of my father's main principles in waging war involved leaving his opponents completely unprepared. With Lavenai, he wedged himself in with crime lords, building a dormant army. By the time the former Laven Colum caught on, the momentum was too great to stop. It's why my father never allowed any major base to truly sleep. He never wanted the same thing to happen to him.

The Imnicus he protected most of all. Even now, the command center hums with watchfulness, each posting filled despite it being nearly three in the morning in Heidl. I should be asleep, but my thoughts keep me restless. I keep dreaming of my downfall. I dream of running. I dream of *her*.

I blink my eyes clear, knowing I missed the words of the rookie soldier standing before me. She holds a paper in her hands. It's the standard letter of recommendation the Imnicus doles out for post changes. I remember this rookie but not by name. Shy but capable.

I wave for her to hand over the paper, swiping a pen from a nearby desk and scrawling my signature upon the bottom. It's bold to ask the Colum himself to sign it, but it'll likely get her a prestigious position when she's finished here.

Commander Aisil approaches us while I dot the last I, stamping this woman's career into existence. "Ahh, Miss Laurel, is it that time already?"

The rookie smiles and snaps off a crisp salute. "Next week, sir."

"I'm sure you have a good posting lined up?" he asks.

"I'm keeping my options open, sir."

"Wise indeed," Aisil says before turning my way. "Forgive me, Colum, but I must disturb you for a moment."

"If you must." I hand back the letter and rookie scurries away. Aisil leads me out of the control room, and I can already feel the polite lecture coming.

Yesterday, I neglected my usual rounds in favor of interrogating Margot. There's probably another fire to be put out, one that could've been prevented.

Instead, I was seconds away from sliding my fingers down my prisoner's waistband. From holding back my own gasps when her hand would have evidently reached behind and palmed me.

"I have a few updates," Aisil starts. "A few hours ago new Ashtanaban defectors were caught protesting in one of the Ralia region's larger cities. Thousands were gathered to watch in the city center before proditors and guards were deployed to break it up. It was unusual. We're used to protests on Laven, but Ashtanabo? That hasn't happened in years."

"Were they detained?"

"It got violent. The proditors had no choice but to make an example of them, which sent the gathered masses into a stampede in fear that they would be next. Three of them were executed and one of them was taken in for questioning before being sentenced to nymbing by Chancellor Ekon."

I don't let my jaw so much as twitch. "What else?"

Aisil's hands are laced behind his back. He waits to speak until a pair of guards pass us and round the corner. "I received correspondence from Arbitor Monicas today."

"Regarding?" I ask.

The commander hesitates. "Margot."

I stop suddenly and turn to face him.

"He heard from Imnicus guards visiting Heidl that she's supposedly out of treatment. Now he insists on seeing her here for supper tonight."

A pane of glass shatters inside my mind and all I can hear in my mind is Knox's chuckle. "Tell him no."

"Remember, Monicas is the type to abuse emergency meetings. If you don't accept, he may force both of you to Ashtanabo, regardless."

This is an impossible scenario. Margot may not be her usual rebellious self, but it doesn't mean she won't crack in the middle of dinner and get me nymbed, even at the risk of damning herself.

Monicas and all the other arbitors truly believe Margot is my wife. They have no idea she's Laven and think she's been in medical containment due to the terrorists poisoning her to near psychosis on her last mission. I'm drowning in lies at every side.

"Might I propose a suggestion, Colum?"

"You may."

"The actress is still on the ship and recovered, based on my reports from Alarik. Margot hasn't seen her yet, so perhaps you can use their reunion as a bargaining chip."

I frown. In all the years I've known him, Commander Aisil has been the definition of adequate, always preserving his post and little else. According to the histories, he was a force during my father's rise to power, but only now do I catch a glimpse of that man.

His suggestion could work. Not to mention, Lleu is the only person who can transform Margot into the Columess again. The only maid, if I can even call her that anymore, who knows Margot's true secret.

"Tell Monicas I won't deny him."

"Certainly, Colum."

After Commander Aisil goes about his way, I stay put, flexing and relaxing my fist. Trying to trick Arbitor Monicas, and convincing Margot to play along, is going to be a nightmare. But first, I have to get Lleu on board.

I arrive at the medical bay, garnering a few surprised stares from staff. In my father's day, people were in and out of here constantly. Now, it's really only used for rare emergencies or cuts and bruises. Or when a proditor trains too hard and needs to be doused in a bath of quick-healing ice. When Margot first woke with her memories wiped, there were more than a few medical transfers from Ashtanaban hospitals to further add to the narrative of the attack.

Lleu's hospital room is locked with restricted security clearance. I hold Margot's ring to it and the door opens with a hiss.

Alarik is sitting on a chair next to Lleu's bed, visibly startled when my eyes meet his. He stands quickly, looking to Lleu's sleeping form before approaching me. "Colum, I wasn't expecting you."

"Is there a problem?" I ask.

"Not at all," Alarik says in a hushed tone. "It's just that she needs her rest."

"Her condition is the concern of the medical staff, not yours. Wake her."

Alarik hesitates before approaching her bedside, shaking her shoulder until her eyes flutter open.

Lleu tenses when she sees me, though she should know by now that I'm the least of her worries. She's far from recovered—bags under her eyes, her arms heavy. It makes me want to strangle Knox. I forget Lleu is the target of my death stare until Alarik takes a step closer.

"How is your condition?" I ask Lleu, keeping Alarik in the corner of my eye, wary of his strange protectiveness. Did his failure to keep her safe once really damage his pride so badly? That he's even cautious of me?

Lleu shrugs. "I should have left the bay yesterday but Alarik—" Her eyes widen. "I mean, the medics thought another day may do me good."

"You'll leave within the hour then. You're not any safer in the medic bay than in the prison cells."

Lleu presses her lips together before nodding slowly. Though raven magic is incredibly strong in the moment, it doesn't leave quite the same long-term imprint. If Knox had actually been able to touch Lleu himself, instead of watering down his power through the use of another proditor, her and I may not even be having this conversation now.

"Why the rush for discharge?" Alarik asks.

I shoot a glare at him for speaking out of turn. "Arbitor Monicas is visiting the Imnicus tonight. He's insisting on seeing Margot for dinner, and the only person I trust to get her ready is you, Lleu."

Lleu sits up quickly. "Wait, Margot is on the ship?" She first looks shocked then ecstatic, like that final wave of happiness burnt away the rest of Knox's crows.

"I didn't want to overwhelm you," Alarik says to her, his arms folded.

"She'll need to look like a Columess again, which I'm sure you can manage," I say.

Lleu straightens her shoulders. "I'll do it for my freedom."

"Yes, help me with Margot, and *then* tell me who wrote you that letter, and you'll be free to go."

Lleu frowns.

I continue. "Besides, what I'm asking isn't a request. It's a demand. You have no choice in the matter."

"But what of Knox?" Alarik asks.

"I'm thinking of having him sent to Lavenai a second time, but there would be no way to do that before tonight. You'll need to be vigilant. Communicate with the security center to disable cameras and take the back hallways."

"But his ravens—"

I spin to Alarik. "Stand down, Proditor. One more out-of-turn word and I'll have you sent on your own Laven mission. Got it?"

Alarik nods and takes a few steps back. My crows relay his bounding pulse and increased blood pressure. Why is he so damn concerned about Lleu? For now, I let it go.

"Bring Lleu to Margot's dressing room in an hour and not a second later," I command.

Chapter 26

Margot

Inside my cell, I sit in the corner, hugging my legs. Sometimes I'm not sure if it's Milo or Knox who haunts my thoughts most.

I almost lost control of myself with Milo. I could argue I did go too far, melting into his touch, craving every part of him. What would have happened if I did give in? Would he have spun me into the pillar after Onyx left? Would I have wrapped my legs around his hips while he consumed my mouth? If he hadn't shown his own hesitation, I don't know that I could have stopped myself from grinding against him. Or from letting him peel the clothing from my body.

But, by the gods, reality leaked through. I know who he is and who I am. I'm thankful for that knife that sliced straight through our desires, grounding us both in our purposes.

Purposes that involve taking down the other. Lethally, if possible.

In terms of Knox, Milo didn't seem to notice anything off about me. It took everything in me to hide the post-crow state. He doesn't know that Knox temporarily re-enabled the security on my ring to lure me to him. He doesn't know Knox was in my head, tormenting me with pure crows. My body trembles at the memories of my parent's lifeless faces. Knox didn't go nearly as far as he did when I was tortured, but it's difficult to keep myself in one piece.

Even after a short time of being imprisoned in this small cell, I'm losing track of the hours, and if it weren't for my meals, time would leave me completely. It's not being imprisoned that's the torture. It's how so much time alone in complete silence brings every pain to light. The horrors of my past breath down my throat, its claws wrapped around my neck, squeezing me until I acknowledge its existence.

When the cell doors slide open, I don't move from the familiar shadow that looms over me. I already showed him my hand once, revealing how much power he still has over me. How my body still responds to him. It's a mistake I can't make again.

"You'll join me for dinner tonight." Milo stands a few feet in front of the threshold, but this time he's not alone.

Off to the side, Proditor Dune stands at attention. He doesn't have a black eye, so I can only assume Milo doesn't care in the slightest that his proditor kissed me.

When I say nothing, he speaks again. "Dune will take you to get dressed."

I stay put. "Is it typical for Imnicus prisoners to dine with you?"

Milo's jaw hardens. "It's typical when we both have something we want."

"And what do I want?"

He's quiet for a second before answering. "Lleu."

My body tenses when her name leaves his lips. She still takes up so much of my headspace. Every hour, I ask myself the same questions. *Is she really okay? Has Milo been treating her well?*

Milo continues, "If you do me this favor, I will let you see her."

"And all I have to do is join you for a meal? I don't see how you benefit from this at all."

"Arbitor Monicas is visiting, and he insists on seeing you."

"Monicas?" An arbitor wanting to meet with me after everything that's happened? How would I not slip up? My memories have returned, which will make filtering my words that much harder. With Dimitri and Oliver stuck on Ashtanabo, I'm not sure I'm ready to die until I know they're safe. "I see."

"So you'll do it?"

"I didn't say that. How would you ensure I wouldn't rat you out and get you nymbed? I no longer have anything to lose," I lie.

When I say the word nymbed, Milo's entire body tightens. "Because Lleu is still at my mercy."

My smile falls, and my heart follows. Any warmth left over from our time in the conference room turns to ice, and I fully hate him once again. How could I have let my guard down? Sure, he's treated her better than the usual Imnicus prisoner, including me, but he's still Milo. An Arris. No matter what my heart tries to tell me, he's still Balistar's son.

"Then, in exchange for Lleu's safety, I will do it. But don't expect me to dote on you or for me to be some perfect fake wife. I will sit for dinner, cordially answer Monicas's questions, and then after I expect to be brought back to my cell and away from you."

"That will be arranged."

Dune looks between us. "We should go now. Lleu is waiting, and you know how Monicas likes to be fashionably early."

Milo doesn't say goodbye as he whips around and strides out of the cell.

"This way." Dune motions to the opposite hallway.

I follow the proditor, keeping him in the corner of my eye. There was once a time where Dune was the silent and unsuspecting proditor. The mysterious one who spent little time on the Imnicus. Little did I know he was likely seeking out my rebellion while Milo and the other proditors kept up the false narrative on the ship.

Even compared to the other five, I now know he's the one truly willing to go all the way to complete a mission, literally and figuratively. He stuck his tongue down my throat just to fulfill Milo's wishes, even though he would've preferred not to. Maybe I should be as fearful of him as I am of Knox or Crux. Then again, he strikes me as someone who is obedient to a fault, not someone who is needlessly cruel.

"Should I be surprised the Colum assigned you to escort me?" I ask to break the silence. "You seem to be his favorite."

"I was the one who was surprised. I didn't think he'd involve me in any assignments concerning you ever again after he punched me."

My lips part. "What?"

"When he first slept with you, I assumed it was another method to manipulate the code from you . . . "

I interrupt. "Why, because that's something you'd do?"

Dune ignores my comment. "Maybe I'm dense, but I really didn't think he'd care in the slightest that I kissed you, especially now. He wanted the rebel who jaded him apprehended at any cost, and I brought him those results." He shakes his head in disbelief.

I replay his words over and over again until we're in front of the dressing room, a weight heavy in my stomach.

When the dressing room door opens, and I see Lleu's face, I forget all about Milo and Dune.

She stands from one of the chaise lounge chairs, her eyes welling.

Hot tears run down my face as I run to her and squeeze her so tightly that I'm worried she'll tell me to stop.

"Are you real?" I ask with a shaking voice.

Lleu nods. "Flesh and blood."

It takes all my effort to pull away from her, and I wipe my tears away. I can hear Alarik behind me, exchanging words with Dune until Dune dismisses himself.

"I really thought Knox had—" I can't bring myself to say the words.

"He nearly did," Lleu answers, pulling up her blouse to reveal the wound on her stomach.

I shake my head. "I can't believe you took a bullet for me."

Lleu shrugs. "You would have done the same."

I smile. Because she's right. I would have.

Alarik is in my line of sight, standing there quietly. I step toward him, fiddling my fingers together. "I haven't told Milo anything. And . . . thank you. I wouldn't be standing if it weren't for you. But I'm sorry for what Crux made you do to me."

"Don't ever apologize for that." He places his hands on my shoulders, holding them firmly. "If I had regretted saving your mind, I wouldn't have helped you escape."

I can't help myself. I wrap my arms around his torso, giving him a tight hug that rivals the one I gave Lleu. He risked everything for me. Now, he's risking it all to protect Lleu too. I don't know why he's helping us, or the reason he's so treasonous, but without him I'd be nothing. I owe him everything.

He hugs me back gently. "I just . . . couldn't stomach watching them do that to you."

I break away from the hug. Lleu wipes away a tear from her own cheek.

The three of us are in this together now, all of us with secrets Milo would kill to know.

"Nobody outside of this room knows who wrote the letter." I turn to Alarik. "But I'm worried about Lleu. Milo says he won't hurt her, but he's unpredictable and—

Alarik puts a hand up. "As long as I'm kept as Lleu's guard, Milo won't find out."

"You need to get her to Msanii."

"If I could send her back this second, I would."

Lleu walks near the bathroom. "Not to stop this reunion, but we only have so much time to get you ready, Margot."

I hold Alarik's hands in mine, squeezing his palms tightly. "If you think for a second Milo will change his mind, then defy Arris law and get her the hell off the Imnicus."

"You have my word, Margot." He nods low, almost like the small head-bows he'd give me when I last played the part of the Columess.

I follow Lleu into the bathroom, giving Alarik one last look before disappearing inside with her.

She sets out a robe and toiletries. The last time I showered was at the hotel in Susuku and I bask in every second I'm under the warm water, sweat and grime leaving my skin.

Not long after, I sit at the vanity and listen to Lleu and Alarik's conversation while she applies makeup to my face. Unlike the last time I watched them interact, she's more comfortable around him now. It makes me wonder . . .

"You two have gotten a lot closer." I smile.

Lleu yanks on one of my curls. "What is that supposed to mean?"

Alarik laughs from where he leans onto the back of the couch. "There's no use in hiding it."

She bites down on her bottom lip. "Yes, we're together. Of course Milo has no idea."

Part of me wondered when they would finally let down their walls. I suppose it took being in close quarters for it to happen. For them to unite over a common front.

"Soon enough you'll be the one at a vanity donning a large gown," I say.

Lleu blushes before unease washes over her face. It's only then I realize it was an insensitive thing to say. A world where Lleu and Alarik could get married is one that's nearly impossible. But it's a world in which the rebellion and myself have been working toward for decades.

I change the topic before either of them can muster up an awkward response. "Having you attend to me feels like old times."

Lleu smiles. "The mornings were always my favorite part of the day. Getting into the role and dolling you up felt so . . . real. It was better than the daily meetings Milo had with the proditors and me about our tasks to ensure you were buying it. It always felt so wrong, and the closer we grew, the sicker I felt. But when I would pretend I was truly your lady's maid, it felt like I could breathe again. It wasn't real, but I liked to pretend it was."

Though I hate admitting it, I enjoyed it too. I could always blame it on how I had little growing up and that, subconsciously, I liked living in luxury. But Lleu became more than my maid. Not even Milo could have stopped our friendship from happening.

After she helps me into a blood-red gown, Lleu smooths out the skirts and takes a step back. "I think you're all ready."

Like always, Lleu has turned me into something unrecognizable. Between the dress and hair and makeup, my heart skips a beat from the mirror's reflection. Not from pride or vanity, but because the little girl in me could only dream of being dressed like this. Guilt flickers in my chest, every version of myself warring against one another.

"Lleu, thank you." I give her a death-grip hug. "I don't know when I'll see you again."

She takes a deep breath. "I know. Somehow, my heart tells me this won't be the last time."

Part of me hopes she's right. The other part hopes Alarik sneaks her off the Imnicus, even if it means never seeing her again.

As I say my goodbyes, I give Alarik a look. One that says everything he needs to know: *Get her to Msanii.*

I meet Dune outside the dressing room and he escorts me through the Imnicus and into the docking bay.

When I see Milo waiting for me, I stop breathing for a second. Dune steps off to the side.

He's dressed extravagantly, forgoing his uniform-like attire. Silver hems accent the dark-gray fabric. His rough demeanor breaks the second his eyes lock on me, his lips parting.

It must be strange seeing me dressed like this again. But not as much of a shock as the first time I met him after the memory wipe. A girl he had left half-dead on the torture room floor stubbornly eating the best food money could buy while he looked on. Back when the biggest problems in my life were amnesia and marriage quarrels. In a way, I long for that ignorance again.

Milo quickly turns his head away and stands facing one of the landing pads of the docking bay. "I see Lleu hasn't lost her touch."

I take my place to his left. "Milo Arris, are you complimenting me?"

He frowns. "Not in the slightest. I meant you look believable enough to play the part of my wife."

There's a pang in my chest as my walls shoot up from the ground once again. "Well, I look forward to being back in my prison cell after this charade is over."

"And I can't wait to throw you in it."

Before I can toss another remark at him, a ship becomes visible in the distance and technicians scramble to prepare for landing. I watch as it passes through the translucent oxygen shield.

Even from a foot away, Milo's body heat radiates over to mine. It's enough to bring a skip to my pulse.

Monicas's brass ship lands and yanks me out of my head, the draft breezing along my dress.

As the ship's ramp touches down, I straighten my posture, as does Milo.

Monicas comes into view, eyes crinkled in a smile, his gray hair free of recede. An attendant helps him over the threshold before he barrels down the ramp with giddiness in his posture.

Seeing Monicas like this, with my memories back in focus, brings a sour taste to my tongue. Even more than Milo, the arbitors are the ones who pass many of Lavenai's most stringent laws, and Monicas is the one who rules over them all. But he's so jolly and fatherly, it's hard to accept he's more of a dictator than Milo is—a wolf hiding in sheep's clothing.

"Ah, Colum, always a pleasure! I am most thankful you accepted my request."

Milo forces a smile. "It didn't feel like much of a request."

The arbitor ignores Milo's comment and immediately locks onto me, his eyes softening in concern. He takes my hands in his like a caring father would. "Lady Arris, how are you? I still can't wrap my mind around what happened!"

"I am better now, Monicas, thank you. According to Milo, I was in a state of psychosis for some time. I promise there is nothing to be concerned about anymore."

Monicas peers at my face. "Have you been eating? You're thinner."

I can feel Milo's eyes resting on me, reminding me of Lleu's fate. "I'll admit, my appetite has been a little off since the mission."

He holds my hands tighter. "You must understand, we arbitors worry about you."

"And I am forever grateful."

"Well, know your only job for the rest of your life is to be our beautiful Columess. Promise me, Lady Arris?"

I swallow, sensing Milo's gaze. "Yes, Arbitor."

"I am so glad to hear it!" Monicas moves over to Milo and shakes his hand. "And you better be taking care of her. You hear me?"

Milo's eye twitches. "Of course, Monicas."

"Good." Monicas moves his hands to the sides of Milo's face and gives him a kiss right upon his forehead.

"Monicas!" Milo flinches back and his face pales. He wipes the kiss away like a scorned child would.

I cover my mouth as laughter rushes through me. Milo's frown deepens as Monicas pats Milo's face. Even Dune is suppressing a chuckle.

"Goodness, my boy, loosen up a little!" Monicas slaps Milo's back.

Milo's fists tighten. "Dinner is ready. We shouldn't delay the staff any longer than we already have." As he turns, his cape whips and hits Dune.

Monicas offers me his arm. After I accept it, he leans close and lowers his voice. "Takes after his father but is not quite as charismatic."

My neck stiffens at the mention of Balistar. That horrors I experienced in Knox's proditor trance. The way my parents hung by their necks while he forced me to watch, the gold flecks in his eyes flickering. "The Colum has his days. Though a few drinks may loosen him up."

Monicas pats my shoulder with his free hand. "Ah, that's more like it, my girl. Now you're learning."

Milo strides ahead of us all the way to the north wing, huffing and puffing, probably murmuring death threats under his breath. Dune follows a way behind us.

"I knew I shouldn't have let you go on that mission." Monicas mutters a few curses. "I had a feeling, you know? Something was off."

"Please don't stress. The sacrifice was worth it. Yes, I lost my mind for a while there. But the medics have been phenomenal and

I feel as good as new. The mission went as planned, much to the rebels' dismay."

"Rebels?" Monicas raises an eyebrow.

Oh no. I slipped up. No, this can still be rectified. "That's what they like to call themselves, anyway. They didn't appreciate it much when I called them 'terrorists.' Perhaps if I omitted that word in my altercation with their leader, she wouldn't have sprayed me with that mind-breaking substance."

For a second, it's like I'm truly the Imnicus spy I was coerced to believe I was. The lies roll off my tongue so effortlessly that it's almost scary. My mind wars with the girl who begged Monicas to be sent to Lavenai.

A few heartbeats pass before Monicas's face softens. "Such horrible people. How could anyone have the gall to hurt a beautiful girl like yourself? It's madness."

I bite down on my lower lip and look at the back of Milo's head. "Yes, madness indeed."

"You'll eat well tonight, won't you?"

This time my nod is genuine. In fact, once I sit at the table to eat, it will take everything in me not to be ravenous. After starving on Ashtanabo for multiple days and then barely eating on the Imnicus, I'm always hungry now.

For the rest of the stroll, Monicas gushes about his nieces and nephews, and their accomplishments. One of his nephews just got into a prestigious Ashtanaban university that specializes in galactic war. Another one of his nieces was the top of her primary school class and one day dreams to become an arbitor. I do my best to congratulate him, but every word off my tongue feels coated in poison.

Upon entering the dining room, we head to our seats. Before I can sit far away from Milo, he grabs my wrist, pulls me to the head of the table, and seats me to his right.

I suppress the glare that creeps onto my face.

Milo pushes my wine glass closer to me while Monicas is busy rattling off extra requests to a servant. "Follow Monicas's lead for both our sakes."

I roll my eyes and grab my water glass instead. The last thing I need is to be inebriated during this dinner.

Milo glowers.

For the first few courses, Monicas goes on tangents about Ashtanabo's bustling economy, trade deals, and political talk that go over my head. Still, I memorize every detail he says. Information is a weapon, and I doubt Milo considered that when having me join him for dinner. One day, I could use this information to my advantage, if I ever escape. I stuff more food down my throat.

Milo whispers to me while Monicas is busy chugging a second glass of wine. "You could stand to be a bit more ladylike."

I wipe a few crumbs off the side of my lips. Every course, I've finished my food before the two men, no matter how much I've tried to pace myself. Eating is making me even hungrier.

"And you could stand to feed your prisoners," I bite back in a whisper and then direct my attention at Monicas, raising my voice. "So, how have things on land been? I haven't been caught up on everything."

Monicas swallows his food. "Oh my, where to begin. Well, there are a few bases that we're planning on building in Lavenai, permitting the land we chose stays under favorable conditions. They will be used to house technology to increase our civilian-monitoring efforts."

"How fascinating." My lips curl. If we can destroy the land where they plan to build those bases, they'll have no choice but to delay construction. "Which cities?"

Milo's head shoots in my direction. "Actually, I don't think we should talk about work at the table."

Catching on now, Colum?

"Heavens, you're right. We keep going on and on when we should keep things light." Monicas's face is flushed with inebriation. "So tell me, Colum, where did your marriage ceremony take place? I never got to ask you about it."

Milo's fingers curl against the table and I freeze.

How are you going to answer this one?

"It was . . ." Milo starts. "Just the two of us, as you know. I found a place in Zreath for us to go near the waterfalls. An officiant met us there, and we eloped. There's nothing more to it."

Monicas's face falls into disappointment. "Surely you can tell a better story than that." He looks to me. "Shall we get a woman's perspective?"

All the food in my stomach turns sour. Even when my memories were gone, I never fantasized what my alleged wedding day with Milo was like. I have to think of something.

"Well, Monicas." I'm a spy. I've been trained to spin stories, so why is this lie stumping me? I think back to the love stories Lucinda used to tell me about her and one love. It's those butterflies her storytelling once gave me that guide my next words. "Our fling had been going on for a few weeks at that point. I thought to myself, if two people are truly meant for each other, why wait for the stars to align? But it was him who spoke first by saying, '*My star, my light, you've ruined me past eternity.*'" Lucinda's exact words ring in my ears for that last part.

Arbitor Monicas chokes on his wine. "Our Milo said that? Why, I never knew he was such a poet." His words are slurring more now. "Please continue."

The story is too overdone. I need to tone it down. "I wasn't sure what he meant until he grabbed my hand and hauled me onto a ship. Before I knew it, we were in Zreath surrounded by waterfalls with nothing but nature and an officiant surrounding us. He got down on one knee, placed a ring on my finger, and we were wed the same hour."

It doesn't even sound like us. But, to my surprise, tears stream down Monicas's face while he dabs them away with his napkin. "That was beautiful, Lady Arris. A story written by the gods."

The muscles of Milo's neck tighten. Maybe because he knows how far it is from the truth. Or because, if Monicas hadn't drank, he wouldn't be asking such invasive questions or sobbing at a made-up love story.

"Though . . ." Monicas starts and I stiffen. "Aren't the waterfalls crowded with travelers? How did you manage to find a section without citizens around, Colum? And where did you land your ship?"

Milo doesn't move. He should know his own planet like the back of his hand. How could he forget such an important detail? Unless he's always been too busy to visit that area of Zreath for himself.

Monicas places his finger on his chin, considering something. "It just doesn't make sense."

Milo clears his throat. "To be completely honest, there are details we aren't sharing about our wedding because they wouldn't be . . . appropriate . . . to share at the table." Before I can process what's happening, Milo leans over and kisses me on the cheek.

My chest contracts. It's just a peck, but it feels like a lifetime. *What is he doing?*

"Oh!" Monicas covers his mouth coyly. "Say no more, Colum."

As Milo pulls away, I catch his dark gaze before he holds my chin and presses another soft kiss to my forehead. He pulls back and his eyes bore into my soul, pulling the truth of my feelings out better than torture could. My palms grow clammy and my pulse is on the brink of stopping all together.

It isn't until he sits back in his chair and takes a drink that I can breathe again.

I have to consider his actions like a spy would. Public displays of affection and intimate stories make people uncomfortable. It was the perfect way to ward off Monicas's questioning. They were just pecks. In some cultures, kissing isn't even considered romantic.

Then why is it that, of all things, this shed light on how . . . how . . .

How much I truly miss him? That I wasn't just the center of his carnal lust but also his tender affections? This threatens to break me. My heart splits in two. My ears ring. No, I can't feel this for him. *Feelings are how you get killed.*

My eyes are drawn to the steak knife next to my plate. How razor-sharp the blade is. An idea sparks.

Monicas laughs and places a palm on his belly. "My, I never took you for the romantic type, Colum." Monicas raises his glass. "Shall we toast? To your beautiful marriage?"

"There's no need," Milo says.

"Lighten up, Colum! It's all in good fun. What is it your father used to say? Oh, yes, I believe it was, '*Why let the wine go to waste?*'" He taps his fork against his glass.

Milo holds his drink tightly."If it will get you to stop that racket."

I follow suit, raising my glass for the toast. I'll have to time my plan perfectly for it to go unnoticed.

Arbitor Monicas raises his glass. "To Milo and Margot, the lovesick crows that made me believe in love again. To Arris Reign," Monicas says.

"To Arris Reign," Milo grumbles back.

While both men's heads are tipped back, and servants are caught up in their tasks, I reach for the knife while I drink and pull it discreetly off the table and into my lap. Quickly, I slip it into the pocket sewn into my dress.

After we finish dessert, Monicas insists on strolling the north wing halls with us. The man surely knows how to overstay his welcome. Milo doesn't even pretend to be interested as Monicas goes on and on about planetside life.

The two have a strange dynamic. Monicas somehow reveres Milo while also treating him like a naïve boy. On the flip side, he also seems more than used to the Colum's moods. Immune, even. It's refreshing.

Milo intentionally manipulates our path for us to walk by his bedroom. Once we're in front of the door, he stops.

Monicas looks to Milo and then to the door. I mentally sigh in relief as the arbitor finally takes the hint.

Monicas chuckles. "Ah, yes, enough of my rambling. It's late, and I know you and your bride are ready to get some rest."

Milo forces a smile onto his face. "Dune will escort you back to the docking bay. I hope for safe travels on your way back to Heidl."

"Thank you, Colum. And Lady Arris, best of luck to you. I will be checking in often that you're well."

"I appreciate that, Monicas." I smile, praying to the gods I won't ever have to do this again.

Now leave. *Leave so I can be as far away from Milo as humanly possible.*

When the bedroom door slides open, Milo grabs my arm and pulls me into the room with him.

"Have a good night, Monicas," Milo says.

"Don't have too much fun!" Monicas shouts as the electronic doors slide shut.

Chapter 27

Milo

As the doors shut behind us, both of our postures lose their tone. I rub my temples while Margot audibly signs and places her hands on her hips.

She studies in the room, taking in the lounge area and the window she used to stargaze through. It isn't until now I realize how much of this space she claimed.

When her focus lands on the bed, she frowns. "This wasn't part of the deal. Take me back to the cells."

I pull off my cape and drape it on the bed. "I can't exactly drag my wife to the prison cells in front of an arbitor, and Monicas has a habit of sticking around and getting sidetracked. I have no doubt Dune will spend the next hour trying to get him off the Imnicus."

Margot scoffs. "So you expect me to spend an hour alone with you?"

I frown. "I don't want this any more than you do. But what choice do we have?"

"Gods, is there any point in fighting you?" Margot rolls her eyes and pulls out her bobby pins. "You're stubborn. Once you put your mind to something, you're impossible to convince otherwise."

"I'm not the only one who's stubborn, you know." My breath softens as her curls fall one by one, tumbling over her shoulders.

She's so . . . so . . . infuriating, and it takes everything in me to tear my gaze from her glowing skin.

The last time she was in my room, our bodies were tangled together, hate and infatuation coursing through both our bloodstreams. She seduced me while simultaneously betraying me.

My arousal bulges and I turn quickly, pretending to look at the window.

Gods, I need to stay as far away from her as possible for the next hour. She's nobody to me. Nobody. If I let myself feel an inkling of desire, I'll dissolve before her. I must contain it and morph it into anger if I have to.

Margot's heels click along the tiled floors as she paces the area between me and the bed. "I don't think it's wise for us to be alone together."

"Why? The servants don't know any better." I focus on a star in the distance, ignoring the blood coursing under my pants.

"You *know* why."

I press my lips together, my heart pounding. I remember the way I sucked on her neck as we hid from Onyx. How I almost took her on my dining room table after Dune apprehended her. She's right.

Anytime we're alone together is dangerous and we can't deny it, though I know both of us refuse to say the actual words out loud.

"How about this: Tell me who sent you the letter and I'll let you and Lleu go tonight. I'll even drop you off in Merth instead of imprisoning you on Ashtanabo. It would beat going back to your cell or being stuck in this room with me."

"That will never happen," she says. "And what makes you think I trust you enough to hold your end of the bargain?"

"Sooner or later, you'll have to speak. You may not value your own life, but I know you value Lleu's."

I hear Margot run at me and I quickly spin.

With her eyes fierce, Margot presses one of my dinner knives against my skin. One movement of her wrist and I'll be finished.

"Do it," I say, my pulse thumping violently but not from fear. Her body is so close now, inches from touching mine. My gaze passes over her cleavage and down to her waist. Gods, this is an impossible game filled with lethal temptations.

I grab her wrist. Her bottom lip trembles as I move the blade's tip to the hollow of my throat.

"You can't do it, can you?" I ask.

"I can and I will!" Her eyebrows furrow.

"Then what's stopping you?"

"It's just . . . " She bites down on her tongue. "Even if I kill you, it won't matter. I'd have to kill all the arbitors and who knows how many politicians and commanders. In the end, nothing will change."

I don't give her a second to regroup or re-plan. With the flick of my hand, I disarm her quickly, turning the blade, pressing it against her neck.

Margot's eyes widen. She swallows against the blade. "Damn you."

"Margot, I won't go easy on you anymore. Tell me who wrote you the letter."

"Never. I won't let you hold Lleu over me."

"It's not personal. It's politics."

"And everything in politics is personal," Margot bites.

"That's the difference between you and me. You make it personal."

Margot tries to pull back. I snake my hand around her waist, pulling her flush to my chest.

Big mistake. She's so warm and all I can imagine is being on my knees before her, tossing her leg over my shoulder, and dragging my tongue between her thighs.

Margot is a good fighter. Even in the large dress, I'm sure she could push me away.

But she doesn't. Instead, she turns her head.

I grab her chin and force her gaze. Her warm skin burns into my hand. It takes everything in me to keep my face neutral. She can't know I'm breaking.

Margot swings at the side of my head. I curse, quickly catching her forearm before it lands. I pulse my powers through her, weakening her crows.

Her eyes widen. "Milo—"

I haul her back toward the bed and shove her onto the mattress. She yelps as I crawl up her body.

Margot kicks at me and I catch her ankles, throwing them out of the way and pinning her arms down. Though it's no easy feat. Even with all her crows gone, her strength is significant.

As I contain her, something primal overtakes me. It's impossible to ignore the feeling of her clothed breasts against my chest and that sweet, perfumed scent. Her skirts have ridden up to her hips, her smooth thighs on display.

Before all self control leaves me, I move her wrists above her head, ignoring the way her back arches under me.

"You look troubled, Milo," Margot says with a thousand emotions behind her voice. Even through her confidence, my crows relay the heat growing between her legs.

I have to get back on topic and her off her back before I explode. But her body against mine feels like a vice that I'm incapable of removing. "Was it a man or a woman who helped you?"

"The letter didn't say," she says breathlessly.

"Were they a servant?" I should adjust my body to get off of her but am drawn closer instead, my hardened length pressing into her heat. Sweat forms along the column of my neck.

"Maybe?" Margot quivers.

My hands are slicker against her wrists, our voices growing softer by the moment. How I wish she'd break free and punch some sense into me.

I release one of her wrists, eagerly awaiting her fist, but it never comes. *Margot, hit me, for both our sakes. I don't know if I can stop myself if this goes on a second longer.*

She makes no moves to fight me.

I hold her wrists again, squeezing them tightly, more so to stop my own thoughts. But it doesn't stop my hips from unconsciously rolling once then twice. *Gods, this is a mistake. Stop me, Margot. Just one word is all it will take. Don't let us do this.* "A soldier?"

Margot closes her eyes, and it takes her seven inhales before she finally answers me. "Possibly." Her clothed pelvis grinds in tandem with mine.

"Are you lying?" I can't stop rocking into her, and I'm barely concealing the low groans forming in the lower parts of my throats.

"Of course." Margot bites down on her bottom lip as she moves in sync with me. With her eyes still closed, I lean forward until our faces are inches apart. And when she does open them, her gaze flickers slightly. She moves her head to the side, elongating the side of her neck.

I lean closer into her. When my lips gently press against her pulse point, she sucks in a breath. It's a sound so sweet that it shoots more heat between both our legs where we instinctively press together.

"Whoever they are, I hope they do what I could not," Margot says breathlessly. "That they will end the Arris Reign."

If we don't stop what we're doing, she'll be the reason it continues.

I let go of her wrists and undo the fastens of her dress, pulling the neckline down. My length strains against my zipper at the sight of her exposed chest. It's enough for me to finish right then and there, but I hold back.

Her face softens when I cup one of her warm breasts, wiping the over-confident look off my face.

"You'll be the end of me," I say.

I kiss her. It isn't tender. It isn't gentle. It's furious. I grow harder, plunging my tongue into her mouth, capturing hers in a tangle. She moans, wrapping her arms around my neck.

I grip the back of her hair, pulling on it slightly as our mouths devour one another. If kisses could kill, it would be this one.

I won't forget who I am, even if it means claiming her while I do my duty. I break away from the kiss, panting, before undoing my clothing and throwing the top layers behind me in a pile.

She reaches for her skirts, pulling the dress over her head. When it's up past her chest, I grip the fabric and tear the dress up and away, discarding it on the floor before sliding her panties down her legs.

"Margot, I won't spare you. Tell me who wrote you the letter."

"Never."

I snake down her body, kissing across her inner thigh, dragging my tongue along the apex. "Why do you have to be so difficult?" I move my mouth between her legs, my tongue meeting her heat.

"I-I will never submit to—" She gasps, gripping the comforter.

I can't help but smile against her. I suck and nip, moving my own hips against the bed just for some friction. I need to be inside her.

I don't taste her gently like I would have once upon a time. I consume her, gripping her hips while her bottom half can hardly stay pinned on the bed.

Before she can finish, I break away. Panic flashes across her face. She thinks I'm going to just leave her like this? Well, if I were crueler, then maybe I would.

I slip off my bottoms, both of us bare for each other. My arousal pulses for her, begging for a release that only this woman who threatens my reign can bring.

I wrap my arm around her waist, pulling her onto my lap, taking a breast into my mouth. She tastes indescribable.

"One more chance, Margot," I say between licks.

"Shut up," she moans. Her fingers tangle in my hair.

I grab my length, positioning it under her. She fits herself around me and sinks down fully. I groan low before my lips meet hers again.

We forget who we are and the things we've done to one another. The creeds we've committed ourselves to. We forgo every alliance and every moral. For just right now, only our hands exist, which can't seem to touch enough of one another.

As my tongue caresses hers and her fingers grip my hair, and even as I move up inside her, I still want her closer. No matter how much I kiss her, no matter how deep I go, it's not enough. I want to consume her fully.

Margot cries out and I hold back my own release. I want her again. And again. And again. Even if it means starving myself.

I place her on her back. My hand wraps gently around her throat as I help her chase a second release. And then her fingers grip the headboard as I claim a third from her. I'd suppress my own pleasure for eternity if it meant seeing her break like this again and again.

It's the fourth time, when I have her on her back again that I know I've exhausted her. Her kisses become gentler and her eyes grow tired. The fourth time, lust fades into something else. My forehead rests against hers and my desire to hold her as strong as it is to bed her.

That's when I finally break.

The heat rushes through me and I spill out, groaning into her mouth. The pleasure doesn't stop. My teeth find her shoulder, biting down to contain the sounds that would wake every star in the galaxy.

Finally, the rush fades. I slowly slip out of her and pull her by the waist into my chest. I can feel her heartbeat and I'm sure she can feel mine too.

Gods, I feel like I used to around her—protective and constantly craving. Wondering how I was ever cruel enough to do what I did to her. Monicas's words come back to haunt me. How anyone could have the vitriol to hurt someone like her.

Our orgasms fade and reality hits like bolts of lightning. Holding her like this feels more forbidden than bedding her.

Margot pulls away from me, lying on her back and intentionally leaving a few inches between us. She stares at the ceiling like she can see the galaxy through it.

I can't let her go. Not yet. I find her hand, running my pinky finger along the side. She doesn't pull away, even as she covers her mouth with her other hand. Her gaze darts between the designs engraved in the ceiling.

As a tear runs down her face, my heart hardens and I push down the ache as far as I could go. The ache that tells me she can never be mine. That our duties will always come before each other.

Margot takes my hand, lacing her fingers through mine and squeezing tightly. She lets a few more tears fall before she rises and sits on the edge of the bed.

I don't move from where I lie as I listen to her find her dinner clothes and get dressed. And I don't stop her as she pages the guard to fetch the proditors. Even when Dune comes to get her, I do little more than cover myself with the comforter as he exchanges a few words with Margot at the threshold and takes her back to the prison.

And once she's gone, I find myself the same man I've always been.

A man who's completely alone.

Chapter 28

Milo

Two whole days pass and I haven't seen Margot once. Everything I do, from signing pilots' documents to meeting with Commander Aisil, feels completely meaningless. My heart hardened a second too late. Her claws were already embedded and now she'll be impossible to dislodge. If I could get her out of my head for a single second, I would.

I scan through the ledgers in my rarely-used office, forcing myself to focus.

How is she holding up in the prison cell? Has she had enough to eat? She's not growing ill, is she?

The door opens and I set the tablet down, rubbing my temples. I don't acknowledge the new presence until he clears his throat.

I furrow my brows as Knox leans as arrogantly as ever on my desk. My longing for Margot turns into fury toward Knox, both emotions the same degree of intensity. There's nothing I want more than to wring his neck. If it weren't for the desk separating us, I may have already lunged at him. The few punches I got in weren't close to enough.

Instead, I do my best to keep my composure as I set down the ledger. "I'll save you some time. Stop interfering with my plans and erase Lleu and Margot from your mind."

Knox tilts his head with a slight smile. He holds his mask in one of his gloved hands. "Not even a 'hello'? I've been planetside on a mission you assigned, and you don't even bother to ask how it went? Why, I'm hurt."

"I'm considering reassigning you off the Imnicus for good."

His playful demeanor sharpens, and his brows furrow. "For what? Following Arris law, unlike the Colum himself?"

"You've been nothing but insubordinate. Most people would be corporally punished for striking the Colum."

"If I remember correctly, you struck first, Milo."

My muscles tense at the use of my first name. It's not as if he doesn't use it often, but this time feels different. Demeaning. "Have you ever thought about the consequences of following through on your threats? If you have Monicas nymb me, it will affect both of us. He may want to make more drastic changes on the Imnicus, down to which proditors are stationed here. His favor for you is minimal. A posting in a remote prison would be your fate. Is that really what you want?" I ask.

Knox's face hardens. "You have no idea what I want."

"You want pain. You want suffering. But you fail to see the consequence of your actions because of . . . because of me." I go numb. For my entire life, all I've done is protect my cousin from everyone except himself. I've used the guise of his sick crows to pity him and to let him off the hook. For what? To let him murder people? To let him torture people who were never prisoners?

I didn't want to see him get nymbed or worse—executed. It's very rare a proditor is given capital punishment, but in his case, he would be at the front of the line for it. With him being my only living relative, I didn't want anyone to hurt him or to take him from me.

But at what cost? The cost of being nymbed myself for hiding his crimes? The cost of letting him hurt the girl I'm in—that I'm fond of?

I shake my head. "This can't happen anymore, Knox."

"What can't?"

"Your crows. I can't protect you anymore."

Knox stays silent for a second while he grips his mask harder in his hand. "Meaning?"

"When you hurt or kill people and I turn a blind eye, I may as well be responsible. You want to tell Monicas of my insubordination? Fine. But how will you obey your crows without my pardons? How will you ensure I don't tell Monicas what you've been doing?"

His expression swirls, like he never expected this coming. Like he thought, just because he is older, he has more control than me. But I'm a man as much as he is.

"You really think you can keep her from me?" Knox asks softly.

I slam my hands on the table and shoot to my feet, keeping my hardened gaze locked on him. "I don't care who or what she is, Knox. She's mine to touch. Mine to imprison. And mine to conquer. Whatever I once promised you, consider it null. I'll never hand her over to you as long as I live."

His eyes flash. "Is that so?"

My voice grows lower, yet louder, mustering the same authoritarian gloss my father once used. "The same goes for Lleu and the rest of the servants. You will not lay a finger on any of them, so help me gods, or I will personally see you ejected out of an airlock. Do I make myself clear?"

Knox nods once then twice. "I understand completely, Colum." He replaces his mask and heads to the door. "I swear to never touch Margot again, as long as you are the Colum."

I keep my sights pinned on him and my heart in my throat. With Knox, the less he says, the more that's going on in his head.

And nobody wants to know what's in Knox's head.

Chapter 29

Margot

I sit on the edge of my bed in prison clothes, reveling in what I did—what *we* did—even though it's been days now.

I slept with Milo Arris . . . willingly . . . again. But this time, I wasn't trying to escape. This time I had a choice, and I let him have me completely without so much as a resistant thought. The second he touched me, a fire lit beneath me and only he could put it out.

Not only that, but I cried in front of him. Showed him a weakness he didn't deserve to see. I had the dagger to his throat; I could have ended his immediate family line then and there. Not only did I hesitate, I let myself be disarmed and I barely broke a sweat because I knew he wouldn't kill me either.

He's driving me insane, which only means one thing—I need to try even harder to escape.

When Dune walked me back to the room, he wasn't thorough while patting my clothing and hair down, and I suspect it's because he saw the evidence of what transpired—Milo only covered by the comforter, my hair and outfit in complete disarray. He seemed uncomfortable touching my body knowing what Milo just did to it.

Because of that, he missed a pin. I grab it from under my pillow and move to the cell door, poking it inside the crevices, trying to find any sign of weakness.

"Come on," I mutter. "Unlatch."

If it weren't for the injections I started getting from Lucinda when I first returned from the Imnicus, I would curse at myself for being so uncareful with him in bed. It's a miracle I'm not already swollen with an Arris heir from the last time I was here.

How ironic would that be? To be the reason Balistar's reign was extended even further. I shudder at the thought.

Milo will never give up his father's dream. It's why he let me pull away from him. It's why he said nothing as he watched my tears drip onto his comforter.

The only hope I have is that I've not heard of any news involving Dimitri, Oliver, or any of the temple points. Maybe they gave up and found a way off Ashtanabo. Maybe Anali decided traveling with them was too risky. At this point, as long as they're alive, I don't care.

When the door doesn't budge, I throw the pin across the room and fall back onto the cot.

The cell door whips open, and my heart leaps slightly. I should be ashamed of myself for hoping Milo would be standing on the other side.

Instead, I shrink away at the borderline-murderous eyes.

"It seems the Colum has granted you recreation access under my watchful eye," Crux says, throwing a stack of training clothes in my direction.

I barely catch the clothes in time. Though stretching my legs and getting out of this cramped cell sounds wonderful, I would rather wither away than go anywhere with Crux. "I don't need it."

Crux narrows his eyes. "This isn't optional."

"I'm not going with you."

"Too bad. I have orders, and you're coming even if I have to drag you by your hair like the rat you are."

I bite down on the inside of my cheek until it draws blood. "I don't see why Milo would want me to train."

"Maybe to keep you strong and conscious if he ever wants to use *real* interrogation tactics against you."

My heart pangs at his words. I know Milo would never do that to me again, but I also wouldn't put it past him to have a change of heart, especially after the way I left him yesterday. Maybe he realized I have too much power against him and he needs to remove the head from the snake.

When I don't move, Crux stomps closer and grabs my upper arm, yanking me to my feet.

If I had a death wish, I would slap him.

He pushes me, and my back rams into the wall. "Put the damn clothes on."

"Fine, but get out!"

Crux surprisingly obeys and steps out of the room while I slip into the training clothes.

Once I'm ready, he hauls me out of the cell and out of the prison ward, unhanding me before any servants see his rough treatment. He side-eyes me the entire way to the recreation room, as if being in my presence infuriates him.

Inside the room, I go straight to one of the treadmills. There are mirrors so I can keep him in my line of sight while I jog. If anything, this will help me stay in shape for when I can eventually escape. But I don't understand Milo's logic. Has his heart softened and he can't bear the thought of my muscles atrophying in a small cell? Or is what Crux said true about interrogation? That Milo will veer back to his old tactics to get me to talk?

I don't know much about Crux, besides from what I learned that night when he and Onyx drank with Lleu and me—he was once a Vicar and doesn't like to talk about his past, which mostly involved being beaten relentlessly in the Vicar temple. Truth be told, Vicar culture is still very foreign to me, even with my memories back. My whole life, I've been taught about the vileness of the proditors without knowing much about their religious counterparts. If they had the audacity to beat a child, maybe they aren't quite as innocent as history paints them.

Ten minutes later, when I study my sweaty reflection, I notice that Crux's eyes are still on mine from where he sits on a weight bench. His disguise is off, his angular face stricken with disdain.

This time, I can't stay silent. "Problem?"

Crux folds his arm. "No problem. I'm just wondering why the Colum ever found you desirable."

My stomach tightens. I could say something similar to him about any woman who has been blind enough to bed him. No amount of beauty can hide how horrible Crux truly is.

"That's behind him now," I say, also for my own benefit. If word got out about what Milo and I did last night, it could harm us both. "He used my emotions against me, as did all of you."

Crux smirks and stands. "It doesn't take a scientist to deduce that he's still fucking you."

I miss a breath. How could he know that? Did Dune tell him? I turn the speed on the treadmill up, as if jogging faster will help me escape this conversation. Why can't he just stay quiet? Why taunt me?

Crux walks toward me and I watch him carefully through the mirror, keeping my hand on the treadmill controls. My pulse bounds, and I'm not sure if it's from jogging anymore.

Something isn't right. His eyes call for blood.

I turn the treadmill off and jump off it with a wide stance as Crux approaches arms reach.

"Stay away from me." I raise my fists.

Crux's eyes darken. His communicator beeps and he pulls it out, checking it once before smiling and stuffing it back in his pocket.

My heart pounds. "Why am I really here?"

He lets out a breathy laugh before taking quick steps forward and grabbing my forearm, and I thank the gods he's still wearing his gloves.

"It's time for things to change around the Imnicus," Crux says.

The Nexus immediately kicks in, strength filling my muscles. I twist out of his grasp and jump away.

"Milo didn't send you, did he?" I walk backward between exercise equipment, too cautious to turn my back to him.

"It would be in your best interest if you stood down."

"And let you hurt me? Never."

Crux's eyes focus on my scarred arms. "But haven't I already hurt you?"

I have to get out of here, prisoner or not be damned. He's going to do something horrible. Maybe something worse than when I was being interrogated.

I turn on my heels and sprint down the rows of equipment. It only takes a second before he's mere steps behind me.

There's only one exit, and I'll have to slow him down if I want to make it out of here in one piece. If it weren't for my sharp turns between equipment, he'd already have me.

I whip around a weightlifting machine, grabbing chains hung over the side and yanking them off. I stop running and spin to face him, catching him off guard. Crux stops briefly before he charges at me, taking the bait. I duck under his arms and swing the chain around his ankles. With all my might, I tug on the chains and he falls hard on his back.

He reaches out and grabs my ankle, tripping me to the floor with him. I grunt, losing my grip on the chains.

Crux climbs over me, placing his body weight on mine to subdue me beneath him. I yelp as he presses his wrist bone into my sternum. Crux grabs a dagger from his boot. The same dagger he forced Alarik to carve me with. He captures one of my hands, placing his boot on my palm to keep my inner arm immobile.

My fear overrides my strength as the horrific memories pulse to the surface. "No."

Crux brings the blade to my forearm. "Yes."

This can't happen. I won't let it. I forcefully toss out the gut-clenching memories—the cuts, the alcohol, Alarik's heartbroken face.

The Nexus ignites, and my face hardens.

I scream, the Nexus flowing through me, my body strength and flexibility amplifying. I whip my legs around his torso and throw him off me.

He lands hard on his side. I don't give him a second to process his next move as I grab the chain off the ground and lunge for him, wrapping it around his neck and pulling it tightly.

Crux's eyes bulge as he claws at the chain, trying to fit his fingers underneath it without any luck.

All I can think about is what he did to me and the demons I live with because of him. He deserves to know what it's like to not know if today is his last.

The crows caw within my mind, their wings brushing the back of my neck as their whispering thoughts become my own. Thoughts I normally resist.

Finish him, Margot. This is your chance. We will reward you. End his life. There is no fear. No pain. Only power. Only euphoria.

Against my will, my body buzzes and my muscles fill with ecstasy.

Is this what Knox feels? The feeling of taking a thousand shots with no consequences? The feeling of the most breathtaking dreams exploding into tangible life?

I press my lips together as blood leaves Crux's face. As terror and fear unite with him.

Don't do this, Margot. It's Lucinda's voice begging me before switching to Dimitri's.

When Crux goes blue, the ecstasy turns into an addicting and throbbing ache. The buzzing fades, and I crave more. At the end of this is an ocean of pleasure, so all I have to do is not let go.

I fear it. Fear the depths of that ocean, knowing I would drown in it. Knox would crave it. He would not hesitate, but I stand at the cliff knowing there will be no going back. I'm no murderer, no sadist. I do not get off on the pain of others.

But I won't stop, no matter how much I tell myself otherwise. I can't make myself. Oh gods, I'm going to kill him.

The blood in my body rushes into my lower belly, the addicting ache amplifying. It slams my mind back into reality. I want to sob. I want to vomit.

I quickly unhand the chains like I just touched a stove, falling backward and barely catching myself.

Crux gasps for air, resting his shoulder against one of the machines. He can barely move or even speak as he holds his neck, his brunette curls flattened.

To even obey the crows for a few seconds . . .

Tears well up in my eyes.

It doesn't matter that Crux deserves it. It doesn't matter that it was self-defense.

I stand and stumble back until something stops me and I can't move any further. I sob, my muscles screaming at me to run and my mind telling me to collapse.

Crux just watches me. For once, he doesn't give me that terrible look. The one that amplifies how weak I feel. He stays quiet as he regains his breath while I cry, shame riddling my body.

"It felt good, didn't it?"

My entire body tenses as a bare finger runs along the side of my neck. My back is suddenly aware of his body heat. His chest that's been pressed against my back for a while now.

The crows disappear all at once.

I'm mortal again. Vulnerable.

But without the crows' strength protecting me, my cries turn into sobs. I sink to my knees, tears staining my palms. I feel his hand on my shoulder briefly.

Knox shuffles around me and I lift my head in time to see him crouch in front of me. Crux's stays still, his breaths losing their wheeze.

"You win." My face is hot and sticky from the tears. "Take them back. Please, I don't want them anymore. I don't care if I lose every fight from now until the end of my life. Just do it!"

He holds my chin with his fingertips, stroking my jaw with his thumb. "That comes with a price." His expression is delicate and soft, almost caring. He moves his mouth closer to me. I try to back up, but it only makes him hold my face tighter.

"Don't," I whisper.

He smiles and laughs, quickly dropping his hold. "You think I have any interest in your body?" But he nears me again, this time his nose grazing against my jaw. "Though I am quite good at it."

I gather my wits and place my hands on his chest, shoving him away.

Knox's expression turns to poison. "If I had the power to take this from you, I would have forced it from you by now. You stole more from me than I ever thought possible. I'm a selfish man. I don't share."

"It was you who infected me with this in the first place!" I say sharply.

"Crow transfers are a fickle thing. Unpredictable at best. Impossible at worst. My uncle only did them when they benefited him most. Do you remember the Laven drug wars?"

Lucinda told me all about them, as her former organization dealt heavily with pills and tinctures that brought temporary power to the veins of mere humans. But none of it was permanent the way my crows are.

The doors to the recreation room open again.

Onyx circles around the equipment and tenses as he takes in the three of us—Crux's blue skin, Knox's devious face, and the tears running down my cheeks.

"What is this, Knox?" Onyx holds onto the end of a racked barbell.

"It's about time you showed up." Knox folds his arms.

"The Colum almost killed you the last time you defied him. Are you out of your mind?"

It's only then that reality snaps into me like a band. Something about Crux having me exercise didn't feel right, then Knox showing up at the inopportune time, and now Onyx having been told to meet him here . . .

I jump to my feet, but Knox quickly catches my waist and pulls me into him.

"Ah, the Little Fennec senses something is off." Knox laughs.

I struggle against him but he holds me even tighter. I should have known something was amiss the second Crux entered my cell.

Knox could have used Crux's clearance to ambush me in my cell, but he didn't, meaning he wanted me to burn with desire at the caw of his crows. He wanted me to fall into the temptation he bears every day.

Crux finally manages to speak, his face now gray. "It's what she gets."

Onyx is still stiff. "Knox, I don't understand—"

"You're as like-minded as me and Crux. Our Colum has strayed too far off the path. He's gone soft. As Balistar's protégé, there is no way I can let this go on either further. Onyx, today marks the beginning of my siege."

Onyx's eyes widen. "And you'll use her as leverage?"

"Precisely."

My hair stands on end. Knox is planning on betraying Milo, and somehow he's going to use me to do it. "Just because Crux follows you, doesn't mean the rest of them will. The entire Imnicus is loyal to Milo!" I can't believe the words coming out of my mouth. I'm actually defending Milo's reign for once in my life. But whatever Knox has planned may be even sicker than Balistar.

Knox moves his thumb over my abdomen. "Oh, I don't doubt they'll try. But I have abilities nobody will see coming, Little Fennec. Abilities no other proditors have because I am obedient to my crows."

"You can't go along with this, Onyx," I say. "You're loyal to Milo, aren't you?"

His eyes sink, his forearm tightening. "It's . . . complicated. My father—"

"Would have chosen whichever side aligned with Balistar's ideals," Crux interrupts. "And, as it is, Milo is straying from his father's footsteps where Knox wants to reestablish them. Besides, Onyx is loyal to whichever side holds the most pleasure. The most comfort. And where I go, he goes."

Onyx turns his head away and my eyes well up. I should have suspected Onyx would be pragmatic.

I have to fight them or at least get away long enough to warn Milo.

"So what do you say, Onyx? Will you join me and Crux?" Knox asks.

Onyx closes his eyes for a second, and I can hear him muttering something under his mask. "As if there is ever any choice with you two."

A sudden pain slams into my skull. I fall over, gripping the back of my head where the blow landed. My temples pound as I teeter the edge of unconsciousness, but there's enough of me awake to keep going. My head slumps as I press myself up to my hands and knees, crawling away.

Knox doesn't even try to stop me as I listen to Onyx's endless follow-up questions. Their words gunk up my ear like mud, increasingly difficult to decipher.

"You can't. Raven magic is forbidden. We have our creed to protect," Onyx says harshly.

"A creed that has a habit of changing overtime. It was once the creed of a Vicar to serve the gods, and it is the creed of a proditor to serve ourselves."

Their voices become more muffled, my vision flickering from the blow. I make it halfway across the room before a boot presses into my spine and slams me to the floor with enough force to knock the wind out of me.

One set of hands forces me to my feet while another set grips my hair.

Knox tucks a few of my curls behind my ear. "In time, Margot, I'll show you what a Colum should be like. Whereas Milo was decreed to be a ruler, I was molded to be one."

Those words are the last I hear as my mind caves in, hiding itself behind walls as thick as iron. I know what lies at the end of this. I barely feel the blows as they rain down upon me. I ride upon the fear like an ocean wave, only hoping they accidentally kill me before Knox truly has his fun.

Chapter 30

Milo

I stroll through the command center while officers work tirelessly at their stations, monitoring events on Lavenai and Ashtanabo. The day has been slow and, besides my nagging thoughts, relatively calm.

Private preparations for transferring Margot off the Imnicus and into a VIP prison are already underway. After she's gone, I'll tell the arbitors we simply grew apart. Because as long as she's here, she can control me. And the more time that passes, the less I'm able to protect her from the law.

An officer stands at his desk. "Colum, I have a report. May I speak?"

"You may."

"A guard may have eyes on the fugitives you spoke of."

It takes me a minute to process his meaning. "Are you telling me they may have found the rebels and Matsumoto?"

"Precisely. They're tailing the three quietly to be certain before ambushing them. Would you like to see the footage to confirm their identities?"

I nod and walk behind his desk. He sits and pulls up the footage of a girl and two guys walking through a city in the region of Zreath.

Immediately, I recognize Margot's cousin, Dimitri. I recall the fury in his face at the sight of me. How he wanted nothing more than to kill me once he realized the true nature of my relationship with Margot.

Now, I have the opportunity to kill him. With a single word, I could have him ten feet under within a few minutes.

I imagine a world in which I walk into Margot's cell after days of not talking. A world in which I break the news that her only living relative died at my command. The way she'd look at me like I'm a monster, the way . . .

The way my father was.

"Don't apprehend them," I tell the officer.

"Pardon?"

"We need more time to confirm their identities before we act."

The officer's lips part and he blinks rapidly. "With all due respect, Colum, we know these are the rebels and Miss Matsumoto. We just have to get your approval before—"

"How did you just refer to me?"

His eyes widen. "I said 'Colum.'"

"Exactly. That's my title. I say that they are not authorized for arrest so nobody will lay a finger on them. Understood?"

I see the words form on the tip of his tongue before he pulls them back. My crows relay his rapidly increasing blood pressure from the frustration.

"Yes, Colum. We will not make any moves against them."

"Good." As I turn around, Commander Aisil stands there, waiting for me.

"Colum, a word?"

I glower. "What now, Aisil?"

"It's Arbitor Monicas again."

A deep frown crawls across my face. He's not due to nag me for at least another few months. "If it's dinner he wants again, tell him I'm away on business."

"You don't understand—he's already here. Along with all the other arbitors and their wives."

My breath catches. "Here? Now?"

"They're waiting in a conference room in the west wing."

"Why was I not informed?"

"It was unexpected for us all. They landed and gave no warning they were coming. We barely had enough time to prepare a landing platform. Whatever they want must be serious."

I shoot Aisil a glare.

He stumbles over his next words. "Or not! It could be . . . a well-intentioned surprise—"

"Enough. Oversee my duties while I'm away." Hopefully I can get them out of here as quickly as they arrived. What if they ask to see Margot? There's no way Lleu will be able to get her ready in a believable amount of time unless I stall.

No, I am the Colum. If they ask to see her I will tell them they should have sent notice and that she's napping.

"Understood, Colum," Commander Aisil says.

On my way to the west wing, servants I pass become rigid or clutch their laundry baskets closer to their chests. I don't care if I'm visibly fuming. There could be a billion and one reasons Monicas wants to see me, and it doesn't help that I just pardoned Margot's cousin and put my entire planet at risk.

I pause just before the doors. My father's words reign in my head. *Milo, always be strong. Always rule with the air of a leader, even when you don't feel like one. And most of all, do not disappoint me.*

When I enter the conference room, Arbitor Monicas stands at the farthest head of the table, chuckling with Arbitor Lorne. Anya Lorne smoothes out her braided hair while she sips on moon tea with Ida Bruis. The women giggle together. Arbitor Bruis stands near the paned glass windows, admiring the planets.

Their ease settles my breath—slightly.

"Colum!" Monicas extends his hands gleefully.

"I hope nothing too pressing has caused this surprise gathering," I say.

Monicas presses a hand to his belly and laughs. "Heavens no, but I need no excuse to be welcomed by a host such as yourself. Your wine is sublime, and your chef is extraordinary! But no, as for pressing issues, I could ask you the same thing Colum, as you called this meeting?"

"You're mistaken."

The arbitors look at each other before Arbitor Lorne speaks. "You said it was an emergency. That we needed to drop any speeches or meetings we had for the day and meet you here at once."

Lady Lorne and Bruis aren't fazed by the conversation in the slightest as they poke at pastries.

Arbitor Bruis runs his palm across the tall leather chairs while he paces toward me. "So tell us, what was so urgent I had to cancel my meeting with the delegates from Zreath?"

This is a mistake. Perhaps an error on the command center's part. They're going to be even angrier when they realize their trip was pointless, but I can't help feeling relieved. "I will speak to our military staff. They must have sent an emergency message by accident."

Arbitor Bruis pinches the bridge of his nose. "And see to it that whoever called us here be terminated immediately. Nymbed even."

His words bring nausea to my throat. That he could even suggest something so casually. It always takes me a little off guard when the arbitors bring up certain punishments without a second thought. Like they don't understand the ramifications, considering how separated they are from normal society.

Monicas claps his hands together, beckoning our attention. "Why not make the best of the day, shall we, Bruis? How often do you get to travel to the Imnicus?"

"Yes, my love," Lady Bruis says to her husband. "We should use this little mishap to enjoy ourselves."

Of course the arbitors would use this opportunity to take advantage of the Imnicus's luxuries. As if they don't have estates and mansions of their own. But as long as it helps aleve their frustrations, I can't complain. With a proper excuse about Margot's absence, all of this will blow over.

Anya Lorne rolls her eyes. "And some of us are in need of a little break, aren't we darling?"

Arbitor Lorne shoots his wife a glare.

The doors slide open. Conversations come to an abrupt halt.

"Yes, enjoy yourselves. After all, it was me who called this meeting."

When I spin around, my cousin's eyes are already locked on me, his glare hardened. A dark energy radiates off him.

I don't know what he thinks he's doing. His presence . . . his *recklessness.* My fists tighten.

If anyone would have done to my father what Knox just did to me, my father would have done the execution himself. Gods know how many people have died in this room at my father's hands. How much stained tile had to be replaced.

Before I find the right words to say, Arbitor Lorne's eyes narrow. "You're telling me that you, a proditor, *a subordinate,* used the emergency protocol to summon us?"

"What better way than to get you here quickly?" Knox folds his arms.

Lorne stomps toward Knox and points his finger straight in his face. "You are out of line, Proditor!"

Bruis joins in. "You have broken numerous laws! Impersonating a political figure; wasting the time and resources of the Arris reign!"

Monicas puts a hand up. "Now, now, before we get angry or jump to conclusions, let's allow the boy to speak. Surely he didn't call us here as a childish prank. Tell us, what do you have to say, Knox?"

I have a stare-off with Knox, shaking my head subtly enough for only him to notice. He can't do this to me. To himself. But doesn't he know I'll tell them about his unsavory hobby if he exposes me? What game is he trying to play?

"You see, Monicas . . . " Knox grabs his mask and throws it off to the side, letting it clatter to the ground. The women gasp and more steam blows out of Arbitor Lorne and Bruis's ears. "I think sometimes we forget I'm not just a proditor but an Arris."

"What is this?" Arbitor Lorne yells. "Breaking your creed in front of your superiors!"

Monicas keeps his reprimands at bay. "Proditor Knox, I don't know what you're getting at." It's only now I realize how much patience Monicas truly has.

"Put your mask back on," I whisper harshly. "Go back to your quarters and we'll forget this ever happened."

Knox ignores me and paces around the room. "Milo is also an Arris. The blood heir of Balistar. Yet it seems he's not quite on board with his father's ideals. Truly, I think if he had his way, he would banish Arris law all together and do things however he wishes. Wouldn't you, Milo?"

Arbitor Bruis's shoulders visibly tighten. "That is a vile accusation to set against our Colum! Colum, have him arrested and remove him from his posting on the Imnicus immediately!"

Finally, Monicas's voice grows more stern. "Don't be cryptic. Tell us what you want to say and maybe we can forget this lapse in judgment."

Knox's eyes shoot to mine once again. "I'll let Milo explain it to you. Tell them, cousin, why a Laven rebel spy is the Columess."

The blood drains out of my face. Part of me was holding on to the hope Knox would remember we are supposed to be like brothers. That he would hold my secrets as long as I once held his.

The arbitors's eyes are no longer on Knox but on me.

Arbitor Lorne shakes his head in disbelief. "Colum Arris, is this true?"

"This is being twisted! There's an explanation for all of this." The words come out too fast.

"Answer the question," Monicas says firmly, and this may be the first time in my life I've seen him with this much suspicion in his eyes. Suspicion against me.

"Yes, but—"

Monicas's eyes sink in disappointment. "Why, Colum?"

I can't face Monicas, so I turn my head to the side. Then I proceed to tell him everything. The entire time I do, Knox stands there with an infuriating smirk on his face. No matter how I word and pad the story, the arbitors's faces grow more and more disappointed.

"So what you're telling us is a Laven spy infiltrated the Imnicus, and you had no sense to report it?" Arbitor Lorne practically yells the words. "Not only that, but you married her on paper to deceive us. It's public record!"

It's a truth I've never admitted to Margot. In the eyes of the law, she really is my wife, and because of my authority as the Colum, no witnesses were required. I simply had to press her fingerprint to the certificate while she was in a coma. That way, if anyone had their doubts about the validity of our marriage, every base was covered.

"What I did was wrong, I get that. But if I hadn't, we never would have gotten as close to the rebels as we did."

"Then why is she still parading around as your wife? Why didn't you kill her the second you completed your own mission?" Bruis adds.

I stay silent for a moment, unable to give them the truth or face it myself.

Monicas breaks into a small grin. "You fell in love with her."

I don't nod, but my lack of response is enough confirmation. It's something I don't even like to admit to myself.

Monicas shakes his head in disbelief. "You know I love you like a son, Milo. I've watched you grow from a boy into the man you are. Your father always saw your potential as a leader, and I was happy to continue on with mentoring you after he passed." He swallows. "That being said, what you did borders on treason to your own crown. But I know Balistar, and I know he would want you to stay on the throne regardless of this. So, effective today, you will be sent to Ashtanabo to be nymbed until you can submit back into the rules of the Arris Law."

Fear rises in me. I've watched nymbing performed on people, but I never thought I'd be subjected to it. I thought I was too loyal to my father's wishes to stray so far. "In the meantime, who will rule?"

"In line with the law, I will be interim Colum until you're fit to rule again, may that be a few months or years," Monicas says.

"And Margot?"

Arbitor Monicas's eyes grow somewhat glassy. "I think you already know."

I can't deny or push out my thoughts or feelings. Worse than being nymbed is the thought of losing her. Can I live in a universe where she isn't breathing? Where emptiness lives in my heart until the day I die?

But I won't go down without taking Knox with me. My own cousin betrayed me. And for what?

Wait . . . and for what?

If Margot is executed, he won't be able to have her. Why would he let that happen? What is he gaining out of all of this?

My eyes sweep to Knox, a twisted grin tugging at the edges of his mouth. "If I can interrupt . . ."

Monicas cuts him off. "I'm closer to arresting you, Proditor Knox."

Knox continues anyway, "I think the best person to replace Milo would be someone with Arris blood, wouldn't you agree?"

I take a step back. This can't be what he wants. He doesn't mean . . .

Monicas places his hands on the table. "Arris Law is clear about the order of succession, both in permanent cases and interim postings. It was Balistar's own will for me to become the Colum if something were to happen to Milo without an heir. If not myself, then Bruis, then Lorne, then their wives, and only then would you be considered for the throne."

Knox chuckles and walks behind the arbitors' wives, leaning his forearms on the backs of their chairs. "Which leads me to my next point . . ."

Lady Lorne turns her head up at him. He winks, and she suppresses a coy smile with a hint of unease.

My body is restless, theories churning in my head. What is he planning . . .

Wait . . . No!

"Knox, get away from them!" I shout.

Before the arbitors can process my meaning, Knox grabs Lady Lorne from behind, yanking her out of the chair and into his chest. He presses a dagger against her throat.

Lady Lorne screams in terror. "Cedrick! Do something!"

This . . . this is why he wanted all of Balistar's successors in the same room.

Arbitor Lorne steps forward, and Knox presses the tip in deep enough to draw a small scratch of blood. Lorne quickly retreats and gets on his knees. Lady Bruis screams and quickly crawls under the table, as if that will protect her.

I put my hands up. "Let her go. We can talk without bloodshed."

"And what makes you think I want to talk? You heard the man. The law is the law. The arbitors are your heirs. Well, that is considering there are any arbitors left."

"Don't!" I yell.

Knox drags the knife across Anya's neck down to the windpipe. Blood flows down her neck and dress like a waterfall. Arbitor Lorne screams bloody murder, falling on his knees and grabbing his head in horror.

Just as I go to lunge at him, the doors fly open. Crux and Onyx drag in a somewhat limp Margot. Her hair is tangled and her face is pale.

How dare he . . . I'll kill him for this!

"I was beginning to wonder when you two would show up," Knox says unamused.

"What did you do!" Before I can even think of throwing my fist, Crux holds a gun to Margot's head.

Margot's head droops, half-conscious, her lids flickering in a post-crow fatigue. Based on the bruises lining her skin, I know they used more than just proditor magic against her. They broke her like they would a man of equal strength. There is a world in which I could see Crux betraying me, but Onyx? My chest tightens more.

Arbitor Lorne is on his knees, crawling to Anya, not caring that her dead body lies at Knox's feet. Bruis is on the other side of the table, trying to coax Lady Bruis out who is crying hysterically.

"Milo, get on your knees and put your hands behind your head," Knox commands.

If I don't listen, I could knock him over long enough for the arbitors to escape. But Crux may blow Margot's brains out before I could take Knox down. It's not like I can defeat three full-proditors myself. I stare at Margot's beaten and bruised body, and I want to murder all three of them for touching her.

I do as Knox says and get on my knees. Choosing a Laven over the life of the arbitors. "My father wouldn't want this."

Knox tips his head back and laughs. "Isn't this how he claimed his throne?"

"There was a reason he didn't make you a primary heir. At the end of the day, he knew you wouldn't be able to control your crows after his death. He knew you would've been a poor leader."

Knox's face swirls into anger. "So says Balistar's afterthought."

I don't let his words sink in. I am well aware of my place with my father.

He continues, "A part of me always felt like Uncle Balistar put me at the bottom for a reason. He wanted me to prove my greatness. To rise exactly the way he did. To rule in the same manner. To carve my own path and not let petty laws dictate my true inheritance in this world."

Knox lurches at the table and grabs Lady Bruis's ankle, dragging her out toward him.

Arbitor Bruis holds onto her wrist tightly. "No!"

But Knox is stronger. He stomps on the arbitor's wrist, hauls her out, and sinks his blade deep into her chest.

Monicas backs against one of the walls, completely speechless.

Bruis loses all logic and composure, yelling in fury. He charges around the table and tries to swing a fist at Knox. But Knox is quicker, more agile. He takes the arbitor's head between his palms and snaps his neck.

Bruis falls in the pile with the ladies.

My knees dig into the floor, and it takes everything in me not to fight Knox. If it were only my life on the line, I would.

I look at Onyx, begging him with my eyes to snap out of Knox's trance. He simply turns his head away as he holds up Margot's left side.

Margot's eyes are still closed, but she's conscious to some degree. Tears drip down her face and onto the conference room floor, mixing with the small river of blood pooling around her knees from the pile of bodies.

"Lorne, move!" Monicas shouts.

But the arbitor is paralyzed as Knox plunges the blade into Lorne's back and he falls onto his stomach next to his wife.

He reaches out for his wife's hand and whispers "I'll see you soon enough, my Anya," before his eyes close for good.

Monicas doesn't try to run in horror as Knox slowly strides toward him. He keeps his feet glued firmly to the ground, tightens his fists, and straightens his back. "I'm not afraid of you, boy. I watched you piss yourself as a teenager when Balistar put you in your place."

"How brave." Knox walks forward and places his hand on Monicas's shoulder.

The arbitor visibly shudders. Still, he doesn't try to run. "I am a servant of the people, and I will never cower. I will die if it means protecting them."

"That's the unfortunate part, isn't it? You won't be helping them. Your death means nothing." Knox steps back and takes a second dagger from his belt. He quickly swipes the blades diagonally across Monicas's neck like an X.

I am completely numb as I watch his body thump onto the floor, lifeless and wide-eyed.

Everything is quiet. Enough for me to hear my ragged breaths and my beating heart. I've seen a lot of bloodshed during my reign but never like this.

Part of me wants to believe this isn't what my father would want. But Knox was right. This is exactly what he would condone. It's only in this moment, watching Knox slaughter with so much joy, that a veil lifts from my eyes. Everything I once believed about my father, and even my own reign, shatters.

My father was never an honorable leader who wanted the best for everyone, even if that's how it started out. He was a killer. A stealer of souls. A man who gave into the lust of wealth and power and would've burned down planet after planet if it meant filling his plate, even at the expense of billions.

And Knox is no different. Though, somehow, Knox is even worse because I know he doesn't care about either planet. He doesn't even care about money. He only cares about control and how he can use it for his own sick desires.

Slowly, Knox turns toward me. Blood streaks his face and his golden hair. It drips off the silver tips of his daggers. "Are we having fun yet?"

"How dare you make a mockery of their deaths," I bite.

"A mockery? Milo, this was a symphony." Knox sheaths his daggers and wipes blood off his face with the back of his glove.

I can't entertain his delusions any longer. All I care about is getting Margot out of here. "I didn't interfere with your massacre, so let her go."

"I don't recall making a deal with you. And in case you haven't noticed, you aren't in any position to be making demands."

My arms shake from pure rage. "Knox, let her go! Take my life instead!"

Margot visibly slumps more from my words. She tries to lift her head to say something, but her neck gives out once again. This time, she looks completely unconscious, only held up by Crux and Onyx.

"Hmm, it doesn't quite go along with my plan." Knox hops up on the table, then crosses his legs.

"And what plans do you have for her?"

"Do you remember in the old days, when a woman became a widow and her late husband's brother was expected to marry her to take care of her? Imagine it, Milo. A tragedy to tell the people. One where a son couldn't follow in his father's footsteps, so there was no choice but to put him down. A Colum who committed treason against his people."

"Knox—"

"Now, I will be their savior. *Her* savior. I'll take her as my own, and everyone will know that I swooped in and cared for her when you could not."

"She will *never* willingly become your wife."

Knox smirks as he looks at Margot and then back at me. "Maybe I'll take a note out of your playbook and erase her memories then.

I'll be the one to console her when she finally wakes from her coma, holding her hand while she processes the chain of events I lead her to believe. Imagine it, Milo—a world in which Margot is mine, riding me in your bed while you can only look down in rage from your place in the stars."

"I'll kill you before you can even consider doing something like that!" I lower my arms before I stop suddenly, remembering Crux's gun.

Knox yawns. "Are you finished, or can we get down to business?"

What more can I say to stop him? My words will mean nothing. Knox is a man of action, and I am helpless. It's how I've always been. A broken, worthless boy among powerful men with superior magic.

Even being the Colum has been a facade. I see it now. Power in name alone that I could toss about like a child playing a ruler. How foolish I was. The only true power I held was in the hands of the two proditors I held closest. One of which is ready to hold a knife to my throat, and the other . . .

Knox laughs and taunts me from across the room, but I've abandoned my focus on his words. I dive deep down into my psyche, breathing out long and steady. My crows flutter in response, feeling out for another. It's a bond I've never truly understood, and I curse myself for not paying attention to the connected crows earlier. I can only hope it isn't the death of me now.

I let the waves of anguish roll over me. The death of Monicas, a man I knew as a father. A more kindly one, anyway. Margot's beaten form and the rage that boils in me at the sight of each bruise.

Even Knox and the searing pain from his betrayal. The emotions rip through me and my crows respond, tipping their beaks to the heavens above, releasing a cry for help from the depths of my soul.

Dune, hear me. I need you, Dune.

Chapter 31

Margot

Fog clouds my head and cotton fills my ears. There are shouts. Screams. Begs. Threats.

I reach for veils, tearing them down one by one, trying to find my path back to the real world as the crows of others' fight against my strength.

One veil is itchy in my hands. When I rip it from the infinite above, everything releases. The pounding in my head amplifies, and every sound pierces through my ears.

Fingers stroke my forehead.

The cool metal of a gun is pressing into my skull, consciousness enveloping me whole.

Knox's vindictive eyes stare down at me. "I want you to watch this, Margot." In his hand, he holds a dagger dripping with thick blood.

He approaches Milo, who's on his knees with his hands behind his head.

No. I try to force my way out of the proditors' grasps, but they only hold me tighter, keeping my crows at bay.

I look up at Onyx, saying everything I can through looks alone. *How could you?*

Onyx tears his gaze from me. Proditor or not, he knows he was in the wrong place at the wrong time.

"Stop it, Knox!" It's barely a shout, my voice hoarse.

Knox laughs. "I'm about to become the Colum, and I can't exactly do that if he's still alive."

"He's your own cousin. Your blood!" As many fights as Dimitri and I have been through, there's not a world where I could betray him.

"It's the price to pay for the world I will create."

I shake from the anger. "A world filled with sadistic pain and misery."

"You don't seem to understand who has the upper hand here." Knox points the dagger at Milo's throat. "So mind your tongue."

I hold back my next words. How can I just sit here and watch this? Lavenai will be in even more danger than it already is if Knox takes the throne.

Milo's neck elongates when Knox presses the tip of the dagger against the hollow of his throat. I stir, my heart pounding. Please . . . don't . . .

"I only have one request—don't make her watch this," Milo says.

Knox tilts his head. "Oh?"

"It's cruel and you know it."

Knox turns to me. "What do you think? Would you like to watch your lover's final moments? Or leave him to meet death alone?"

They're impossible questions with impossible answers. I want to tell Knox to go fuck himself, but before I can, two small ball-like devices roll across the floor between us. I squint. Am I hallucinating?

Onyx's grip tenses on me. "Wait . . . Knox!"

The devices explode, filling every inch of the conference room with a blinding smoke.

Onyx and Crux lose hold of me as they are taken down by seemingly invisible forces. I fall on my side and waste no time, crawling in Milo's direction.

Pained shouts swoop throughout the room. Tables and chairs screech across the floor as strong bodies collide in combat with one another.

I palm around, trying to find any sign of Milo while avoiding the surrounding duels.

Arms wrap around my torso and drag me out of the room. I try to fight back, but my body is still weak.

When the smoky veil lifts, I take in the hallway around me as Milo rests me against the wall.

"My gods, you're still alive" I say. A true relief floods my chest. He's safe . . . thank the gods he's safe.

Milo places his hands on my shoulders. "Are you all right?"

I nod and signal to the room. "Who's in there?"

"I couldn't see, but I can only assume."

Across the hallway stands Lleu, her arms crossed like she's cold, anxiously watching the door. She's on the brink of tears.

"Lleu!" I try to stand but Milo guides me back down. "What are you doing here?"

Alarik stumbles out of the room with a respirator on. Dune follows shortly behind him. The proditors quickly take two more of the smoke bombs and roll them into the room then force the doors shut.

Milo races to the security sensor and taps his ring to the screen. He types in a code. "That should hold them for now. Those are hyssopite bombs, right?"

Alarik nods and peels off the respirator, replacing it with his mask. "It's the only way to maintain our strength and weaken theirs."

Dune crouches beside me. "Get on my back. You're too injured to walk right now."

I want to refuse him since my strength is gradually returning, but I know I will only slow everyone down if I don't accept. I hop on his back.

"Milo, what is happening?" Alarik asks firmly. "Dune said he could sense you were in trouble. Once we got to the conference room, we peeked through the doors only to see a knife against your throat and a pile of arbitors."

Milo waves at all of us to follow him down the hall at a brisk pace. "Knox is after the crown. If you have your communicators, send a message to Aisil. Tell him we need backup on the Imnicus."

Alarik digs his communicator from his belt and taps angrily at the screen. "Communication has been disabled."

Lleu looks like her knees are about to give out. "But if we get to the command center, we can send a message planetside, right?"

Milo shakes his head. "It means Knox took out the communication tower before his ambush. Aisil must already suspect something is off."

"Everyone on the Imnicus is loyal to you," I tell Milo. "You have an entire army here and two proditors on your side. There's no way Knox will be successful now that you got away."

"Let us hope. We need the communication tower repaired in the meantime."

"We should split up." Dune stops his strides. "I can go to the tower and repair it. You four should get to the docking bay and escape to Ashtanabo. The Imnicus isn't safe anymore." He sets me down next to Milo.

With my strength now at fifty percent, I refuse Milo when he offers me his back.

Milo turns to Dune. "Promise me you'll take a ship back to land when you're finished."

"I'll be as quick as I can." Dune bows his head.

Milo nods, and Alarik pats Dune's shoulder once before Dune jogs down the hall, disappearing down the corner.

"Let's go," Alarik says.

The closer we get to the south wing, the more my fears dissipate. Even with proditor magic, there is no way Knox, Crux, and Onyx will be able to take on an army of Imnicus soldiers. When Balistar took over, it took him meticulous planning over a long period of time, becoming a parasite Lavenai didn't even realize they were infected with until it was too late.

Lleu visibly shakes. I take her hand, squeezing it tightly. "We're going to be all right. He won't have you again."

"I don't know if I'll ever feel at ease until he's dead." She lowers her voice, so only I can hear. "He used raven magic on me while you were gone. He didn't even have to touch me."

"How?" I shiver.

"He used Alarik's crows."

I swallow. I know almost nothing about magic complementary to crows. Is it something Knox could use in his favor against an army? Do Alarik and Milo even know how to stop magic like that?

A small shadow crawls in the corner of my eyes and I blink a few times, concentrating on the path ahead. Already, my mind plays tricks on me.

I see it again and turn my head quickly to catch it, but it's gone.

The third time, my knees buckle. "Milo—"

Just as I process their shell-like shape, they fall onto my skin from the ceiling. I yelp.

Beetles. They multiply on the walls and on my skin.

I let go of Lleu, fervently swiping at the bugs. "Get them off!"

Milo and Alarik spin around. Lleu covers her mouth.

"What is it, Margot?" Milo asks with narrowed eyes.

"Is that even a question? Don't you see them!" I've never been overly squeamish about bugs, but this is almost unbearable.

Milo scans the walls, but it doesn't seem like he's looking for bugs. He's looking for something else.

"Alarik," Milo bites. "He's out."

"Got it." Alarik walks straight up to the security camera and slams the hilt of his dagger into the lens, shattering it.

The bugs vanish.

"He can use the cameras?" I ask in horror. There are cameras everywhere on the Imnicus.

Milo inspects for more cameras while he speaks. "My father pursued dark magic complementary to crows and Knox was his willing test subject. Knox can mark you and then use the touch of another proditor to break into your mind. And after killing the arbitors and tormenting you, his power is temporarily amplified. He knows three of the four tenets of dark magic. My crows sense his ravens, the most dangerous of them all, in every hall we enter."

Alarik stays close to Milo, far away from Lleu and me.

"For all we know, Knox may have already marked both of you." Alarik rubs his wrist. "We should be careful not to touch one another."

I want to tell Alarik he's practically covered head to toe, but I know he won't risk Lleu's well being regardless.

I don't hold Lleu's hand again in case Knox can use his own crows against her through my skin.

We follow Milo into a hallway that holds a weapons closet. Milo grabs extra guns and a long metal baton, then he hands Alarik packs of ammo.

"You think guns can stop me?" The presence of a body presses against my back, dark chills crawling up my spine and neck. I whip around, but nobody is there.

Alarik throws a gun my way, and I turn back in time to catch it. "Focus, Margot."

Milo finds another camera and promptly shatters it with the baton, and all remnants of Knox's ravens vanish.

When we approach the outside of the command center, Milo taps his ring, or rather my old ring, to the door, but the doors groan and stay shut.

"There is no way they could have disabled your security clearance this quickly," Alarik says.

Milo looks through the windows of the door. His face falls. "It's barred from the inside. Not only that . . . but they're slaughtering each other in there."

I gather with Milo and Alarik and watch the massacre through the windows. Soldier turns against soldier. Guard against guard. Commander against commander.

"Why are they doing this? Were half of them working for Knox all along?"

Milo presses his ear to the door. "No, Knox is deluding them with ravens. Threatening them."

I follow suit and listen to the muffled sound of an isolated intercom where Knox speaks commands over the barred room.

"Submit to me."

I see it now. The glaze over the eyes of those who are choosing Knox over Milo. They are looking at things in the room that aren't even there. Knox is using ravens and fear as weapons. Fear great enough to commit treason.

Those brainwashed fight with panicked strength, and those who are fighting for Milo only last so long before the ravens overtake them too, the invisible horrors revealing themselves.

Milo backs away from the door. "We don't have long before he does the same in the docking bay. Let's go."

Chapter 32

Margot

We enter the docking bay where crates and overturned furniture create an impromptu barrier. Two dozen soldiers have their guns trained at the wide entrance.

Behind them, like a tall spire of rock amongst the spraying waves, is Commander Aisil. His orders cut through the chaos, bringing a strange stability to the pilots and technicians rushing in a flurry around him. He pulls his shoulders back, his stance unwavering. My steps slow at the sight of him. Not unlike Lucinda in moments of crisis, he's an unwavering anchor to latch onto. It's hard to process that it's the same Aisil I remember.

But I know the truth behind the panic. Any minute, the soldiers Knox converted to his side will be upon the bay, and no amount of preparation can prepare for overwhelming numbers. It appears Commander Aisil knows this.

At the far end of the hangar, Milo's ship is being prepared for an escape, along with a few other troop transports. Milo strides through the barricades, briefly resting his hand upon the shoulders of guards as he passes. Each stands a little taller, the fear in their eyes resolving to determination just at the recognition. Commander Aisil turns to face him as we walk up, his eyes set with a resolve I've never seen from him.

"Colum, only brief reports came through before the communication tower went down, but I hope you have better news. Men turning on each other . . . chaos within the command center. How much of this is true?"

"Knox is attempting a coup d'état," Milo says flatly. "He's using forbidden magic to indoctrinate our men. I need every camera in the docking bay disabled. Break them if you must."

"Understood, sir. And what of the arbitors?"

"Dead."

Aisil's jaw clenches. Grief passes over his eyes.

"And we will be too if we don't control this," Milo says but hesitates, glancing around at the soldiers gathering at the barricades. When they're not focused on the doors, they're staring at us. At him. "Keep their spirits up, Aisil. They'll need all the motivation they can get."

One of the technicians rushes up to Milo and motions to the ship farther up on the tiered platform. "Your ship is ready, sir."

Milo grabs my hand and the four of us ascend the metal steps.

"Are we really going to leave Dune here?" I ask Milo.

His jaw twitches. "He's strong and will find his own way to safety."

Shouts and the heavy stomp of more than one-hundred boots leak from the hallways into the docking bay.

"He's almost here, Milo," Alarik warns.

We approach the ship, and Alarik quickly helps Lleu up the ramp. Milo stays on the balcony, watching carefully.

The lines of soldiers resist the urge to step back as Commander Aisil shouts more commands.

"Ready!" Aisil yells. "Protect our Colum. Protect the Arris Reign. Do not let your gaze falter. Stay alert!"

Most soldiers here are under the age of thirty, and no wars have been fought since they were children. For nearly all of their military careers, they've never engaged in a real battle, especially if they've only ever been assigned to the Imnicus.

One soldier takes a step back, dropping his gun and grabbing his ears.

I grip the railing. "What's going on?"

Another screams and then another. All of them drop to their knees one after the other.

A few soldiers look around and yelp at nothing, as if there were invisible monsters surrounding them, ready to swallow them whole. Blood drips down the ears of several men.

Milo stays still, his eyes darting between each soldier who falls for the spell.

"Milo, Knox can see them!" I shake his arm. Knox may not be watching us from the cameras, but he's stalking from somewhere.

Man turns on man, grabbing each other's throats or raising their guns at the person to their left, as if they weren't comrades just seconds ago.

A funnel of new soldiers stampede into the docking bay, adding even more chaos to the mix.

"Do not falter!" Aisil shouts.

Bullets ricochet off metal. Milo and I drop to our knees, shielding our heads.

"Milo, you have to let me help them," I say. "My crows are back, and I could fight him. I could—"

Milo's eyes meet mine, furious, like I offended him by even asking. "Get on the ship, Margot."

"You can't expect me to just stand here!"

Milo pulls me into his chest and picks me up under my knees, carrying me up the ramp of his ship.

I could fight Milo on this and maybe even defeat Knox. But instead I strain my neck to watch the battle over his shoulder before the ramp shuts. I quickly shimmy out of his arms and over to the control panel.

Through the ship's windshield, my body shakes as Knox emerges.

Holding a firearm in one hand and a dagger in the other, he moves as if he's not worried about bullets in the slightest. Blood streaks his face—a fallen beauty amongst carnage.

He joins in the fight, taking down soldier after soldier. This time, he rarely spares those who beg to follow him in exchange for their lives—enacting punishment the way Balistar did to Lavenai. He's gaining energy and strength with every sadistic kill, and he fights with a skill I'll never be capable of replicating.

I will never kill to increase my powers. It's why I will never be able to match him while he's in this state.

Aisil shouts to the squadron. "Do not fall back! Fight without mercy!"

Soldiers cower to the floor, kneeling from mere eye contact with Knox, submitting to his demands.

"Enough of this. The Imnicus has been sieged. We need to move," Milo says. He and Alarik work at the control panel, flicking switches and pressing buttons.

I take a step back to give them space. But what about Dune? Commander Aisil? The servants? All of them will be stuck here under Knox's rule if they survive past today.

As the ship ascends, Knox stops in his tracks and narrows his eyes right at me through the windshield.

I can't hear his words but can read his lips well enough. *"Shoot the ship!"*

Bullets bounce off the ship's exterior.

"Get down!" Milo shouts over his shoulder, ducking his head.

Lleu gets on her stomach, but I stay put, unable to take my eyes off Knox.

Milo curses as he gets ready for launch, hovering the ship just outside the Imnicus.

Knox sprints up the balcony, and with the power in his steps, I believe he'd be capable of bringing the down ship all by himself if we weren't already outside the oxygen shield.

He stands on the edge of the bay, just by the purple octagon shield. His gaze locks on mine, hands gripping his weapons so hard that his knuckles bulge from under his gloves. With blood staining his golden hair, he's a painting of the treasonous sadist I know him as.

I tear my gaze from him and kneel on the floor next to Lleu.

Milo turns the ship around. He pulls back a lever then slams his palm down on a button. The ship launches away from the Imnicus.

Lleu shakes while I rub her back. I'm unable to find words of comfort. Incapable of overriding my own numbness.

I rise, standing between Alarik and Milo at the control panel.

A sphere of purple appears in the distance, and I take a step back. "You're taking us to Lavenai?"

"At this rate, Knox will have all of Ashtanabo convinced of my treason within a day. It will be easier to hide out on Lavenai," Milo answers.

"You're joking right? There are cameras everywhere!"

"And there was a time when you flew under my radar even while your face was in the database. Regardless, going to Lavenai will buy us a few extra days before that happens, if it happens at all. Knox isn't the brightest in certain regards, and it will take him longer to realize I didn't go to Ashtanabo.

I narrow my eyes. "I will not take you to the rebellion. I refuse." Not only that, but *his mother* is there. His mother who he believes abandoned him with Balistar. She never told me the full story, but I know her well enough to conclude she was never given a choice.

Milo takes a deep breath. "The only way to fix things is if we work together—you and me. And if you allow us to seek shelter and aid from the rebellion, then them too. It will only be a matter of time before Knox turns both planets into ruin."

Somehow, against all odds and possibilities, I am on the side of Milo Arris.

But that's not true, is it? I will never agree with the Arris Reign, or anything Milo has done. If anything, a civil war in Ashtanabo is the perfect distraction for the rebellion to get their foot in the door of restoring Lavenai. I should be happy . . . but I'm horrified. Ashtanabo will face utter destruction, and Lavenai will be next.

At the end of the day, Milo has virtually no power anymore. Not just over me but over the entire galaxy. He's merely a human stripped of his crown. There's no reason for him to betray me, though I can't let my guard down around him, even now.

I look at Alarik. "And how do you feel about this?"

He shrugs. "I guess I'm just looking forward to the tour."

I force a laugh. "Then to Lavenai it is."

Epilogue

Dimitri

"Are they still following us?" Anali asks quickly.

"No, I think we lost them." I slide down against the stone alley wall.

Ever since Margot disappeared, we've been tailed. Sometimes we lose the guards and spies for a few days, only to sense someone stalking from the shadows the next. Time and time again, we've nearly been caught.

Oliver sheaths his dagger in his boot. "At this rate, we won't make it to the next temple point before we're thrown into the clutches of a proditor. We already had to skip the second point in Susuku."

Anali grabs day-old bread out of her bag and takes a large bite.

"You're eating now of all times?" I narrow my eyes.

She shrugs. "We haven't stopped to eat for half a day now. I'm just being time efficient."

I murmur something spiteful under my breath, though I suppose I can't blame her for being so socially inept. She's been trapped in a prison for years, and obviously they didn't teach her any manners. Or maybe I'm just letting the hunger get to me.

We find shelter later that night in a cottage along the lake in the region of Zreath. An older couple rents it to us for half the cost, and thankfully so. Anali's thievery has been subpar at best recently, and stealing digital currency is no easy feat. It's not exactly the most ideal place to stay, but for once since Margot disappeared, I finally feel like we're not being watched.

When we first went looking for Margot, after it was clear she wasn't going to arrive at the meeting point, a set of guards started chasing us. It was at that moment I knew, deep down, the Colum took her again.

And I was furious. Inconsolable.

I hate myself for it. Knowing I failed her again. I shouldn't have let us split up. I should have stayed by her side the entire time. It took hours for Oliver to drag me out of the city after we lost the guards, but he was right. She may not be dead, but she was no longer in Susuku.

Rain falls against the roof, the cabin echoing like a false oasis. Oliver takes a crossed-legged position on the wooden floors and Anali slumps onto the couch.

I pace around the room. "We have three options. One, we try to save Margot on the Imnicus. Two, we find a way back to Lavenai." I swallow at my next words. "Or three, we stay on Ashtanabo, and take down the temple points."

"Well, I know which option you prefer." Oliver shakes his head.

My jaw tightens. "She's family. Or course my first choice would be to save her."

"But is that what she would want?" Anali interjects. "I didn't know her long, but I'm willing to bet she'd be pissed if you chose her over the mission." Anali finds a remote and turns on the holographic television, clicking through the channels.

Anger burns in my chest because of course she's right. Our mission was to find Anali and destroy the temple points. It's still not an impossible task, just a difficult one with the Colum on our tail. "How am I supposed to finish the mission knowing full well they may be doing horrible things her?"

"You see your problem?" Oliver sighs. "You're choosing your personal issues over the fate of the planet. Sure, let's say we find some elaborate way to get on the Imnicus. She could be already dead for all we know."

I tighten my fists.

"But more than likely," Oliver continues, "she's simply imprisoned, and the second you free her she'll slap you. Then we'll have to find an even more impossible way to get off the Imnicus. All the while, we'll be back to square one."

Anali stops suddenly on one of the news channels and shoots up, as if sitting isn't even appropriate anymore.

"What is it?" I stand by her and immediately go numb at the headline.

The Ashtanaban newscaster faces the camera with widened eyes as text scrolls across the bottom of the screen.

Colum Milo Arris dethroned after arbitor assassination. Accused of treason.

I can't believe what I'm hearing. The Colum killed the arbitors? That doesn't make any sense.

The newscaster begins her speech. *"It is a sad day for all here on Ashtabano to report that Arbitors' Monicas, Bruis, and Lorne, along with their wives, have been killed by our former Colum. It's not clear yet what his motive is, but he has escaped along with three accomplices: Proditor Alarik Walsh, Lleu Todd, and the Columess, Margot Arris.*

I look at Oliver whose jaw is just as agape as mine is.

"He will be succeeded by Balistar's nephew, Knox Arris, a more distant heir to the throne. If you see any of the perpetrators, please report them immediately to your local enforcement office. To Arris Reign."

Margot escaped the Imnicus on her own? With the Colum himself? And a proditor?

But she's alive and off the Imnicus, thank the gods. The tightness in my chest releases.

The name of the new Colum interrupts my relief. Knox Arris. My heart palpitates.

Margot mentioned him when she first returned. The way he sadistically tortured her. His bloodlust. I never thought anyone could be worse than Milo Arris, but from how Margot described this Knox guy . . .

All three of us look at one another. A somber acknowledgement that we aren't leaving Ashtanabo anytime soon. There is still work that needs to be done for the rebellion. For Lavenai. Our mission is more critical than ever before. With Milo Arris now a defector, fewer eyes will be focused on the temple points during the transition of power.

We will destroy every last one of them or give our lives trying.

Acknowledgements

Thank you to all my readers. Whether you found me on TikTok in 2022 or through Netgalley in 2024, you guys are what keeps me going. Anytime I get a comment or DM, it motivates me to keep writing even when things get hard. You guys are my glue.

To my husband, who truly helped me make this book even better, you are my Alarik. Thank you for being my shoulder to cry on and the person who loves me through my dark days. You sacrifice your own writing time to leave me content and prose suggestions, and I couldn't do it without you.

To my Seattle bestie who coworked with me online during the later drafts of this manuscript, thank you for helping keep me diligent, especially on the days I didn't want to write and edit.

To my beta readers, for being honest with me on issues with the manuscript. Your feedback makes me a better author.

To Taylor, thank you for proofreading this book and combing over any grammatical errors and spotting any last minute issues. I couldn't do it without you!

About the Author

Growing up, Abelia wanted to work in film and would make movies with her siblings and friends. In high school, she wrote screenplays and short stories. She decided to become a nurse after her younger brother passed away, but a year into the profession, she left nursing and currently works in marketing. She writes every spare chance she gets. Currently, she lives in Ohio with her husband and has a vision board the size of a novel.